Andrea Laurence ~~porary romances fi~~ ~~a lover of reading~~ ~~A dedicated West C~~ ~~she is thrilled to sh~~ ~~sarcastic humour wi~~

Karen Booth is a Midwestern girl transplanted in the South, raised on '80s music, Judy Blume and the films of John Hughes. She writes sexy big-city love stories. When she takes a break from the art of romance, she's teaching her kids about good music, honing her Southern cooking skills or sweet-talking her husband into whipping up a batch of cocktails. Find out more about Karen at www.karenbooth.net

Four-time RITA® Award nominee **Joanne Rock** has penned over seventy stories for Mills & Boon. An optimist by nature and a perpetual seeker of silver linings, Joanne finds romance fits her life outlook perfectly—love is worth fighting for. A former Golden Heart® Award recipient, she has won numerous awards for her stories. Learn more about Joanne's imaginative Muse by visiting her website, www.joannerock.com or following @joannerock6 on Twitter.

Precious Surprises

ANDREA LAURENCE
KAREN BOOTH
JOANNE ROCK

MILLS & BOON

First Published in Great Britain 2019
by Mills & Boon, an imprint of HarperCollins*Publishers*
1 London Bridge Street, London, SE1 9GF

PRECIOUS SURPRISES © 2019 Harlequin Books S. A.

Little Secrets: Secretly Pregnant © 2017 Andrea Laurence
Little Secrets: Holiday Baby Bombshell © 2017 Karen Booth
Little Secrets: His Pregnant Secretary © 2017 Joanne Rock

ISBN: 978-0-263-27654-1

0619

MIX
Paper from
responsible sources
FSC® C007454

This book is produced from independently certified FSC™ paper to ensure responsible forest management.

For more information visit: www.harpercollins.co.uk/green

Printed and bound in Spain
by CPI, Barcelona

LITTLE SECRETS: SECRETLY PREGNANT

ANDREA LAURENCE

To Dan
Thanks for the inspiration

Prologue

Fat Tuesday

Everyone was dancing and having a good time. Everyone except Emma. That wasn't unusual, though. Emma Dempsey had forgotten how to have fun a long time ago.

After her recent breakup, she was beginning to wonder if something was wrong with her. Her ex, David, had said she was boring both in and out of bed. She made the mistake of telling that to her friend and former sorority sister, Harper Drake, and the next thing she knew, she was at a Mardi Gras party at a loft in Tribeca.

She'd tried. She wore a pretty butterfly mask and a tight skirt, but this just wasn't her cup of tea. Perhaps she should just call a cab and go so she didn't ruin Harper's night. She nibbled absently on a carrot stick as her gaze fell upon a tequila bar that had been set up on the kitchen island beside her. That was always a second option.

Emma knew she had to make a choice. She could either go home and join a local Red Hat Society at the ripe age of twenty-seven or she could take this bull by the horns and have some fun for once.

Feeling brave, she abandoned her plate and moved down the island. There was an assortment of small paper cups, slices of lime, a salt shaker and several bottles of tequila laid out. She prepared a shot and held it there, knowing once she leaped off the cliff, there would be no turning back.

Being with you is like dating my grandma. The memory of David's painful words pushed her over the edge.

Without further hesitation, she licked, drank and sucked the lime furiously to cover the flavor of the liquor. It burned her throat as it went down, splashing in her stomach and sending a scorching sensation almost immediately through her body that a beer couldn't even come close to.

It tasted absolutely terrible, but within seconds, she could feel a pleasant change. Almost as though her spine had loosened. Slinky. Maybe feline. This wasn't bad at all. With a smile of satisfaction, she poured a second shot as someone else came into the kitchen. A quick glance confirmed her worst fears.

"Hey there, beautiful," a creepy guy in a Batman-like mask said, leaning against the counter.

The compliment fell flat considering 75 percent of her face was covered in an ornate Mardi Gras mask. Emma sighed and slammed back the second shot of tequila without salt or lime. She needed it. She started pouring a third, blatantly ignoring him.

"Would you like to dance? I've got some sweet moves."

She doubted it. "I don't dance, sorry."

Batman frowned. "Well, then wanna blow this party off for someplace quiet and dark where we can…talk?"

A shudder ran down Emma's spine. Being alone with him was bad enough. Alone in the dark was downright frightening. "No, I'm here with someone. Sorry."

Batman straightened up, his body language projecting the anger his mask hid away. "Who?"

She opened her mouth to answer him when someone came up behind her and set heavy, warm hands on her shoulders. He leaned in, placing a kiss against her cheek, and Batman finally took a step back.

A deep male voice rumbled near her ear. "Hey, baby, sorry I'm late."

Emma fought the urge to pull away from this second, undesired suitor, but the fingers pressing insistently in her shoulders begged for her cooperation. He wasn't putting the moves on her; he was trying to save her from Batman. Relieved, she turned to face the man and moved without hesitation to say hello.

Whoa. He was taller than she expected, a few inches over six foot, but she couldn't look surprised and convince Batman to bugger off. She strained on tiptoe to reach up and kiss the lips that were the only part of his face visible with a gold-and-green Venetian mask obscuring the rest.

The instant their lips touched, the simple greeting turned into something else. The electricity of the kiss nearly knocked her backward, but his firm, yet gentle grip on her arms wouldn't let her fall away. Her senses were instantly overloaded by the scent of soap and a spicy men's cologne, the soft brush of his lips against hers and the heat of his skin.

Emma wasn't sure if it was the tequila or his kiss, but she was suddenly very aware of her body. The nearness of the man made her skin tingle and her breath quicken. She felt her body leaning into him without her consent. It had to be the tequila. No wonder people got into so much trouble with this stuff.

Regaining some of her senses, she pulled away to break the kiss, but he didn't immediately let go. Batman must still be watching. "I've missed you," she said, snuggling suggestively into him.

His arms wrapped around her and hugged her tightly against the solid wall of his chest. He leaned in, breathing the scent of her hair and whispered, "He left, but he's watching us from the other side of the room. Keep it convincing if you don't want him coming back."

Emma nodded and pulled away. She reached up to affectionately rub a bit of lipstick from her white knight's mouth. The gesture was intimate and quite convincing, she was sure. Once away from him, she had a better view. The mask obscured most of his face, so all she could really decipher was his tall, broad build, tightly fitting jeans and his attractive and bright smile.

"Are we doing tequila shots?" he asked.

"I was, but I think I'm done." She'd had just enough to make this scene authentic, but too much more was trouble for sure.

"Don't be a quitter." He poured himself a shot, and then paused only for a moment to smile wickedly before leaning forward and licking a patch of exposed skin just above her cleavage. Emma sucked a ragged, surprised breath into her chest and held it there. She couldn't respond. Every impulse in her brain was telling her to step back and stop him, but she just stood there, the tequila rendering her mute.

He hesitated, the salt shaker in his hand. His dark blue eyes connected with hers, awaiting her permission. Could she give it? She wanted to. This was what she'd set out for tonight, even if she hadn't known it. Grandmas didn't do body shots with strangers at parties. But the words still escaped her. All she could do was tip her head back to let him sprinkle the salt gently over the swell of her breasts and place the wedge of lime delicately between her lips.

He came closer, shot in hand. Her entire body ached with anticipation as his hot breath hovered over her skin. He licked slowly, taking longer than she ever expected to remove every grain from her chest. Surely Batman wasn't watching that closely. When he tipped the glass back, swallowing the tequila in one sip, she was finally able to release the air she'd held painfully in her lungs. Then he set the cup down.

Emma tensed, not quite sure what to do aside from holding perfectly still as his hand slipped around her neck to cradle her head and tip her mouth up to him. He dipped his head, his lips brushing hers briefly before biting down and sucking the lime juice. A cool, tart stream of it flowed into her own mouth before his teeth tugged the rind away.

When he took a step back, Emma did the same. It had taken everything she had not to moan aloud when he'd touched her this time. The best thing she could do was to get out of this situation before she lost what little control he'd left her with. Never mind that her face had to be flushed with embarrassment and unexpected arousal.

Her hand self-consciously came to her face and

brushed the rough, glittery surface of her mask. She'd forgotten he couldn't see her. Even if she was beet red, he wouldn't know it. She was anonymous tonight. Somehow the knowledge made her bolder and she fought her flight reflex to hold her position by the bar.

He picked up her full paper cup from the counter and held it up in a dangerous and silent offer. It was her turn.

A quick glance confirmed that Batman had disappeared and there was no reason to continue with the show. Aside from her not wanting to stop. "He's gone," she said, giving him the opportunity to stop if this was still just a ruse.

"I know," he said, and handed her the salt shaker.

Given that he was wearing a long-sleeved button-down black shirt, the only real option she had was his neck. She stood on her toes, straining in her heels to reach him. Emma leaned in and left a moist trail from the hollow of his throat to just over his Adam's apple, where her tongue ran across the rough stubble that had grown in since his morning shave. She could feel his pulse quicken as she hovered near to him. This time, she noticed his skin smelled more distinctly male. Salty and slightly musky. She couldn't help lingering to take in a deep breath and commit the scent to memory. Her body's reaction to it was almost primal, parts deep inside of her clenching with a building need.

"Here," he offered as she pulled away to apply the salt. He lowered onto his knees and looked up at her with big blue eyes, his hands resting on the swell of her hips.

Emma could hardly see enough of his face to piece together an expression, but his intense gaze urged her on. As he knelt, it almost felt as though he were worshipping at her feet. She liked it.

She tried to focus on doing the shot properly before his skin dried and the salt wouldn't adhere. She didn't want to give away her inexperience with this. She'd never even dreamed of doing anything as blatantly sexual as body shots. She didn't think she had it in her.

She sprinkled the salt on his throat and positioned the lime between his full, soft lips. Nervously gripping the tequila in one hand, Emma leaned in a second time to lick off the salt. She could feel the vibration of a growl in his throat as her tongue slid across his skin. Pulling away, she quickly threw back the drink and placed her hands on each side of his face. Just before she was able to bite into the fruit, he spat out the lime. Emma didn't have time to stop and their lips met with another unexpected spark.

She didn't pull away. The old Emma would have. In her mask, she was someone else.

The second kiss blew the first out of the water. His fingertips dug into the flesh of her hips as he tugged her close against him. She melted against his mouth, slowly slipping down until she, too, was on her knees in the kitchen. The island shielded them from the crowd only feet away. She wrapped her arms around his neck, her lips clinging to his as he probed and explored her with his tongue.

It was deliciously naughty. In that moment, Emma wanted his kiss more than anything else in her entire life.

Just when she'd convinced herself that the kiss might never end, they parted. His quick breath was hot on the skin of her neck as he pressed his cheek against hers and sat there for a moment to recover. Their arms were still tangled around one another, neither grip loosening. There was an intensity in him that excited and frightened her, but she matched it with her own.

"Come with me," he whispered, then stood and offered his hand.

Emma wasn't ignorant. She knew what he was offering and every inch of her body urged her to take him up on it. She'd never done anything like this. Ever. And yet there was something about her hero that insisted she go with him.

So she did.

One

"**W**here the hell is Noah?" Jonah Flynn growled into his telephone and gripped his coffee mug fiercely in his free hand.

"He's…n-not in, sir."

His brother's administrative assistant, Melody, was audibly startled by his tone and he immediately chose to correct it. Jonah didn't raise his voice to his employees, ever. Honestly, the only person he ever shouted at was Noah. And he would direct his anger at his brother if he could find the bastard.

"I'm sorry for yelling, Melody. I didn't think he would be there. He's never in the office. What I really meant was do you know where he's gone to? He isn't answering his home phone and his cell phone goes directly to voice mail like he's got it turned off."

Melody hesitated on the line for a moment. Jonah could hear the clicking of her keyboard as she checked his calendar. "His calendar is wide-open, but he mentioned as he left that he was headed to Bangkok."

Jonah nearly choked on his latte. He swallowed hard and moved the cup out of his reach. "As in Thailand?"

"Yes, sir."

He took a deep breath to swallow his anger. He would not, could not, take this out on Melody. She'd already called him "sir" twice, which just felt wrong. Yes, he was the CEO, but he was also wearing jeans and a Monty Python T-shirt. Everyone just called him Jonah.

"Any idea when he'll be back?"

"No, but he did send me the number of the hotel he's staying at. You could probably reach him there."

"That would be great, thanks, Melody." She read off the number and he quickly scratched it on his desk blotter before hanging up. He dialed it, getting transferred to his brother's suite without much trouble. Of course Noah didn't answer. He was probably frolicking with some exotic beauty. Jonah forced himself to leave a voice mail message that didn't betray the true reason for his call and hung up in disgust.

Thailand.

If he'd had any second thoughts about Noah being involved in his current mess, they immediately dissipated. If the preliminary accounting reports he was looking at were correct, his little brother had just taken off to Southeast Asia with three million dollars that didn't belong to him.

Jonah leaned back in his leather chair and gently rubbed his temples. This was not good.

The timing was never good for embezzlement, really, but his brother had just royally screwed him over in more ways than one. Noah didn't spend much time in the office; his role in the company was to please their mother and nothing else. But Noah knew—he *knew*—that they were close to wrapping up the deal with Game Town. The auditor they'd hired was showing up today. Today!

This could ruin everything. It wasn't a huge amount in terms of the numbers that ran through the company, but his brother wasn't smart and took it in one big chunk, transferring it to some offshore account he had in the Caribbean. Anyone with an interest would run across it eventually. Game Town was hiring FlynnSoft to manage their monthly game subscription service. Who would want the company handling their money to have issues like that? Jonah certainly wouldn't do it if the roles were reversed.

This needed cleaning up and fast. As much as he didn't want to, he could rearrange his assets for some cash and cover the loss. He would take it out of his brother's hide later. Maybe make him sell his overpriced European sports car. Perhaps even make him do some actual work at FlynnSoft for free until he paid off the debt.

But Noah *would* pay for this. By the time Jonah was done with him, his little brother would wish he'd simply called the cops.

But he wouldn't. Not on his brother. And not for any love he had for his useless sibling, but for concern for their mother. Angelica Flynn had a degenerative heart condition and couldn't take much stress. If Noah, the baby and undoubtedly favorite child, ended up in jail, she'd have one hell of an attack. If she found out Noah was turned in by his own brother, he had no doubt she'd drop dead from the strain and embarrassment. In the end, it would all be Jonah's fault and he refused to be the bad guy in this.

He would handle his brother without their mother ever finding out.

Publicly, Jonah could deal with this however he wished. As a privately owned gaming company he had that luxury. Thank heavens he hadn't taken people's advice to go public. The move could make him a fortune overnight, but he'd also have shareholders and a board of directors to answer to. He could even be fired, losing control of the empire he'd started in his college dorm room.

No way. FlynnSoft was his and Jonah didn't answer to anyone, especially some pompous suits who thought they knew better than he did how to run his company. He'd bail FlynnSoft and his brother out one way or another. His employees deserved as much. And they deserved the money this new contract could bring in. *If* Noah hadn't just blown it.

What a mess.

Jonah flopped back into his executive chair and let his gaze drift over to the framed photograph that sat on the edge of his desk. In it, a Blue Morpho butterfly sat sunning itself on a clump of bright yellow flowers.

He'd gotten more than a few odd looks since he'd brought the picture into the office. Jonah wasn't exactly a nature buff. He'd spent his entire adolescence focused on video games and girls, both of which could be enjoyed in the climate-controlled comfort of his bedroom.

Of course, he couldn't tell anyone why it was really there. How do you explain a night like that to people? You just couldn't. They wouldn't believe you. If it wasn't for the proof inked into his skin, he might've believed she was a tequila induced hallucination. His gaze dropped to his right hand and the tattoo etched into the web of skin between his thumb and index finger. His fingertip grazed over the slightly raised design, tracing it as he'd done that night, only then it was across the silky skin of her chest. His half of the heart.

The other half had disappeared with the woman in the butterfly mask. He'd never anticipated a company Mardi Gras party at his loft would turn into an unforgettable night of body shots, anonymous sex and late-night tattoos. But for some reason, she, whoever she was, had gotten under his skin almost instantly. Everything from her soft gasp as he licked the salt from her throat to the way she'd begged for him to take her was etched into his mind.

Even with all the crap going on with Game Town, he couldn't help but let his thoughts drift to her again. She'd asked him for one night. No names, no personal details. Pure fantasy. Her multicolored glitter butterfly mask had obscured everything but her sleek, brunette ponytail, the full pout of her lips and the bewitching emerald green of her eyes.

How, exactly, had he decided that letting her walk out of his life was a good idea?

Jonah had been an idiot. He could see it now. For years, he'd gone through a lineup of women. They were all beautiful. Many were successful or talented in one way or another. They were drawn to his business success and the glamorous lifestyle he could provide. Most men would be content with the kind of woman who would throw herself at them, but he never was. He would inevitably get bored and move on. He'd actually earned a reputation as one of Manhattan's Most Eligible and *Elusive* Bachelors.

But his butterfly had kept his interest. Even three months later, he still found himself thinking about her. Wondering where she was. Who she was. Trying to figure out if the real woman could ever measure up to his memory of her. She'd insisted that the next morning he wouldn't want her anymore, like she would turn into a pumpkin at the stroke of midnight. Was it just the fantasy he craved? If he'd seen her face and known her name, would she have been relegated to the list of women he'd loved and forgotten? He didn't know.

Jonah ran his hand through the long strands of his dark brown hair and gripped the back of his skull. He needed to let this go. Let her go. If he kept looking down the blouse of every woman he met searching for that tattoo, eventually he'd get slapped. Or sued. Maybe arrested.

He simply couldn't help it.

With a sigh, Jonah turned back to his computer. He needed to focus. Noah would eventually come home and suffer mightily, but until then, he needed to clean up the mess. He searched through his contact list for his accountant, Paul. He'd be able to move his assets around and get the cash he needed. He always made sure his money worked as hard for him as he did for it and invested heavily, unlike his brother, who burned through money buying silly toys.

He could get the cash; it just might take a few days for the wheels of finance to turn.

In the meantime, he'd have to find a way to stall the forensic accountant Game Town was sending over. Someone would be showing up this afternoon at two. No one had mentioned the auditor's name, so he had no idea who, or what, to expect. His strategy would rely heavily on who showed up.

If the auditor was male, Jonah would drag his dusty golf clubs from the closet and take the guy out. He hated golf, but found it to be an important social tool in the business world. Few company honchos got together to play *Madden* on their Xbox. It was a pity. Instead, they would play eighteen holes; he'd buy the auditor some drinks. Steaks. Whatever. Perhaps if the guy was hung over enough, the numbers would take longer to crunch.

If the auditor was a woman, there would be a different tactic. The golf clubs would stay in the closet, but the charm would be on in full force. Regardless of whether she had three eyes and a hunchback or looked fresh from the Parisian runways, Jonah's charisma would carry him through. Since the age of fifteen, he'd had a way with women. A gift, he supposed, and one he made good use of. Dinner and drinks would still be involved, but the ambience would improve greatly.

He wouldn't have to lay a hand on her. The last thing he needed was the woman running back to Game Town with that tale. No, Jonah wouldn't go there. The right smile, some intense eye contact and a few compliments would go far, especially with a mousy accountant who wasn't used to the attention. If he planned this right, he'd have her so hot and bothered she wouldn't be able to remember her own name, much less see the problems with the financial reports.

No matter what, Jonah would come out on top. If he had to sit down with Carl Bailey, the CEO of Game Town, and explain what was going on, he would, but if it could be avoided, he'd gladly play eighteen holes or take a lonely accountant to the theater.

He made a note to ask his assistant, Pam, what shows were playing on Broadway at the moment. He wasn't a big fan of musicals, but he found most to be tolerable enough. Except *Cats*. He wasn't making that mistake a second time. That was a phenomenal waste of four hundred dollars, which was saying a lot, given he'd easily spend that much in a week on supplies for the gourmet coffee bar they added on the twenty-third floor.

Speaking of which, he eyed his now-cold coffee with dismay. He'd get a refill and a bagel after he talked to Paul. Picking up the phone, he dialed his accountant and mentally cleared his calendar for the next week. He'd be busy courting the Game Town auditor.

Jonah just prayed it was a woman. He really hated golf.

Surely her boss was a closet sadist. There was no other explanation for why he'd send her to FlynnSoft for two to three weeks. Tim could've sent anyone. Mark. Dee. But no, he had to send Emma. She was the only one who could handle herself in that environment, he said.

Slipping her hand inside the doorway to her closet, she flipped on the light switch and stepped inside. Tim was full of it. He just wanted to see her squirm. She liked to think that she'd been hired for her top grades at Yale and her recommendations from professors, but she had a sneaking suspicion her father had gotten involved and made it happen.

Tim likely resented some rich kid getting dropped into his department against his will and enjoyed making her miserable as a result. It made her more determined than ever not to give him that satisfaction. She was going to do a good job. No—a *great* job. She would not get sucked into FlynnSoft's corporate hippie attitude. She would not fall prey to *Jonah Flynn, Golden God* and his seductive smile.

Not that the notorious CEO would waste any of his smoldering looks on Emma. She wasn't bad to look at, but the last gossip blog she'd seen had him coming out of a restaurant with a model she'd recognized from her lingerie catalog. She simply couldn't compete with abs of steel and breasts of silicone. And she wouldn't even try.

A man like Jonah Flynn was of no interest to her, anyway. He embodied everything her mother, Pauline, had warned her about. *Don't make the same mistakes as Cynthia did*, she'd say. Her older sister hadn't died because of poor choices—a plane crash had done that—but when those choices came to light after her death, the family had been scandalized. Emma had grown up as her sister's polar opposite as a result.

If Tim was being absolutely honest with her, she'd bet that's why she got the job. Dee, although competent, was a tall, thin and attractive woman easily distracted by men. If Flynn even looked at her sideways, she'd be a puddle at his feet. Forensic auditors could not puddle. Emma probably wouldn't earn a second glance.

She eyed the neatly hung rows of clothing in her closet. Although FlynnSoft was a pioneer of the übercasual work environment, there was no way she was walking into that building while wearing jeans and flip-flops. Even if she stuck out like a sore thumb amongst the laid-back software designers, she was wearing one of her suits with high heels. Her sole concession to the casual environment would be leaving off the hosiery. Summer was just around the corner in New York and she preferred staying cooler in the heat.

She pulled a charcoal-gray suit and a light blue top from the rack and smiled in approval. There was just something about the crispness of a freshly starched blouse and a smartly tailored blazer that gave her a much-needed boost of confidence.

It was just the armor she needed to go into battle against Jonah Flynn.

Battle was the wrong word, really. He wasn't the enemy. He was a potential contractor for Game Town. FlynnSoft had managed to build an extremely robust and efficient system for handling subscriptions and other in-game purchases for their addictive online game *Infinity Warriors*. Recently, they'd branched out offering the management of other online game system subscriptions to companies that needed help handling a high number of users or providing additional monetizing options. It allowed small software start-ups to focus on designing the game and let FlynnSoft manage the back end.

Before they went to contract, it was customary for the companies to have a forensic accountant review the vendor's records to ensure everything was shipshape. Carl Bailey, the man who started Game Town twenty years earlier and now headed up the board of directors, hated surprises.

Although FlynnSoft had a sterling reputation, the old man had a general distrust of a company where a suit and tie were not standard issue. Bailey wasn't getting into bed with any company he didn't think was up to snuff, even if paying Flynn was cheaper than developing the capability in-house. She was to go over everything with a fine-tooth comb.

Emma would be welcomed and provided everything she needed to do the job, but at the same time, no one liked an auditor nosing around. She might as well wear a big red button that read I Can Ruin Your Life.

That was a pretty unfair generalization. She could only ruin their lives by calling to light their own misdeeds. If they were good boys and girls, she couldn't get them into trouble.

Her mother had pounded that much into her head as a teenager. *Never say or do anything you wouldn't want printed on the front page of the newspaper*, she was always saying.

Before her sister, Cynthia, died in a plane crash, she'd been engaged to the owner of the *New York Observer*, Will Taylor. He was also the business partner of their father, George. That newspaper was delivered to her childhood home every morning, and to this day, Emma lived in fear that something she did might actually turn up there. The scandals of the remaining socialite daughter of the Dempsey family were news worth printing.

So far, so good.

With a quick glance at the clock, Emma left her closet and started getting ready. She had to be at FlynnSoft at two to meet with Mr. Flynn at his insistence.

Normally, she would've simply worn what she'd put on to go to work that morning, but she came home at lunch to change. It was nerves. Her outfit that morning was more than suitable, but she felt this need to put on something else before she went over there. To get every hair in place.

After thirty minutes of primping, Emma gave herself one last inspection. Her brown hair was twisted into a tight bun. After David moved out, she chopped it off at her shoulders in typical female defiance, but it was still long enough to pull up. Her makeup was flawless—fresh looking, not too heavy. She could still see the faint specks of freckles across her nose, which she hated, but could do nothing about.

The suit was loose because of her recent stress-induced weight loss, allowing it to hide any unfortunate bumps she didn't want to share. The blouse she wore under the coat was a flattering shade of blue and more importantly, the neckline was high enough to hide her tattoo.

The half of a heart that was inked into her chest above the swell of her left breast wasn't the only evidence of the night she'd made the mistake of letting herself go, but at the moment, it was the hardest to hide. That wouldn't be the case much longer.

Like a little devil sitting on her shoulder, Harper told her to have fun that night. And she certainly did. She hadn't intended to take it that far, but there was something about her masked hero that she couldn't resist. Before she knew it, they were having fantastic sex in the laundry room and walking down the streets of New York in the middle of the night in search of adventure.

Every time Emma washed her clothes and felt the cold metal of the washing machine against her skin, a flush of embarrassment would light her cheeks on fire. She had done her best to forget about it and the tequila had done a good job turning the experience into a fuzzy, dreamlike memory, but still, it crept into her mind from time to time. If it hadn't been for the bandage on her chest when she awoke the next morning, she might've convinced herself it had never happened.

But it had. She'd allowed herself to do anything and everything she wanted to do. She'd let David's words strike too deeply and questioned everything about her life, when in truth there was nothing wrong with the way she lived. She did everything a proper Upper East Side woman was supposed to do. She was educated, well-spoken, polished and elegant. She took pride in her work as a CPA. It was true that no one would ever describe her as the life of the party, but her escapades would never show up on the front page of the local paper, either.

In retrospect, it took one uninhibited night to prove that she was okay with being that kind of woman. There was no glory in being like her older sister, who followed each pleasurable impulse and left her family mired in scandal after her death. Then again, that one night was enough for the repercussions to echo through her entire life. She could keep it under wraps for now, but eventually everyone would find out.

And of course, the tattoo remained. Emma had considered getting it removed, but it had become her personal reminder of how dangerous the wrong choices could be. Every time she even thought about breaking out of her shell, she could look at her tattoo and remember what a bad idea it was. It was a slippery slope she was determined not to go down again. She would not become her sister and shame her family. It didn't matter how good or right it might feel in the moment.

But in keeping it, she had to work hard to ensure it stayed covered, especially in a professional setting. Or near her mother, who felt tattoos were only for bikers and inmates. Emma had tripled her ownership of high-collared tops the last few weeks. She worried about the challenge of her summer wardrobe as the temperature climbed, but she had to deal with the FlynnSoft job first.

Emma was just thankful she'd gotten hers in a place she could hide easily, unlike her hero with his tattooed hand. There was no way he could disguise his half of the heart, although she wondered how he would explain it. He was at a FlynnSoft party, so he was potentially an employee, like Harper was. She supposed that in the laid-back corporate environment, a tattoo was no big deal. Might even be a requirement.

It was just another reason to be nervous about her assignment.

At any moment, he could appear. An engineer, a programmer, hell, even the janitor. She didn't know a thing about him and had no real way to find him other than the tattoo. She'd shared a few choice details of the night with Harper, and her friend had been on high alert to discover the man's identity since then. She hadn't been as willing to let the romantic fantasy go, especially when Emma confided in her about her predicament.

A few weeks after the party, at the family Easter dinner, Emma took one look at the spiral ham and went running down the hallway to the powder room. After two more weeks of denial and antacids, she realized she had more than a tattoo to show for her wild night—she was having her anonymous hero's baby! And had no way to contact the father and tell him.

In the last three months, there were no tattooed hands to report at FlynnSoft, at least in the marketing or accounting departments, where Harper spent most her time. The odds were that even if the man worked at FlynnSoft last February, he was gone now if Harper hadn't found him. That meant Emma was on her own with this baby, whether she liked it or not. She would tell her family soon. Eventually. When she couldn't hide her belly any longer.

Another glance at the clock proved that she couldn't

delay any longer, as much as she might want to. She brushed her fingers over her hair and grabbed her purse from the table by the front door. With a fleeting look down her blouse, she opted to button her shirt one notch higher.

Just in case.

Two

It was an easy trip down to the FlynnSoft building, as she'd been there several times meeting Harper for a lunch date. They occupied the top five floors of one of the high-rises a few blocks from her apartment. The lobby was like many others with sleek, modern furniture and large LCD screens playing video clips about the company and scenes from the various video games they produced. The only difference, really, was the receptionist, who was wearing khaki shorts and a tank top. Her brown hair was pulled up into a ponytail that highlighted the multiple piercings in her ears.

If this was the first face of the company, she had no doubt things would go downhill from here. After checking her in, the woman gave her a temporary access badge and walked her back to the elevators. She showed her how to wave her badge over the sensor, allowing her to select the twenty-fifth floor, where the executive offices were located.

Emma considered stopping on the twenty-fourth-floor business wing to see Harper, but she didn't have time. They'd see each other plenty over the next few weeks, she was certain. Instead, she pushed the button that read 25 and closed her eyes. As the elevator rose, Emma could feel her anxiety rising, as well. She wished she knew why. She was more than capable of doing this job and being successful. She was an excellent auditor and accountant. Harper had done nothing but praise the company and everyone she worked with. Everything would be fine.

Exiting onto the twenty-fifth and top floor of the building, Emma headed down the hallway to the right as she'd been directed. Pausing in one of the doorways with a placard that read Gaming Lounge, she watched a couple of employees playing foosball. In any other company, the large space would be a conference room, but here, there was a pool table, a *Ms. Pac-Man* machine and some beanbag chairs arranged around a big-screen television.

The players stopped their game to look over at her, staring as though she were wearing a clown suit instead of well-tailored gray separates. Emma quickly started back down the hallway to avoid their gazes. As though they had room to judge with their Converse and baseball caps.

She finally came to a large desk at the end of the hallway. A woman in a spring sundress with reddish-blond hair sat at it, talking into a headset and typing at her computer. She gave a quick glance to Emma and ended her call.

"You must be the auditor sent by Game Town." She stood and grinned, offering her hand over the desk.

Emma accepted it with a self-conscious smile. "Yes, I'm Emma Dempsey. How did you guess?"

The woman laughed, her eyes running over Emma's professional outfit a second time. "I'm Pam, Jonah's assistant. He stepped down the hall, but he should be back any second. Can I get you a drink while you wait? A latte or a soda or something?"

Emma arched a confused eyebrow and shook her head. She didn't want any of the staff going to any trouble on her behalf. Some companies went to great lengths to kiss up to auditors and she didn't want to start out setting that kind of precedent. "No, thank you."

"Okay, but if you change your mind just let me know. We have a coffee bar on the twenty-third floor in addition to a Starbucks on the ground level. I'm sure you'll get the full tour, but while you're here, we hope you'll make use of all our employee amenities. We also have a gym, several game rooms and a pretty decent cafeteria with a salad bar where employees can eat at no charge. All the vending machines are also free to keep our programmers awake and productive."

"Wow." There wasn't really a better word for it. Emma had read in magazines about how Jonah Flynn was some sort of modern business pioneer who was changing everything. That he strived to create a workplace where people wanted to go so that staff would be happier and more productive. A casual work environment was only one piece. Apparently, a foosball table and free caffeinated beverages were another.

"This is a great place to work. Hopefully you'll enjoy your time with us." Pam walked out from behind her station and Emma noticed she was barefoot with sparkly, hot pink nail polish. At this point, that detail was no longer a surprise. Padding softly across the plush carpet, she escorted Emma to a set of double doors a few feet away. She pushed one of the heavy oak panels open, and then stepped back and gestured for her to go inside. "Have a seat and Jonah will be with you shortly."

The door closed silently behind her, and Pam and her toes disappeared, leaving Emma alone in Jonah Flynn's office.

As instructed, she quickly settled into one of the black leather guest chairs, crossing her ankles and holding her portfolio across her lap. She couldn't help but look around as her fingers nervously drummed against the notebook.

The office was massive with impersonal executive-type furniture that was very similar to the decor of the lobby. Glass and chrome, black leather, bookshelves with awards and books he'd probably never read. There was a large conference table that ran along the length of the floor-to-ceiling windows overlooking an amazing view of Manhattan.

She wasn't quite sure what she was expecting to find in the notorious CEO's office—perhaps a stripper pole and a *Donkey Kong* machine—but it all seemed to fit the space in a generic way aside from the giant cardboard cutout of what must be one of his video game characters. Emma was unfamiliar with it, but it looked like some kind of blue troll in battle armor.

There were only a few unexpected details. A photograph of a butterfly on his desk. A world's greatest boss trophy on the shelf behind his chair. A child's crayon drawing addressed to "Mr. Jonah" pinned to his cork-board. She was pretty certain he didn't have children, but she only knew what the gossip bloggers reported, which could be far from the truth.

"Miss Dempsey. Sorry to keep you waiting," a man's voice called out to her from over her shoulder.

With a nervous smile, Emma got up from her chair and turned to face him. He was standing in the doorway, taking up most of the space with his broad shoulders. Shoulders that were covered in a clingy brown T-shirt with what looked like some cartoon knights on the front. He was wearing loose-fitted jeans with a torn-up knee and well-broken-in high-top Converse sneakers. And a Rolex. She could see the large diamonds on the face from across the room as he held his drink.

What a contradiction. Software. Foosball. Jeans. Diamonds. You didn't run into this kind of CEO every day.

As he came closer, she only had a moment to register the face she'd seen in so many magazines: the distinctive dark brown hair with the undercut shaved on the sides, the deep blue eyes that seemed to leap from the glossy pages, the crooked smile that was endearing and arousing all at once. All of it was coming at her, full speed ahead.

Letting her business training kick into gear, she held out her hand. "A pleasure to meet you, Mr. Flynn," she said.

Jonah reached out to her, gripping her with a warm, firm shake. His dark eyes seemed to be appraising her somehow, a faint smile curling the corners of his mouth. If she didn't know better, she'd say he looked pleased about something.

"Call me Jonah. And the pleasure is all mine," he said, his voice as deep and smooth as melted dark chocolate with the hint of a British accent curling his words.

"Emma," she reciprocated, although the word barely made it across her tongue. Emma suddenly felt very aware of herself. Of him. Of the newly uncomfortable temperature of the room that made tiny beads of perspiration gather at the nape of her neck. His cologne tickled her nose, a spicy male scent that was infinitely appealing and somewhat familiar.

She tried to swallow, but a thick lump had formed in her throat. She couldn't even speak while he continued to touch her. Did he have this effect on every woman or was she just that desperate after three months of celibacy and her pregnancy hormones conspiring against her?

Jonah Flynn was everything she expected him to be and then some. The magazines truly hadn't done the man justice. He was handsome without being too pretty, with hard angles and powerful, lean muscles flexing beneath the cotton of his shirt as he reached out to her. His every move was smooth and deliberate, exuding power and confidence even in a T-shirt and jeans. You just couldn't capture that in a picture.

She was blushing; she knew she had to be. How embarrassing. This was not going well at all. She had set out to prove to Tim that she could handle this assignment and here she was, practically mute and drooling after only a few seconds in the CEO's presence. Her clothes should be too big, since she had instantly transformed back into an infatuated twelve-year-old girl.

She needed to pull it together—and now. Emma broke eye contact to collect herself. Casually gazing down, she caught a glimpse of red, then recognized the other half of her tattoo etched into Jonah Flynn's hand.

Emma immediately began to choke.

* * *

Perfect. He'd never get the contract with Game Town if he killed the auditor on the first day.

Jonah quickly escorted the woman to a chair and buzzed Pam to bring her a bottle of water. He wasn't quite sure what just happened. One minute, she was smiling and shaking his hand, the next she was hyperventilating and turning bright red. Maybe it was an allergic reaction. He'd have Pam take the flower arrangement on his conference table to her area just in case. Wasn't there an EpiPen in the kitchen first aid kit? That would be his next move.

She'd calmed down a bit once she sat. Maybe she'd just swallowed her gum. No. She had pearl earrings and crossed ankles despite her inability to breathe. She definitely wasn't the kind of woman who chewed bubble gum at work. If at all.

Pam breezed through the door with the water, which Emma gratefully accepted. Jonah held out his hand for Pam to stand by until he was certain the woman would recover.

Emma took a few breaths, a few sips and closed her eyes. Things were improving. He waved Pam off, but knew she'd be poised and ready if she were needed.

He knelt down in front of Emma, watching with concern as her breathing stabilized and her color began returning to normal. At least, he supposed it was normal. The woman was awfully pale, but his expectations were skewed by spray-tanned celebutantes who usually sported an orange undertone to their skin. No, he decided. Pale was normal.

Once she was no longer deprived of oxygen, he had to admit she was quite pretty. She had silky brown hair that begged to be hanging loose around her shoulders, but she'd forced it into submission in a knot-like bun. She had an interesting face, almost heart shaped, with full lips and creamy skin she didn't hide under a ton of makeup.

From what he could see of her figure beneath that dowdy suit, she had ample curves in all the right places. Although he'd been photographed with the occasional model type, he gravitated toward the lingerie and swim-suit girls because they were equipped with the assets he was looking for.

Completing his inventory, he noticed her nicely mani-cured nails and naked ring finger. A single woman would be much easier to work his charms on.

This might not be the worst couple of weeks after all. Keeping Emma's mind off the books could turn out to be a pleasurable experience for them both.

"Are you okay?" he asked once she'd drained half the water bottle and he was certain she could speak again.

Emma swallowed hard and nodded, although her eyes were glued to his hand as it rested on her knee. "Yes, I'm sorry about that."

Following her gaze, he immediately removed his hand and stood up, allowing her some personal space. "Don't apologize. Is there anything Pam or I can do? Move the flowers, perhaps?"

"Oh no," she insisted. "I'm fine, really. Please don't worry about me."

She was the kind of woman who didn't like to be fussed over. Jonah made a mental note. "Okay, well, back to business, then." He rounded his desk and sank into the soft leather of his chair. "The Game Town people said it should take you a few weeks to go through everything."

"Yes." She nodded. "Perhaps less if the records are

easily accessible and someone on staff can assist me with questions."

"Of course. I'll alert the finance people to have everything ready for you tomorrow. I'm sure they'll be happy to assist you with anything you need. You have our full cooperation. Everyone is very excited about this potential partnership with Game Town."

"I'm glad to hear it. I'm ready to get started."

Jonah arched an eyebrow, but quickly dropped it back in line. What was the rush? He *would* get an auditor who was hell-bent on getting the job done when it was the last thing he wanted. "How about we go on a tour first?"

"That's not necessary," she said, her answer almost too quick. "I'm sure you have more important things on your agenda. If Pam can point me to my desk, I'm sure I can make do."

If Jonah didn't know better, it sounded like she was trying to dismiss him. Women never dismissed him. He wasn't going to let this one buck the trend. "Nonsense," he insisted, pushing out of his chair to end the argument. "I've got some time and I want to make sure you're settled."

Emma stood, somewhat reluctantly, and walked out of the office ahead of him. Despite her stiff manners, she moved fluidly and gracefully as a woman should. The curves of her rear swayed tantalizingly from left to right as she walked in her high heels to the door. Maybe that suit wasn't so bad after all. It fit nicely, hugging her hips just tight enough. He'd prefer to see her in a pair of clingy jeans and a tight little T-shirt, but the suit was growing on him. As were other things.

He took a deep breath to stifle the thoughts and pulled up alongside her once they started down the hall. "I'm sure you saw our gaming lounge on your way in. Each floor has one." They paused at the doorway and he couldn't help but beam with pride. It was one of his favorite innovations. He probably spent as much time in these rooms as anyone. It was good for the spirit to break away for a while. It was refreshing and gave new enthusiasm to tackle the workload.

"That's very nice." Emma's voice was cold and polite.

She seemed decidedly disinterested and it annoyed him. She should be impressed like everyone else. *Forbes* magazine had done an article on his game lounges and sky-high productivity levels. It was groundbreaking territory. Certainly it should evoke more interest than her watery, patronizing smile suggested. Perhaps if he made it more personal? "What's your favorite video game? We have quite a collection here outside of the ones we produce in-house."

"I'm sorry. I don't play video games."

Jonah tried not to frown. Surely in this day and age everyone had a favorite game. Even his grandmother played bridge on the computer. "Not even *Super Mario Brothers* when you were a kid? *Sonic the Hedgehog*? *Tetris*, even?"

She shook her head, sending a dark strand of hair down along the curve of her cheek. It gave her a softness he found quite a bit more attractive than the uptight accountant thing she had going with that bun. Wearing her hair down around her shoulders would be infinitely more appealing. Seeing the brown waves tousled across one of his pillowcases would be even better. Although that couldn't be a part of his plan while the Game Town deal was pending and she worked under his roof, it didn't mean he couldn't continue to pursue her later.

Emma immediately tucked the rogue strand behind her ear and opened her mouth to ruin the fantasy he'd built in his head. "I was raised not to waste time in idle pursuits."

This time he had to frown. Idle pursuits. *Hmph.* His video game obsession as a child had blossomed into a multimillion-dollar video game empire. Not exactly idle. He wondered what she did with her time that was so superior. She certainly couldn't spend all her weekends feeding the hungry and knitting blankets for the homeless. Sweet ass or no, she was starting to work his nerves. "All work and no play can make for a dull girl."

Emma turned to him with a blankly polite expression. "There's no sin in being dull. Is it better to have scandal chasing your tail?"

"No, but it's certainly more fun." He couldn't help the sarcastic retort. The tone of condescension coming from her full, soft peach lips was a contradiction that set his teeth on edge. It was public knowledge that Jonah had scandal chasing his tail on more than one occasion. If nothing else, it kept a man on his toes.

Emma turned away from the game room and continued down the hall.

This time, watching her walk away was not nearly as enticing, as he'd been dismissed again. Containing his aggravation, he moved quickly to pull alongside her. Taking a breath, he decided to start over. She might be grating his nerves, but Emma was his pet project for the next few weeks.

"You'll be sitting on the twenty-fourth floor with the finance group while you're here. Before we go down there, let's stop by the twenty-third floor and I'll show you the coffee bar. I know I always need something to perk me up midafternoon."

"Mr. Flynn—"

"Jonah," he pressed with the smile that always got him his way where women were concerned.

"*Jonah*, this really isn't necessary. I'm sure someone other than the CEO can show me the coffee bar and the gym and the cafeteria. Right now, I really just want to get out of your hair and start to work."

He mentally amended his prior statement—his smile usually got him his way. Emma seemed immune. He sighed in resignation and held out a hand to escort her to the elevators. How was he supposed to charm this woman when she wouldn't let him? It was downright frustrating. "I'll just show you the area where you'll work, then."

They were silent as they waited for the elevators, which were running slowly just to spite him today. He had to admit he preferred her quiet. When her mouth was closed, she was attractive and graceful with just a touch of mystery in the green eyes that appraised him. When she spoke, it became abundantly clear that they came from two very different schools of thought where business and pleasure were concerned.

Jonah didn't know if it was better or worse that he found her perfume so appealing. Actually, as he anxiously watched the digital numbers of the elevator climb, he began to wonder if it was a perfume at all. The scent was more like a clean, fresh mix of shampoo and a lady's hand cream. It suited her more than the heavy stink of the perfumes that made his nose twinge. Much more delicate. Like the line of her collarbone that was barely visible at the V of her blouse.

The reflex to glance down her top for a tattoo was stifled by the blue dress shirt she wore. One less woman to slap him with a harassment suit, he supposed. Besides, Miss Goody Two-shoes was the least likely candidate to be his butterfly that he'd run across yet.

The doors finally opened and they took the short trip to the twenty-fourth-floor finance department. As they walked, he noticed Emma's gaze didn't wander like so many other visitors. Normally people were interested in the untraditional workings of FlynnSoft. Emma's vision was fixed like a laser in front of her. Her intensity was both intriguing and a touch disconcerting. Would she be this focused on the financial reports?

He stopped at a visitor's office and opened the door. The small L-shaped desk took up much of the space with the computer setup and phone occupying one whole side. There was a corporate lithograph framed on one wall and a ficus shoved in the corner. It wasn't intended for long-term occupancy, but certainly it would be adequate for the short time she required it.

"This will be your home for the next few weeks. The desk is full of supplies, the phone is activated and there's a docking station for your laptop. If you need anything, the finance assistant, Angela, can help you. She's down the hall and to the left."

Emma watched him gesture, then nodded curtly. Another annoyingly dismissive gesture. The woman just couldn't wait for him to go away. What exactly was her problem? She was tight as a drum, every muscle taut, and anxious as though she itched to brush past him into the office and shut the door in his face. Why would such an attractive woman be wound up so damn tightly? She needed a drink. Or a good lay. Both couldn't hurt. He'd be happy to oblige if she'd give him the opportunity.

"Are you all right, Emma?"

Her head snapped toward him, a slight frown puckering the area between her eyebrows. Her green eyes searched his face for a moment before she spoke. "I'm fine."

The hell she was. But pushing her probably wasn't the best tactic this early on, so he let it slide. He didn't have to claim victory on the first day. He'd do it soon enough.

"You just seem a little uncomfortable. I assure you none of us bite." He planted his right hand on the door frame and leaned closer to her to emphasize his words. "You might even find you enjoy your time with us."

Emma's face went pale, her eyes focused on his hand and completely ignoring his persuasive charms. When she turned back to him, she flashed a saccharine smile. Sweetly artificial. "Of course. I'm just anxious to get settled in."

His hand fell heavy at his side. This wasn't going as well as he'd planned. He wasn't sure if she was deliberately being difficult or she was just like this normally. Paul had better be rushing that transaction because his wine-and-dine plan might not pan out the way he hoped. He'd just been assigned the only woman in Manhattan who was immune to him. Possibly even annoyed by him.

Maybe it was just the work environment. It was possible she stuck to strict business protocol and the casual interactions he was used to made her uncomfortable. All the better to get her away from the office, then. Give her the chance to let her hair down, kick off those heels and relax. He'd drop the dinner invitation, then leave her alone for the rest of the afternoon to stew over the possibilities. The anticipation alone would do a great deal of the work for him.

He glanced at his watch to lay it on thick. "I'd love to talk to you some more about your assignment, but I'm afraid I have a meeting in a few minutes. Would you be interested in having dinner with me tomorrow night?"

"No."

Jonah opened his mouth to suggest a restaurant and stopped cold. Had she just said no? That couldn't be right. "What?"

Her pale skin flushed pink and her eyes grew wide for a moment as she seemed to realize her mistake. "I mean no, *thank you*," she corrected, turning on her heel and disappearing into her new office with a swift click of the door.

Three

The following morning, Emma met Harper at the twenty-third-floor coffee bar before work. She'd barely slept the night before and was seriously in need of some caffeine.

"You look like hell," Harper said, always the honest one. When they'd first met at the sorority house, Emma wasn't quite sure what to think of her. Now she'd come to appreciate her candor. Most of the time.

"Thanks. Good morning to you, too."

They got into line and waited to place their orders. "What's wrong?" Harper asked.

"I just didn't sleep well last night."

Harper nodded and took a step forward to call out her customized coffee to the guy at the counter. Emma watched her, her brain trying to decide what she wanted to drink, but it simply refused to function like it should. She hadn't slept. Of course, she hadn't told Harper why.

She'd been in a nervous tizzy. Jonah Flynn. The playboy millionaire of the software world had the matching half to her tattoo. Fate had played a cruel joke. There was not a worse match on the planet for her, much less to father her child. It was just as well she'd kept her identity a secret. He most certainly would've been disappointed to see who she was beyond the tequila and the mask. And fatherhood for the most elusive bachelor in the five boroughs? Yeah, right.

And yet, as she lay in bed that night attempting to sleep, all she could think about was him. How he'd saved her from the creep. How a thrill of excitement had raced through her when he kissed her for the first time. She remembered his hands running over her body as though he couldn't get enough of her. After everything with David, it had felt incredible to be desired like that. It was a feeling that could easily become addictive and that meant it was dangerous.

She'd tried to forget about that night and had been mostly successful, but her body remembered. Being in the same room, touching him and breathing in his familiar scent had brought it all back. With a vengeance. In the dark of her bedroom, she could easily recall the sensations he'd coaxed from her body. Not once, in two years with David, had she ever responded like that. It was something raw, primal.

"Ma'am?"

Emma turned to the man at the counter, who was patiently waiting on her drink order. "Hot tea," she blurted. Although she probably needed the jolt of a black cup of coffee, she knew she wasn't supposed to have too much caffeine. That was a cruel irony for pregnant women everywhere.

The area was as miserably crowded as any Starbucks, so when their drinks were ready, they took them and their pastries, and went on their way back to their offices.

Harper seemed quite pleased with her new work arrangement. "I can get used to having you working here. I'd finally have someone to talk to. Everyone here is pleasant and all, but most of them have their heads in the clouds or their noses in a computer."

Emma had noticed that. Software designers were definitely different than most of the people she'd worked with. They were intensely focused, usually not even making eye contact or saying hello in the hallway. They were all on some mission, be it to fix a software bug or beat their nemesis at some video game. That or perhaps they just didn't know how to speak to women.

"Then why do you stay?" Emma asked. "We both know you don't need to work."

Harper narrowed her gaze at Emma, then shrugged. "I get bored doing nothing."

"You could always help Oliver. He might like having his sister there at the family business."

"Oliver doesn't need my help with anything. Besides, this place is fun. You'll get spoiled quickly. I save so much money with the free food. I was able to drop my gym membership, too, which saved me a bundle. Now I can use that money for Louis Vuitton handbags and trips to Paris, instead. I enjoy having income I earned on my own, not because of my last name. You couldn't get me to leave here and I hope you'll feel the same. We do need to make some adjustments to your wardrobe, though."

Emma looked at Harper's khaki capris and silky, sleeveless top, then down at her conservative suit and frowned. It was her favorite. She'd always thought the dark green had complemented her coloring. "I can't help it if everyone here dresses like college students. I refuse to assimilate. And don't you get your heart set on me being here past a few weeks. The minute I can get out of here, I will."

They paused at the elevator and Harper pushed the button. "Why are you so anxious to go? Is it that bad?"

It wasn't, but staying here a moment longer than she had to was courting disaster. Emma wondered how much she should tell Harper about yesterday. Harper was one of her best friends, but she was lacking in social couth. Anything she told her would instantly be passed along to their friends Violet and Lucy, as well. From there, who knows who would find out. Emma wanted Jonah to stay in the dark about her identity for the time being and the best way to make that happen was to keep her friends out of the loop.

"I'm just not comfortable here."

"You're afraid of running into *him*." The remark hit a little too close to home for her taste. Harper always had a way of seeing too much where Emma was concerned. It made her an excellent friend, but left Emma little privacy, even in her own head.

There was no sense in denying it. "Yes, I'll admit it. It would be awkward, at best, to run into him. And at worst, a conflict of interest if anyone at Game Town found out. My entire report could be compromised if anyone thought I was personally involved with someone here."

"Or it could be the most wonderful thing ever. I thought you wanted to find him. You know, for the sake of the *B-A-B-Y*." She mouthed the last part silently.

Emma didn't respond. Harper was too wrapped up in her romantic ideas to see the situation objectively and there was no sense in explaining herself any further. She just stepped onto the elevator when the doors opened and sipped her hot tea.

"You've already seen him!" Harper accused.

She snapped her head to the side to confirm they were alone in the elevator. "What? No, of course not."

Harper was unconvinced by her response. "Who is it? Is he cute? What department does he work in?"

The doors opened to the twenty-fourth floor and Emma waved at her friend to be discreet as they stepped out. "Would you keep it down? I don't want everyone to know."

"Okay, but you've gotta tell me. I can keep it a secret."

Emma eyed her with dismay. She loved her friend, but honestly… "No, you can't."

Harper frowned and planted a hand defiantly on her hip. "Oh, come on. Why not? I mean, it isn't like it's the CEO or something. Bagging Jonah would be quite gossipworthy, but anyone else is just run-of-the-mill office news. I don't know what the big dea—"

Emma could feel the color drain from her face and there was nothing she could do to stop it. Harper halted in her tracks, forcing Emma to turn and look back at her. Her friend's jaw had dropped open, her perpetual stream of words uncharacteristically on hold.

"Oh my God," she finally managed.

"Shh! Harper, really. It doesn't matter."

"The hell it doesn't!" Her voice dropped to a hushed whisper that was still too loud for Emma's taste. "Jonah Flynn? Seriously?"

Emma nodded. "But he doesn't know who I am or know anything about the baby. And I intend to keep it that way for now. You understand?"

Harper nodded, her mind visibly blown by her friend's news. "Jonah Flynn is the hottest man I've ever seen in real life. He and my brother are friends, and it took everything I had not to throw myself at him every time he came to the house. I can't believe you two… How did you not jump into his lap when you realized who he was?"

"Have we met?"

Harper frowned. "You're right. A damn shame, though. What a prize to land. He was totally smitten with you."

"He's a player. I seriously doubt that."

"If you believe the gossip, then yes, Jonah Flynn is a notorious womanizer. But that's not the guy I've known over the years. And the guy you were with was willing to tattoo himself after one night together on the off chance it might reunite you someday. A playboy wouldn't have an inch of skin unmarked if that was what he did with everyone. You were special to him. Special enough for a guy that goes through women like tissues to take serious notice."

That was true. Emma hadn't spied another tattoo on what she'd seen of his body, then or now. But she refused to believe there was any kind of future with him. Even if he was interested in starting something, he wanted the woman she was that night. Not regular old Emma. And she swore she'd never be that woman again. So what was the point? Telling him who she was would just torture them both and ruin the memory of that night.

And yet she had to. Or did she? Her hand dropped protectively to her belly. If Jonah rejected Emma and their child, it could scar the baby forever knowing its father didn't want him or her. Would it be better to keep quiet? The idea was unsettling to her, but until she decided, not a word could get out. "You have to keep this a secret, Harper. No one can know. Not Violet, not Lucy, not your brother and especially not Jonah."

"Cross my heart." Harper sighed in disgust and Emma could see it was almost physically painful for her to say the words. "You'd better keep that tat of yours under wraps, though."

Emma straightened her collar nervously and started back down the hallway. "I don't make a habit of displaying my décolletage and have every intention of keeping it hidden. I'm here to do my job and get out."

"But what about the baby?" Harper trailed behind her.

"I don't know, Harper. What happened between us is over. Never to be repeated. Ancient history. I don't know that the baby will change that." Emma reached out and opened the door to her office. Sitting on her desk was a large crystal vase filled to overflowing with white lilies in full bloom. The warm scent of them was nearly overwhelming in the small space, making her happy that she was past her morning sickness. She'd never received a more beautiful bouquet of flowers in her life.

She stepped inside and plucked the card from the plastic prong. As she flipped open the envelope, she couldn't decide if she wanted them to be from Jonah or not. His attentions, although flattering, were pointless and even dangerous if he knew who she really was. Yet her impractical, inner girl couldn't help but wish they were from the handsome businessman.

"'To Emma,'" she read, her stomach aflutter with nerves and excitement. "'Welcome to FlynnSoft. I look forward to getting to know you better.' It's signed *Jonah*."

"Ancient history, eh?" Harper said, leaning in to sniff one of the flowers. "Are you so sure about that?"

* * *

Jonah came down the hallway from the elevator, coffee in one hand, bagel in the other, and paused outside his office. There was a large and quite stunning crystal vase of white Casablanca lilies sitting on Pam's desk. He frowned. He'd specifically ordered that type of lily for Emma because he felt they were a reflection of her: elegant, pure and refined. They didn't make any flowers that were stuffy and aggravating.

Plus, he thought she'd see right through roses. Lilies were different, exotic. He'd spent enough on them to catch the attention of even the most difficult to please female.

He would be the first to admit he typically didn't have to work that hard to woo the ladies. He'd been told that with his good looks and irresistible charm, the panties of every woman within a fifty-yard radius simply flew off. It made for an amusing visual, one he'd like to witness really, but he wasn't naive. He figured their interest in him probably had more to do with the fact that he was filthy rich rather than charming. Panties were consistently repelled by obscene displays of money.

But Emma was different. Her iron underwear stayed firmly in place when he was around. And given her stiff, overly polite demeanor and cutting tongue, they were probably chafing.

That was just not acceptable. The one time he needed his way with women to work without fail… The auditor Game Town hired was priority one even if charming her would take everything he had. He was willing to shift his tactics and restrategize his game plan, but in the end, he would be successful.

Even if right now, things didn't appear to be going so

well. Emma had rejected the flowers and in record time. The odds of Pam receiving the same flowers on the same day were slim to none.

"Did Miss Dempsey bring those up here?" he asked.

Pam was beaming with the large bouquet perched on her desk. She seemed to really take pleasure in having them there where everyone who passed by, including her, could see them. Well, at least someone was enjoying them. The money hadn't gone entirely to waste.

"Yes," she said. "She told me she was allergic and I should enjoy them. Aren't they pretty?"

He made a mental note to buy his assistant flowers more often. Make that all the administrative assistants. The occasional flowers probably appealed to them more than the *Ms. Pac-Man* machines, and he probably catered too much to the programmers with his corporate innovations. They couldn't function without the admin staff and something like that would be great for their morale.

"Lovely indeed." He continued past her desk to his office with his breakfast in hand and let the door slam behind him. Allergic, his ass. She swore yesterday that her choking fit had nothing to do with the flowers and he believed her. This was about her being stubborn. Never in his life had he run across a woman so resistant to him. It didn't make any damn sense.

Jonah settled into his chair, set down his food and fired up his computer with a stiff punch of his finger. It almost made him wonder if he'd romanced her before. Or one of her friends. She had the attitude of a woman who'd been loved and left by him or someone like him in the past.

But that couldn't be the case. Despite the lengthy list, Jonah had a great memory for names and faces. He'd never laid eyes on Emma Dempsey before yesterday. If she was bitter about men like him, it wasn't his doing.

But it would be his job to change her outlook. The deal with Game Town was riding on it. Even if he could get his hands on Noah and wring three million dollars from his neck, the transaction would be in the records.

His phone rang, an unknown number lighting up the display. Pam had put the call through, so he figured he wasn't about to be assaulted by a telemarketer.

"Jonah Flynn," he said into the receiver.

"Hey, it's your favorite brother."

Speak of the devil. Jonah took a deep breath before he said anything, choosing each word carefully. "I've told you before that Elijah is my favorite brother, but Noah, you're just the man I was looking for."

His brother chuckled on the line. They both knew the operations of FlynnSoft had nothing to do with Noah. He occupied an office. Drew a paycheck. On a rare occasion when he was bored with his other mysterious pursuits, he helped with charity golf tournaments and presented large, cardboard checks.

"What's so important that it couldn't wait until I came back from this trip? This call is costing me a fortune."

"What?" Jonah asked. "About three million dollars?"

The silence on the end of the line told him everything he needed to know. Noah had taken the money but didn't think anyone would notice it so quickly. Maybe any other time they might not have noticed it before he replaced it. But his timing sucked and Emma would find it, Jonah had no question.

"Listen, I don't care whether you blew it on hookers and fruity drinks or built schools for poor children. It doesn't matter. But I want it back right now."

"Yeah, that's a little iffy at the moment. I don't exactly have it right now. But hopefully I will by the time I come home."

"And when will that be?"

"Two weeks at the most."

"Okay, fine. But if it isn't back in my hands—*in full*—within fifteen minutes of you arriving in the US, I'm going to take every penny out of you with my fist."

"Jonah, I—"

"I don't want to hear your excuses. You come up with three million bucks or I will make you so miserable you'll wish you'd stayed in Thailand. Am I clear?"

This time, Noah didn't try to argue. "Crystal. Have you told Mother?"

Now it was Jonah's turn to laugh. "No. And I have no intention of doing it unless I have to. You and I both know her heart can't take the stress, although it doesn't stop you from pushing the boundaries."

"I would never deliberately hurt Mother," Noah argued.

Jonah shook his head in dismay. "It doesn't matter whether it's deliberate or not, you still do it. You never think of anyone but yourself."

"And you don't think of anyone but your employees and your company," Noah countered. "You practically ignore the whole family. When was the last time you went to the estate to visit her? Or came to my apartment? Or Elijah's place? You accuse me of blowing money on Thai hookers and you spend every bit of time and money you've got on vapid supermodels."

Jonah's jaw grew tighter with every word out of his youngest brother's mouth. If he had the time, he'd fly to Thailand right that instant just so he could punch Noah in the face. His brother seemed to think that this company had appeared out of thin air. That Jonah hadn't had to pour his heart and soul, in addition to all his free time, into building it and making it a success. When he did get to play, he played hard. Yeah, he didn't spend much time with his family, but they all had their own lives, too. None of them had knocked on his door recently, either.

"The company is important to me, yes. It supports a lot of people, including you in case you've forgotten. I have pride in what I've built and I'm not about to lose it because you're a thoughtless little prick. You do know the auditor from the Game Town deal is here, right? That your little stunt may have cost the company a huge, lucrative contract?"

"Oh hell," Noah swore. "I completely forgot about that. I didn't think—"

"No, you didn't think, Noah. You never do."

There was an awkward silence on the line for a few moments while Jonah took another deep breath.

"Do you think they'll find it?" he asked.

"Probably. You did everything short of highlighting the withdrawal with a yellow marker. But I'm trying to clean it up. Paul's moving some money around. Temporarily," he emphasized, "to cover the gap until you pay it back."

"I will pay it back, Jonah."

"Yeah, yeah," he sighed. "Just don't make me regret trusting you."

"I promise you won't."

"I'll see you when you get back," Jonah said, hanging up the phone.

He wanted to believe his brother, but it was hard. He was never a bad kid, just one who was used to getting

ANDREA LAURENCE 57

his way. As the youngest, his pouty lip would melt their mother's heart in an instant, especially after Dad died. When he got older, people seemed to go out of their way to give him whatever he asked them for.

If Jonah was smart, he'd put Noah to work full-time on corporate fund-raisers. His best job fit might be applying that skill to encourage rich people to part with their money. In this economy, FlynnSoft wasn't able to raise as many outside dollars for charity. Noah might make the difference.

That is, if his unorthodox loan didn't cost them a huge contract and put all their donation programs on hold.

Jonah leaned back in his chair and took a bite of his bagel. The day was so complicated already and it wasn't even 9:00 a.m. yet. Two weeks. He had to figure out how to replace or bury the stolen money until Noah came back. And then find some way to put it back in without raising more flags.

Until then, he had to find a way to get around Emma's defenses. The direct approach wasn't working and he didn't want to strong-arm her. He'd never had to beg or coerce a woman to go out with him in his life and he wasn't about to start now. It didn't exactly set the right mood. He wanted her ready and willing, not even more stiff and distant than she already was.

It really was a shame. Emma was a beautiful woman. A sensual woman, although she seemed determined to keep that fully under wraps. He could tell by the luscious sway of her hips and the way her full lips parted slightly when he leaned near to her. She had a reaction to him. Certainly. She just wasn't willing to do anything about it. Yet.

But he could plant the seed. Get under her skin. Whether

or not she agreed to let him wine and dine her, he was going to do everything in his power to make sure she went home every night and thought about him. Whether it was with irritation or suppressed lust, he didn't care. Either would be enough to help her lose focus, and that was the most important part.

It would take Paul a couple more days to get the money. Until then, he had some unofficial FlynnSoft business to tend to.

Popping the last of his bagel in his mouth, Jonah got up from the desk and went in search of his curvy, up-tight auditor.

Four

Emma had rarely been as happy to get home as she was tonight. It seemed like no matter where she went or what she was doing, she would run into Jonah. Not like he was following her; he was just always there. She'd look up from the copier and see him down the hall talking to someone. He'd look at her and smile, the charming grin chipping away at her defenses before he turned back to his discussion. He was in the cafeteria, the coffee bar, passing her in the hallway...*constantly.*

And when Jonah wasn't there, she found herself thinking about him anyway with a confusing mix of irritation and, if she was honest with herself, desire.

She didn't want to admit it, but no red-blooded woman could resist Jonah's charms. Emma had tried her best, but he was infuriatingly persistent and wearing her down. Their past didn't help. Knowing what he could coax from her body, knowing what it felt like to cling to him, un-inhibited and anonymous, made it that much worse. She couldn't concentrate. The lines of the financial records blurred together, the math not adding up in her head no matter how many times she ran the figures. Her focus was not on the audit and it absolutely had to be—charming, sexy CEO be damned.

It was a relief to get home, the one place where she knew she was safe from Jonah Flynn. There was something about the feminine fabrics, soft throw pillows and cheerful colors that instantly made her entire body and mind relax. She'd decorated her Upper East Side apartment to look like a cozy retreat out of *Country Living* magazine, casual and inviting.

And yet, when she slipped out of her work clothes and into something more comfortable, she realized she wasn't even safe from Jonah here. As she stood in the bathroom, clutching a worn T-shirt to pull over her head, she caught a glimpse of herself in the mirror. There, just above the bare swell of her breast, was the blasted tattoo staring back at her.

She could still see him standing there, his mask obscuring everything but the same boyish grin, sharp jaw and dark blue eyes that seemed to rid her of all her good sense.

"Let's get a tattoo," he'd said.

Emma hadn't realized they'd stopped on the sidewalk outside a tattoo parlor until he said that. It wasn't the kind of place she typically took notice of. Or had any interest in going to.

"Two halves of one heart," he'd lobbied and pressed the palm of his hand against the bare skin of her chest exposed by the low neckline of her top. His fingertips had gently curved around the edge of her breast, sending an unanticipated wave of pleasure through her. He had the uncanny ability to render her brain butter with the simplest touch.

"Right here." He'd traced his skin at the juncture of his thumb and index finger, then across her skin, showing how their touch would make the heart whole. "If we're meant to be together after tonight, I'll find you. And this heart will be how we'll recognize one another."

Emma's heart had swelled in her chest. His suggestion had been romantic and spur-of-the-moment and completely stupid. Not once in her life had she ever considered getting a tattoo, but that night had included a lot of firsts for her. With his hand gently caressing her and those ocean-blue eyes penetrating her soul, she couldn't help but follow him into the shop.

Looking in the mirror now, she let her fingertip trace the heart the way his had done. Just imagining it was his hand instead of her own sent a shiver of longing through her body and her skin drew tight with gooseflesh. He'd been the last man to touch her, three long months ago. Her realization that she was pregnant with the stranger's child had been a big enough disruption, making her physical needs easy to ignore, but now, knowing how close he was, it was as though her libido had flipped a switch.

Flustered by her wanton response to the ghost of a man she couldn't have, she pulled the T-shirt over her head and marched back into the living room to make dinner.

It was Tuesday and if she kept daydreaming, the girls would arrive and she wouldn't be ready.

Every Tuesday, Lucy, Harper and Violet gathered at Emma's apartment for dinner and their favorite television series. They took turns cooking or buying takeout. Tonight, she'd promised Lucy she would make her favorite baked ziti and she hadn't even boiled water yet.

In the kitchen, she busied herself by preheating the oven and gathering the ingredients for the family recipe. The ziti recipe was one of the few valuable things her older sister had taught her before she'd died.

Everything else she'd learned from her sister was more of a cautionary tale. She'd been sixteen when Cynthia died, barely dating herself, and yet the truth of her sister's secret life had scared her parents enough to clamp down on Emma with an iron fist. She was hardly a problem child, but of course, Cynthia had always seemed perfect on the surface, too.

When she was old enough to be in charge of her own life, she'd thought about rebelling. Her hunt for a sorority had been a start, but instead, she went the other direction and chose Pi Beta Phi, the sorority of proper, well-off ladies out to do community service and build sisterhood. She'd seen how her sister's scandal had hurt her parents and she didn't want to be the one responsible for putting that look on their faces ever again. When she finally lost her virginity in college, it was to a well-groomed, polite premed major she'd been dating for nearly six months and had hoped to marry. She pretended to be the proper, sophisticated society darling her parents wanted, and after a while, it just became who she was.

She'd only really, truly let herself go that once. Emma let herself do shots of tequila with a stranger, licking salt from the musky skin of his throat and sucking a lime from his full, soft lips. From there, it was a slippery slope that led to the tattoo on her chest and a positive pregnancy test on the back of the toilet. One night had ruined a decade of good behavior. She had no idea how she was going to tell her parents.

Emma opened the box of pasta and dumped it into a pot of boiling water with an unsatisfying splash. It had been so easy to let herself get carried away that night. Too easy. There was a part of her that understood how her sister could get so wrapped up in a passionate and illicit relationship while she was engaged to someone else. The pleasure and the excitement were enthralling. The other part of her knew there was nothing worth derailing her whole life for.

There was nothing she could do about the choices she'd made in the past, but she certainly wasn't going to make the same mistakes twice. Jonah Flynn was just the kind of man who could make her priorities get all out of whack. That made him dangerous. She would tell him about the baby once the audit was complete and she had done her job. He couldn't know the truth about her identity or the baby before then, which made it imperative that she not let her guard down around him.

"We're here!" Violet called out from the living room.

"I'm in the kitchen," she replied, giving the pasta a stir and setting the timer. Since she'd added the girls to the approved guest list with the doorman, they tended to show up with little warning. "It's nowhere near ready, sorry."

The girls came around the corner with paper sacks and set them on the counter. "We're not in a hurry," Harper insisted. "Anyway, I brought a bottle of chardonnay and Violet picked up some cheese and crackers to keep us busy until dinner is ready. The wine is just for us, of course."

Her best friends unpacked the items from the bags

and set them on the counter. "Oh, and tiramisu," Harper admitted, pulling the seductive dessert from the bag. "I had to."

Emma groaned inwardly. "You said FlynnSoft has a gym, right? After all this I'm going to have to find it or I'll gain fifty pounds with this kid. Now that I've gotten my appetite back, I'm hungry almost all the time."

Harper smiled and nodded. "It's on the ground floor near the rear entrance. You can't miss it. There's usually no one in there after six or so. You can have it all to yourself."

"I don't know what you're complaining about," Lucy said. She reached out and put her hand on Emma's slightly rounded belly. "You look like you had a big lunch, not that you're over three months pregnant. I think you can afford some indulgent carbs."

"I'm glad you think so," Emma quipped. "Now open those crackers. I'm starving."

Violet opened the box of crackers while Lucy pulled wineglasses from the cabinet and the corkscrew from the drawer.

"So how is the FlynnSoft assignment going?" Lucy asked after Harper opened the bottle and poured her glass.

There was something about Lucy's tone that worried Emma. She turned away from the marinara sauce she'd made and frozen to look at Harper and knew instantly that she'd spilled the secret about Jonah to the others. Emma swore under her breath and returned to mixing the cheeses and seasonings into the bowl.

"I'll just presume you all are caught up on who Jonah is—thank you, Harper—and jump right into it. I have never met a man so persistent in my life. You should've seen his face when I told him I wouldn't go to dinner with him. It was as though I was the first woman in his life to ever tell him no."

"You probably were. I sure wouldn't tell him no," Violet spoke up.

"Well, someone needs to," Emma responded. "He's not a god. He can't get his way all the time. That kind of arrogance makes me crazy."

"I've never really thought of him as arrogant in the years I've known him," Harper said, shrugging. "He's confident, sure, very smart, of course. He knows what he wants and he goes after it. I find that attractive. But you're determined not to like him, so he could save puppies from burning buildings and you would find a reason to hate him for it."

Emma opened her mouth to argue, but knew there wasn't much point. It was true. Mostly. She didn't hate him. She couldn't feel that way about the father of her child. But she had to find things wrong with him for her own protection. And if he was perfect, she'd make up lies in her head about all of Jonah's evil doings and pretend they were true. "It's better this way, trust me."

"Why, Em?" Lucy settled into a chair at the kitchen table. "And don't give me some story about your sister. We've all heard it before and know better than anyone that you're not your sister. You certainly aren't going to disappoint your parents with anything you do. You're a better person."

"There's no sense in punishing yourself for sins you've never committed," Lucy said.

Instead of answering right away, Emma drained the pasta and started mixing it with the sauce and cheese to put in the oven. What could she say to that? Was that really what she was doing? "I'm not punishing myself."

"Yes, you are," Harper insisted. "If not for your sister's sins, then for whatever you did at that Mardi Gras party. I think the punishment far outweighs the crime."

"That night was a mistake and I'll never be able to put it behind me. Don't you think getting impregnated out of wedlock by a stranger at a party will disappoint my parents?"

"They might not be thrilled, but grandbabies become a joy no matter what," Violet said.

"I'll remind you of that when you accidentally get pregnant by a man whose name you don't know, Violet."

"Listen, honey," Harper interjected. "I've made plenty of mistakes where men are concerned. But not even one of my best moments were as sexy or romantic as what you told me about your night with him. You jumped in with both feet and scared yourself. Okay, I get it. But that doesn't mean you have to stay out of the pool entirely. If you're not ready for the deep end, at least put your feet in. Test the waters. Letting your hair down every once in a while won't hurt anything. It might be good for you."

Popping the casserole dish in the oven, Emma dusted her hands off on her yoga pants and eyed her friends' wine with a touch of jealousy. If she didn't put an end to this discussion, her friends would continue to badger her and they'd miss the show they'd come over to watch. "That is all well and good, but I'm not getting in a pool of any kind with Jonah Flynn. Not that he'd want to once I'm huge and pregnant anyway."

"With *his* baby!" Lucy pointed out.

"It doesn't matter. Does he look like the paternal type to you? I've told you my reasons for avoiding Jonah, but if nothing else I've said convinces you, know that it's a major conflict of interest. I'm auditing FlynnSoft. If even so much as a whisper of a relationship pops up about Jonah and me, past or present, my credibility is shot. I'd probably lose my job and permanently damage the reputation I've worked so hard to build. No man, not even Jonah Flynn, is worth that. Not to me."

"Well, they're going to find out when the baby is born and everyone figures out what happened between the two of you. There's no avoiding that. Your only option is to tell Tim you can't do it. That would be the most forthright answer," Violet said.

"Technically. But *can't* isn't in my vocabulary. I refuse to back down from this challenge, even if there's a risk."

Harper nodded in resignation and Lucy sighed. Emma hoped her friends would leave it alone, at least for the next two hours.

"Of course," Harper said with a smirk, "if I was going to sully my reputation and ruin my career for a man, it'd be for him."

Jonah was sitting at his desk Wednesday afternoon when his phone rang. He recognized the number as his financial advisor, Paul. Hopefully it was good news.

"Paul," he said. "Tell me what I want to hear."

There was a hesitation on the line that instantly told Jonah he was out of luck. "I'm sorry to tell you, Jonah, but it's going to take me at least two more days to get everything handled. We could look into getting a short-term loan to get you the money, but the banks are really tight on those lately with the market the way it is. I doubt it would come through any faster. Any chance you could borrow it from…um…"

"From my mother?" Jonah asked.

"She does have more liquid assets than you do. That's the only reason I would even suggest it."

Jonah sighed and shook his head. He wanted to keep this situation as close to his vest as he could. "I don't want Mother to know what Noah's done. Ask someone for three million dollars and they'll sure as hell want to know what it's for. At least she'd ask *me*. She'd give it to Noah without blinking."

"Then why didn't he just borrow it from her in the first place?"

Jonah ran his fingers through his messy hair. "I have no idea. The less I know about what he's up to the better. Listen, just move things as quickly as you can and I'll do what I have to on this end."

They wrapped up their conversation and Jonah hung up. He'd given Emma some space this morning, hoping maybe the money would come through and he wouldn't need to continue pursuing a woman who was clearly disinterested in him. It was fun for him, a challenge he'd never had to face before, but he couldn't spend all his time trying to woo the ice princess. He still had a company to run.

Apparently that task was back at the top of his to-do list for the day. He had some time on his calendar, so he slipped out from behind his desk and went in search of his elusive prey.

He spotted her on the twenty-fourth floor down the hall from her office. She was leaning over the copier, pressing buttons and eyeing the pages as they spat out. Jonah was tempted to come up behind her and whisper something in her ear, but nixed the idea. Somehow he thought that might earn him a slap or a knee to the groin.

Instead, he just watched her from a distance, admiring the curve of her calves highlighted by her knee-length skirt and four-inch heels. She held a pen gently to her full, soft lips, the lower one pouting just slightly and urging him to reach out and brush his mouth across hers.

The best thing about watching her from here was that her defenses were down. She was relaxed, a faraway day-dreaming look in her eyes as the constant rhythm of the copier lulled her mind into thoughts about something other than accounting. He didn't know what she was thinking about, but the corner of her mouth curved in a smile. It made her face light up in a way he hadn't seen before. She was always so proper and guarded around him.

It was then that she turned to glance down the hallway and spotted him. Her green gaze ran over the length of his body for just a moment, her tongue darting quickly across her bottom lip. He thought he caught the slight-est hint of something other than derision in her eyes, but before he could be certain, she snatched her papers from the copier, turned on her heels and started off in the other direction.

She was avoiding him again. No more avoiding.

Jonah marched up behind her. She was easy to catch with those high heels slowing her escape. He spied one of the janitorial closets just to her right and got a bad idea. Without so much as a hello, he wrapped one arm around her waist and opened the door, tugging her inside.

"What on *Earth*—" she shrieked in surprise, but quickly silenced when the door slammed shut and they were suddenly cloaked in the darkness of the small space.

The room was slightly musty, smelling of industrial cleaner and old cardboard, but the subtle scent of her lotion cut through it all and sent a spike of need down his spine. Memories of the night with his butterfly flooded his mind in an instant. He'd made love to her in the small, private space of his laundry room when no place else was available. If he'd had a second chance with her, he would've made up for it with a bed covered in satin sheets and rose petals. That's what she had deserved.

Again, like the laundry room, the janitorial supply room wasn't the best or most romantic choice, but he would take what he could get. He had no intention of trying to seduce her here, but if this was the only way he had of getting her alone to talk, so be it. He was tired of this game.

He tightened his arms around her waist and tugged her close to him so she couldn't get away. The closet was filled with any number of dangerous things she'd likely hurt herself with if she took a step back from him. She needed to stay right where she was. They were going to talk about what was going on whether she liked it or not.

So far, he was pleased enough with the situation. She was very still and quiet in his arms, albeit a touch stiff. He could hear the soft sound of her breathing, the rise and fall of her chest as she pressed futilely against him with her palms. He liked the feel of her in his arms more than he expected to. It felt natural and familiar somehow.

As his eyes adjusted to the dim light coming under the door, he was able to make out her silhouette and the soft contours of her face. What he could see of her was fighting this tooth and nail. Her eyes were squeezed shut, her lips tightly pressed together. Emma's shoulders were drawn up around her ears. She was strung tight as a drum, the comfortable woman from minutes ago completely forgotten.

"Relax, Emma. I'm not going to bite."

"I need to get back to work," she said, but there was half-heartedness in her voice that betrayed her. There was a part of her that was open to him. He didn't know why she was fighting it so hard. It could be quite an enjoyable experience for them both.

"I want to talk to you first. You've continued to avoid me and have left me with no choice but to abduct you and make you listen to what I have to say."

"I'm not talking to you in a closet with the lights off. It's inappropriate." Emma struggled against him in earnest, gaining little traction and succeeding in doing nothing but rubbing her belly back and forth against his rapidly hardening desire.

Jonah had to swallow a groan as her movements sent a wave of pleasure radiating from his groin. "Stop. Wiggling," he managed through gritted teeth. "I just want to talk. I have no intention of taking advantage of you in here, but if you keep grinding your hips against mine like that, we may have to make some impromptu changes to the agenda." The thought had undeniably crossed his mind, but even *he* had boundaries in the workplace. "I can tell you don't think that highly of me and my reputation with women, but I can assure you that I much prefer the king-size bed in my loft for that kind of thing."

"I don't want to talk. Or to see your king-size bed."

"I hadn't asked you to."

Emma stopped struggling and looked up at him. He could see the dim light reflecting in her eyes as they searched his face for something. Sincerity, maybe. She must've found it because eventually her body relaxed in his arms.

"Then what is it you want, Jonah?"

He couldn't very well tell her that he wanted to distract her until he could clean up his brother's mess. And in that moment, that wasn't his biggest motivation. There was something about the way she said his name that sent a fire raging through his veins and made him want to pull her close and kiss her. It was different from the run-of-the-mill lust most attractive women lured from him. It was more powerful. Potent. And it demanded he take action.

"I just want to get to know you. There's something happening here... I can't explain it, but I want to see where it goes." Jonah released her waist with one hand to reach up and caress her face. He just had to touch her, even if it earned him a slap.

Instead, he heard Emma's sharp intake of breath and decided he wasn't the only one whose plans were crumbling under the strain of their attraction to one another. "Tell me I'm crazy, but I know you feel it, too. You're just determined to fight it. Stop fighting."

"I..." Emma began to protest, but words seemed to escape her in that moment.

They escaped him, too. And words wouldn't fill the need building inside him. Jonah leaned in and pressed his lips against hers. He expected resistance, but he found none. There was only a slight hesitation, then surrender. Maybe it was the safety of the dark, but his uptight auditor melted into him instead, matching the enthusiasm of his touch.

He'd been correct in his assessment of her. Under that straitlaced veneer was a sensual female looking for an outlet. Jonah would gladly provide it.

Deepening the kiss, he let his tongue slide across hers, drinking in the taste of spicy cinnamon. The flavor was sharp, biting him unexpectedly. He liked the surprise contrast. Emma was full of them.

She wrapped her arms around his neck, tugging her body closer to him. The darkness and the familiar feel of her in his arms roused thoughts of his butterfly again. If he didn't know better, he'd swear he was with her, in his laundry room. Without thinking, he let his right hand drift to her chest, stopping short of groping her breast, but aligning his hand where his butterfly's tattoo would be.

She must have misinterpreted his intentions because Emma instantly stiffened in his arms and jerked away from his kiss. "What the hell are we doing?" she whispered.

"Wait," he protested, the distance between them suddenly painful. Jonah let go of her to fumble for the light switch, but the instant he did, he felt her pull away and scramble for the doorknob. The door flew open, flooding the small room with light so he could see her dash away from him and down the hallway to the ladies' room.

Flopping back against the wall, Jonah ran his hand through his hair and wished away his erection. That hadn't exactly gone to plan.

So pulling her into a dark room and pinning her against him might've been the wrong tactic if he'd really just wanted to talk. And he had, at first. His body just had other plans. So had hers, but he went too far, as always. Damn.

He shook his head. Something about her just wasn't quite right. She was nervous around him. Avoided him at all costs. Refused to accept gifts or dinner dates. He'd watched her interact with other employees, and the stiff, overly polite veil dropped. She was still professional, just not militantly so.

Emma was just insistent on keeping the wall up between them. A wall that in the dark, crumbled in an instant. She'd let him in for a brief moment, then regained her senses and ran as fast as she could in the opposite direction.

For some reason, he absolutely repelled her and had since the first moment they met. He didn't understand at all. Yes, he was a force of nature when he wanted something, but he was also friendly, laid-back and fairly easy to get along with. Why would she fight something her body so clearly wanted?

Unless…

Jonah swallowed hard and looked out the door to watch Emma peek out, then dash down the hallway back to her office. Maybe his plan was too little, too late. Perhaps his enterprising accountant had already found the discrepancies in the books. If that was the case, it would explain a lot.

Who would want to date a man they were about to report to Game Town for keeping sketchy books?

Five

Jonah was forced back to his office for a teleconference after the closet incident, but he wasn't about to let that whole thing go. Either she knew about the missing money or she didn't. She liked him or she hated him. But he was going to find out the truth either way.

The next morning, he found her sitting in her temporary office. Jonah watched her silently for a few minutes as she sat hovering over her paperwork, studying it with unmatched intensity. Her nose wrinkled just slightly, a line of concentration settling in between her brows as she scrutinized every number.

Even at her desk and fully immersed in her work, her posture was not slouched over. She sat quite upright, her shoulders back, her breasts pressing insistently against her pink, silk blouse. Her brunette hair was pulled back again, a stray piece framing the curve of her face.

Without looking up, she tucked the strand behind her ear and started to make notes in a spiral notebook. She had some of the neatest penmanship he'd ever seen. Programmers were not known for their handwriting. He typed nearly everything aside from signing his name to contracts and checks. Her handwriting was precise and delicate with full, curling loops and sweeping letters. It suited her, he thought. Rigid and controlled at first glance, but inherently feminine and open if you took the time to study and understand her better.

Audit or no, Jonah was genuinely interested in Emma and it surprised him. She got under his skin and irritated him, but at the same time, she was a fascinating puzzle to try and solve. Yesterday's encounter just made it that much more intriguing. Figuring her out and breaking down her defenses would be an achievement on par with the first time he'd beaten *Legend of Zelda* as a kid.

"What's the matter, Mr. Flynn? Run out of women to abduct so you thought you'd stop by my office and try again?"

The sound of Emma's voice pulled him from his thoughts. She was watching him, but he didn't see the tension in her shoulders that was there before. There was even a touch of amusement in her voice, which surprised him. Giving her some space had been the right thing to do.

"I'm sorry about yesterday. I hadn't intended—"

"That's fine," she interrupted. "It's not a problem. Let's just pretend it never happened."

Jonah didn't expect this. He expected her to be wound tight and ready for a fight, or at least, a harassment suit. Instead, she was insistent on keeping things professional and putting it behind them. Perhaps she hadn't found Noah's indiscretion after all. "Can we talk about it?"

"I'd rather not."

A blush lit her cheeks and Emma let her gaze drop back to her paperwork. She actually looked embarrassed. Jonah had no idea what that was about. It had been virtually impossible to make most of the women he'd dated blush, much less embarrass them with talk of romantic embraces. He wanted to see her porcelain complexion flush pink again, this time after they kissed. Kissing in the dark had robbed him of that tantalizing visual.

"Let me make it up to you."

At that, she rolled her eyes and pushed away from her desk. The sweet blush was gone. "Please…"

"…go to dinner with you? Very well, I accept. How about o ya for sushi? I haven't gotten to try there yet."

Emma stopped in her tracks, seemingly startled by his turn of the conversation. "What? No."

"No sushi? You're right. That's not everyone's cup of tea. How about a steak house?"

"No. I mean, *no*, I don't want to go to dinner." Her face blushed a deeper red this time; she was clearly flustered with irritation. She brushed past him into the hallway. He took a moment to admire the tight fit of her black pants as she sauntered away, then jogged a few steps to catch up to her.

"Why not?" he asked, pulling alongside.

"It would be inappropriate," she said over her shoulder.

"Says who? I'm not your boss. I don't see anything wrong with taking you to dinner as a friendly welcome to my company. I take clients out to eat all the time."

"You haven't built a reputation like yours on simply being *friendly* to women."

Her sharp words jabbed at Jonah. It sounded like her concerns were less about it appearing inappropriate to others and more about her less-than-flattering opinion of his love life. "Ah, so you don't want to be seen in public with a man whore like me, right? Would it damage your sparkling reputation, Emma?"

Emma picked up her pace, quickly turning a corner and heading down an empty hallway, probably to the copier again. "Honestly, yes. I've worked very hard to get where I am. I'm not interested in men like you or the kind of 'friendliness' you offer."

They stopped outside the elevator and she pushed the down button, refusing to look him in the eye. It made him wonder why. Those words didn't jibe with the woman who had kissed him in the dark supply closet. "I don't know..." he teased, letting a sly smile curve his lips. "You might like sullying your reputation a bit with me. It didn't seem to bother you so much yesterday."

Her head snapped around to look at him with a frown pulling down the corners of her pink lips. "Or I might end up in one of those gossip rags and have everyone talking about me."

Jonah hated those publications. Why anyone was interested in his life, he didn't know. "Who cares what other people think about what you and I do?"

The doors opened and Emma rushed inside with Jonah in her wake. "I care. You might be a millionaire playboy, but I'm a professional. Something like that could cost me my job."

"Would your boss really care about the two of us being seen together? Why would you want to work for someone that uptight? Come work here. I could use a new finance officer."

Emma finally looked up at him, her green eyes widening in surprise, but then shook her head. "That's a nice offer, Mr. Flynn, but I don't ever want it to be said that I earned my job on my back."

She'd called him by his formal name again. They were regressing, if that was even possible. "I never said anything about you being on your back, Emma. All I suggested was dinner. You filled in the rest based on your biased presumptions about me."

A chime announced their arrival on the next floor and she shot out the minute she could fit through the doorway. "They aren't presumptions anymore. Now they're from personal experience. Yesterday is all the proof I need to know that even something innocent can go astray when you're involved, Mr. Flynn."

That was three times now. "Please call me Jonah. Mr. Flynn is my father. And he's dead. Besides, I already apologized for that. I told you I didn't know what got into me. I won't do it again unless you ask me to. Just have dinner with me."

Emma turned suddenly and planted her hands on her hips. "Why are you dogging me so hard? Why me? Don't you have some underwear model to keep you entertained?"

Jonah shoved his hands into his pockets in frustration and made a mental note: no more models. They gave him a bad reputation and intimidated other women. He had a universal appreciation of the female body in all its forms. Women rarely understood that, though. They just measured themselves against this perfect ideal and didn't think he could desire them, as well.

"What if I truly, genuinely, was interested in you, Emma? That I thought you were smart and funny and attractive and wanted to see what could happen between us? Is that so bad?"

"In any other time and any other place, maybe not. But as it stands, no dinner. No dates. Just, no thank you." Emma turned and marched into the coffee shop.

It was fairly empty at this hour, so Jonah followed her, refusing to end this conversation until he'd won. "Let me at least buy you coffee."

Emma chuckled and crossed her arms protectively over her chest. "It's free in here."

Jonah arched a brow in amusement. "Not for me, it isn't. I pay for it all. As a matter of fact, I've bought you several meals since you've been here. What's the harm in one more? The only difference is that we eat it at the same time at the same table."

She narrowed her green gaze at him and sighed. "You're not going away until I at least agree to have coffee with you, are you?"

"Coffee is a good start."

"Fine," she said. "I'll have a tall hot tea with two sugars, one cream, and a cinnamon roll. I'll be waiting at a table. And when we're done, I don't want to see you for the rest of the day. Got it?"

Jonah grinned wide, the small victory seeming bigger when Emma was involved. "Absolutely."

He found her seated at a table in the back corner of the coffee shop a few minutes later. Jonah watched silently as she doctored her hot tea and removed the bag. "What got you into accounting?" he asked. This wasn't the time or place for bold moves or hard questions.

"I dislike ambiguity," she responded. "In math, there is no gray area, no questionable decisions. Two plus two equals four. I liked having a career based in something I could depend on. It also seemed to be a respectable profession. My parents were both pleased with my decision."

"And what if you'd wanted to be a fashion model or a rock star?" Jonah asked. "What would they have thought about that?"

Emma only shook her head. "I would never want to do something like that. For one thing, I'm not pretty enough or talented enough. And even if I were, I wouldn't do it. Those kinds of people end up in the magazines right beside you."

Jonah frowned. He didn't like the way she spoke about herself. "It's not so bad," he countered. "People read those magazines because they want to live vicariously through people like me. They want to share in the glamour and excitement."

"My sister was the one destined for the spotlight, not me."

"And what does your sister do?" Jonah asked.

"Nothing. She's dead." Emma put the lid on her cup and picked up her plate. "I'm sorry, Jonah, but I've got to get back to work."

Emma flopped back into her desk chair and buried her face in her hands. This was not going at all to plan. Before she'd come to FlynnSoft, she'd been confident that its handsome CEO wouldn't want anything to do with her. Finding out Jonah was the father of her unborn child made it even more critical that she maintain her distance until her audit was complete. There was tiny, living proof that she'd slept with the FlynnSoft CEO at least once, and that was too much. And yet in the last twenty-four hours, she'd made out with him in a dark closet and agreed to have coffee with him.

What the hell was wrong with her? Kissing Jonah? She wished she could say she lost her mind in that dark room, but what was her excuse today? Chatting with him over breakfast pastry and caffeinated drinks seemed harmless, but they both knew it was anything but. If she gave him an inch, he'd take a mile. There was no such thing as harmless where the two of them were concerned.

Despite her accusations to the contrary, she was fairly certain all Jonah had intended to do yesterday was get her somewhere private and force the conversation she was adamant to avoid. But somewhere things just went wildly off course. Again.

It was just like Mardi Gras all over again. Whatever powerful, magnetic force drew them together and lured them into a night of hedonistic pleasure was still in play. Being pressed against Jonah again, his warm, male scent teasing her brain with arousing memories... It was like the last three months without him never happened.

But they had happened. And for a reason.

The minute his hand came near her chest, the cautionary reminder of her tattoo sent a spike of panic through her. He couldn't see and didn't know he was inches from completing their tattoo, but she knew. And it was far too close for comfort. All she could do was turn and run. Like that night, she couldn't change what she'd just done, but she could put a stop to it and make sure it didn't happen again. He could be a part of her life as the father of her child, but nothing more. And not yet.

This was all her girlfriends' faults. They'd sown the seeds of doubt and discontent in her mind when they came over for dinner. Emma lay awake for hours thinking about the night she'd spent with Jonah and the lonely, miserable ones that had followed since.

She'd convinced herself that a man like Jonah would never be satisfied with a woman like her. The woman who fell into his arms that night didn't really exist. Keeping their romance anonymous was what kept it special, what made it into the fantasy she couldn't forget. It could never be ruined by the reality of who they really were, come daylight. And yet, the child they'd created that night would make destroying that fantasy a necessity.

After the last few days working with Jonah, she was beginning to wonder if ruining the fantasy would matter to him. Inexplicably, there was a draw between them that had nothing to do with masks and secrets. He had no idea who she really was and yet Jonah Flynn seemed genuinely interested in her. He was going out of his way to get her attention and she couldn't understand why. He couldn't possibly want her as she was. She seemed to do nothing but irritate him, based on the crease that was constantly present between his eyebrows.

Was he simply trying to woo his way into a favorable audit finding? It wouldn't be the first time someone had tried to bribe or coerce an auditor. It had never happened to Emma before, so maybe she was being naive about his attentions. Perhaps a man like Jonah preferred the more pleasurable option of seducing them over laying out cash. The spark between them might simply make his job easier.

Of course, if he was going to that much trouble, it meant he had something to hide...

A deep feeling of unease pooled in Emma's stomach. This was a huge and very important contract for Flynn-Soft. If he was afraid she might uncover something that could risk it, she had no doubt he'd go out of his way to distract her. He didn't necessarily have to think she was smart or pretty to pull it off. How could he, when he was used to dating fashion models and pop stars? Emma was just the rich daughter of someone far more important than she was. If all he really cared about was nailing the deal with Game Town, he would be willing to do it by any means necessary. Suspecting his motives would make it easier to ignore his advances, right?

At least for now. He'd certainly wanted her back in February when there were no audits, no accounts and no contracts. But then she wasn't herself that night.

Emma tried to push that thought aside and focus on the numbers the rest of the afternoon. While her work might seem boring to some, what she'd said to Jonah about math was true. It never lied. It was a constant, and she found working with numbers to be soothing. She could lose herself for hours in the books, and today was no different. When she looked up, it was after six. Jonah had thankfully kept his promise to stay away for the rest of the day and she'd managed to get a lot done.

She considered packing up and going home, but restlessness still plagued her. She decided she'd been sitting for too long and headed straight down to the FlynnSoft gym. She'd packed a bag of workout clothes and brought them in after the guilty tiramisu consumption.

Tonight wasn't about calories, though. She needed an outlet for the frustration and nervous energy threatening to bubble out of her, and some pounding on the elliptical machine was just the thing since pounding Jonah was not an option. She honestly wasn't sure how much of this she could take. He was relentless, absolutely aggravating and refusing to take no for an answer. Her afternoon of peace would be the exception, not the rule, she was certain. Especially now that he knew he could wear her down after a while and get his way.

It made her wonder if he knew who she really was. Maybe it wasn't about the audit at all. She hadn't found a single questionable thing in the books to warrant a distraction. And yet, it would be impossible for Jonah to recognize her from that night. Not a bit of her tattoo had seen the light of day. Their conversations offered no clues to her identity or their past. And yet he was constantly in pursuit of her.

Before she headed down to the gym, she stopped at the desk of Jonah's assistant, Pam. "Is Mr. Flynn gone for the day?" she asked.

"Yes, he had a five-thirty dinner engagement."

Perfect. "Thank you."

Emma made her way down the hall, thankful that she would be able to work out in peace. In the locker room, Emma changed quickly into her standard gym clothes, which consisted of a tank top over a sports bra and a pair of jogging shorts. The top left the tattoo partially exposed and clung to the barely rounding belly of her pregnancy, making her frown in the mirror. She hadn't thought about that when she packed her bag, but the time of baggy clothes and maternity outfits was right around the corner.

She considered changing back into her regular clothes and just heading home for the night, but she was actually looking forward to the workout. Emma glanced into the still-empty workout room and decided it was safe enough since Jonah wouldn't be around to see it. No one else would understand the significance of either the tattoo or the belly.

The coast was clear. Harper was right. Apparently,

software programmers were more likely to make use of the coffee bar and pinball machine than the exercise facilities. She jumped onto the closest elliptical machine, putting her water bottle into the cup holder and plugging her earbuds into her phone to listen to her favorite workout music.

Emma selected an upbeat seventies playlist and started moving to the disco beat that thrummed through her body. She closed her eyes and gave in to it. The sweat running down her spine and the ache of her muscles were welcome distractions from the confusion and arousal that had been her constant companions the last few days. She hoped that if she worked out long enough, her attraction to Jonah would seep out her pores and she would be better prepared to deal with him.

At least that was the idea.

Emma had always been a fan of exercise. You wouldn't think it to look at her, but she recognized it as an outlet for her body's impulses. The all-girls private school she attended for high school had encouraged them to be as active as possible. The nuns insisted that sweat was purifying and there was no desire that couldn't be suppressed with a good workout.

She had reason to be a believer in its powers and fell back on it instead of eating when stress took over her life. She lost ten pounds after her breakup with David in February. Between him leaving and the fallout of her twenty-four-hour rebellion, she'd clocked in serious overtime at the gym. She'd finally regained those ten pounds due to her blossoming pregnancy, but she continued to work out, nonetheless. She didn't want to get too large and spend valuable time postpartum worrying about extra pounds instead of enjoying precious moments with her newborn.

ANDREA LAURENCE　　　　87

When her body was about to give out from the strain, Emma slowed her pace to cool down and opened her eyes. She smiled, pleased with her workout stats on the console. She may well have earned herself a treat after dinner. Maybe some nice dark chocolate would provide a pseudosexual chemical release to back her down from the edge.

Emma silenced her music and stepped onto the padded floor with gelatinous kneecaps. Her plan had worked. She was exhausted, sticky and thirsty. Sex with Jonah was the last thing she wanted at the moment. She reached for her water, taking a healthy swig, then began wiping her face with her towel.

The sound of a man's laughter startled her. She yanked the towel from her face, pulled out her earbuds and looked around the gym, but found it to be just as empty as it had been before. Her only guess was that it must've been someone in the hallway walking past the gym. Or maybe her imagination was getting the best of her.

With another quick glance around, she gathered up her things and headed to the locker room just to be safe. Originally, she'd planned to shower and change here, but the unknown man's laughter left her unnerved. What if Jonah had seen her? She had taken a huge risk tonight and she couldn't repeat it. She needed to bring some gym clothes to work that wouldn't leave her so exposed next time. Jonah might be out tonight, but that wouldn't be the case every time she came down here.

Instead, she grabbed her tote bag, slipped a hoodie over her clothes just in case and headed to the exit.

She could bathe in private at home where she didn't have to worry about who might be watching.

Six

Jonah ducked into a corridor and watched Emma as she headed toward the back exit of the building. When his dinner meeting was canceled earlier tonight, he was already at the restaurant waiting. He opted to get a to-go order and take it back to the office. There, he planned to get in some weight training—it was legs day—and eat his dinner as he went over some emails.

The gym was usually empty in the evenings and he enjoyed the solitude. He spent all day in meetings and on phone calls. His time at the gym was an hour out of the day where he could lose himself in some music and let his sore muscles distract him from his worries. He never expected to find Emma there. She seemed like the kind of woman who didn't like to get dirty, much less sweat. Yet there she had been, going to town on one of the machines, music pumping into her ears, her eyes closed.

If he didn't know better, he'd say she was trying to work something out of her system. Perhaps he'd done a better job of sexually frustrating her than he thought. Maybe she only resisted him on the surface.

He'd almost opened his mouth to say as much to her when she suddenly came to a stop and climbed down from the machine. He watched her from the doorway, unnoticed, as she sipped her water and wiped the sweat from her flushed face. It was then that he spied a flash of red peeking out from her black top. He took a few steps farther into the gym and could clearly see half a red heart tattooed on her left breast. Jonah had stopped, looked at the tattoo on his hand, then at her tiny, rounded stomach in disbelief before choking on a nervous laugh and darting out of the gym before she saw him.

Could it be?

Never. Never in a million years would he have pegged Emma as his butterfly. His butterfly had been free, uninhibited, wild. On the surface, Emma appeared to be anything but. She'd told him she was acting out of character that night, but he didn't really believe her. Everyone said something like that when they found themselves in an awkward situation.

She must've been telling the truth. His butterfly had also told him that he wouldn't want her in the morning, like she'd turn into a pumpkin at sunrise. Instead, she turned into an uptight accountant. A beautiful, graceful, aggravating, uptight accountant who looked as though she might be carrying his child.

He was no expert in that department. What he did know was that three months ago, her belly had been flat as a board, trembling as he planted kisses across it. Emma wouldn't show much at three months, but it was hard to hide a belly in workout clothes. Could she really be having his child?

That was something Jonah had never really considered. He wasn't opposed to children as a whole, but he'd not envisioned his life as one where he would settle down and have a family. Maybe one day, but one day always seemed a long way off. It certainly wasn't six months from now.

Jonah let his head roll back against the wall with a dull thud that did little to help the situation. A baby. Was it really possible that Emma was having his child? They'd used protection. He always used protection. He wasn't stupid. There were plenty of women who would be happy to carry his heir to inherit his money along with his blue eyes. Emma didn't seem at all like that kind of woman.

Of course, if you'd asked him an hour ago, he would've told you she was the kind of woman who would tell a man when she was having his baby. And yet she hadn't.

Jonah shook his head and started back down the hallway to his office. He couldn't work out now. His head wasn't in it. Besides, this revelation changed everything.

His pursuit of Emma had been purely business at first. Yes, distracting her would be a pleasurable chore to cover his ass and Noah's until the finances were cleaned up, but still business. When she rebuffed him, it had become a challenge. He always enjoyed conquering impossible tasks.

But now it was a matter of pride. Emma knew who he was. Had known almost from the moment they'd met. She'd seen his hand, seen his tattoo and yet had said nothing despite the fact that she was carrying his child. Why? The tattoos were supposed to help bring them together. The only link from the night of fantasy to their reality. Seeing his tattoo should've been a sign to her, a pleasant surprise, especially since she had no other way to contact her baby's father. If he'd found her first, he would've instantly told her who he was. Unless she thought their night together was a mistake. Or that she didn't want him in her or their baby's life now that she knew who he really was.

Impossible! What woman wouldn't be thrilled to find the father of her child was secretly a rich, successful and attractive businessman? There were plenty of outcomes to that scenario that weren't nearly as positive.

Jonah reached his office and spied a copy of a recent entertainment magazine on Pam's desk. It was flipped open to a page that featured a picture of him with a woman he'd only gone out with once or twice. The by-line read "Software playboy romances lingerie model." He frowned.

Okay, so maybe his celebrity status wasn't helping his cause. He had a reputation for being a badass and he liked it. Women were just part of the package. Most women didn't mind getting a piece of him, no matter how brief.

Emma was different. He knew that much. She wasn't the type of woman to tolerate that kind of crap from a man. She was an old-fashioned woman who expected the romantic overtures that were practically dead in this day and age. Not flowers and jewelry, but time and attention. The kind of woman who made him cringe. *Needy* and *clingy* were two adjectives that quickly axed a woman from his address book.

And yet she was also the woman who had filled the last three months with erotic fantasies he couldn't shake.

The one who had occupied his thoughts and forced him to compare every other date to the high bar she'd set. So far, no one had measured up.

Pushing the door open and entering his office, he threw his exercise towel over the back of his guest chair. She'd sat in that very chair when she'd had her panic attack.

The attack that had immediately followed their shaking hands. That had to be the moment she realized who he was. Not exactly the romantic response he'd pictured in his mind when they'd sat in that tattoo parlor and held hands while getting inked.

All this time, he'd been worried that her nerves and avoidance of him had been related to the audit. That she'd found out about Noah's indiscretion already. Instead, there had been a bigger issue—she was trying to keep him from uncovering the truth about her. Apparently they both had secrets to hide.

For whatever reason, Emma wasn't interested in Jonah and didn't want him to know who she was. She'd resisted his every advance like no other woman had before, even knowing she was carrying his child. Why would she be so determined to keep that from him? Wasn't he good enough to be her baby's father? Would she prefer some quiet, unassuming banker or insurance broker who would provide stability and no passion?

He didn't believe that for a second. The woman he'd spent Mardi Gras with had been complex, with layers that included passionate minx. Sure, he had a reputation for being wild, too, but he was an adult and knew there was a time and place for everything. Being a responsible father was a duty he wouldn't shirk, no matter how low her opinion of him might be.

Their recent time together proved that she was also a strong-willed, stubborn woman who thought she could outwit him. Emma really thought she could keep this secret from him.

Jonah twisted his lips in thought as he reached for his butterfly photo. He'd imagined the moment he found her would be like taking his first breath, starting his life anew with the amazing woman he'd longed for all this time. Instead, his mystery lover thought he was nothing more than an irritating pebble in her shoe.

But she hadn't seen anything yet.

It wasn't that long ago that he'd coaxed her into a wild night of uninhibited passion and recklessness. Considering the uptight accountant he'd come to know, that was no small feat. Knowing he'd done it once, however, Jonah was confident he could do it again. Before he was done with Emma, she'd be putty in his hands, all too eager to confess her identity and fall into his arms for good.

Until then, the torture would be sweet.

Emma couldn't shake the sensation of being watched. It had been that way since the night before at the gym. Every time she felt the urge to pull her gaze away from her computer screen, she expected to see Jonah loitering in her doorway with his smug, cat-that-ate-the-canary grin. But he wasn't there. In fact, she hadn't seen or heard from him since the coffee shop encounter the day before.

She knew better than to let her guard down, however. She'd made that mistake last night and couldn't do it again.

More importantly, Emma needed to focus on the

books. Something wasn't adding up right and unless she could shut down every part of her brain but the one that dealt with numbers, she'd never be able to determine if this was a real issue or one caused by her own distraction.

The third time she tried running through it and got the same result, she sat back in her chair with a groan. She'd obviously made a mistake a few pages back. A huge chunk of money was missing. "Damn it," she cursed, pushing the unruly strand of hair from her face for the twentieth time today. She needed to buy a barrette.

"What's the matter, Miss Dempsey?"

Startled, Emma sat bolt upright in her seat and clutched her hand to her chest. As she looked over this time, Jonah was loitering in her doorway when she'd least expected him.

"Nothing," she insisted. Even if she had found something of concern in the financials, she wouldn't mention it to anyone until she was absolutely certain. You didn't pull the fire alarm until you saw the flames. Right now, this was just a little smoke. No one was stupid enough to do something that obvious. Smart people took money in small chunks. There had to be an explanation.

She took a deep breath to steady herself and looked back up at Jonah. There was something different about the way he carried himself today. Emma couldn't quite put her finger on it, exactly, but something had changed. Perhaps it was the sly twist of his full lips and the knowing twinkle in his eye. She had no idea what would have pleased him so greatly this afternoon, so she chose to ignore it and the deep-down pangs of desire it caused inside of her.

"Well, I just got off the phone with your boss."

At the mention of her supervisor, the desire immediately melted away like an ice cube dropped into boiling water. "You spoke with Tim? Is there a problem?"

Jonah shook his head. "No, not at all. He was just calling to see if you had settled in okay."

Emma held her breath as she listened to his response. Tim never just called to see if an employee was settled in. He didn't care that much. Knowing him, Tim was calling to see if Emma had fallen for Jonah's charms yet. "And what did you tell him?"

Jonah pursed his lips for a second, drawing out her torture with obvious pleasure. "I told him that you were the most polite and professional worker in the building, myself included. Why? What did you think I would say?"

Emma shrugged. "I don't know," she admitted. "Hopefully nothing related to the supply closet."

At that, he chuckled and gripped the door frame of her office, flashing his tattoo at her. "I didn't build a successful company by being a fool, Emma. And despite what you seem to think, I'm not out to put your job in jeopardy."

She expelled a sigh of relief that was premature.

"It did occur to me," he continued, "that your boss seemed like a bit of a hard-ass. I get why you're so concerned about appearances. And that's why I'm offering you a compromise."

Emma tried not to frown. There was nothing to compromise over.

"You don't want to be seen with me because it's inappropriate. I get that. But I am going to take you to dinner one way or another. So I can either find a way to blackmail you into having dinner with me here in town, or you can accept my offer of having dinner with me out of town, where no one will find out."

Blackmail? Emma leaped up from her chair. "I don't know what the hell you're playing at, Jonah, but there's nothing to blackmail me with."

He didn't seem fazed by her sudden bravado. "So you say. And maybe that's true. But there's nothing stopping me from telling Tim some fabricated misdeed. He'll believe me over you, don't you think?"

Emma's jaw dropped. "You wouldn't. Why would you even consider such a thing?"

Jonah crossed his arms over his chest, wrinkling the fabric of his flannel shirt. "Because I get what I want, Emma. And I want you to have dinner with me. If I thought for one second that you weren't sincerely interested, I would let it drop. But you can't fool me with your tight hair buns and your formal demeanor. The woman that was in the supply closet with me wants to have dinner. And who am I to deny her?"

"You don't know anything about me, in or out of a closet, Jonah."

"Don't I?"

His blue eyes challenged her, and that made her instantly nervous. She self-consciously reached for the collar of her blouse and pulled it tighter to ensure she hadn't given away her identity.

"I certainly don't want to take it this far, which is why I'm offering you an alternative that will make everyone happy. Tomorrow night, meet me at the Wall Street Heliport at six sharp. From there, I will whisk you away to a location where we won't run into anyone we know. We can have a nice, private dinner without you needing to worry about your job. You can just relax for once and enjoy your time with me."

It wasn't an ideal scenario, but it was certainly better than losing her job over a lie. She couldn't believe a man that high profile could just disappear like that, though. "And what about your little paparazzi friends?"

Jonah shrugged. "They only take pictures when I allow them to know where I am. When I want privacy I'm more than capable of arranging it. I assure you that no one will know where we're going tomorrow night, even you."

That was one less concern, but it still left several on the table she wasn't ready to discuss with him. Like how being alone with him turned her knees to butter and how if she fell prey to his charms, she'd run the risk of him finding out all her secrets. It was too soon for that. But did she really have a choice? "And if I go to dinner with you...just dinner...you'll leave me alone?"

"If at the end of the evening that's what you want, then yes."

Emma would make sure that was how the evening ended, even if she regretted every word out of her mouth. While she didn't anticipate much to come out of her attraction to the infamous CEO, she didn't want even a whisper of it to happen before her job here was completed.

"Okay, fine," she said in a huge rush of breath before she could change her mind. "What shall I wear?"

Jonah grinned wide with unmasked pleasure. "Excellent. Now you might be surprised to hear this, but I plan to take you somewhere that requires a jacket and maybe even a tie on my part."

Emma's eyebrows shot up in surprise. "You mean you own a suit?"

"I own several. I'm not antisuit under the right circumstances, despite what my mother would say if she were asked. I just don't need them to feel important or in control like some people do. I like to be comfortable and a T-shirt with a video game reference on it is far more representative of my personality than a boring old pin-striped tie."

Emma tried not to get excited by the idea of seeing Jonah in a suit. He obviously underestimated what a sharp suit on the right man could do to a woman's resolve. "Then I'll meet you at the heliport tomorrow at six."

Jonah gave her a curt nod and disappeared from her office. Once he was gone, Emma was finally able to take a deep breath and realized what she'd just agreed to. She peeked out around her door, and when he was nowhere in sight, dashed down the hallway to Harper's cubicle.

"Help!" she said as she rounded the corner.

Harper looked up with wide, surprised eyes. "What's the matter?"

"I've got a date tomorrow. With *him*."

"Him?" Harper leaped up from her chair. "I thought you refused to go out with him right now."

"I know, but he shot down every excuse I could think of. I agreed to it this time on the condition that he would leave me alone after that if I asked him to."

Harper just shook her head. "How could you ever ask a man like him to leave you alone?"

"Well," Emma sighed, "at the moment, I have bigger problems than that."

"Like what?"

"Like I have no idea what I'm going to wear. Most

of my clothes are somewhere between business casual and business professional. I need date clothes. You're the fashion diva. I need you to go through my closet and tell me what to wear."

"I doubt there's much in there we can use," Harper said with obvious dismay. "Especially with junior playing havoc with your waistline. I think we need to go shopping."

Emma frowned. "I don't think I have time to—"

"Right now," Harper interrupted. She reached into her desk drawer and pulled out her Kate Spade purse. "Get your things. We're going shopping right now."

Emma let Harper shove her down the hallway as she protested. "It's three in the afternoon."

"You need all the help you can get."

Emma couldn't argue with that. The next thing she knew they were in a cab and on their way to Fifth Avenue. As they strolled along the sidewalk, Harper had her gaze narrowed at every window scanning for just the right thing. They had stepped into about seven or eight stores, but left with nothing. Harper was searching for something special—a standout look—she said.

Emma was happy to hang back and let Harper decide what was best. After all, that was what Harper lived for— designer clothes, cute shoes, a fabulous handbag—she didn't need much else in life. Her apartment was paid for, so Emma was pretty sure that her entire paycheck from FlynnSoft went directly to Neiman Marcus or Saks Fifth Avenue. Thankfully, she was raised by a father with more money than he, or she, could ever spend.

And that was coming from Emma's point of view—a girl who'd never wanted for a thing in her life.

"That!" Harper came to a sudden stop and pointed at

a mannequin in the window. "That's what you're wearing." She snatched Emma's hand and pulled her into the boutique before she had really even gotten a good look at the dress. All she saw was a blur of blue.

When they stopped at the rack inside the store, Emma realized it wasn't even a dress. It was a jumpsuit. "Are you serious?"

"Absolutely. Jumpsuits are very in right now. Any woman he's dated could wear some slinky little dress to dinner. That's what he expects. Blow him out of the water with this instead."

Harper held up the royal blue silk jumpsuit and Emma's eyes got big. It was sleeveless with wide straps that went over the shoulders and a neckline that dipped down to her sternum. She'd need a specialty bra to pull this outfit off, for sure.

"What about my tattoo?" Emma whispered.

"It will cover it. The wide straps are perfect."

That was one concern dealt with. "And where's the back of it?" she asked.

"The fabric crisscrosses in the back and leaves the rest bare. Just enough skin to be sexy, but not overtly so. Pair it with some silver heels and a silver chain belt and you're going to look fabulous. Ooh…maybe even a chunky bracelet."

Emma frowned at the dress—*er*—jumpsuit. She wasn't ready to talk about accessories yet. She'd never even worn a jumpsuit before. She wasn't entirely sure she could pull it off. Then again, it would make it easier to get in and out of the helicopter if she wasn't worried about her dress blowing up over her head. She could appreciate the practicality of that.

"So what do you think?" Harper pressed.

It was also the same blue as his eyes. She could almost feel his warm hand brushing against the bare small of her back as he escorted her into a restaurant. It sent a chill through her whole body and she finally came to appreciate Harper's genius.

"I think we need to try it on."

Seven

Emma anxiously stepped out of her cab outside the Wall Street Heliport. Before she headed inside, she made certain to adjust her jumpsuit and ensure everything was in place. It was all fine. She looked amazing in the jumpsuit, something she never would've believed until she looked in the mirror at the store and noticed her jaw had dropped along with Harper's.

She took a deep breath, swung her uncharacteristically loose brunette waves over her shoulder and headed inside. Looking around the small waiting room, she didn't see Jonah anywhere at first. Only a few of the seats were taken, mostly with families awaiting helicopter tours around Manhattan. Then she noticed a tall, slim man in a dark gray suit at the window with his back to her. Could it be?

As though he sensed her arrival, the man turned

around to look at her, and she was surprised to see it *was* Jonah standing there. He was wearing a royal blue dress shirt, almost the same shade as her jumpsuit, but it was unbuttoned at the collar, with no tie in sight. Even then, the effect was amazing. The suit coat highlighted his broad shoulders and the narrow hips she remembered cradling between her thighs. The blue of the shirt made his eyes an even deeper shade, like the darkest waters of the ocean.

Standing there with his hands casually stuffed into his pants pockets, he looked every inch the powerful CEO of a software empire. And yet, he had been right about it being an unnecessary accessory. He didn't need an expensive suit to command the attention of every person in the room. The crisp lines and exquisite tailoring on his body were just the delicious icing on the man cake that made her heart race in her chest and her resolve weaken.

Emma had to remind herself that although this felt like a date, it wasn't really. He didn't know who she was and she couldn't be certain of his motives for asking her out. Besides, being blackmailed into dinner was not a date. And yet she couldn't help preening as he took his turn looking her over from head to toe. She went with it, ignoring everyone else in the waiting area and giving him a little spin to showcase the bare back and the fit that clung to her curves. If he was a little uncomfortable all night, all the better.

His pleased smirk convinced her it was the right choice of outfit for the evening. When he was finished admiring her, she approached the window and closed the gap between them. "Good evening, Mr. Flynn."

"Tonight, of all nights," he insisted, "it's Jonah. You can call me Mr. Flynn at work tomorrow if you insist."

"I suppose that depends on how tonight goes," she added with a smile, and then turned to look at the helicopters waiting just outside. "So when will our ride be ready?"

"It's ready now." Jonah turned to the desk and gestured to the man at the counter. The attendant buzzed them out and Jonah pushed open the door that led to the helipad. "Just waiting on you."

Stepping outside, she was glad it was a calm day, not too windy. Emma had been in a helicopter twice with her parents. Sometimes her father needed to be able to get back from the Hamptons for a work emergency faster than a car or train would allow. It had never been her favorite mode of travel, but the unsteady movement didn't bother her, thankfully. Even so, she was sucking on a ginger candy to soothe her stomach just in case. She would not be remembered by Jonah as the woman who puked in the helicopter.

As they approached the sleek black helicopter, the pilot waved to them. He and Jonah helped her up inside and once she was buckled in, Jonah climbed in beside her and shut the door.

"Where are we going to dinner?" she asked as the blades started to spin overhead.

"It's a surprise."

"Of course it is," Emma muttered, but her voice was drowned out by the sound of the helicopter.

Jonah offered her a headset to wear and she accepted it. It muffled the engine sounds and allowed her to speak to the others without shouting. She didn't have much to say at first. It was a clear day and she was too busy admiring her city. New York by helicopter was a truly amazing sight. You could get up close to the architectural wonders, unlike taking a plane, and without getting bogged down by the traffic and the noise of being on the ground.

She thought they might be heading toward Long Island, but then the helicopter turned and headed farther north. They could be heading to Boston, perhaps. Or Martha's Vineyard. It was high season there.

"Stop trying to guess," Jonah said to her through the headsets. "I can see it all over your face. You're not going to be right and it will make you crazy trying to figure it out. Just relax and enjoy the flight."

Emma smirked and flopped back against her seat. She supposed he was right. Instead of looking for clues, she glanced out the window to take in the view. When she turned back to Jonah a few minutes later, she noticed he was intently watching her instead of the landscape speeding by.

"I suppose the view bores you when you've seen it repeatedly."

"Not at all," he said. "I've just got something more intriguing to look at this time."

Emma gasped softly, but didn't know what to say. Instinctively, she held her breath as he leaned close to her and put his arm around her shoulder. She started to worry that he would be able to see down her top from this angle, but it was hard to focus on that when she could smell his cologne and feel the warm press of his leg against hers.

"Thank you for agreeing to have dinner with me."

"You didn't really give me a choice," she replied, mostly in jest.

Jonah only shrugged. "I know. And I apologize for that. I guess I just wasn't sure what to do when you kept turning me down."

"Taking the hint was always an option."

"Yes." He laughed. "And I would have if your eyes were sending the same message as your mouth. But I could see you were conflicted, so I thought I'd give you a little push in the right direction."

"Threatening to get me fired is not a little push. That's blackmail."

Jonah winced. "Agreed. It was a drastic step on my part. But I wouldn't have called your boss, for the record. I was bluffing."

Emma crossed her arms over her chest, realizing too late that it gave him a tantalizing view of her cleavage. His blue eyes flickered down for only a moment before returning to hers. She was surprised by his restraint.

"Even if you're mad at me, by the end of the night, we will have kissed and made up," he said confidently.

Emma couldn't help but arch an eyebrow at him. "You're just used to getting your way, aren't you?"

"Usually."

She eyed the full swell of his bottom lip as he spoke, remembering those lips as they sucked salt and lime juice from her body at the Mardi Gras party. The memory sent a flush of heat to her cheeks that she was certain he could see. She turned away from him, looking out as the sun started to set and lights began twinkling in the distance.

"Perhaps not this time," she said, both hoping she was right and knowing she was wrong. Every minute she spent with Jonah, the more convinced she was that she wouldn't be able to resist him much longer.

"Mr. Flynn, we're about five minutes from landing."

Jonah smiled and pulled away from her. "Excellent. See, now it didn't take very long to get here, did it?"

Emma glanced at her phone in her purse. It had been a little over forty minutes. Not far enough for Boston. Too far for the Hamptons. She didn't recognize the skyline, but it was a smaller town on the water. She could see the shore. Within minutes, they came to a gentle, bouncing landing on top of a bank building.

"We're going to a bank?"

"Very funny. I'm actually friends with the president of this bank. He's the only one that uses the helipad and said we were welcome to make use of it tonight. It's that or fly all the way to the outskirts of town to the airport and charter a car to drive us right back here. This way we're only a block from the restaurant."

They slipped off their headsets and unfastened their seat belts. The pilot opened the door of the cabin and they stepped out onto the tarmac. "I'll be waiting on you, sir," he said.

"Thank you," Jonah replied before taking Emma's hand and leading her to the rooftop door. They took the elevator down to the lobby and exited onto a quiet street in a quaint-looking seaside village she didn't recognize.

They walked about a block before she saw a taxi go by advertising a place that claimed to have the finest seafood in Newport. Newport, Rhode Island? She'd never been there before, although she knew it had once been a very popular summer retreat for the wealthy of New England. It was famous for its huge mansions only blocks from the sea.

Emma kept her suspicions to herself until they reached a building just off the harbor that looked like an old Georgian-style inn with white siding, dormer windows and the charm of an old-fashioned seaport village. The sign hanging overhead read Restaurant Bouchard & Inn.

"Here we are," Jonah announced as they climbed the

short staircase that led inside. "The best French restaurant I've found on this side of the Atlantic."

The maître d' greeted them, noted their arrival in his book and escorted them to a table beside one of the large bay windows. Once they were alone with their menus of the day, Jonah leaned across the table. "Anything you order here will be amazingly delicious and beautiful. Their chef makes food into art. Tasty art at that."

Emma scanned the menu, desperately hoping her three years of high school French would assist her in not sounding foolish tonight when she ordered. Madame Colette would be so disappointed in her for mangling such a beautiful language. She had finally decided on a ratatouille ravioli starter and the rosemary lamb chops when the sommelier arrived at the table.

"Wine?" Jonah asked with a pointed look.

Emma was about to request a dry red to go with the lamb when she realized she wasn't allowed to drink. The last week of her life had been so different it was easy to forget about her situation. "None for me, please. I'd just like some seltzer with a twist of lime."

Jonah ordered a single glass of cabernet for himself. When the waiter came to take their order a few minutes later, she made her selections and he opted for the stuffed lobster starter and the sautéed duck breast with brandied balsamic glaze.

Emma was surprised by his flawless French accent as he ordered. As the waiter stepped away, Jonah turned to her with a mildly amused expression on his face. "What? Do you think that just because I wear jeans every day and play video games for a living that I wasn't properly educated in expensive British preparatory schools like most ridiculously rich kids?"

Emma frowned and looked down at the glass of seltzer in front of her. She was bad at making presumptions where he was concerned. He was just so different from what she was used to. It made her wish she did have wine to drown her embarrassment. "No, I'm just a little surprised—and jealous—of how flawless your accent is."

"You should hear my Japanese."

She looked back up, truly stunned this time. "You speak Japanese?"

"If you want to be successful in the Japanese video game market, you have to. I also speak Spanish and I'm learning Mandarin as we expand further into the Asian markets. I'm an accomplished pianist and was the captain of my rowing team at Harvard, although that was just to appease my parents. I would've much rather been indoors playing games or romancing the ladies. As you can see, there's a lot more to me than meets the eye, Emma. The same could be said of you."

"What do you mean?" she asked, feeling suddenly anxious at the turn of their discussion. "I'm just boring, uptight Emma the accountant."

"You're selling yourself short. For starters, you're great at keeping secrets."

Emma stiffened in her seat and swallowed hard. "Secrets? I don't—"

Jonah raised his hand to silence her protests. "Now that we're away from New York and the prying eyes of anyone that might care besides the two of us, I can say as much. And you can finally be truthful with me. Because you've known. All this time, you've known who I was and you didn't say anything to me about it."

The steely edge in Jonah's voice sent her spine straight in a defensive posture. When she looked into his eyes, however, she didn't see the anger she expected. Just hurt. The jovial, carefree CEO had a tender spot and she'd managed to find it without trying.

"We had something special and you don't seem to care about it at all. Why didn't you tell me the moment you realized who I was?" He slipped his hand, palm down, across the white linen tablecloth to expose his half of the tattoo, then wrapped his fingers around her hand.

It was happening. The moment she'd been dreading since he walked into his office and turned her world upside down. "I couldn't," she said in a hushed whisper.

"You absolutely could! You've had dozens of opportunities to speak up."

"No." Emma pulled her hand away into her lap and sat back to regain some of her personal space. "Up until this moment, we weren't just Emma and Jonah, we were the Game Town auditor and the CEO of FlynnSoft. Yes, I knew the moment I shook your hand, but I wasn't sure what to do. I know it's hard for you to understand, but I wanted to do my job first. I've been doing my damnedest to finish this audit, despite your constant distractions, so I could put it behind me and finally come to you and tell you the truth about everything."

Jonah nodded, acknowledging her struggle. "You mean about the baby."

Emma's green eyes widened in panic and Jonah felt his own pulse speed up in his throat. She wasn't expecting him to say that at all. He'd uncovered all her secrets, it seemed.

"How did you...?" She shook her head in denial.

"I saw you in the gym the other night after work."

She continued to shake her head, letting her gaze drop

to her lap. "I knew I heard someone as I was leaving. It was stupid of me to wear that outfit, but I didn't even think about it as I packed it. No one was around and I've really just started to show recently, so I didn't think anyone would notice. Especially you. You were supposed to be out at dinner." She glanced up with an accusing look in her eye.

Jonah felt his chest tighten more and more the longer she spoke. Not because of her pointed look, but because up until this moment, the baby had been a suspicion, not a fact. Yes, she skipped the wine, but she could just not like it. Yes, she had a little tummy, but she could've overindulged. He was no expert where pregnant women were concerned.

Now it was confirmed.

He was going to be a father. *A father.* He'd taken every precaution, and yet fate had laughed in his face and put him in this position anyway. He reached out to brace his hand on the edge of the table and squeezed his eyes shut. "My dinner meeting got canceled, so I came back to lift some weights. I'm usually alone in there. And yes, I sure as hell noticed. I noticed the tattoo and I noticed the... stomach. I wasn't sure until now, but I noticed."

Emma slumped back against her seat and dropped her face into her hand. "This wasn't how I wanted you to find out, Jonah. I'm sorry. I wasn't keeping it from you forever. I was going to tell you."

Jonah's head snapped up and his gaze pinned hers. "Were you?" He wasn't so sure. Sometimes she looked at him as though he were something stuck to his shoe, not the father of her child.

"I swear I was. Like I said, I wanted to finish the audit, do my job without any whispers of impropriety, but then yes, I was going to tell you who I am and that I'm pregnant. If I'd known how to contact you two months ago, I would've done it then, but by the time I figured it out, I was already involved in the audit. That said, I've been scared to death to tell you the truth."

Jonah swallowed hard and furrowed his brow. He was far from a hulking, intimidating person that people were scared of. He picked up his glass of wine and took a large sip to slow his spinning brain. "Why?"

Emma pulled her gaze from his and crossed her arms protectively over her chest. "It's like I told you that night—I'm not the woman you think I am. I knew that you wanted *her*, the wild and passionate anonymous stranger, not me. I couldn't bear to see the look on your face when you realized that I was that girl and the fantasy was shattered forever. I'm just boring old, stick-in-the-mud Emma. And to make matters worse, then I'd have to tell you that we were stuck together for the sake of our baby."

"Stuck together?" Jonah flinched at her choice of words. Is that how she saw her situation? She was *stuck* with him because they screwed up and she got pregnant?

The waiter returned with imperfect timing, placing each of their appetizers in front of them and disappearing silently when he sensed the tension between them.

"You know what I mean!" Emma leaned in and whispered harshly across the table at him. "Even if you were disappointed beyond belief to find out it was me, even if you never wanted to lay another hand on me again, I'm having your child, Jonah. I would hope that you would want to be a part of his or her life, even if I'm just on the periphery."

Jonah didn't know what to say. He honestly didn't

know how he wanted to move forward where Emma and the baby were concerned. His thoughts were spinning too quickly to light on one in particular. His strict up-bringing nagged at him to marry her on the spot. Mother would insist when she found out. Noah could embezzle three million dollars, but it would be Jonah's scandal of an out-of-wedlock child that would be the biggest family disgrace in her eyes. Emma wasn't the only one constantly worried about gossip.

At the same time, his rebellious nature insisted that people didn't get married in this day and age just because they were having a baby. He and Emma hardly knew each other, much less loved each other. Coparenting was a more popular thing for people who didn't want to make the previous generations' mistakes and stick out a miserable marriage for the sake of the children.

What did he want? Jonah had no idea. He'd barely become accustomed to the concept of fatherhood, but he certainly never imagined that Emma would just be on the periphery, no matter the scenario.

"Emma…to start off, you're not a disappointment. Look at me," he demanded, and then reached across the table and took her hand, gripping tightly so she couldn't pull away from him again. Once she reluctantly met his gaze with her own, he continued. "I mean it. While this is all a surprise, I can assure you that disappointment has never crossed my mind."

She studied his face with disbelief lining her weary eyes. How had he not noticed how tired she looked? He'd been blinded tonight by flawless makeup and the silky jumpsuit he wanted to run his hands over. Now that he was really looking, he could see the sense of overwhelming stress and exhaustion in her eyes. She was working too much, and too hard, in her condition. They'd discuss that before long.

"But I'm not the woman you wanted, Jonah. I'm not wild and sexually adventurous. I'd never done body shots or had a one-night stand before. I'd certainly never have a tattoo if it weren't for that night. Everything you saw and liked about me was out of character. I mean, I...I don't even know what I'm doing here. Coming with you tonight was a mistake."

Emma moved fast, slipping out of the booth and taking the nearest door out to the back patio that overlooked the water.

"Emma?" Jonah rushed after her, catching her wrist as she leaned over the railing seemingly looking for an escape. What was she going to do? Swim away from him? All the way back to New York?

"Emma! Would you just stop and listen to me?" he demanded as she tugged at his grip. She finally turned around to face him, leaning her back against the railing. He instinctively wrapped his arms around her waist. He knew immediately that pressing against each other like this wasn't the best idea to keep his focus, but at the very least, he could convince her that he was attracted to her.

"Jonah, I want to go home."

"If that's what you want, I will, but not until you hear me out. I sat there and listened to all your excuses for lying to me. You owe me the opportunity to tell you how I feel, whether you believe me or not."

Emma finally stilled in his arms, although her gaze was fixed on the buttons of his shirt. He breathed a sigh of relief that he could finally focus his thoughts on telling her how he felt. This was important.

"I want you to know that you're totally and completely wrong." Jonah pulled aside the blue silk strap of her jumpsuit to expose her shoulder and upper chest. He placed his hand over the curve of her breast as he'd done that first night. Their tattoos aligned, creating one heart again at last. Emma looked down at the heart with tears shimmering in her eyes, but she didn't say anything.

"These tattoos weren't just something I suggested on a whim, Emma. They were supposed to be instruments of fate. This heart becoming whole again would only happen if it was meant to. Yes, we don't know much about each other, but now is our second chance to make that happen. Not just because of the baby, but because we've been brought together again to do just that."

"Jonah…" she started to argue.

"No," he silenced her. "From the moment I saw you sitting in my office, I've had this pull towards you that I couldn't explain. It was the same feeling that led me to rescue a pretty stranger from a creep at a party. I didn't know why then and I don't know why now, but I know I'm not letting this second chance slip between our fingers. I don't know how it's going to end. No one ever does. This might not be forever. It might not turn into the love affair of the century. But we owe it to ourselves, and to our child, to at least try and see where it can take us."

She sighed and relaxed into his touch. "And what if my company finds out? I'll lose my job. They'll never believe that I can be impartial. I have a vested interest in the successful business dealings of my baby's father."

Her mention of the audit was enough to remind Jonah of why he started romancing his auditor to begin with. Yes, he'd been drawn to her, but he'd stuck it out to cover Noah's ass and keep from botching the Game Town deal. He hadn't heard from his accountant in days, and that wasn't good. Sooner or later, she was going to find the discrepancy. If he couldn't keep it from her, there was a part of him that hoped maybe she wouldn't mention it in her report as a favor to him. That he could explain it away somehow.

"Can you be impartial, Emma?" he asked.

Her green eyes met his with a hard glint shining in them. Her spine straightened and her pointed chin thrust forward in the defiant response he seemed to coax out of her so easily. "Yes. Despite what Tim thinks, I'm first and foremost a professional and I will do my job."

Jonah didn't doubt that at all. That's exactly what he was afraid of. But for now, he needed to salvage tonight and worry about Noah's mess tomorrow. "Then there's nothing your boss could say or do to prove otherwise. Now come back inside and eat that amazing-looking dinner with me."

Emma sighed and nodded. She slipped the strap of her jumpsuit back over her shoulder, hiding away the tattoo and removing the temptation of her bare skin.

They went back inside, crisis averted, and yet Jonah couldn't help but feel a new sense of worry. The audit for Game Town was at risk and it had nothing to do with Emma and everything to do with Jonah.

Eight

Thankfully, the rest of the dinner went well. Jonah had been worried that the whole evening would be ruined, but the opposite turned out to be true. Uptight Emma seemed to finally, truly relax. All her secrets were out in the open and lifting that burden had an almost-physical impact on her. She smiled more, flirted happily through dinner by sharing bites of her food and making eyes at him, and didn't once refer to him as Mr. Flynn.

All their issues weren't behind them, but they were able to at least focus on enjoying each other's company tonight and worrying about the rest tomorrow. With that thought in mind, Jonah directed the pilot to land on his building's rooftop instead of returning them to the heliport.

When they touched down, Emma frowned out the window. "Where are we?"

"My place." He opened the helicopter door and offered his hand to help her.

Suspicion wrinkled her nose, but she still accepted his hand and stepped out onto his rooftop with him. They hustled away from the helicopter and over to the door. He led her down a set of stairs and out onto the landing where the entrance to his penthouse loft was located.

"Wait a minute," Emma said as she stared at the door.

"What?"

"This was your place? Where the Mardi Gras party was held?"

"Yes," he replied as he reached out to unlock the door. Jonah didn't hold many parties at his loft in Tribeca, but the Mardi Gras shindig had been one of them. "You don't think I'm tacky enough to seduce a woman in someone else's laundry room, do you?"

Emma's cheeks flushed bright red at the mention of their impulsive encounter. "I didn't really think about it. Although now that you mention it, I think Harper did say that party was at her boss's place. I assumed she meant the head of finance, not the CEO's apartment."

"I was right under your nose the whole time," Jonah said. He pushed open the door and gestured her in ahead of him. He followed behind, watching her as she studied the open, industrial space he'd fallen in love with the first time he toured it.

"It looks different without a hundred people crammed in here. It's huge."

"It takes up the whole top floor," Jonah explained. "Originally, I think this building was some sort of textile factory. When I bought it ten years ago, part of it had been converted to offices and shops and the top two floors were a storage warehouse. I ended up turning the whole thing into loft apartments with shared common areas on the ground floor."

Emma stopped and turned to face him. "You own the whole building?"

Jonah nodded and slipped out of the suit coat that had been irritating him all evening. He was hot-blooded and the suit on top of the long-sleeved shirt and glasses of wine had him almost at the point of sweating.

"If I listened to nothing else my mother, the great Angelica Flynn, told me, I did learn to diversify my investments." He tossed the jacket over the back of a dining room chair and spread his arms out. "This was my foray into the real estate market. She thought I was crazy, of course. She prefers stuffy uptown mansions with marble and gold inlay. I like exposed brick and ductwork. Fortunately, I'm not the only one. The other lofts were rented with an extensive waiting list within weeks of being on the market."

Emma set her purse on the concrete countertop of his kitchen and ran her fingers across the slightly roughened surface. "It's definitely a different style. Not my style, but I know plenty of people who would like it."

He followed behind her as she strolled through the living room and dining area, nearing the door that led into the infamous laundry room. As a true loft, there were only three doors in the whole space. One for the laundry and utility room, and the others for the guest and master bathrooms. Even if he'd wanted to take her to his bed that night, he wouldn't have been able to. The space was wide-open to the party. It wasn't ideal but the laundry room had been his only real option.

Emma hesitated for a moment, then reached out and turned the knob of the door. Was she really heading straight for the scene of the crime? He'd brought her back to his place with the intention of tasting every inch of her skin, but he'd anticipated using the bed this time.

She went straight to the washing machine, running her hand over the same top that he'd lifted her onto. Emma turned and pressed her back against the machine, then looked up at him with a sly smile curling her lips. "That night was…"

Mind-blowing? Crazy? Amazing? Passionate? Life changing?

"…unforgettable."

Jonah took a step closer, narrowing the gap between them. "That it was. Every minute I spent with you was seared into my brain. Every soft moan and cry permanently etched into my memory."

Emma made a familiar sound, barely louder than an intake of breath. He remembered that gasp. She'd made that same sound of surprise when he pushed up her skirt and pressed his fingertips into the flesh of her upper thighs.

He moved closer with that thought in mind. His every nerve tingled in anticipation as they remembered that moment. His blood rushed through his veins as his heart pounded loudly in his ears. "Over these last few months, I've thought of little else but having my butterfly back in my arms again."

Emma looked up at him as he came near enough to slip his arms around her waist. For once, she didn't fight or squirm. Instead, she pressed into him and clutched at the fabric of his dress shirt. "I've thought about that night a lot, too. I've wondered what I would do if I were given a second chance to be with my hero."

"Any ideas?" Jonah asked with a wicked grin. He leaned into her, pressing her back against the washing machine and imprinting his desire for her against her stomach.

"I have a few." Emma laced her fingers behind his neck and pulled his mouth down to hers.

As their lips made contact, Jonah realized this was the first time that he'd kissed Emma knowing who she really was. The kiss they'd shared before, aside from being slightly antagonistic, was just a kiss from the up-tight Game Town auditor. There were no real expectations there, unlike a kiss from his butterfly.

He worried that this moment might be tainted by shaded memories of that night that no mortal woman could ever live up to. The minute they touched, however, it was no longer a concern. Her scent, her taste, the feel of her in his arms—it all combined in a familiar tidal wave that washed over him all at once. Before, there had been things about her that seemed familiar, but it had been like a déjà vu moment with one piece missing, the piece to tie it all together.

Now he had the tattoo to bring it all into focus and suddenly everything was right in the world.

He pulled her tight against him, loving the feel of her silken tongue as it glided along his own. Her touches weren't as bold as they had been that night, but tequila did that to a person. Yes, it made her wild and uninhibited, but with her in his arms again, he realized that wasn't the part of her that he craved. Emma was wrong to think that he wouldn't want her the way she was. Who she was, was the core of what he was after. The inner woman; the one who felt free to be herself for the first time in her life.

Jonah's hands spanned her hips and he slid one up the soft fabric of her jumpsuit to caress her breast. He took advantage of the low neckline to slip his hand beneath the cups of her strapless bra and happily mold her flesh in his palm until the peaks of her nipples dug into him.

He'd never gotten to see what her breasts looked like. If he had one regret about the night they'd spent together, it was that he'd had to rush things. It wasn't the time or the place for a leisurely exploration of a woman's body. Most of their clothes stayed on in the process.

That was not going to be the case tonight.

Taking a step back, he drew in a lungful of cool air. He braced his hands on the washing machine, trapping her there while he took a moment to collect himself.

"What's the matter?" she asked softly.

"Not a damn thing." And it was true.

"Then why—"

Jonah shook his head, interrupting her question. When he looked in her eyes, he saw confusion and disappointment mixed into the emerald green. Did she honestly think he was pulling away because he didn't want her? Nothing was further from the truth.

"Emma, I am not about to take you on this washing machine a second time. Tonight, I'm going to take my time and do it properly. I'm going to strip you naked from head to toe and press my mouth against every inch of your skin. I plan to make your body quiver and your throat go raw. So, nothing is the matter. I'm just taking a moment to keep myself from ruining my plans for tonight."

"They're good plans," she replied, and let her pink tongue snake across her bottom lip. Easing up from the washing machine, she laced her fingers behind his neck and pulled him close to her again. "You should show me where your bed is so we can implement them immediately."

* * *

Any anxiety Emma felt about this moment with Jonah vanished when he looked at her like that. He gazed at her so intently she couldn't help but believe he would do everything he promised, and then some. That was the look of a man who kept his word, and she couldn't wait.

He'd taken her hand and led her out of the laundry room and back into the main part of the loft. There, to her right, she saw the bed. Without all the party guests to block the view, it was easy to see the massive king-size bed along the far back wall of the loft.

It was placed in a niche between the bathroom and the closet to give it a little privacy despite it being out in the open. The plush, black velvet headboard rested against a wall of exposed, worn red brick. The comforter, like so much else in the loft, was a soft, steely gray that almost looked like liquid mercury pouring across the bed.

She couldn't take her eyes off their final destination. This was the moment she'd fantasized about, feared and longed for. How could it ever live up to either of their memories of that night they shared? David had told her she was a wet noodle in bed. She didn't want to be that for Jonah. She wanted to be the wild, passionate woman she'd been for him once. But how long could she maintain that facade? Was it better that she not try so hard and let him see the real Emma?

Jonah stopped in front of the bed and wrapped his arms around her waist. "Stop it," he chastised.

That snapped Emma out of her worried fog. "Stop what?"

"Stop overthinking it. Maybe that's all the tequila accomplished for you. It kept you out of your head, allowing you to just feel and go with the moment."

That may have been true. Emma found herself almost too nervous to move the more she thought about being with Jonah. She wasn't about to make love to a mysterious, heroic stranger. This was millionaire playboy Jonah Flynn. He was a man who'd romanced some of the most beautiful women in the world. She couldn't wrap her head around why he would want her. How could he not be disappointed with plain, boring old Emma? The thought was paralyzing.

Jonah seemed to notice the hesitation in her and compensated for it. His hands sought out the zipper on the side of her jumpsuit and pulled the tab to the end at her hip. "I guess I'll just have to overwhelm you with pleasure so you have no choice but to stop thinking."

His words coincided with his fingertips brushing along the sensitive bare skin of her side, making Emma gasp. He gripped the fabric at her shoulders and pulled it down. The silky material slipped over her arms, exposing her satin strapless bra, and then the slightly rounding curve of her pregnant stomach.

Emma instantly felt self-conscious about it. She had always been relatively slim, but never had the hard abs of someone who worked out at the gym doing core exercises. Jonah had seen her stomach when he was spying on her at the gym, but this was different.

He seemed to realize it, too. When he pushed the fabric of the jumpsuit over the curve of her hips, his eyes seemed fixated on her midsection. Jonah dropped down onto one knee, helping her step out of the outfit and slip out of her heels. Even then his eyes never flicked away.

When she was wearing nothing more than the bra and matching satin thong that wouldn't show through her jumpsuit, Jonah gripped her hips and pulled her to him. It reminded her of that first night where he'd done the same thing in his kitchen, looking up at her through his mask.

This time, as he leaned in to unfasten her bra and cast it to the floor, he pressed a kiss against the swell of her stomach. The gesture was simple and sweet, so unlike the man she envisioned from the newspapers. Emma closed her eyes to hide the glimmer of tears that started to gather there. Despite her worries and fears of Jonah rejecting his child along with her, it seemed as though she'd judged him too harshly. He would be a good father. That was all she dared ask of him for now.

She felt her panties slide down her legs and was too anxious to open her eyes again. There she was, completely naked in a well-lit room for his inspection. Jonah didn't seem to mind what he saw. He continued with his work, letting his hands and lips roam from her inner ankles up to her thighs. He stopped when he reached the exposed skin where her panties had once been. With a gentle nudge, he knocked Emma off balance and she sprawled back onto the bed with a shout of surprise.

Emma's eyes flew open in time to see the exposed beams and ductwork overhead. Before she could sit up and yell at Jonah, she realized he was kneeling between her spread thighs. She bit anxiously at her bottom lip as she felt his hot breath against her exposed center.

"I never got to taste you," he said. "Do you know how much I've regretted that?"

She covered her face with her hands to keep him from seeing her bright red cheeks. A moment later she felt one hand close around her wrists, pulling them away. He pinned them to the bed and when she finally opened her eyes, he was hovering over her. His shirt was unbuttoned now, showing off his lean, muscled torso.

"Does it embarrass you when I say things like that?" he asked.

Emma could only nod. How else could she explain that she was twenty-seven but about as comfortable with sexual topics as a twelve-year-old? She liked sex. And she'd had a good bit of it. But talking about it so blatantly? She just couldn't take it.

"Well, then I'll stop *talking* about it," he said, releasing her hands.

Before she could breathe a sigh of relief, she realized what he meant by that. He slipped down off the edge of the bed and pressed his palms against the inside of her knees to spread her legs wider.

The first touch was light, like a flicker over her skin that set off sparks under her eyelids. Every muscle in her body tensed in anticipation of the second contact. This time, his tongue lingered, moving slowly across her skin and making Emma squirm. After that, she lost count. Her hands gripped at the comforter as his lips, teeth and tongue feasted on her without showing signs of letting up.

Emma had done this before, and yet, she felt as though this were a totally new experience. Nothing any man had ever done to her had felt this amazing. She couldn't think, not really. Not when the waves of pleasure were coming at her from all sides. The only clear realization she had was that perhaps her lack of enthusiasm in bed with other partners was more of a reflection on them than on her.

It was as though a burden was lifted from her shoulders. Yes, perhaps David was just crappy in the sack and she accepted that because he was the kind of man she should want on paper. Successful, respectable, boring… The fears of becoming her sister had sent her on a path of living half a life. What else had she missed out on?

Emma looked up at Jonah and realized that he could definitely be the one to show her what was missing from her life. It might not ever be love or marriage or romance, but it would certainly be something more exciting than what she'd had. With a baby on the way, she had years of 2:00 a.m. feedings and runny noses in her future. She was excited to start that new part of her life, but there was no reason why she couldn't relish every second with Jonah now.

The thought released the last of the barricades she'd put up in her mind and she finally was able to relax and thoroughly enjoy the pleasure Jonah was giving her. She'd been holding tight to the release that was building up, somehow afraid to give in to it until now. When he slipped a finger inside of her and flicked his tongue over her swollen flesh, she couldn't hold back any longer.

Arching her back, Emma cried out. Her whole body convulsed against her will as the pulsating pleasure radiated through her. She clutched hopelessly at the blankets as Jonah continued his assault on her body, but there was nothing to hold her down.

This wasn't a release like she'd had before. Not even like the one he'd coaxed out of her the night of the Mardi Gras party. This blew them all out of the water and she found she couldn't control her body while it was happening. Only once the sensations finally faded away was she able to take a deep breath and lick her parched lips. She drew her legs together and melted into the bed like butter on a warm biscuit.

"That's my butterfly," he soothed as he stood up with a pleased smile curling his lips.

Emma could only watch him, the energy completely drained from her body, as he slipped out of his shirt, then went to work removing the rest of his clothes. Watching him was enough for now. There was so much of him she hadn't seen. He was lean and hard with the build of a marathon runner. Were there more tattoos he kept hidden beneath his clothes? In addition to their shared tattoo, she'd seen one peeking out from the sleeve of his T-shirts, but nothing she'd been able to study closely. Even now, she didn't really have the mental capacity to focus too much. Her body and her mind were gelatin.

"You seemed to enjoy that," he said. Completely nude, he offered his hand to help her sit up on the edge of the bed. "I'm anxious to hear you make those sounds again."

"Again?" she said, bewildered. She pushed herself back until she was centered, closer to the headboard.

Jonah crawled across the mattress until his body was covering hers. "Maybe even three times," he teased, pressing a kiss to her lips.

Emma couldn't imagine, but she wasn't about to argue with him while he was hovering between her thighs. With his lips still locked on hers, he pressed his hips forward, slipping inside of her with little resistance.

Now this, Emma remembered. She could hardly forget. He had been the perfect size for her, filling and stretching her body without being overwhelming. She drew her legs up to wrap around his hips and give him a better angle to go even deeper. The movement forced Jonah to pull away from her lips and curse softly with his cheek against hers. After a moment, he pushed up onto his arms with tightly closed eyes and a clenched jaw to maintain control.

"I don't know how you do this to me," he said as he withdrew and surged forward a second time. "It's like your body was just made for me. Everything about you…

your scent, your taste, the way you feel wrapped around me…I've been obsessed with experiencing this moment again. I can't believe I finally found you."

Emma couldn't believe they found each other, either. Or that despite everything, they'd ended up back in this place. She wanted to savor every moment they spent together so later she could use these memories to keep her warm on lonely nights. She reached up and cupped his face in her hands. The stubble of his beard was rough against her palms. She looked into his eyes, those blue, mesmerizing eyes, and drew his face down to hers so she could kiss him again.

"Stop talking and make love to me," she whispered against his lips.

Jonah grinned and kissed her full and hard before focusing on the task at hand. Adjusting his positioning, he settled into a slow, steady pace guaranteed to make them both crazy before too long. Resting on his elbow, he was able to dip his head down to nibble at her throat and taste her breasts, drawing hard on them until she arched her back and cried out.

He quickly adjusted his pace after that. They both knew that neither of them were patient enough to drag this pleasure on for too long. Jonah lifted her leg and hooked her knee over his shoulder. As he increased his speed and depth, Emma could only press her hands against the headboard to keep steady. That only made the thrusts more intense.

She couldn't imagine she could come again after the orgasm he'd just given her, but she felt the buildup start in her belly. She tensed her muscles and bit at her bottom lip as the pressure increased. She whispered soft encouragements between harsh gasps and groans as she got closer and closer.

"Oh Emma," he growled, planting a rough kiss against her inner knee.

Hearing her name on his lips was enough for her. She wasn't his butterfly, or his anonymous lover anymore. She was Emma. The one he wanted. And she came undone with her name on his lips.

As Emma cried and bucked her hips beneath him, Jonah finally gave in to his own pleasure. With a loud groan, he thrust hard and poured into her.

With his arms quivering, he kissed her, and then rolled to her side and collapsed back against the mattress. There was a long period of silence filled by ragged breathing and the occasional sigh of contentment.

Emma was wondering if he'd expect her to make her exit soon, when he rolled onto his side and tugged her body against him. She snuggled into the comfortable nook he created for her and felt herself start to drift off to sleep.

When she was on the edge of unconsciousness, she heard Jonah's voice whisper into her ear.

"I know you think that we're not good together and can't be a family. I'm here to tell you, Emma, that I worked too hard to find you and get you back in my bed again. I may not be willing to let you go this time."

Nine

Jonah was awakened the next morning by his cell phone ringing. He untangled from his grip on Emma's naked body and rolled over to grab his phone from the nightstand. It was Paul, his financial advisor. With everything else going on in his life lately, it was easy to ignore the fact that he was trying to cover up his brother's embezzlement.

"Hello?"

"It's done!" Paul said, triumphantly. "The money is in your accounts so you can move it wherever you need to."

Perfect. Of course, now he had to do that with Emma's eagle eyes watching the books, but what was done, was done. If he had to explain it to her, he would. He just didn't want to until the money was back where it belonged.

"Thanks, Paul. How much did it cost me to liquidate that quickly?"

"Er…" Paul stalled. "Perhaps a conversation better suited to a weekday at my office where we can look at all the figures."

That meant he'd taken a huge loss. "I'll be sure to take it, plus interest, out of Noah's hide."

"And we can hopefully make some of it back when we reinvest the funds."

Ever the optimist. "Okay. Thanks again, Paul." Jonah hung up the phone and scowled at the black screen. His advisor was working under the presumption that Noah was going to pay him back. He didn't have as much faith in his brother. Their mother would argue that he always treated Noah unfairly. Jonah would say the same of her. She coddled him, turning him into the monster that the rest of the family had to cope with.

"Is everything okay?"

Emma's voice drew him back to the here and now. "Yes, that was nothing. Just business."

"It's awful early on a Sunday morning for business." Emma yawned and curled into a ball against his chest.

Jonah wrapped his arms around her and clenched his jaw to hold in the angry words that had nothing to do with her. "Luckily we can go back to sleep," he said instead.

At first, his worry had been that Noah would screw up the Game Town deal. Covering up the stolen money had been at the forefront of his mind until he realized who Emma was. Then he'd nearly forgotten about why he was pursuing her in the first place. Now everything was different. Emma was more than an auditor; she was the mother of his child. She was the one who had held his interest, the one he couldn't forget about, the one who could make his blood race with a simple touch. It was possible that she could be The One.

How would she feel about what was going on with Noah? If she uncovered the truth, would she question every moment they'd spent together? Could she trust Jonah knowing he had been lying to her about this the whole time?

Jonah might very well lose the Game Town deal because of Noah, but if he lost Emma... He would never forgive his brother for screwing this up for him. This was the closest thing to love he'd ever experienced before and he didn't want it ruined by another one of Noah's wild ideas before it even had a chance.

"What are you thinking about?" she asked softly.

"Nothing important. Why?"

She placed her palm against his bare chest. "Your heart is pounding like mad. I was thinking you were upset about something."

He wasn't going to ruin this moment with Noah's nonsense. If he had to tell her, he would do it later. "Did it ever occur to you," he said, tugging her tight to his chest, "that I just woke up to a beautiful naked woman curled against me? That can make a man's heart pound pretty hard. As well as other things."

Emma's eyes widened, teasing him. "You mean you want to do it again?"

Was it teasing? He wasn't so sure now. "Emma, I would make love to you ten times a day if you could take it and we could get anything else done. Does that surprise you? I don't know how it could."

She pulled out of his grasp and sat up in bed, tugging the sheets to her chest. "A little. I mean...this is going to sound ridiculous. I'm just not used to all that. I went to Catholic school and got my sex education from nuns. I was raised to be more conservative. Not so conservative as to wait for marriage, obviously, but I've never really had the wild kind of nights you're probably used to."

"Were all the guys you dated just that boring?"

Emma frowned, a crease forming between her eyebrows. "Yes, in a way. But I suppose that was what I was looking for."

Now it was Jonah's turn to sit up. "You were looking for someone boring?" He couldn't imagine someone like Emma wasting her life with someone like that.

"Not *boring*. More like…responsible. Respectable. The kind of man you'd be happy to take home to your parents."

"You mean the opposite of me?"

"No!" she insisted. "Well…not exactly."

Jonah tried not to be offended. He knew he wasn't the clean-cut lawyer or investment banker some parents wanted for their daughter. "Do your parents know you're having my baby?"

Emma shook her head. "They don't even know I'm pregnant yet."

"Emma! How could you keep that a secret?"

"Easy. I assure you that it was far simpler to avoid my parents than to tell them I'm pregnant but don't know who the father is. And I didn't until a week ago. Listen, my parents are very overprotective of me. My sister ended up being an embarrassment to the family. I was just a teenager when she died and my mother was constantly on me not to make the same mistakes Cynthia made. So I guess I've been more worried about pleasing them than pleasing myself. It wasn't until my ex said those horrible things that I gave myself permission to rebel for just one night."

"And look what happened!" Jonah said jokingly, but he could instantly tell by the pained expression on Emma's face that she felt exactly that way. He was used to scandal, but he sensed that Emma was out of her element with this entire situation. He opted to change his tactic. "Listen, I'm sorry about all this, Emma. I certainly didn't expect you to suffer permanent consequences from our night together. At least outside of the tattoo. I know how you feel—"

"How could you possibly?" she interrupted.

"Well, you might be surprised to know that my parents were very conservative and very strict. I wasn't allowed to do anything. Me and my younger brothers got sent to a boarding school in England when my father died. I only had a year or so left, then I returned for college. There, I realized that I could live my life the way I wanted to, and everything changed for me. I think my professional success is due in part to my rebellious management style. It doesn't work for everyone, but it really worked out for me."

"And what does your mother say about how you live your life?"

"She said plenty at first, when she thought I still cared. Then she realized I was a grown man, a CEO of my own company, and she finally let it go. At least until Thanksgiving rolls around. It wouldn't be a family holiday without Angelica Flynn putting her two cents in."

"I don't know that it will ever be that easy with my parents. Once they lost Cynthia, I was all they had left. I've never wanted to disappoint them."

Jonah put his arm around Emma's shoulders. "I don't know how you could possibly disappoint anyone."

Emma brought her hand to her stomach and rubbed the small bulge there unconsciously as she stared off across the expanse of his loft. "They won't be happy about the baby. My mother has been waiting years to put together a huge society wedding for me. Cynthia died before she could get married, so I'm her only chance to be the mother of the bride at an outrageous affair at The Plaza Hotel. You don't have a big affair like that when the bride is obviously pregnant. And there's no hope of a wedding at The Plaza, or otherwise, when the baby is the result of a one-night stand and they have no intention of marrying."

There were a lot of things about Emma's pregnancy that he really hadn't taken into consideration until now. He'd only thought about how fatherhood would affect his life, not hers. Not really, and that was stupid and selfish of him. "Will your parents insist you get married?"

Emma shrugged. "They can try, but they can't force you into it. My father doesn't own a shotgun, so you're safe there. I'm certainly not going to force you into it. The pregnancy was a mistake. I'm not going to compound it by demanding that we add a marriage into the mix."

The last few days with Emma had changed a lot of the ways Jonah looked at the world. Once, long before she walked through the doors of FlynnSoft, Jonah told himself that if he ever found his butterfly, he wouldn't let her go. That hadn't entirely changed when he realized Emma was his fantasy woman. When he saw her, he saw a future without a line of women outside his door. Yes, he would absolutely stand up and be a father to their child, but for the first time in his life, Emma made him consider more—more than this cold, empty loft, trysts with random actresses and lonely nights working late at the office.

The idea of coming home after work to a nice, comfortable apartment and spending time with his very own family was suddenly more appealing than it had ever been. Having a family was something he'd never put much thought into, perhaps just because at heart he was still a teenager rebelling against his parents at every turn. As a grown man with a child on the way, things were different.

But it didn't sound like a future together held the same appeal for Emma. "You don't want to marry me?" he asked.

She turned to look at him with wide green eyes. "No, I don't."

Jonah had never asked a woman if she wanted to marry him before, and although it wasn't really a proposal, he was a little hurt by her blunt rejection. "Why? Am I not good enough to be your husband?"

"Of course you're good enough," she chided. "It has nothing to do with that. Despite the fact that we're having a child together, we hardly know each other, Jonah. *That's* why. We agreed to give the relationship time to develop and see what—if anything—happened, and I'm fine with that. If one day, you decide you're truly in love with me and want to marry me that will be completely different. But I'm not going to rush things because of an artificial ticking time bomb that ends with this kid entering the world. My mother and her dreams of a big Plaza wedding will have to just be dreams."

Emma had hoped that the weekend would clear her mind and she could return to work Monday ready to wrap up this project at FlynnSoft. Instead she found herself just as baffled by the discrepancy in the financials as she was the week before. If her calculations were correct, and she'd checked them three times, someone had taken out three million dollars without logging the expense properly. The money had been transferred to an offshore account she couldn't find any record of, nor did it have any relation to the corporation that she could find. It looked very fishy. And yet who would be foolish enough to steal such a large amount? Someone was bound to notice it.

This was the part of Emma's job that she didn't like. She had to tell the CEO that someone was stealing from him. Then she had to hope the finger didn't point back at Jonah himself. He had that right, she supposed—it was his company, after all—but it wouldn't look good. Then, worst of all, she had to report it back to Game Town, where the stodgy owner would likely pass on the contract. This wasn't going to end well for anyone but the creep who made off with three million.

With a heavy sigh, Emma picked up her phone to call Mark, one of her coworkers at the firm. She needed some advice on how to handle this so she could make certain she wasn't letting her relationship with Jonah cloud the issue. Mark had been doing this job for twenty years and had seen it all. He would know what to do.

"Hey there, Emma," Mark said as he answered. "How're the crazy kids over there at FlynnSoft?"

"It's definitely a different kind of company," Emma admitted. "Listen, I'm about to wrap up but I've come across something questionable that I wanted to run by you." She went through everything she found as briefly as she could. "Do you think I should speak to the CEO before I make my report?" she asked when she was done.

"You can. And I would. It's possible he can find an explanation and documentation for it that you haven't thought of. But if there's the slightest whisper of funds mismanagement, you need to report it back to Game Town. It's not your job to protect FlynnSoft from themselves."

Emma's stomach sank. "Of course. I just wanted a second opinion. Thanks for your time, Mark."

She hung up the phone and gathered some of her papers to take upstairs to Jonah's office. She hadn't seen him yet this morning. She tried not to think about what that meant. He'd said a lot about a potential future for the two of them, but she didn't believe it. Not really. It sounded good; it was the right thing to say, but would he follow through? Or would he chase the next shiny thing that caught his eye?

His secretary, Pam, wasn't at her desk when she came upstairs, so Emma went ahead and knocked on his door.

"Come in," she heard him yell from inside.

Emma pushed the heavy door open and slipped into his office. The moment he laid eyes on her, his eyes brightened and he smiled. Jonah leaped up from his seat behind his desk and rushed over to her. Before she could stop him, he swept her up in his arms and pulled her into a passionate good-morning kiss.

Emma tried to untangle herself as delicately as she could. "Jonah, please," she fussed, straightening up her paperwork and taking a step back.

"No one can see into my office, butterfly."

"Don't call me that at work, Jonah. And someone could walk in and catch us together at any time."

Jonah frowned and leaned back against his desk. "I guess. But what if you worked here?" he asked. "Would you still worry all the time?"

"What do you mean?" she asked.

"Well," he explained, "I told you before that I need a new financial director. From everything I've seen of your work thus far, I think you'd be great for the job. And besides that, if you worked for me instead of this pesky third party, you wouldn't have to worry about the impropriety of it all."

It was a little more complicated than just that. She'd thought he was only joking when he'd mentioned the job last week. "No, I'd only have to worry about people saying I slept with the boss instead."

"Well, to be fair you did sleep with the boss," Jonah said with an impish grin. He leaned in and whispered "multiple times," like he was sharing a secret.

Emma shook her head. It seemed like everything was a joke to Jonah sometimes. "I'm serious."

"So am I," he countered. "I need a finance director and I want you to take the job."

"I'm not taking the job, Jonah. I don't like the way it would look."

"My brother works here. He collects a paycheck and doesn't do a damn thing. Everyone knows that and no one cares. Nepotism is alive and well in the corporate world."

"Yes, but if we continue to date, if everyone finds out I'm having your baby... I just don't like it. You know how I feel about that sort of thing. Reputations are important to me."

Jonah sighed. "Okay, fine. You won't kiss me. You don't want to work for me. I suppose that means you won't give yourself to me on the conference room table. So tell me what it is that brings you here today, Miss Dempsey."

Emma ignored his sexual comments and tried not to bristle at his sudden use of her formal name. A week ago she would've preferred it, but now things were different. Now she knew he was only doing it to get a rise out of her because he was irritated.

She clutched the paperwork tight to her chest and tried

to focus on what she needed to say instead of the dark blue eyes that were watching her curiously. "I'm finished with my audit."

"Oh, excellent. You're very efficient, considering how much I distracted you. Does that mean you'll be free to be seen with me in public? Or do we have to wait for the Game Town deal to go through?"

"Well, the Game Town deal is what I came to talk to you about. I've found a significant discrepancy in the books."

The curiosity on his face instantly faded. His brow drew together with a serious expression of concern that seemed out of place on his face. "What did you find?"

Emma took the pages over to him where she'd highlighted the withdrawal. "Exactly three million has been taken out and wired to this offshore account in the Caymans. I haven't been able to figure out who it belongs to, but I can't make any connection to a legitimate business expense or account."

Jonah nodded, his face unusually blank of its usual emotion or amusement. His gaze simply flicked over the pages as she spoke without really seeming to take in the data. She wasn't sure what to think, so she continued to nervously prattle on.

"Do you know anything about this? I was hoping you might have some kind of insight that would keep it from looking as bad as it does right now."

Jonah turned his gaze to her and he nodded curtly. "I do have some insight, but unfortunately, it won't improve the circumstances. Please have a seat."

He returned to his desk chair and Emma lowered slowly into the guest seat where she'd first met the infamous Jonah Flynn a week ago. So much had changed and yet she was just as anxious talking to him now as she was then. "Am I missing something?" she asked. "Is this some kind of third world charity outreach in the Caribbean?"

Jonah shook his head. "I'm pretty sure we document our charity funds appropriately. You haven't missed anything, and I didn't think you would. The truth of the matter is that my younger brother Noah is a vice president here, as I mentioned earlier. He transferred the money out to one of his private accounts—an unauthorized loan of sorts. A member of the finance department brought it to my attention the day you arrived to conduct the audit. Had I known about it earlier, I would've disclosed the issue, but instead, I hoped that perhaps I could resolve it. I spoke with Noah last week and confirmed my suspicions."

Emma's stomach felt like the baby was flittering around with butterflies. Unauthorized loan? That was a nice way to say stealing. She'd never even met Jonah's brothers and now she was learning that one of them was a thief. Her *baby's uncle* was a thief. As though her parents weren't already going to have a meltdown over this.

"And?" she pressed.

"And, he's returning it all. I can't tell you what he needed the money for—I didn't ask—but he swore he would return it when he got back into the States. At the moment, he's in Southeast Asia. In the meantime, I have deposited enough money to cover the withdrawal. The accounts should register it as of this morning. Since this is a privately owned company with no board of directors to answer to, I've covered the loss and opted not to publicize the theft outside of the company."

"You still have the president of Game Town to answer to," Emma pointed out. "When I disclose this, I'm pretty sure Carl Bailey is going to back out of the partnership deal with FlynnSoft. He was suspicious enough of your company and its unorthodox methods going into it. I don't see him as the kind of man that would want to do business with a company that could potentially lose money it's handling on his behalf."

"We won't lose Game Town's money. I guarantee it."

"How can you do that?" she asked. Was he willing to use his own money to replace every dime his brother or anyone else decided they could take?

"I can guarantee it because I intend to make my brother's life so miserable he'd sooner stab himself in the eye with a butter knife than touch a penny of this company's funds again. When I'm done making an example of him, neither he, nor anyone else in this company, would even consider it."

"Well, hopefully when you meet with Game Town, you can convince Carl of that. I'm not the one you need to sell it to."

"That's where you're wrong. I need you to understand that this is really a private matter between my brother and I, and I would like to keep it that way. I covered the loss and would do so again if necessary."

The unease returned. It all sounded very nice and good, but Emma couldn't shake the feeling that this was bad news. She believed Jonah and what he said about the money, but the implication was clear. "Are you asking me to leave the stolen money out of the report?"

Jonah looked her in the eye for a moment, as though he were silently pleading with her. But he didn't say the words. "I can show you the records of the deposits, Emma. Would that make you feel better?"

It would. To a point. "I would like to see those records.

Then I can and will include in my report that the funds have been reinstated. But I won't be a party to covering this up. If someone were to find out, I would lose all credibility. I would be fired. I wouldn't be able to get a job anywhere in my field." Emma placed a hand protectively over her stomach, which seemed to grow a tiny bit every day now. "As it is, my impartiality will be questioned when the truth about the baby comes out. If anyone were to uncover that I knew about the theft and hid it…"

"You know you don't need to work, Emma. I can take care of you and our baby."

Emma shook her head adamantly. "Support your child because you want to and it's the right thing to do. I don't want it to feel like a kickback. Please don't ask me to do something that compromises my integrity, Jonah."

With a sigh, Jonah set aside the financial paperwork and walked over to her. She reluctantly let him wrap his arms around her and pull her into his protective embrace. "I won't. Report what you need to report, butterfly. FlynnSoft will recover, no matter what happens with the Game Town deal."

Emma eased back to look him in the eye and see that he really meant what he said. "You're okay with this?"

He nodded with a soft, reassuring smile. "I'm okay with this. In the end, it is what it is, right? You have to tell the truth and I have to be willing to stand in front of Carl and explain to him why he can still trust us to do a good job, despite it."

A sense of relief washed over her. She didn't like what she'd found, and she didn't like that Jonah and his employees might be punished for someone else's actions, but thankfully it would be out of her hands. "Thank you."

"When you get done typing that report up, I insist you

let me take you out to dinner tonight. Anyplace on the island you want."

"I'm still not comfortable with us being seen together. It's not over until my report is filed, I'm back at my old office and the deal is done, Jonah."

"Okay, fine," he relented. "How about some very privately consumed takeout at your place, then?"

"Perfect," she agreed, letting him pull her tight against him again. Even now, when it felt like things were unraveling, she was okay as long as she was in his arms. Hopefully she'd be able to stay there and weather the upcoming storms.

Ten

Jonah wasn't sure what to expect from Emma's apartment, but it wasn't what he got. Her work persona was so strait-laced and uptight, he anticipated her home would be boring, neat, with a place for everything and everything in its place. But the large and spacious apartment was flooded with daylight through large picture windows and the decor was relaxed, comfortable and filled with personality.

He followed her inside clutching a bag of Thai food from the restaurant up the block. Once he made it in far enough, he closed the door behind him and just stopped to take it all in. The fabrics on the curtains and the furniture were soft and romantic with florals and lace. The furniture itself looked comfortable like you would want to settle in and read for hours. It was soft, feminine with a touch of rustic country charm, telling him more about the real Emma than he expected to uncover.

"What's the matter?" Emma asked.

"Your apartment. It just wasn't what I was expecting." He followed her into the kitchen with its white Shaker cabinetry and gray-washed wood floors. A vase of multicolored zinnias sat in the middle of the kitchen table, likely from the flower shop on the corner.

"Not enough chrome and glass for your taste?" she asked. "Industrial chic isn't exactly my thing. I get enough concrete and steel walking around Manhattan every day. When I got my own place after college, I decided that I wanted something softer and more comforting to come home to."

"It's nice. Certainly more inviting than my place, but I'm more about function than anything. Here, I keep expecting a chicken to run across the hallway."

"You quit it," she chided, taking the bag away from him and unpacking cartons of Thai food onto the butcher-block countertop. "I don't have any pets, and that includes chickens. I think that's against the co-op restrictions," Emma added with a chuckle. "This is still the Upper East Side, you know."

They both made plates and bypassed the dining table to sit together in the living room on the couch. As they finished their food, Jonah found himself more curious about Emma's personal hideaway. He wanted to see it all and gain more insight into her.

"May I have the rest of the tour?" he asked as she set her mostly empty plate on the coffee table.

Emma shrugged. "If you want. There isn't much left to see. Two bedrooms, one bath." She got up and he followed her down a little hallway where she pointed out the black-and-white retro bathroom. "This," she said as she opened the opposite door, "used to be my office. I've cleared all that out to uh…for the nursery."

That was right. This wasn't just a cute bachelorette pad any longer. This was where she intended to raise their child. They stepped inside the room together. There wasn't anything in it yet.

"I thought it was too early to buy much. I had the walls painted a soft gray. I thought that was neutral enough for whatever I…*we* end up having."

"It's a pretty small room, Emma. The baby is going to outgrow it fairly quickly."

"I know," she said with a sigh. "I didn't buy this place expecting to raise a child in it. When the baby needs more space, I'll look at something larger. I want to save money while I can. If my parents haven't disowned me, perhaps they can help with a down payment."

It baffled Jonah how she continued to talk about the baby as though she was having to do this entirely on her own. "Or I could."

"Well…yes, maybe. I'm just not used to thinking about it that way. Up until a week ago, the baby's father was not in the picture. I had no idea how to find you, so I was having to make plans to do this all on my own."

"I may need a new place, too," Jonah said, thinking aloud. His loft didn't have any walls. How was a baby supposed to sleep without walls to block out noise? "Perhaps…perhaps we could look at getting something together."

Emma froze on her way out of the nursery. She looked at Jonah with wide eyes. "You want to move in together?"

"Uh…" When she said it that way, it was a little terrifying, but still accurate. "Yes. If we both need a bigger place, we could look into something large enough to accommodate all of us. Then the baby doesn't have to move back and forth between us. We could even look for something where you could have your own room, if that would make you more comfortable."

She took a ragged breath before pushing past him into the hallway. "That's something we could talk about," she said in a noncommittal tone he'd gotten used to with her. It was better than a complete dismissal. "We have time."

"Do you have a due date?"

"The doctor told me it would be November twenty-first."

With every detail, the baby became more and more real in his mind. Now he knew when to expect his life to change forever—before the holidays rolled around again. "A Thanksgiving baby?"

Emma nodded. "Seems like a long time from now, but it will probably be here before we know it." She continued down the hallway to the last door. "This is my bedroom."

They stepped into a room that was much larger than the nursery. A queen-size bed sat along one wall with a white wooden headboard that was worn and gouged to reveal the darker color of the wood beneath the paint. The bed had an eyelet coverlet and easily a dozen pillows, all different. An antique oval mirror, a dresser and an old cedar chest at the foot of the bed finished it off.

The place was nice, but the addition of a baby, plus a stroller, high chair, bassinet, toys and all the other accessories a child came with, would eat up the space she had left. It was a lovely, spacious apartment for a single woman, but that wasn't what she was anymore.

"We need to get a new place. This just seals the deal. Your apartment is too small and mine is too impractical. I'm going to call a Realtor next week to have him start looking for apartments. How do you feel about the Village?"

Emma turned around to face him and placed a cautionary hand on his chest. "Slow down. I'm not ready yet, Jonah."

"Not ready to get an apartment or not ready for everyone to know we're together?" He asked the question knowing the answer. Emma and her blasted reputation. "When?" he pressed.

"Once the FlynnSoft deal is done. And we tell our parents. Then, if they haven't killed us, it should be okay to let others know about us and about the baby."

"It can't happen soon enough. I don't like hiding. I'm used to living my life out in the open. I can't wait until I can touch you whenever I want to. Kiss you whenever I want to."

Emma turned to him with a sigh. "It won't be too much longer. Until then, you'll just have to take advantage of your opportunities when they arise."

Jonah sat down on the edge of the bed and looked at her. He had an opportunity right now he wasn't going to pass up. "Come here."

Emma took a few steps toward him, stopping when she was standing just between his knees. She placed her hands on his shoulders and looked down at him.

God, she was beautiful. The fact that she didn't think so just made her that much more attractive. Even when the mask had hidden most of her face, there was a beauty that shone out of her from the inside. Perhaps that was what he'd been drawn to all this time. No mask, no boxy suit, no stuffy demeanor could suppress it.

Jonah ran his palms along the outside of her legs, down and back up to her hips. There, he pulled her dress shirt out from where she'd tucked it into her waistband. He immediately sought out the silk of her skin beneath it, stroking her elegantly arched back and sides that seemed to quiver at his touch. She was content to let him explore, closing her eyes and just feeling him.

He unfastened her dress pants, sliding them over her hips to the floor. Once she'd stepped out of them, Jonah hooked his hand behind her knee and pulled her toward him. With little resistance, she crawled into his lap, straddling him on the bed. He ran his hands over her smooth thighs and hips before turning his attention to her blouse. One by one, he slipped the pearl buttons through the holes until Emma was astride him in little more than a lacy peach-colored bra and panties.

Emma reached up and pulled a few pins from her hair. With a shake of her head, the dark brown waves broke free of their restraints and tumbled down around her shoulders. The scent of her shampoo swirled around him. Jonah could only wrap his arms around her waist to hold her securely in his lap as he leaned in and buried his face in her creamy, lace-clad breasts.

She gasped and wove her fingers into his hair, pulling him closer as he teased and tasted her sensitive skin. His tongue rubbed across the rough lace that kept her nipples confined, over and over until the fabric was damp. Frustrated by the impediment, he tugged the straps down her shoulders until her breasts were exposed. He kissed the inside of each one, then placed a kiss on the ridge of her sternum between them.

"Why are you wearing so much clothing while I'm wearing so little?" Emma asked. "I feel like I'm at a distinct disadvantage here."

"You're prettier naked than I am," Jonah replied with

a grin. He immediately followed his words with action, tugging his shirt up and over his head. He wanted as much of his skin to touch hers as possible. He wrapped his arms around her and pressed his bare chest against hers before meeting her lips with a searing kiss.

He couldn't get enough of her. Not then and not now. She was unlike any other woman he'd ever known. She was his and he was hers in more ways than he could even describe. His butterfly had changed everything. And even if the thing with Game Town ended badly, he knew that if he made it out of this situation with Emma still in his arms, everything would be okay. She was his anchor, holding him steady so he wouldn't drift out to sea. He couldn't lose her.

Emma pulled away from his kiss, shifting in his lap and grinding against his erection with a wicked grin lighting her face. "Now," she pouted.

He wasn't about to deny her. Emma rose up onto her knees while he scrambled out of his jeans and kicked them away. And then, she slowly lowered herself back down, taking in every inch of him at a deliciously slow pace.

"Oh Emma," he groaned into her hair, pulling her close as her heat enveloped him. "I'm never letting you go. Never."

She didn't want him to let go. She was content to stay right where she was forever. Emma had never felt so close, so connected to a man before. As she raised her hips and lowered them, rocking back and forth in his lap, the delicious friction her movement generated hit in all the right places.

A heat that started in her belly seemed to spread

through her whole self. As her temperature shot up, the close proximity of their bodies made her skin break out in a thin sheen of perspiration. Each time Emma moved, her moist skin glided across his. Jonah only clutched her tighter as the sensations they were each experiencing grew more and more intense.

Emma wanted to find her release like this. She wanted to come apart wrapped in his arms. She wanted him to feel every tremble, every aftershock, and then she wanted to experience the same thing for him. This closeness was what she truly craved with Jonah. Here, in this moment, she could truly believe that they were supposed to be together. She could open her heart enough to let him in, if just for a moment.

She was roused from her thoughts by Jonah's encouraging whispers in her ear. "Ahh, yeah. That's my beautiful butterfly. Come apart for me, baby."

The low rumble of his voice against her ear and neck sent goose bumps through her body. She moved faster, rocking her hips hard until her muscles ached and her knees burned. It was when she almost had nothing more to give that she reached her goal. As suddenly as a snapping of fingers, her body gave in and the pleasurable sensations rushed through her.

Jonah held her tight, continuing to whisper to her as her body shuddered and spasmed in his arms. When the rush subsided and she barely had the energy to hold on to him, he thrust hard from beneath her until with a final groan, lost himself in her. Jonah collapsed back onto the bed, taking Emma with him. After a moment, she rolled off and flattened into her mattress, drawing in a lungful of cooler air. They shifted around until Jonah could pull the covers up over them both and they snuggled together in the plush softness of her bed.

Lying there, looking up at her ceiling and listening to Jonah's heartbeat pound in his chest, she wondered if this could really be what her life would be like now. With the audit behind her, she would soon be free to be with Jonah. She wasn't sure how things would turn out, but even if they didn't marry, surely her parents would be happier about the pregnancy if they were together. If they *loved* each other.

Did she love him?

She had questioned her feelings for Jonah repeatedly over the last few days. Now, lying in his arms, making love to him again, it was easy to admit to herself that she did. She had loved him since that first night. She'd just been afraid to acknowledge the truth, even to herself. Love was a scary proposition, and love with a man like Jonah could be downright terrifying.

He was everything she thought she shouldn't want. Exciting, spontaneous, rebellious, passionate… For some reason, she'd lumped all those qualities in with irresponsible and dangerous, when that was hardly the case. She didn't need a man to be boring. She just needed him to be there for her. Jonah might very well be that man.

Emma was so content in his arms and so deep in thought that when her cell phone rang, she was tempted not to answer. And she wouldn't have except for the fact that it was her work ringtone. It was awfully late to be fielding calls from the office. Then again, they wouldn't call her if it wasn't necessary.

She answered the phone, seeing her boss's name on the screen. "Hello?"

"Emma. We have a problem," Tim said.

Her stomach instantly felt as though it had twisted into a knot. How could they have a problem? She hadn't even filed the report yet. And she'd disclosed everything. She sat up in bed and grabbed her robe off the hook. "What's wrong?" she asked as she nervously walked out of the bedroom and tied her belt. She needed to focus and couldn't with Jonah's nude body sprawled on her bed.

"I spoke with Mark not too long ago. He told me about the conversation you had with him today. I really don't appreciate being left out of the loop on something so important. You should've come to me with this issue first."

Emma's free hand curled into a fist at her side. She went to her coworker for support and he'd ratted her out before she'd had a chance to do what she needed to do. "He gave me some advice and I'm following it. I'll have my report to you first thing in the morning. I wanted to read over it again before I submitted it."

"And what will the report say?"

"It will say that I discussed the issue with Jo—*Mr. Flynn* and he provided an explanation. Both the discrepancy and how FlynnSoft handled the issue will be included in the report for Mr. Bailey to handle as he pleases."

There was a long pause on the phone that Emma didn't like. When Tim was quiet, he was preparing his words, and they usually weren't good. "So you're on a first name basis with *Jonah*, are you, Emma?"

She swallowed hard, measuring her words carefully and trying to ignore the heat of Jonah's naked body that still warmed her. "The environment at FlynnSoft is very casual, sir. You know that as well as anyone."

"You know, Emma, I sent you because I thought you

had some sense. More than Dee. I should've sent Mark, though. I underestimated Mr. Flynn's allure. I see that now."

Emma's mouth dropped open. "Sir, are you accusing me of some kind of wrongdoing? I assure you that my report is as accurate and impartial as Mark's would have been."

"So you're willing to sit there and deny any type of personal relationship with Mr. Flynn?"

Could she lie? No, she couldn't. But could she convince him it wouldn't matter? "No, I can't do that, sir. But I can say with complete confidence that I did my job as well as anyone."

Tim groaned loudly over the phone line. "Can't you see that he just used you, Emma? I'm willing to bet that he turned on the charm the minute you walked in the door. Did he offer to give you a personal tour of the building? Did he take you out to dinner and welcome you to the company? Just to be friendly, of course? He dates models and actresses, Emma. You're a pretty girl, but do you really think a man like him would be interested in a woman like you if he didn't want something from you? I'm pretty sure his entire plan from the beginning was to distract you from your work so you wouldn't find the problem in the books. Or if you did, to convince you not to disclose it. Now that it's done, he's going to drop you like a bad habit."

His sharp words hit their target, bruising her ego, but she wouldn't back down on her report. "But I *did* disclose it," she insisted. "I don't understand why you're saying all this when I haven't even submitted my report yet."

"Yes, you disclosed the problem, but then you followed it up with the recommendation that the deal still go through because Jonah had handled it in a fiscally responsible manner."

"How...?" She hadn't submitted her report yet, and he'd just quoted her own words back to her.

"I pulled it off our server and read your draft when I got off the phone with Mark. I couldn't believe what I was reading. Would you have made that recommendation with anyone else, Emma? Tell me the truth."

Emma couldn't answer. She didn't know. Perhaps she wasn't as impartial as she thought. Perhaps Jonah had managed to get his way in the end without her even realizing he was doing it.

"You've lost your objectivity because you've gotten romantically involved with him, just as he'd planned. If I can't count on you to do your job, Emma, I have no choice but to let you go. Come in tomorrow and pack up your office."

She couldn't believe what she was hearing. It was everything she'd feared and dreaded since the moment she laid eyes on Jonah. She thought she'd been so cautious, so careful, and yet it was all falling down around her. "Are you serious? You're firing me?"

She heard the bed squeak and Jonah's heavy footsteps coming down the hallway. He must've heard her say she was fired. Panic started to close her throat. She couldn't deal with Tim and Jonah at the same time.

"I am," Tim said. "I'm sorry, Emma."

The line disconnected, leaving her dumbstruck. The phone slipped from her hand to the living room floor, where she left it.

Jonah appeared in the room wearing nothing but his boxers and jeans. "He fired you?" he asked, but she didn't answer.

She couldn't. Tim's words were swirling in her head and muffling Jonah's voice. She was pregnant and unemployed. She'd just lost her medical insurance. What was she going to do? Turn to her baby's father? The same man who may have very well used her to close the deal with Game Town?

That was the part that really ate at her insides. She wasn't the kind of woman Jonah was known to date. He'd pursued Emma from the moment he walked into his office and first laid eyes on her. Well before he knew who she really was, he was asking her to dinner, to coffee, buying her expensive flowers and pouring on the charm layers thick. Maybe Tim was right. All of this was just his way of securing the contract by any means necessary.

"Emma, what did he say? What's happened? Did he find out about us? We were so careful."

"Jonah, please," she said, holding out her hand to silence him. "Just answer one question for me. That's all I want to hear right now."

Jonah's jaw flexed as he held in his own questions and nodded. "Okay. What do you want to know?"

"Before you knew who I really was, why were you pursuing me so doggedly? The truth. Were you only feigning an interest in me in an attempt to distract me and keep me from finding that Noah stole all that money from the company?"

"Is that what Tim told you?" he asked.

"Just answer the question, please."

Jonah's blue eyes focused on her for a second before they dropped to the floor. "Yes," he said after a prolonged and uncomfortable silence.

"Oh my God," she said, tears rushing to her eyes.

"Emma, no. Listen to me. Yes, that was my original

intention, okay. I wanted to charm you a little to see if it would help things. I don't want to lie to you about that. But once I knew who you were, I was nothing but sincere. You're my butterfly. I—"

He reached out to her, but Emma dodged him. "Don't. Just don't. I can't have you touching me and calling me pet names when I'm trying to come to terms with the fact that you were just using me."

"Emma, please. You've got to listen to me."

"No, I don't. The only thing I have to do is pack my office tomorrow and update my résumé. I need medical insurance and a way to support my baby."

"Our baby," he corrected.

Emma only ignored him. She couldn't think about that right now. A future of dealing with him as her baby's father was too painful a thought. "I need you to get your things and go home, Jonah."

He took a step toward her, but she backed away and he stopped short. "I told you I'd never let you go and I meant it, Emma."

His eyes pleaded with her, the deep blue tugging at her heartstrings, but she didn't dare back down. He'd used her to get what he'd wanted and she couldn't forget that. He'd destroyed her career and her reputation just to save his own ass. "I'm not giving you the choice, Jonah. I need you to leave. Right now." Her voice was as stone cold and unemotional as she could make it with her feelings threatening to explode out of her.

This time, he didn't bother to argue. He returned to the bedroom, gathered up the rest of his clothes and pulled them on without another word. Emma followed him to the front door, fighting to hold in her tears until he was gone.

"I didn't mean to hurt you, Emma," he said before stepping out the front door.

She closed and locked it behind him, and rested her forehead against the cold wood. The tears started flowing freely then.

"Well, you did," she whispered.

Eleven

"Someone is looking awfully grumpy this morning."

Jonah looked up from his desk to see his brother Noah standing in the doorway. Just the sight of him was enough to send his blood pressure rocketing.

His brother had chosen the wrong day to come strolling into his office with that smug grin on his face. He hadn't slept for days after the fight with Emma. He couldn't eat. The worst part was that he knew he'd handled the situation with her all wrong. He didn't know how he would fix things, if he even could. But he could get some justice by making the culprit that put him in that position pay.

Without responding, Jonah slowly stood up from his desk with his hands curled into fists at his sides. He had no doubt the waves of anger were rolling off him with the way the perpetual smirk on Noah's face faded.

Jonah stalked his brother around the room like a panther toying with his cornered prey. Slowly. Deliberately. Silently. He would savor this punishment. Weeks of frustration, heartache, not to mention millions of dollars—all because of his reckless, stupid younger brother.

"Jonah…" Noah held his hands up and backed away toward the conference room table. "Let me explain first, please."

"Oh, you're going to explain," Jonah said. "But you're going to do it with a split lip and a bloody nose."

"Oh, come on, Jonah. Physical violence? What would Mother say? I'm going to see her tonight. Do you want me to look like I've been in a fight?"

Normally, the mention of the grand dame would've given him pause, but not today. "Nope," he replied. "I want you to look like you've lost a fight."

Now Noah looked worried. He moved until the conference table was between them. "Why are you so angry? Did the Game Town deal fall through?"

"Did the Game Town deal fall through?" Jonah said with a near-hysterical edge to his voice. He had no idea. He hadn't heard a word on the deal since he left Emma's apartment Monday night. He laughed and continued to circle the table. "That's the least of my worries at the moment, Noah."

That puzzled his younger brother. "Well, wait. Really. What has happened? Because I spoke with the Game Town CEO yesterday and he sounded like he understood and everything would go through just fine."

Jonah froze. He hadn't. Noah hadn't gone to their potential partner and spoken with him without even telling Jonah he was back in the country. He wouldn't. "You what?"

"I'll tell you everything if you sit down and promise

not to hit me. That's why I came here after all. I'm not stupid."

Jonah sincerely doubted that, but he was more curious about his brother's story at the moment. He couldn't fathom a scenario where he could explain the theft to Carl and have everything be okay. "Fine. But I still might hit you."

"Fine," Noah agreed. "Please sit down and let me finish first."

Jonah returned to his desk, his eyes never leaving his younger brother as he crossed the room and sat in his chair. Noah took a seat in the guest chair, perching on the edge as though he were preparing to make a quick getaway.

"Talk," Jonah demanded.

"I got back from Thailand two days ago," Noah explained. "The jet lag is unbelievable, really. I spent the first day in bed, and the next day Melody called me and told me there were whispers in the halls that the Game Town deal might not go through because of me and the money. I felt bad about the whole thing, so I went to Game Town and talked to the CEO myself."

Noah Flynn was not known for his initiative, so Jonah refrained from interrupting him to see exactly what his angle was with all of this. There had to be an angle. Had to. Noah always had an angle.

"I explained to him what the money was for and that it was extenuating circumstances that would never happen again."

Every word out of his brother's mouth made Jonah angrier. "And what, exactly, was the money for, Noah?"

"Ransom."

Well, that was certainly not what he was expecting. Was he serious? "Ransom for whom?"

"For my son."

Jonah didn't think his younger brother could shock him any more than he already had, but Noah was always full of surprises. "What son? You don't have a son."

Noah sighed. "So, about a year and a half ago, I met this doctor named Reagan Hardy at a charity event. We spent a week or so together, but not long after that, she took her next Doctors Without Borders assignment in Southeast Asia. She found out she was pregnant after she left and never told me. Her high-profile work in the community made her a target of the *chao pho*, the Thai mafia. They kidnapped Kai from the clinic where she was working. I didn't know he even existed until she called and asked for help. They demanded three million dollars in seven days or they would kill Kai. If Reagan contacted the police or told anyone, they would kill Kai. I had to act quickly, so I took the money and got on a plane. I'm sorry it caused you trouble, but I'd do it again in a heartbeat."

Somehow, the knowledge that his infant nephew had been in the hands of dangerous criminals made everything else seem trivial. "What happened?"

"I paid the ransom, and they returned him unharmed. The cops picked the kidnappers up the next day and we recovered most of the money, so I have it to pay back, as I promised. When I told Carl about it, he was understanding. It's not the kind of thing that happens very often. He said that he wouldn't hold that against you under the circumstances. Did he change his mind?"

Jonah shook his head. "I don't know. I haven't heard from Game Town. And at this point, I don't really care."

Noah studied Jonah for a moment with a curious look on his face. "The guy that nearly pummeled me a few minutes ago cared quite a bit. If you're not angry about the Game Town deal, what is it?"

Jonah didn't even know where to begin. How could he explain what he'd had with Emma and how he'd lost it?

"A woman has gotten to you," Noah stated.

Was it that obvious? "It hardly matters anymore, Noah. She was the auditor involved in this whole mess and she lost her job because of me."

"I'm sure you could help her find a new job. Hell, just hire her to work here."

Jonah shook his head. He knew Emma would say no, even now. Especially now. Everything blowing up in her face was just proof that she was right all along. "She wouldn't accept my help—I know it. Her reputation was the most important thing to her and I ended up ruining everything. Not just her job, but I screwed up us. She was the one, Noah. I love her. She's having my baby. And what did I do? I lied to her, trying to cover up the missing money and save our asses. It all blew up in my face."

"Is this the same woman from the Mardi Gras party? The one with the tattoo?"

Jonah could only nod. Just the mention of that night made the whole thing that much worse.

"Well, then you've got to fix it."

Jonah frowned. Things were always so simple to Noah for some reason. Even a harrowing kidnapping seemed to go smoothly for him. "How? I don't even know where to begin. I don't think she wants anything to do with me anymore."

"Probably not, but that doesn't mean it can't change. You said the most important thing to her was her reputation. So step up. Talk to her boss, tell them it wasn't her fault and get her job back. Taking the blame and making things right for her again is something you can offer her."

That all sounded good, but was it really enough? "What if she doesn't forgive me? Or does, but doesn't want me back?"

"Then you'll have to be content knowing you did the right thing."

For once, Jonah had to admit that Noah's idea was a good one. He might never win back her trust or her love, but he could make things right for her reputation and her career.

"Unless, of course, you're ready to make your big move."

Jonah's brows went up. "My big move?"

Noah held up his left hand and waggled his ring finger. "Give her everything she could possibly want from you in a two-pronged approach—restore her job and her reputation at work, and then restore her personal reputation and faith in you by declaring your love for her and asking for her hand in marriage. If she's that concerned about what people think of her at work, how does she feel about the fact that she's having your baby out of wedlock?"

"I already asked her to marry me. She said no."

"Well, ask again. And not because of the baby, but because you love her and you want to spend the rest of your life with her."

Once again, Noah was right. Jonah wouldn't say it out loud, though. Instead, he turned to his computer and looked up a few numbers. He had quite a few calls to make to put all this to rights.

"Who are you calling?" Noah asked as Jonah picked up his office phone.

"Everyone."

* * *

Emma was moping and she knew it. It had been a week since she'd been fired. At least she thought it was. She'd honestly lost track of time spent wallowing. She was pretty certain she'd worn the same cartoon-clad pajama pants three days in a row and hadn't washed her hair. She couldn't work up the enthusiasm to care. What did it matter? She had nowhere to go. No one to see. She was unemployed, single, pregnant and miserable.

Her phone rang just then, but she ignored it. She knew who it was just by the ringtone. Harper, Lucy and Violet all seemed to be taking turns checking in on her unsuccessfully. This time it happened to be Lucy calling. Emma had no doubt that before too long, they would show up at the door. They were on the visitor list and Violet had a key, so there would be no putting them off in that scenario.

It didn't matter. It felt almost as though little did. At least for now. After a few more days, she'd have no choice but to pick herself up, dust herself off and move on with life. There were bills to pay and soon, a baby to feed. She could borrow money from her parents, she supposed, but that would require her to confess what a mess her life had become lately. She wasn't ready for that yet.

That meant she had to work.

Emma had been looking at jobs online. Her only hope was that perhaps she could find another position before word got out about why she'd left her last one. They would eventually call a reference and her company would disclose that she was terminated and ineligible for re-hire—she couldn't help that—but that would be better than the rumors that would build as they circulated. Especially once she could no longer hide her baby bump.

So far, she hadn't run across much of interest. There was a financial analyst position at Sandlin-Kline. That was probably a demotion, but she'd take it if they offered because they were a big firm where she could grow. They even had a day care for employees, which she would need before too long. There was also a CPA position at a large tax firm, which she could do, but it was a last resort. Taxes were not her favorite.

The only other job that had piqued her interest was the finance director at FlynnSoft. She'd giggled with hysteria when she saw the posting. Obviously she was a masochist for that to catch her eye. There was no other excuse as working with Jonah on a daily basis would be pure torture.

As it was, she would have to deal with him where the baby was concerned. Seeing him day in and day out, having him as her actual boss this time… That was out of the question. She was qualified for the position, and he'd already offered her the job twice, but that door had closed for them both when he lied to her. She would bag groceries at the corner market before she'd go crawling back to him for a job.

George and Pauline Dempsey would have a stroke if they caught their pregnant, single daughter bagging fruits and vegetables. But she'd do it, because if nothing else, she still had her pride and she would work to support her child. At least once she got out of this funk and moved on.

Emma was pondering eating ice cream for dinner when her phone rang again. This time it was Tim's number. She frowned as she picked it up and studied the screen. Why would Tim be calling? Her last check was coming via direct deposit. She'd already cleaned out everything from the office. If he thought she'd be willing to answer questions about her accounts after he fired her, he would be sadly mistaken.

Unable to resist finding out what was behind the call, she broke down and answered. "Hello." She tried to hide the displeasure in her voice, but failed.

"Emma! Hey, this is Tim."

"I know."

"Do you have a second to chat?"

Emma sighed. "Not really, Tim. I've got an interview with Sandlin-Kline Financials first thing in the morning. I've got to pick up my suits from the cleaners before they close," she lied. She hadn't even submitted her résumé anywhere yet. She wasn't about to let Tim know that, though.

"Well, then I'll be brief, Emma. The truth of the matter is that I think I acted prematurely the other day in firing you. I was upset about being left out of the loop and I came down too hard. I shouldn't have let you go for that."

Emma slowly lowered herself down onto her living room sofa. Was Tim apologizing? Tim never apologized. There was something fishy about this. "I'm glad you recognize that," she said. She wasn't about to read any more into it, though. She hadn't known of a single person cut from the company that ever returned.

"Things have been pretty chaotic the last few days. I think I underestimated how much work you actually managed here. There's no way we can handle this workload without you. I know I've made a terrible mistake. I'd like you to come back, Emma."

Her jaw dropped silently as she tried to absorb the information. He was giving her the chance to come back. "Are you serious?"

"I am. I really shouldn't have blamed you for Flynn's

actions. There's no way you could've known what he was doing. He's a very charismatic and persuasive man. You did everything I'd asked you to do."

Emma paused. This didn't sound like the manager she knew. "Tim, did Jonah talk you into giving me my job back?"

There was a long silence on the line.

"Tim," she pressed. "Did Jonah Flynn call you and tell you to give me my job back?"

Tim sighed heavily. "He did. He came into the office in person this morning. He explained about the kidnapping and how the management at Game Town wasn't holding FlynnSoft accountable."

"Kidnapping?" Emma was suddenly very lost. "What kidnapping?"

"Flynn's nephew. That's what the three million was for. Did he not tell you that? Anyway, he said the whole situation was entirely his fault, that he pressured you into going along with it and that I was a damn fool if I let you go."

"A damn fool?" All she could do was repeat what Tim was saying because she couldn't grasp the conversation at all. Jonah's nephew was kidnapped? What nephew?

"Yes, that's a direct quote. And since I am not a damn fool, I decided I needed to call and ask you to come back. What do you say, Emma?"

She didn't know what to say. The fact that Jonah had gone to Tim and stood up for her was amazing. And unexpected. She hadn't heard a word from him since he left her apartment. After throwing him out like that she didn't really expect to hear from him until it was time for the baby to be born. He hadn't had to do this for her. And yet he had.

Perhaps he'd meant what he said that day.

Emma had been too upset in the moment to really listen to his protests. As far as she was concerned it was all just excuses to cover up the fact that he'd been caught. But if he'd really been sincere once he knew who she really was... If he really truly cared about her and their baby... He probably thought she wouldn't believe him, so he did what he could to at least undo the damage he'd caused.

Jonah knew this was important to her. But the job and her reputation suddenly weren't as important as they used to be. In that moment, they shifted to a distant second to the future of her family. Her future with Jonah.

"Emma?"

"What?" She realized she wasn't listening to her phone conversation like she should.

"Will you come back?" Tim repeated.

Emma thought about it for a few moments, but she already knew her answer. "No thank you, Tim. I appreciate the offer, but I think it's time for me to move on to other things. Good luck to you. Goodbye."

She hit the button, disconnecting the call before she could lose her nerve. And she did almost instantly. The second she dropped the phone on the couch beside her, she felt the panic well up inside of her. She'd just turned down her job. It frustrated her, but it was a good job. It paid well. What the hell was she thinking?

Was she thinking she didn't need it because Jonah loved her and wanted her back? If that was the case, she'd just taken a huge gamble. He may have only been trying to be nice. Or to put things to rights. And she'd tossed that gift back in his face. Now what was she going to do?

The chime of her doorbell drew her attention from her

worries. What was the point of being in a building with a doorman when people could just trot up to her apartment unannounced? Who could it be, now? People just seemed unwilling to take the hint. She approached the door cautiously and peered out the peephole.

It was Lucy and Harper. As expected.

"What do you want?" Emma shouted through the closed door.

"What do we want?" Harper repeated. "It's Tuesday at seven, Em. What do you think we want?"

"I've called three times today, Emma," Lucy chimed in. "If you'd answer your phone this wouldn't be a surprise. It's girls' night!"

Shoot. Emma had totally and completely forgotten about girls' night. With a groan, she unlocked the door and pulled it open. "I'm sorry," she said. "I've lost track of the days, apparently."

Harper's appraising gaze ran over Emma's sloppy bun, oversize T-shirt and Eeyore pajama pants. "I can see that. Lucky for you, Lucy picked up everything for dinner tonight, so we won't starve."

Emma stepped back to let them in the apartment. "I don't know if I feel up to this tonight, you guys."

"Well, too bad," Lucy quipped. "Alice refuses to pay for cable despite her millions in the bank, so I don't get this channel at my place. I need to know what happens this week on our show. So I'm not leaving."

Lucy and Harper pushed past her and started setting up in her kitchen. Apparently this was happening whether she wanted it to or not.

"I'll go clean up a bit while you guys are getting dinner ready." Emma cruised through the living room, quickly snatching up tearstained tissues and empty snack cartons, and tossing them in the trash before she headed to the bathroom. She opted for a quick shower. By the time she emerged about fifteen minutes later, she felt a little more human and dinner was ready.

They gathered in the living room as they always did. This time, they each had plates of Greek food from a restaurant down the block from Lucy's place. Emma took a few big bites, savoring the first real food she'd eaten in days. It was so good it took her a moment to notice the other girls were looking at her with expectation on their faces.

"Where is Violet?" Emma asked, hoping to shift the discussion away from her for the moment.

"She's been MIA the last couple of days," Harper explained.

"I think she and Beau had another blowup," Lucy added. Violet had been dating an investment banker named Beau on and off for the last three years. "Who knows with those two? What's more important is what's going on with you and Jonah?" Lucy asked.

Emma told them about the phone call and how she'd just turned down the job offer from Tim. Lucy looked as stunned as Emma felt, but Harper seemed pleased by her reckless decision.

"Good girl," Harper said. "Tim deserves to suffer for turning on you like that. I bet he's up to his ears in your work right now."

Emma wasn't quite as convinced. "You think it was the right thing to do? I wish I was that certain. I mean, what the hell am I going to do now? I've got to work."

Harper nodded with a wicked glint in her eyes that made Emma uneasy. "Of course you have to work. And I have the perfect job in mind for you."

Twelve

Jonah eyed the tiny Tiffany blue box on his desk. Today was the day. He'd made things right with Tim and hopefully Emma had gotten her job back. He'd talked to Carl Bailey at Game Town and Noah had been right—things were smoothed out there. All the broken pieces from the last week had been glued back together except for one.

Tonight, when Emma got home from work, he was going to her apartment. He would beg her forgiveness, swear his love for her and their baby, and then present her with the shiny two-and-a-half-karat Soleste emerald cut ring set in platinum that he'd picked up on Fifth Avenue yesterday evening. He would ask her to marry him—the Big Move as Noah had suggested—and hopefully, the last piece would fall into place.

Hell, he'd even worn a suit and a tie for the occasion. A classic, black Armani suit with a green silk tie that reminded him of her eyes. Every employee he passed in the hallway made a joke about him having a job interview somewhere today, as though he didn't own the place.

A soft knock at the door caught his attention. Jonah snapped the box closed and scooped it off the desk and into his pocket. "Come in," he replied.

Pam stuck her head into the room. "I've got the stack of résumés for your interviews today."

Jonah had forgotten about that. He'd agreed to interview a few candidates for the financial director position. His human resources team had already narrowed it down to the top three candidates for him to talk to today. Fine. Whatever. If they could keep his brother from stealing from him again, they were hired.

Pam carried the papers into his office and set them down on the blotter. "Today is the big day, isn't it?"

Jonah nodded. Pam always knew his business because she made his business possible. She'd called Tiffany's and set up a private, after-hours appointment to select a ring. She'd made sure a car picked him up on time so he didn't miss it. She was the one who saw to it that his suit went to the cleaners so he'd have it to wear today. She was pleased as punch to be part of such a big moment for her boss.

"She's going to love it," Pam insisted. "Don't be nervous."

"I'm not nervous," Jonah said with a smile, but Pam didn't seem to buy it.

"Of course you're not. You've just got to keep it together through a couple of interviews and you'll be fine. The first candidate should be here at ten."

Jonah looked down at his watch. He had about ten minutes. Just enough time to scan the résumé, finish his coffee and think up a couple of intelligent-sounding questions for the interview. He hated doing this kind of stuff. Hiring smart, capable people was his goal. It was also his goal to do so well at that, that the smart, capable people could handle hiring more smart, capable people without him.

This was a director-level position, though. After the minor scandal with Noah, he needed to be really cautious about who he chose to head up the finance department. He needed Carl and any other CEO who might want to work with FlynnSoft to be completely confident in their decision.

With a sigh of resignation, Jonah took a big sip of his coffee and picked up the first résumé. As his eyes scanned the top, the coffee spewed from his mouth, coating the paper in mocha speckles.

Emma Dempsey.

Jonah reached for a napkin and wiped up the coffee, dabbing her résumé carefully so he could still read it. Never in a million years did he expect her to actually apply for this job. He'd offered it to her more than once and she'd turned him down. Of course, now the Game Town audit was over, maybe she felt freer to make that decision.

He tried to scan over her qualifications and education, but the only thought that kept running through his mind was that Emma was going to be here. In his office. In five minutes. He had her engagement ring in his pocket. Could he hold on to it for the entire interview and not give it to her? Play it cool?

Yeah, no. He was pretty certain he wouldn't make it through the meeting playing the coy interviewer and interviewee.

How was it that no one mentioned Emma applying before now? Someone had to have known. At the very least, Pam. Perhaps that was behind the twinkle in her eye earlier. He'd thought she was just excited about colluding over the engagement, but perhaps she knew something he didn't.

Another knock sounded at the door. It was exactly 10:00 a.m. and that meant she was here. "Come in," he repeated, and stood up at his desk.

Pam pushed the door open with a devious grin and behind her was Emma. At least it looked a bit like Emma, but not in any way he'd ever seen her at the office before. The stuffy suit and severe hair bun were gone. Her hair was down in loose brown waves around her face like it had been on their date. She was wearing a pair of dark denim skinny jeans with comfy-looking ballet flats and a T-shirt with a navy corduroy blazer over it.

It was the perfect mix of dress and casual, as though Emma had merged her style with his and finally found her niche here at FlynnSoft.

It looked good on her. Amazing. It made him want to reach out and stroke the waves of her hair between his fingertips. But he knew better. First and foremost, this was an interview and even if she had forgiven him, Emma would want to keep things professional.

"Jonah, this is your first applicant, Emma Dempsey." Pam grinned and disappeared from the office as quickly as she could manage.

He smiled and reached out his hand to greet her properly. "Hello, Miss Dempsey."

"Call me Emma, please," she said with a soft, knowing smile as she shook his hand.

It took everything he had for Jonah to let her go, but

he had to. "Please have a seat," he said, indicating the guest chair she'd sat in many times before.

Once they were settled, Jonah picked up her résumé and tried to think of something intelligent to say. He decided to continue as though they'd never met before and start with his basic opening question for any interview. "So. Emma, please tell me a little about why you want to work here at FlynnSoft."

Normally, this question would help him pinpoint whether or not the applicant had the same core values as most FlynnSoft employees. A love of gaming and graphic design, joy for their work, hell, even an interest in free coffee was worth a mention. People who appreciated his workplace innovations before they even started would be much happier and more productive employees later on.

"Well," Emma began, "I recently had an opportunity to work with some of the FlynnSoft family as part of an audit I conducted for my previous position. It was not at all what I was used to in a corporate environment, but after I adjusted, I really learned to appreciate what FlynnSoft offers their employees."

"And what is that?"

"Freedom to work at their own pace on projects that excite them. All the tools they need—traditional or otherwise—to get their jobs done. Time and amenities to recharge and maintain their enthusiasm for their work. Also, an owner and CEO that truly cares for his staff. At first I thought he was all about the money, but I realized that so much of what motivated him was the success of his company for the benefit of the employees that depended on him."

"So you understand that despite how things might look, he was just trying to protect them?" he asked.

Emma nodded.

"And you realize that he would never deliberately hurt one of his employees, even if they were just on a temporary assignment?"

Emma looked at him with her big green eyes and he was happy to see no hurt hiding there. "Yes. I can see that now. At first, it was hard to believe, but I've had a little time to think about it and I've really come to appreciate what he was willing to do."

She understood why he did what he did. Jonah wanted to sigh loudly in relief and thank his lucky stars, but he wouldn't. Not yet. "Okay, great answer. Now, what skills and experience do you have that would be an asset to FlynnSoft if we were to bring you on board?"

At this question, Emma grinned. "Well, I am very structured and organized. I like to keep things professional in the workplace, but I also know when to let my hair down. I think that with my experience, I am the perfect candidate to keep not only the FlynnSoft financial department in line, but to keep the CEO himself in line, as well."

"Oh really?" Jonah's brows rose in curiosity. Now things were getting interesting.

"Yes. He has some weaknesses that I can exploit when necessary to keep things on track."

"What kind of weaknesses?" Jonah asked.

Emma's soft pink lips curled into a smile. "Me, for one thing. I happen to know that the CEO has a soft spot where I'm concerned."

Jonah leaned forward onto his elbows, getting as close to her as he could with the massive furniture between them. "That's true. You could probably negotiate an amazing benefits package with that kind of leverage."

"I'm mostly interested in maternity leave," Emma responded. "Flexible schedules and telecommuting are always good with little ones, as well. If my office was big enough, I would also like to be able to bring my daughter in to work with me."

Jonah opened his mouth to respond, but found there were no words. He had been following along until suddenly—*wham*! Did she just say *daughter*? They were having a girl? How could she know so soon?

Emma reached into her portfolio and slid a grainy black-and-white photo across the desk to him. He'd seen normal ultrasound pictures before, but this one had amazing detail.

"I had a 3-D ultrasound done yesterday. Fourteen weeks is still a little early to be absolutely sure, but the technician was very confident that I, we, are having a little girl."

Emma was fairly certain the interview was over. Jonah had managed to maintain as professional a face as he'd ever had, but the minute she slid the photo of his daughter across the desk to him, it was done.

Sitting there, she had the rare opportunity to actually watch a man fall in love with his child. It was something she thought she might never see before now, and she was so relieved she could almost cry. But she wouldn't. She could already see the sheen of tears in Jonah's eyes and the whole meeting would devolve into sobbing if she started.

Jonah stared at the picture for a few minutes before gently wiping at his eyes and setting it back down on his desk. "I am fairly certain we can accommodate whatever needs you may have to bring our daughter into the office.

I'll kick Noah out of his office and turn it into a nursery if you want me to."

He smiled and stood up, walking slowly around his desk to her. He stopped just short of touching her, sitting down in the other guest chair beside her so they were at eye level. "I love you, Emma," he said without the slightest hesitation. "I love you and I've missed you so badly. I'm so sorry that I hurt you. I never meant to do that."

Emma reached out and covered his hand with her own. She gave it a gentle squeeze, reveling in the touch of his skin against hers once again. "I know. I love you, too. And I'm sorry, as well."

Jonah frowned at her. "Sorry for what? You didn't do anything wrong."

"Yes, I did," she insisted. Emma had put a lot of thought into this the last few days and she wanted to make sure he knew how she felt now. "I let my worries about what other people think of me interfere with living my life and loving you the way I wanted to. I've spent my whole life more concerned with what other people thought than what I thought of myself. I didn't like the uptight, boring woman I'd become, but I thought that's who I should be.

"You loved the parts of me that I was ashamed of, and it helped me to realize that what other people think of me is none of my business. All that really matters is that I'm happy and living my life the way I want to live it. And I want to live it with you. I want to make a family with you, Jonah, however we decide to have it."

Emma didn't care if they got married with a big Plaza wedding, eloped at the courthouse or didn't get married at all. The big wedding was her mother's dream anyway, not hers. A wedding and a marriage was only important if they put importance on it. All Emma wanted was Jonah in her life, and in her baby's life, every day. She wanted to love him and be with him. That was what would make her happy.

Jonah looked at her for a moment and she could swear there was a flicker of nervousness across his face. Before she could say anything else, he reached into his coat pocket and slipped out of his chair onto one knee.

He kept a tight grip on her left hand as he moved, so Emma had to clutch the arm of the chair with her right. Her entire body tensed up as she watched him and realized what he was doing. "Jonah…" she gasped, but he ignored her.

In his left hand, he held a Tiffany blue jewelry box. Before he opened it, he looked at her and said, "I know you said you didn't want to marry me the last time I mentioned it. You said we hardly knew each other and that if, given time, I fell in love with you and wanted to get married, you would reconsider." His thumb anxiously stroked the back of her hand as he spoke, making it hard for her to focus on his words.

Finally, he let go long enough to pull the black jewelry box out of its bright blue container and pry open the lid. He held the ring up for her to see it. Nestled in the velvet was the ring of her dreams. Emerald cut, surrounded in tiny diamonds and with a delicate band inset with even more. It picked up the morning sunlight in Jonah's office, displaying a dazzling show of rainbow colors. It was simply breathtaking.

"I'm hoping that you've reconsidered, Emma. I know that not much time has really passed, but this week without you has felt like a lifetime. I couldn't let another day, much less another week, go by without telling you how much I love you. And that I want to make you my wife." Jonah paused for a second to look her in the eye and swallow hard. "Will you marry me, Emma?"

How had she gotten to this point in her life? From her lowest moment before that Mardi Gras party, to the thrill of romance with a stranger, to the crushing loss of everything she held dear… And now love. Marriage. A family.

"I will. Of course I will, Jonah," Emma managed with tears filling her eyes.

With a cheer of satisfaction, Jonah leaned in and gave her a firm, soft kiss. Emma held his scruffy face with both hands to keep him close for as long as possible, but eventually he pulled away. Taking her hand in his, he plucked the ring out of its velvet bed and slid it onto her finger. It was perhaps half a size too big, but with her blooming pregnancy, she had no doubt it would be snug before too long.

Emma admired the glittering stone on her finger, then turned her attention back to her fiancé. "Thank you, Jonah," she said. "You're amazing and I'm so lucky to have found you."

Jonah stood up and shook his head. He pulled Emma to her feet, then wrapped his arms around her waist. "I'm the lucky one, butterfly."

They would have to agree to disagree. Emma put an end to the discussion by pressing her lips to his and losing herself in his kiss. Somehow, despite the odds being against her, everything had come together and she couldn't be happier. Sometimes the scary decisions in life reaped the greatest rewards, and today, her reward was marrying the most amazing man she'd ever met.

A chime sounded over their shoulder from Jonah's

computer. "Crap," he groaned as he broke away from her kiss and looked down at his watch.

Emma frowned at Jonah. "What's the matter?"

"Well, to be honest," he said with a sigh, "none of this was supposed to happen until tonight at your apartment. I wasn't expecting to see you this morning until I saw your résumé."

Emma wouldn't tell him that she'd sworn everyone, from HR to Pam, to absolute secrecy about the interview. "So?"

"So, you were my first interview of the day. I've got two more lined up after this. Why didn't they schedule you last? I want to take you home and make love to my fiancée."

Emma laughed, pulling back from his snug grip on her body. "Well, that's not going to happen right now, so you'd better get prepared, Mr. Flynn. Even if you marry me, you'll still need a financial director."

Jonah narrowed his blue gaze at her in surprise. "You mean you don't want the job?"

"Of course I want the job!" Emma said. "But I want it fair and square. I told you before, I'm not letting anyone say I earned it on my back."

At that, Jonah laughed. "You're seriously going to make me interview all those people even though I have every intention of hiring you in the end?"

"Yes. I'm pretty sure your HR director would say the same thing. And if you hire me," she said, poking him in the chest with her finger, "it better be because I'm the most qualified." She might be marrying the boss, but Emma still had her pride. She'd worked hard to achieve a director-level position and she wanted it on merit alone.

Jonah studied her face for a moment and nodded. He took a step back and sucked in a deep lungful of air. Then he held his hand out to Emma. "Well, thank you for coming in today, Emma. Pam will see you back down to Human Resources. I'm sure they have some paperwork for you to fill out and they can answer any questions you have about the company and our total compensation package."

Emma grinned as she shook his hand and picked up her leather portfolio. "Thank you for your time, Mr. Flynn. When should I expect to hear back from you about the position?"

With her hand still in his, he leaned in and whispered into her ear. "I'll be at your place by six."

* * * * *

LITTLE SECRETS: HOLIDAY BABY BOMBSHELL

KAREN BOOTH

For my sweet and endlessly patient husband.
I'm writing as fast as I can in the hopes that you can
retire early.

One

With its French-milled soap, lavender-scented shampoo and soft lighting, the finely appointed bathroom in her Grand Legacy Hotel suite might've been the loveliest place Charlotte Locke had ever gotten sick. She closed her eyes, willed herself to stand from the cool comfort of the marble floor and fumbled for her toothbrush. Ten weeks pregnant and mint was one of the few things she found appealing. She scrubbed her teeth clean, straightened her skirt and jacket, and neatened her blond hair. Hopefully, that was the last of today's morning sickness. She had work to do.

Charlotte marched out of her room, determined. "Wish me luck. I'm off to Sawyer's office," she said to her aunt Fran, who was sharing the suite while in New York from London for Christmas.

Fran tucked a strand from her white-blond bob behind her ear, then refilled her mug with room-service tea. Charlotte's beloved papillon dog, Thor, nine pounds of snow-white and chocolate-brown attitude, was curled up at Fran's hip. "You won't need luck. You're more than qualified to sell the Grand Legacy condos."

Charlotte sighed. Okay, no luck. But she wouldn't mind some bolstering. How many times had she gone hat-in-hand and asked a family member for another chance? Too many. Charlotte slipped on her wool coat, a lovely shade of peacock blue, and buttoned up. "I'm glad you're so confident. I think I stand about a fifty-fifty chance."

"You're sure you aren't going to tell Sawyer about the pregnancy? He's your brother. I don't see any way he can say no to you if he knows you have a baby on the way."

Charlotte shook her head. "I don't want anyone's charity. I'm asking him to trust me with millions of dollars of real estate. I don't want to remind him that his little sister has a habit of making colossal life mistakes."

Fran scratched Thor behind the ear. "Everything happens for a reason. It just might not be clear to you yet what that reason is."

"I like your optimism, but being accidentally pregnant by a man who doesn't love me is classic Charlotte. I'm trying to avoid all appearances of the old me." Charlotte leaned down and kissed her aunt's cheek, then grabbed her gloves and handbag and stepped out into the hall, closing the door behind her.

Each impeccable detail of the Grand Legacy—the plush black carpet with ornate royal blue scrolls, the gleaming chrome-and-glass wall sconces, even the tasteful sign directing guests to their room—was a link to Charlotte's past. The hotel had been in her family since the 1920s, long before she'd been born. Now it was solely owned by her brother Sawyer, a detail that displeased their father greatly.

She pushed the button for the elevator. Every time she stepped on board, childhood memories of clowning around in the hotel with her brothers played in her head, like an old movie. The ones where she was youngest were the fuzziest, but the happiest. There had been many games of hide-and-seek in these halls, but only when her mother had been alive. As soon as she passed away, their father never wanted her or her brothers to spend any time at all in the hotel.

"Good morning, Ms. Locke," a bellman said as she emerged from the elevator.

"Morning," she said cheerily. Her heels clicked across the black-and-white marble lobby floor.

"Stay warm out there, Ms. Locke," the front desk clerk said.

"I'll try." She pushed her way through the revolving doors and was smacked in the face with a rush of icy air that felt as though it had been shipped in from the north pole. The doorman hustled to show her to the car Sawyer had sent.

"Thank you." Charlotte juggled her wallet, a five-dollar bill and her gloves.

"That's not necessary, Ms. Locke." He tried to hand back the tip. "Not from you."

"Of course it's necessary. You work hard, and it's the holidays." She smiled, waved him off and slid into the back seat of the car.

The driver knew exactly where they were headed—downtown to Sawyer's office in Chelsea. Charlotte had already practiced her pitch several times—awake in bed last night, in the shower that morning. It wasn't that Sawyer was intimidating. He was anything but. It was more that Charlotte hated to ask for yet another favor. She was already bracing for that look on her brother's face, the one that said he was hesitant to give her responsibility. She'd done so poorly with it in the past.

Charlotte couldn't commit any more time or effort to feeling bad about her current situation. Now was the time for action. The car pulled up in front of Sawyer's office, and she wasted no time climbing out and heading upstairs. Hopefully inertia would be enough to keep her going.

Her brother's admin, Lily, greeted her warmly. "Your brother is waiting. Let me take your coat for you. Remind me when you get out of your meeting and I'll call another car for you."

"Thank you so much." Charlotte smoothed her skirt, trying to ignore the trepidation in her stomach. This was her brother. Sawyer. Everything would be fine. She hoped.

A broad smile crossed Sawyer's face when she poked her head into his office. "There she is."

Waves of relief washed over her. Why she constantly worked herself into a tizzy over things was beyond her. She only knew it was her habit. "Hey, Sawyer. Thanks for meeting with me today."

"Of course. I'm glad you came in. I feel like I hardly had the chance to speak to you at the grand reopening party at the hotel."

"Sorry about that. All sorts of old friends were there." *Plus, pregnancy makes a woman all kinds of tired.*

"I'm just glad you're back in town. It wouldn't have

felt right not to have you there." Sawyer sat back in his chair. "Do you want to tell me what precipitated the surprise junket to see Aunt Fran in England?"

Even though she'd prepared for the question, Charlotte blanched at it. So much had led to that trip. It started with the breakup from Michael Kelly, the man she'd fallen hopelessly in love with, the man who was unable to return the feelings. That had been bad enough, and then came the real powder keg—the pregnancy. She couldn't tell her brother she'd gone to England for those reasons. Charlotte was always falling in love, and it was always getting her into some sort of impossible situation.

"I just needed some time to really think out my long-term career goals. Fran is so good at listening and helping with advice." She cleared her throat. "Plus, I'll be honest. It was stressful to watch the way Dad was fighting you on the Grand Legacy renovation. I hate the family rifts."

"If I could've gone to England with you, I would have. Then again, that might have meant things wouldn't have worked out with Kendall the way they have. So scratch that. I'm glad I stayed and fought through the Dad situation."

Charlotte smiled. She was happy Sawyer had found someone, and Kendall was a very special someone. Charlotte had worried for many years that their home life had left her and her siblings—Sawyer and their brother Noah—incapable of having normal romantic relationships. The fact that Sawyer had finally broken through that particular Locke family glass ceiling gave her hope that some day she'd do the same. Just not any-time soon—she was no longer looking for love. Stability was her number one quest. "I'm really happy for you and Kendall. I'm so looking forward to the wedding. I love the idea of a wedding at Christmastime."

"I know it's soon, but we didn't want to wait. Call us old-fashioned, but we both want to tie the knot before the baby arrives."

"Sure. Wouldn't want your little boy or girl to do the math later in life and figure out you were married after the fact." Charlotte couldn't believe what was coming out of her own mouth. She sounded like her grandmother. Maybe she was just as old-fashioned as her brother. She'd be putting an end to that soon, though, with her very single status while welcoming a new life into the world.

"So, tell me about these long-term career goals. You aren't considering a change from real estate, are you?"

This was a valid question where Charlotte was concerned. The number of careers she'd had in her twenties was enough to make anyone's head spin—interior designer, fashion blogger, party planner, cupcake maven. That last one had been the most disastrous. Charlotte couldn't cook to save her life and she'd gained fifteen pounds tasting buttercream all day long.

"Nope. It's still the right career for me. It's a natural fit with the real-estate development and hotel interests in our family. It allows me to work with people, which I love doing. And the good side of having had so many false starts with various careers is that I've made a ton of contacts." *Watch me make lemonade with my arms full of lemons.*

"I'm glad to hear you've settled on it. That stability will be good for you."

"Exactly. Stability." Charlotte sucked in a deep

breath. *Here goes nothing.* "And that's why I'm here. Now that you've put the finishing touches on the Grand Legacy condos, I'm hoping you'll let me have the listings." Charlotte couldn't help but notice how her brother's expression had fallen. She had to make her case now, or lose out. "I know the building better than any agent you could possibly work with. You know that it will have my full attention, and more than anything, it will give us a chance to work closely together, which is something I've always wanted to do."

"But, Charlotte…you can't just pop in here and ask for the listings now. I've been working on this for months. This is so like you to throw a wrench in things at the eleventh hour."

Yeah, well, I didn't exactly plan on getting pregnant. "I know. I'm sorry about the timing, but nobody expected the units to be ready now. Your original opening date was New Year's Eve. That's still several weeks away."

Sawyer pressed his lips together firmly, seeming deep in thought. "I already have an agent lined up. A fantastic one who will most likely sell every unit in a matter of weeks. He's on his way over right now to discuss strategy and to get the paperwork straightened away."

"But…" Charlotte had already discharged her only arguments. She didn't really have any other means of selling herself. She was, as always, an unproven proposition. "I'm family. Surely that counts for something. It's the Grand Legacy. This isn't some random building you and Noah decided to sink money into." She could see Sawyer's eyes soften and she knew she had to open up her heart. "I love the hotel so much, and being there over the last few days has been amazing. Isn't it important to have someone who really, truly cares?"

"You don't know that this other agent doesn't care. I've had multiple conversations with Michael Kelly about this over the last few months and I can tell you that he absolutely cares."

Charlotte's heart had stopped beating. Or at least it felt that way. Unwanted visions of Michael popped into her head—all six feet and six inches of his trim and muscled swimmer's body. He might have crushed her heart, but he'd looked good doing it, with his thick, dark hair she loved to comb her fingers through, and magnetic blue eyes she could get lost in for days. "Michael Kelly? Seriously?"

"Do you know him? He's a really good guy. Straight shooter. He cares a lot. He's told me so."

Charlotte blew out a breath. Michael Kelly cared, all right—about himself, money and his job. Everyone else was going to have to fend for themselves.

Michael knew he didn't have much more time in the pool this morning. *Just a few more laps.* He touched the tile wall with his hand and took his turn, propelling himself through the water, beneath the surface, to return to the other end.

The rhythm of swimming relaxed him. After tens of thousands of hours spent in the pool, his muscles knew exactly what to do, and he could give his brain some space to roam. This was the only time during his day that he was unreachable, his cell phone turned off and tucked away in his personal locker at the brand-new Empire State Athletic Club, an expensive and exclusive replacement for the old Downtown Athletic Club, which had been converted to apartments years ago. He loved this sliver of his day, when he had a chance to unplug. Owning and running the top residential real-estate agency in the city, The Kelly Group, meant that he was otherwise expected to be available 24/7, 365 days a year.

He made another turn and switched to freestyle, the stroke that had won him three Olympic golds. He always ended his swim this way. It was a powerful reminder of what had once been, of everything he'd worked so hard for and, most important, what it felt like to win. Coming out on top was a high unlike any other, and after his retirement from swimming six years ago, he'd been working his butt off in real estate just to get a taste of that feeling. He lived for that moment when you're invincible, standing at the top of the mountain, looking down at everyone else that couldn't match up to you. There was no roar of the crowd or medals awarded in real estate, but the money helped. And there had been a lot of it, not that there wasn't always more to earn.

He skimmed along in the water at the end of his final lap, came to the surface, pulled off his swim cap and tossed it onto the pool deck. He scooped water into his hair and hoisted himself up out of the pool, grabbing his towel. There was one other person still in the pool—Gabe Underwood. Gabe had taken up swimming a year ago, when he also set his sights on knocking Michael from his perch of top-selling real-estate agent in Manhattan. Gabe certainly knew he wasn't in the same league as Michael when it came to the sport that had won him Olympic medals, but he insisted that he wanted to remind Michael that he was on his heels and closing in.

It was annoying, but Michael couldn't stop the guy

from swimming laps at the same time he did. They were both members of the club, and all the money in the world wasn't going to help Michael put an Olympic swimming pool in a Manhattan apartment. That would have to be for later in life, when he retired out in the Hamptons or Connecticut.

Michael trailed into the locker room and quickly took a shower. The hot water felt fantastic on his muscles. There was definitely a part of him that could have stood beneath the spray for a long period of time, but he had to be on his way. Sawyer Locke and the Grand Legacy apartments were waiting. Towel wrapped around his waist, Michael made his way into the dressing area, where his suit was waiting, freshly pressed by the club staff. His black leather Italian wingtips had been given a polish as well.

"I beat my own time today, Kelly. I'm making big progress." Gabe's voice grated on Michael like little else.

"Yeah? Good for you." *Like I care.* He went ahead with getting dressed, hoping Gabe would take a hint, hit the showers and leave him the hell alone.

"Just like I'm closing in on you in sales. With everything I have lined up for January and February, I'm very close to replacing you as the top agent in the city next year. I have to say, it'll be a sweet reward and very well-earned."

Michael didn't want to take the bait. He wasn't going to take it, but damn, it was hard. Michael fed on competition, but he couldn't let someone see that he cared about their achievements. Focusing on his own was the best way to maintain the steely demeanor necessary for winning. "I'll keep doing what I do, but thanks for the heads-up."

Completely uninvited, Gabe perched on the locker-room bench. "What do you have in the hopper these days? Anything new and exciting? Some big fish on the line?"

"Always. But I'm not about to share that information with you."

"I heard you landed the Grand Legacy residential units."

Dammit. Michael worked his feet into his shoes. He wasn't about to spill the details. It was all sewn up, but there was no point in bragging. He'd let news of the sales filter through the circles of the real-estate world on their own.

"No comment?" Gabe asked. "I get it. Trying to be the mysterious Michael Kelly. Well, I'm psyched for you, but just so you know, I've worked on several properties with Sawyer's brother, Noah. I even snagged an invitation to Sawyer's wedding. Pretty sure those guys are eager to work with me."

Michael cast his eyes at Gabe, but only for a moment. The less he acknowledged him, the better. "I know the game you're playing because I invented it. Don't try to go up against me. You'll only regret it."

"Is that some sort of threat?"

"I don't need to make threats, Gabe. Threats are for people who can't deliver. I always deliver." With that, Michael grabbed his suit coat. "Have a good day."

Michael strode to the elevator and took it down to the parking garage, where his car was waiting. He was one of those guys—the ones who insisted on having a car in the city, even when it was generally a pain in the butt. He didn't like waiting around for other people, he didn't like barking orders from the back seat. He knew the best way to get where he wanted to go, and driving himself was the only way to get there.

Traffic wasn't too heavy, so he arrived at Sawyer Locke's office in twenty minutes and nabbed a spot in the lot next to his building. He took the stairs and still arrived five minutes early.

"Please have a seat, Mr. Kelly. Mr. Locke is finishing up a conversation with his sister. Can I get you a cup of coffee while you wait?"

His sister? Charlotte's back in town? Michael shifted in his seat, finding it more than a bit uncomfortable. "Uh, No, thank you. I've had two cups already this morning."

"It shouldn't be more than a few minutes."

Michael had learned long ago that there's a bump in every road, especially when you're sure everything is going to go smoothly. Apparently, today's bump was going to be Charlotte. He'd probably jinxed himself by daring to think the Grand Legacy was a done deal. Now he had to hope that Sawyer didn't mention who his ten o'clock was with, opening the door for Charlotte to rail on Michael, call him a jerk or insensitive or any of the things she'd called him the day she'd ended it with him.

The thing was, Michael had had no choice but to open the door for Charlotte to break things off with him. Three months of monogamy was a lifetime for him, and all signs were there that Charlotte was taking things much more seriously than he ever would be able to. He just wasn't built for focusing on a relationship. There was nothing to win. He'd be lying if he said he was looking forward to speaking to Charlotte. He could only imagine what she might spout off at him. But he was most certainly looking forward to *seeing* her, even if it might be as she huffed and stormed past him in the lobby of her brother's office.

Lily's phone buzzed. "Yes, Mr. Locke?" She glanced over at Michael. "Certainly. I'll send him right in." She hung up and rose from her seat. "Mr. Locke will see you now." She stepped out from behind her desk and headed for Sawyer's office.

"I thought you said he was meeting with Charlotte."

Surprise crossed Lily's face. "You know Ms. Locke?" She gently tapped her forehead. "Of course you know Ms. Locke. You both work in real estate."

Michael cleared his throat. *That's not the only reason.* "We're acquainted."

"Well, good. Mr. Locke won't need to make any introductions."

Michael was beyond confused, eyeing the door as Lily rapped on it lightly. "I'm sorry. I guess I'm running a step slow today. My meeting was with Sawyer. It's an important one, too. If he's busy, perhaps I should come back another time." *And cut out of here before Charlotte lops off my head.*

The door opened. Sawyer waved him in. "Michael. I understand you've already met my sister, Charlotte."

Two

Michael did not like to go into meetings unprepared, but he did love a challenge. He first saw Charlotte only in profile, her long, golden-blond hair framing her rosy cheeks, full lips and adorable chin. She sat straight as a pin in a dark purple jacket and black skirt, poised on the edge of her seat. That was Charlotte. Beautiful, but always on the edge. She turned toward him, her vivid blue eyes immediately putting him on notice. She was still angry. He not only saw it, he felt it, as if her eyes were slicing right into him.

It was pretty hot.

Just seeing her brought back the day they first met seven or eight months ago, when she'd come to interview for a position in his agency. She'd been professional and polished, but her résumé was thin. As they talked, he became more and more enchanted by her as a woman, but he knew she wasn't cutthroat enough to work for him. She smiled so easily, almost as if she couldn't help it. She laughed in much the same, affable manner. She was clearly beguiling, but he couldn't see her playing hardball in a negotiation, or putting up with an ultrademanding billionaire client. He'd told her as much. That hadn't gone over well. In fact, she'd argued with him about it, giving him that first vision of the fire behind those eyes. In the end, she didn't get the job she wanted, but he called her a few weeks later anyway. He asked her out and she said no, but then she started peppering him with questions about real estate, and the next thing he knew, they'd been on the phone for an hour, the conversation ultimately drifting to more personal topics. Three or four more marathon calls after that, he asked her out again, and that time she said yes. The rest—all three months of it—was history.

"Michael, hello." Charlotte's words were polite enough, but the tenor of her voice was rigid. She'd never taken that tone with him before, not even when she left. That day, she'd only had tears and gasping breaths. Crying was one of his weak spots when it came to relationships. He never knew what to say. So he often didn't say much of anything.

"Charlotte. It's nice to see you." He reached out to shake her hand and it was clear she was thinking twice about it. When she finally reciprocated, she was quick to retreat, but even a lightning-fast brush of her skin against his brought back memories of just how white-hot their connection had been. Charlotte might be a handful, but that was also the reason she was impossible to forget.

She folded her hands in her lap as Michael took the

open chair next to her and Sawyer sat behind his desk. Michael's full attention needed to be on Sawyer at this moment, but he had to steal a glance at Charlotte's legs as she crossed them and sat even straighter. She was wearing jet-black heels today, and he would've been a fool not to take his chance to admire her, while his mind flashed to what the rest of her looked like naked as she did the simplest of things, like padding from his bed to the bathroom and back.

"Michael, the reason I've asked Charlotte to sit in on this meeting is because I've decided to make a change with the Grand Legacy condos. I'm giving half of the listings to Charlotte."

Michael always did everything he could to keep his cool in a business meeting, but he did not like surprises. Not at the last minute. "You're what?" His voice betrayed him. The anger was apparent and quite possibly too strong, but as far as he was concerned, he had every right to be mad. He glanced over at Charlotte, only to see her fighting back a smile. He knew that look—the corners of her plump lips twitching while she was trying everything she could not to laugh.

Sawyer held up his hands in defense. "I know this is a surprise, and it's not the way I like to do business, but the timing just wasn't right on this one. You were already on your way here when Charlotte and I talked about it this morning."

"You do realize I can sell those units ten times faster than she can, right?"

Charlotte's hair whipped through the air when she turned to Michael. "Excuse me?" She was no longer close to smiling. Her mouth was slack and gaping with disbelief.

"It's the truth." Michael shrugged and sat back in his chair, reminding himself to stay cool and calm, however angry he might be.

"Look, I hear what you're saying," Sawyer said. "You're a rock star of an agent. There's no denying that."

Tell me something I don't know.

"But Charlotte is family," Sawyer continued. "And she brings some unique qualities to the table that, quite honestly, I hadn't considered and no one else has."

"Like what, exactly?" Michael couldn't imagine that anyone had a talent that he didn't possess. If he was lacking in some way, it had yet to materialize in his life in a formidable way. If he didn't know how to do something, he learned. Quickly.

Charlotte huffed and shook her head. "I have a history with the hotel. I know it almost as well as Sawyer. And I have the Locke name. That counts for something."

She had him on that. "I can always introduce a client to your brother, Charlotte, if they want to meet a member of the Locke family. Of course, at that point, the only name they'll truly care about is mine. They'll get experience with me. How many properties have you even sold since you became an agent?"

"I didn't come here to share my résumé with you. Sawyer doesn't care about that."

"It's not that I don't care about it. I'm simply willing to see past it in order to make a compromise," Sawyer said.

So that's what this was. *A compromise.* Michael was not a fan. "Sawyer, I have buyers lined up. It's just a matter of giving me the go-ahead, and I can start showing units later today."

"I already have a buyer for one unit in the building

and she's ready to make a full price offer today," Charlotte piped up.

Michael had plenty of potential buyers and other interested agents on the line already, but no one had seen the condos yet. Sawyer had kept everything under lock and key. "She's bluffing."

Charlotte turned, narrowing her vision on Michael. Her jaw tensed. He could only imagine what was going through that gorgeous head of hers. Murderous thoughts, probably. "I'm not bluffing. I don't need to bluff."

"Then where is this mysterious buyer?"

"You're looking at her." She thrust her chin into the air.

Michael laughed and shook his head at the irony. "You sure you want to do that? You might not like your first neighbor."

"What are you talking about?"

"Michael gave me a verbal offer on a unit for himself a few weeks ago," Sawyer said.

"I'm dying to get into the hotel. It's so much closer to my office. My commute takes way too much time."

"Are you serious?" Charlotte asked.

"The more important question is, are you serious?" Sawyer asked. "It's a big commitment."

Charlotte twisted her lips tightly. "Yes, I'm serious. I need a place to live. I gave up my apartment when I went to England. I'm already living and working out of the hotel. I can quite literally do a showing at any time, day or night. And these apartments will be the only thing I'm working on. You'll have my undivided attention, unlike with another agent, who might be such a hotshot that he's juggling hundreds of properties."

"She might have you there," Sawyer said. "You can't deny that's a compelling argument for her half of the listings."

Michael had a long string of counterarguments cued up in his head, but the reality was that Charlotte was Sawyer's sister. In Michael's experience, family won out over nearly everything. Sometimes, it even won out over money. Michael needed to focus on his long game, especially with Gabe Underwood on his heels. Sawyer Locke and his brother, Noah, were quickly becoming some of the most prominent real-estate developers in the city. The sooner Michael aligned himself with them, and elbowed Gabe out of the picture, the better. That meant playing ball.

"I'd never want to get in the way of family," Michael said. "I understand it's important you give your sister this opportunity."

"Thank you," Sawyer replied earnestly. "I really appreciate it. Truly. I owe you one."

Music to Michael's ears. "Happy to do it."

"We can get the paperwork in line later today and be on our way." Sawyer rose from his seat. "I'm ready to get these sold. It's one of the final pieces of the puzzle for the Grand Legacy."

"I'm so excited to work together. Thank you so much for the chance," Charlotte said, embracing her brother. That was the reason Michael hadn't stood a chance when he walked into this room. Family bonds were always the strongest.

Sawyer walked them into the lobby, but didn't have time for long goodbyes, as his admin let him know he had a call. Charlotte was putting on her coat. Purely out of habit, Michael lifted the empty sleeve for her. She yanked it from his hand. "No, thank you. I'm good."

"I'll go down with you."

"I'm taking the stairs."

"Me, too."

"Suit yourself." Charlotte held on to both railings as she descended the stairs, preventing Michael from walking next to her.

He stopped her when they reached the lobby. "Charlotte, hold up for a second." He grasped her arm, but dropped his grip immediately when he saw the disdain on her face. "You gave up your apartment when you went to England? Were you planning on staying?" The timing still seemed odd to him. She'd dumped him, disappeared from his life altogether, and then he'd heard from a friend that she'd run off to Europe without saying goodbye to anyone.

"I didn't know how long I was going to be in London, but my lease was up, so I just put my stuff in storage and left."

Michael shrugged. "Must be nice. Running off at the drop of a hat, no responsibilities to tie you down."

"I was regrouping. And spending time with my aunt."

Regrouping. Michael wasn't sure what that meant, but he knew very well that it was Charlotte's inclination to leave when she had a problem. "You know, you can't run away every time you hit a rough patch. My dad practically drilled that into my head."

"You can stop right there, okay? You don't even know why I went to England. Don't assume."

"So tell me."

"Um, let me think." She set her finger against her temple. "No."

Good God, she was stubborn. "All I'm saying is that you have to keep going when things get tough. This was a problem when we were together. You were always letting the little things get to you. And you were always coming to me with your problems, expecting me to fix everything."

Charlotte nearly blew steam out of her nostrils. "First off, I don't remember asking for your sage life advice. And second, you have a lot to learn about women. I never wanted you to solve my problems. I wanted you to *listen*."

The biting tone she'd taken gave him pause. But only for a second. "Fine, then. I'm listening. Tell me why you went to England."

She glared at him. "It's a little late for listening. Goodbye, Michael." She opened the building door with a shove.

Charlotte. Always the drama queen.

"Dammit," she muttered. "I forgot to have Lily call me a car."

Michael followed her as she shuffled to the curb. "Do you want me to do it? Or I'll call Lily."

She rifled through her handbag, hunched over it while resting it on her leg. "No. I'm fine taking a taxi."

"Then let me give you a ride. I have my car. It's cold out here. You'll freeze."

He took a step toward her and she shot him another one of her piercing looks. Her breaths left her lips in puffs of white and her cheeks began to turn bright pink. "I like the cold."

"No, you don't. You hate it."

"You think you know me, Michael. But you don't. You never took the time."

Clearly, they were having two separate conversations. He didn't have the patience for more of her thinly veiled innuendos about his personal shortcomings. "Okay, then. Have a nice day." He turned and headed for the parking garage.

"I hope you have the worst day ever!" she called back.

Fine. Be like that.

He trudged around the corner and retrieved his car. When he pulled out of the lot, Charlotte was still standing on the sidewalk, looking for a cab. A heavy sigh left his throat. It would be easiest to turn on his blinker, take a right turn and leave Charlotte to fend for herself. But there was this little voice inside him, a voice he normally ignored, suggesting that he might have a few things to make up for, even if he might never know his actual past transgressions because Charlotte spoke in secret code most of the time.

He rolled down his window and the icy air rushed inside. "Charlotte. Come on. I'll give you a ride."

"A cab will come along any minute now," she replied, not looking at him.

The street was dead. *You'd have more luck if you walked over to Seventh Avenue.* "I'll turn on your heated seat."

She glanced back over her shoulder. That flash of her blue eyes was still pretty damn potent from this distance. "Fine."

Shoulders bunched up around her ears, she hurried around to the passenger side as Michael rolled up his window. The instant she climbed inside and closed the door, her sweet vanilla scent hit his nose. Her presence was impossible to ignore in the confines of the car. It sent a powerful wave of recognition through his body. Even with her prickly attitude toward him, if she said she wanted him, he'd go so far as to blow off work for an hour. He never did that for anyone.

"You have to promise you'll drive carefully." She rubbed her hands together in front of the vents. Without asking permission, she reached over and cranked up the heat.

"Charlotte, you know me. There is no such thing as careful."

Charlotte's heart was beating so fiercely, it didn't even faze her when Michael laid on the horn and yelled at the car in front of him. Everything was getting to her right now, like having the air sucked out of her triumphant announcement that she was going to buy an apartment, only to learn from Michael that he'd made an offer to Sawyer weeks ago. It was bad enough that he'd never said a thing while they were together about cooking up a deal with her brother to sell the Grand Legacy units. It was the perfect illustration of the divide between Michael and Charlotte. A normal couple, a *real* couple, would have discussed such things.

She felt like such a fool, but she had to go through with buying the unit. Her brother knew Charlotte as the woman who made bold, sweeping promises and later changed her mind. Plus, she couldn't stand the thought of Michael being one sale ahead of her.

"Dude. You're killing me with this." Michael jammed the heel of his hand into the car horn again. "Just go."

"See? This is why I didn't want a ride from you.

It's more relaxing having a complete stranger take me somewhere."

Michael zipped into the next lane without using a blinker or even looking. "You're in excellent hands."

She slumped back in her seat, unable to ignore the conflicted feelings pinging back and forth between her head and her heart. She hated Michael. Or at least she was trying very hard to. Every logical brain cell in her head knew the reason why—she'd tried harder with him than she had with any other guy, and she still wasn't enough. So why was there some fragment of her that was happy to be in the car with him, even when she also despised his driving? Who had decided that this irrational part of her brain, hopelessly turned on by the vision of his hand wrapped around the gearshift, should have a voice?

She'd spent an awful lot of time during those five weeks in England talking with Aunt Fran about Michael, about the differences between men and women, heartache and the ways in which Charlotte was regularly sabotaging herself. It was good to be open and optimistic, Fran had said, but it wasn't so smart to dive in headfirst every single time. Well, she hadn't quite put it that way. Her exact wording was, *Charlotte, stop picking out your children's names on the first date.* Call it what you will—jumping the gun. Running away with the circus. Going overboard. It was Charlotte's greatest inclination. She knew this about herself.

By all reports, she'd been that way since she was a little girl. Her brothers teased her mercilessly about her endless string of crushes, all of which she'd been stupid enough to identify by name, starting at the age of four with the first boy she ever kissed, Darren Willingham, on the playground in preschool. As the story went, Charlotte had announced her engagement to be married to the unwitting Darren at the dinner table that night. She had no way of knowing if Sawyer and Noah were making up the part of the story where Charlotte produced crayon drawings of her wedding dress, the flowers and the church. The only other witness to the conversation had been their mother, and she'd passed away before Charlotte could ever ask her about it.

Despite the regular razzing from Sawyer and Noah, Charlotte remained undeterred on her quest for love. By the time she was sixteen, she'd figured out that the affection she wasn't getting at home was easily obtained by sneaking out of the house, taking the train into the city and partying all night. It wasn't love, but it was an acceptable substitute, and after a few drinks obtained with a fake ID, a handsome guy flirting with her on the dance floor, wanting to kiss her and hold her and take her home, it sure started to feel like something real. Love had always been Charlotte's drug of choice. She'd wanted it more from Michael than she'd wanted it from any other man.

What a shame she'd invested so much time and effort into the Michael project. She'd killed herself trying to be the perfect girlfriend, making him meals that took hours to prepare because everyone knew what a horrible cook she was. She'd tried to get him to open up about work problems—she could see how stressed he was—but he wasn't big on talking about any of it. Charlotte had been so sure that whatever was wrong, she could make it better. None of her efforts seemed to make much of an impression on him. Maybe it was because he was used to women fawning all over him.

Even if that was the case, it still hurt. Of course, cooking and listening had become the least of her worries when she'd finally decided that the best approach with him was a direct one.

She'd planned a romantic evening at his place, bought a gorgeous silk nightgown and had his favorite meal brought in. They'd had dinner that night, they'd made love and Charlotte had waited for the perfect moment to confess her love to Michael. They were curled up in his bed, warm under the covers, lips inches apart. She was just about to profess her love for him when she was preempted by Michael's own confession. He was getting the impression that she wanted a lot more out of their relationship than he was equipped to give. He was too busy for a real girlfriend. It never worked out. *Of course.* It never worked out for Charlotte, either, just for different reasons.

"So? What's your plan?" Michael asked.

If only he knew the true breadth of that question. Her hand instinctively rested on her lower belly. She had a lot to plan for, and a lot to accomplish. It all scared the crap out of her, especially the notion of telling Michael. If he'd managed to anticipate and fend off "I love you," there was zero chance he was up for the challenge of a child. Even so, the baby seemed like the one truly bright spot on her horizon. Motherhood was going to be a lot of work, and she was in no way confident she was up to the task, but she liked the idea of finally having a deserving vessel for the love she was so eager to give. "My plan?"

"Yes. For selling your half of the apartments."

She wasn't aware she needed a plan outside of getting out her address book and calling her contacts, starting with the wealthiest ones. "I don't really feel like I should share my strategy with you."

"So you don't have one."

He was so arrogant it made her want to scream. And kiss him. Again, confusing. "That's not true. My plans are just more fluid than yours are. It's called being flexible and thinking on your toes. You should try it sometime."

He shook his head, his signature dismissive move. "Being flexible isn't a strategy, it's a coping mechanism. You sell with a strategy. That's the name of the game in real estate. Sell, sell, sell."

Blah, blah, blah. If only he knew that his little lecture on business was like rubbing salt in the wound. She didn't need constant reminders of how he lived and breathed his job. She was collateral damage from the importance of Michael's career.

"You know," he continued, "if you need some help networking, I host a party every year on December twenty-third. I invite other agents, potential clients. Usually some pretty big hitters. I always get a great turnout. I think people enjoy avoiding their families at the holidays."

"Is that what you do? Avoid your family at Christmas?" Michael had never talked about his family when they were a couple, however hard she'd tried to get him to do it. She didn't know anything more than he had a brother, and parents who he'd hinted were perfectionists.

"You might say that."

She didn't want to take his help, but it might be good to keep her options open. "I'll think about it."

Michael pulled up in front of the Grand Legacy and put the car in Park.

"It really is a beautiful building." Michael rested his hand on the center console, leaning over her and peering up at the building. He was so close, she could practically count the hairs in his perfectly tended stubble. She had once loved to hold on to his face right before he kissed her. He had no idea, but it was her way of reminding herself that Michael Kelly actually wanted to make out with her. The man was an Olympian, as shrewd a businessman as there ever was and the finest male specimen she'd had the good fortune to take to bed. She'd wanted to mark the moment and thank the universe.

But that was in the past. And today was all about her future, as well as that of the baby, the two of them on their own. "It is. I love it. I absolutely love it. Which is why I'm going to sell my units before you do. I simply care more." She reached for the door handle.

"Are you challenging me to a race?"

"No," she scoffed, even though she knew very well that she would take extreme glee in selling her apartments before him. She might be forced to take out a full-page ad in the *New York Times*, or at least go to his office, blow raspberries at him and say, "I told you so" a few hundred times. "I'm a grown-up. I'm not racing you."

"Right. I mean, how would we even decide what the prize is?" He bounced his eyebrows at her, his voice so low and husky that she worried she might pass out and knock her head into the dashboard.

"You do your thing. I'll do mine."

"Or I can just tell myself it's a race. To stay motivated."

"What? You can't do that. You need someone else to

race you. I refuse to be that person." *Except I already am that person.*

"I'm pretty sure I can do whatever I want."

"You're being ridiculous." It would be just like him to do this. The doorman appeared and opened Charlotte's car door. "I'm going now."

"You're welcome for the ride, neighbor. Oh, and by the way, we're totally having a race."

Fine. I'll just have to figure out a way to beat your sorry butt.

Three

Charlotte stood inside the doorway of her brand-new luxury Grand Legacy apartment, mesmerized by muscles.

"Ma'am, where do you want this?" Chad, the head of the moving crew she'd hired, blew his sandy blond surfer-dude bangs from his forehead. His lightly tanned brow glistened with sweat. His biceps bulged through his black T-shirt, which was emblazoned with his company's name: Hunks with Trucks.

Charlotte felt giddy. This was the most fun she'd had in months. "In the bedroom, Chad. Thank you. And please, call me Charlotte." Her voice was high and girlie and exploding with flirtation, and she didn't care in the least how goofy it might make her seem.

"Of course. Charlotte." He smiled and winked at the same time, a talent Charlotte did not possess. Chad was getting a really good tip at the end of the day. As was Marco, the tall one with the megawatt smile, Phil, the one with the nerdy glasses whose side job was as a runway model, and James, the brooding serious one with the mysterious tattoo snaking up his arm.

"I can't believe you hired this moving company," Fran said under her breath when Chad was out of view. "But I'm not sorry you did."

"I figure we're entitled to a little fun. Plus, I hate moving." Charlotte had moved thirteen times, more than once a year since she'd moved out of the house at eighteen. That was when her dad had announced that he couldn't "deal" with her anymore—too much sneaking out of the house, and doing things that were unbecoming of a Locke, mostly staying out late and dancing. There was always a lot of dancing.

Charlotte's brothers had done some of the same things, and although their carousing was never on a par with Charlotte's, they were also never reprimanded for it. She despised the double standard and had been glad to go out on her own. She started her party-planning business the next day, and kept at it during her first two years of college, until she eventually flunked out of school and shifted gears out of boredom, the next phase being interior design. "And they're doing a great job." The bonus of hiring Hunks with Trucks was that as a pregnant single woman, these guys might be the only primo male physiques she'd see up close for the foreseeable future.

Fran consulted her watch. "They got here pretty late, though. Aren't you supposed to be done using the freight elevator at two? It's nearly two thirty." She pushed up the sleeves of her pale pink long-sleeved T-shirt. Even helping Charlotte move, Fran was dressed impeccably, like a modern-day Jackie O in slim black capris, flats and pearl earrings.

Charlotte had gone for yoga pants, a camisole and a slouchy T-shirt over that. Her hair had gotten dry shampoo that morning and was pulled back in a ponytail, but she had gone to the trouble of putting on makeup. She was spending part of her day with Hunks with Trucks, after all. She wanted to look good. "I think there are only a few more things for them to bring up."

"Yes, ma'am," Chad said from behind her. "One or two more trips and we'll be out of your hair. The guys are bringing the bigger pieces of furniture up now."

Thor whimpered from his kennel, which had been put in the quietest corner of the living room. Charlotte rushed over to him and poked her fingers between the metal bars. Thor licked her mercilessly with his tiny pink tongue. He wagged his tail so violently that the crate shook. "Sorry, buddy. Just a little longer and I can spring you from jail. I can't let you out when the door's open. I know you and you'll run away." Charlotte turned to Fran. "Let's start getting the plates and glasses unpacked. I have to have something to eat on."

The two made their way to the kitchen, which was over-the-top considering Charlotte's lack of culinary skills, but she loved it nonetheless. Classic white cabinets, white marble countertops, gleaming chrome fixtures and stainless steel appliances, including a six-burner range with a massive hood. She even had a center island, which was practically unheard of in Manhattan, but Sawyer's architect had done an excellent job with maximizing space. Charlotte also had a huge soaking tub in her bathroom, another NYC anomaly, something she was definitely going to break in before the end of the night. The apartments were a new addition to the hotel, as these top floors had been only guest rooms in the hotel's earlier incarnation. It had been Sawyer's idea to bring a residential feel to the building, and Charlotte had to admire her brother's devotion to both carefully restoring the building and not being afraid to try something new. Plus, it meant a business opportunity had fallen into her lap and she was immensely thankful for that.

"I have my first showing on Monday morning," Charlotte said, cutting the packing tape on one of the boxes labeled Glassware. "An old party-planning client. She's newly divorced and got a huge settlement. She wants to move into the city from New Jersey."

"Sounds promising." Fran began helping Charlotte unwrap the paper around the glasses. "Remind me. How many units do you have to sell?"

"Seven, now that I've bought one. It doesn't sound like a lot, but it'll be a big deal. There's so much competition out there and you have to find the right buyer."

"A person with deep pockets."

"Who also likes the idea of living in a hotel. Sawyer was very specific. He wants resident buyers. He doesn't want absentee owners, so it's a little trickier than simply selling them to anyone with money."

"Well, you could sell it as almost like being in a small building. With only four floors, the residential space is relatively small, and access is closed off from the hotel. That could appeal to buyers."

"Of course, you're sharing the elevators with hundreds of hotel guests."

"You don't have to remind anyone of that. You have

a fantastic restaurant downstairs and there will be two bars to choose from once The Cellar is open. You don't get that in most apartment buildings."

"True."

Chad and his big brown eyes appeared in the kitchen doorway. "It seems we have a problem. Another resident was scheduled to move in this afternoon. He's demanding his time with the service elevator and wants to talk to you."

The other resident could only be one person. *Michael.* To her knowledge, no other units had been sold. "Where is he?"

"He's down the hall, arguing with my guys."

Charlotte glanced at Fran. "I'll be back." Reminding herself to stay calm, Charlotte marched down the hall, Chad in her wake. She could hear men's voices before she rounded the corner to the main stretch, where the elevator bank would be visible. Michael's voice, a sound she had once loved, was the loudest.

When she turned, he was standing there, pointing into the elevator. "You guys have to turn the sofa on its side or it's never going to come out." He caught sight of her and simply shook his head. Again with his never-ending dismissiveness. No one was ever as competent as Michael.

She forced herself to smile sweetly. "Problem?"

"These guys have no clue what they're doing. And they won't let me touch your stupid sofa."

Charlotte stepped closer to check out the scene in the elevator. Two of Chad's guys were trying to turn the sofa, but it seemed pretty well wedged in there. "Chad? Can you take charge here? I'm guessing you're enough muscle to make this happen so we can relinquish the elevator to Mr. Kelly."

"You got it, Charlotte." Chad went to work, instructing his men to make some changes in their plan of attack.

Michael simply folded his arms across his broad chest, pacing the width of the hall. He was dressed in jeans and a Boston Celtics T-shirt. She'd always loved it when he dressed down. It was even sexier than him in a suit, which was already out-of-this-world sexy. Perhaps because it made him more approachable, more like an everyday guy. "Nice moving company," he said. "Hunks with Trucks? You've got to be kidding me."

"Don't tell me you're jealous. I didn't think that was possible." He did seem a little green-eyed about the presence of her studly movers. It left her feeling like things were more even between them. She'd stepped out of his car the other day with the distinct sense that he had the upper hand.

"No, Charlie. I'm not jealous."

Just like that, his words cut her down to size. She hadn't heard him call her Charlie in months and it was like a flaming hot poker to the heart. Nobody called her that. It was a nickname he'd bestowed on her, and he rarely used it when they were around anyone else. It'd been reserved for the times when they were alone as a couple. It was such a potent reminder of the reasons she'd been convinced she not only loved him, but that he was also at least capable of falling in love with her. How wrong she'd been. "You could stand to get a sense of humor, Michael. They've been great to work with. Totally professional outfit, top to bottom."

"I think I see the problem," Chad said.

"Oh, good. He thinks he sees the problem." Michael threw up his hands. "You might find them professional, but I have a team of six guys downstairs, waiting to use the elevator, the elevator that I had reserved for two o'clock. You're using up my time."

"I'm sorry. I had no idea you were in such a rush."

"I have a showing this evening. Here."

"Tonight?" Damn him. He was always ahead.

"Yes, tonight. You know I don't waste time."

Yes, she knew all about that. And she hated the way it made her feel like a lesser person.

"I have work to do," he continued. "I can't be standing around here all day waiting for everything to get moved into my apartment." He pointed down to the other end of the hall.

"You mean that apartment, but on the eighteenth floor, right? I was told you bought the corner unit up top. Please don't tell me you're going to be living on the fifteenth floor."

Charlotte's pulse began pounding in her ears. *I haven't even moved in, and I'm going to have to start thinking about moving out.*

Michael was going to have to lie about the location of his apartment. There was no way around it. "I always meant to be on fifteen. It'll be quieter. Those top units are too close to the shared terrace. There will be all sorts of parties up there. I don't want to deal with that." The truth was that he'd asked to have his unit moved to Charlotte's floor. He'd told Sawyer it was because the upper units were primo and would be easier to sell. Hell, he'd told himself the same thing. But the minute he saw Charlotte again today, he suspected that she was the real reason. He was still so drawn to her, but it was an even more pronounced feeling now. Was it because she seemed to despise him so much? Was that what made it so hot? The conversation they were having was a prime example of their incompatibility.

"You're going to be living down the hall. From me." Her voice and expression carried what he could only describe as profound disappointment. Was he really that bad?

"I'm sorry if that's a disdainful idea, but yes."

"Hmm. Okay." She twisted her lips into a kissable bundle. Charlotte made annoyance and anger sexy.

"Got it," one of the movers said, and just like that, the end of the sofa popped out of the elevator.

"Oh, good. Now we can get off Mr. Kelly's naughty list." Charlotte touched Chad the mover's arm with the tips of her slender fingers.

Michael wrestled with the reasons it bothered him so greatly, while trying to ignore Charlotte's sarcastic comment. He had the elevator reserved and she was using his time. She needed to stop acting as though he was being petty.

The movers in the elevator carried the bright turquoise sofa wrapped in a cocoon of clear plastic out into the hall. "Can we give you a lift?" Chad asked Charlotte.

"I'm sorry?" she asked in a voice that rivaled a cartoon princess.

"A ride. Hop on the sofa and we'll carry you down the hall."

She giggled. "Really?"

"Yes, really. We promise we won't drop you. It's fun."

Chad is fun. Good for him.

"Oh. Okay. Great." Charlotte sat on the couch and the men hoisted her into the air. She grasped the sofa arm as surprise and delight crossed her face. They carried her away, Charlotte waving her fingers at him.

At this rate, Michael just wanted them gone. He couldn't stand another minute of Charlotte and the muscle squad.

Time to get back to work. He made a quick call down to his movers, a perfectly normal company called Manhattan Moving, and retreated to his apartment to make a few phone calls while waiting for the first load to arrive upstairs. Without his home office ready, he was forced to set up in the kitchen, his laptop on the counter. His chocolate Lab, Abby, had already made herself at home, stretched out in a sunbeam gracing the living room floor. One of his hopes with now being closer to his office was that he'd have more time to take Abby to the park and out for runs. He had a dog walker, but it wasn't the same. Abby wanted to spend time with him, and he wanted to spend time with Abby. The relationship between dog and master was a simple one, much easier and more symbiotic than most human relationships.

He touched base with three clients about a handful of different properties, including the client who was coming to see the Grand Legacy that evening. The movers were bringing in the first load when he got a call from his younger brother, Chris. They talked or texted almost every day.

"The Islanders won last night," Chris said.

"Sometimes I wish you had a real job so you wouldn't call me in the middle of the day." Michael smiled and leaned back against the kitchen counter. Chris lived in Washington, DC, about twenty minutes from their parents in Maryland. He worked as a lobbyist. As Michael had learned over the last several years, it's pretty easy to get someone to take a meeting with you when you're a former Olympian.

"You owe me five bucks." They were always betting on sports. No longer living in the same house or competing in swimming, it was one way to keep their sibling rivalry going.

"The winning goal was completely bogus. He kicked it into the net."

"Nope. It went off his skate. They reviewed it. A win's a win."

"Fine. I'll pay you when you come at Christmas." Michael stepped aside as a mover brought several boxes into the kitchen. He pointed at the center island, indicating that was a good landing spot. "I mean, if you still want to come."

"What else am I going to do? Go visit Mom and Dad? I don't think so."

Michael and Chris had been spending Christmas together, but separate from their parents, for six years now. Things had always been difficult with their father. The man had all the warmth of a dark night in Siberia. There was no parental affection, only an intolerance for anything short of perfection. It was one thing when that revolved around swimming. It had helped both Michael and Chris get to the Olympics. It was quite another when it came to one of their sons being on the wrong end of a broken engagement.

"Okay. I'm just saying that I'm fine. I don't want you

to feel like you have to come to New York every year and console me."

"Hey. It's not just you. We both sort of lost our parents that day."

Michael did his best to ward off the guilt. Chris had sided with him when Dad went off the rails about Michael's admittedly disastrous engagement party. Mom took Dad's side, which still confounded them both. Their marriage was anything but blissful.

Out of the corner of his eye, Michael saw a small dog rocket through his foyer. Charlotte raced in behind him. "Thor! No!"

"Hey, Chris. I need to run. Talk to you later?"

"Yeah. Of course."

Michael hung up and rushed to investigate. Charlotte's dog was in the living room, straddling a very startled Abby's leg, humping away. "I take it this is Thor?"

Charlotte pulled her dog off Abby and tucked him under her arm, scolding him. "No. Bad dog."

"Does he always do that? Rush into someone's house and try to mate with the nearest canine?" Michael crouched down and showed Abby some love. "I'm sorry, sweets. He woke you up from your nap and everything."

Charlotte blew out a breath. "I'm sorry. He got out of his kennel and bolted down the hall. He's my little Houdini." She lowered herself to the floor and sat with her legs crossed, letting the dogs sniff each other while she petted Abby. "Hi, Abs. Long time, no see." Charlotte had such a sweet side when she chose to let it out, and he'd nearly forgotten what it was like to witness it. It made her even more beautiful, if that was possible.

She cast her eyes up at him. "I think they can get along. I swear Thor's not really like this. I think the move has him out of sorts. He can't figure out what's going on."

"It's funny. I've seen so many pictures of him, but you never brought him to my place. It seems strange that I never met him."

Charlotte shot him one of her looks. He'd said the wrong thing. Again. "Are you serious right now? It wasn't that I never brought him to your place. It's that we always went to your apartment and my dog was never invited. You're lucky I had a lonely retiree living next door to me. Thor spent most of our relationship with my old neighbor."

Michael hadn't really thought about it. It just always seemed easier to meet up at his apartment. "I'm sorry if it seemed that way to you."

"It didn't *seem* that way. It was that way. You never came to my apartment. Not once."

Was that really true? He guessed it was. *Damn.* Michael's phone rang again, saving him from the onslaught of shame Charlotte was likely about to launch at him. He straightened and fished his cell out of his pocket. "It's your brother. Sorry. I need to get this."

"It's Sawyer? Why would he be calling you?" Charlotte seemed once again miffed by Michael's existence on the planet.

"Maybe because we're working together?" Michael pressed the button to pick up the call. "Hey there, Sawyer. What can I do for you this afternoon?"

"Nothing, actually. This call is purely social. I wanted to know if it's best to mail you something at your office or if you're ready to start getting mail at the Grand Legacy."

"What sort of something?"

Michael watched as Charlotte attempted to further acquaint the dogs by placing Thor back on the floor. Unfortunately, the little brute returned to his previous libidinous activity.

"Is he fixed?" he whispered to Charlotte.

"Yes." She frowned at him.

"I want to send you an invitation to my wedding," Sawyer said.

"Oh. Great. I'd love to come to your wedding." Michael said it entirely for Charlotte's benefit, although he wished he could've received this invitation earlier, when Gabe had been bragging about it.

Charlotte's face made the very short trip from shock to horror.

"It's in a week, and I know this is last minute, but it occurred to me after we met the other day that we're working on this project together and you're the first resident of the Grand Legacy who isn't related to me. I'd like to include you that day if you're free. We're having the ceremony and the reception at the hotel, so you won't have far to go. And, of course, you should feel free to bring a date."

Michael hadn't been on a date since Charlotte had broken up with him. Not that he hadn't entertained the idea. There were several women he'd considered asking out. But something stopped him, every time. He just wasn't sure what his problem was. "Sounds great. You can go ahead and put me down with a plus-one. I'll definitely bring a date." Michael watched for Charlotte's reaction, which turned out to be an overblown eye roll.

Michael and Sawyer said their goodbyes, and the

movers brought in another round of boxes along with a few smaller pieces of furniture.

Charlotte scooped up her dog again. "So you're bringing a date to my brother's wedding? Or did you just say that for my benefit?"

Maybe. "Yes and no."

"It wasn't payback for Hunks with Trucks?"

He could admit to himself that he'd been irked that she'd hired an all-male revue to move her into the building, but he wasn't about to own up to it with her. "I don't bother with payback, Charlotte. You're free to do whatever you want. You broke up with me, remember?" He disliked the tone in his voice, the one that said it still bothered him. He knew he should be over it by now, but it still felt like there was a lot unresolved between Charlotte and him. Being around her only brought it to the surface, like scratching a wound that hadn't healed.

"I broke up with you because you practically dared me to do it. Which is probably why we should just agree to be kindly neighbors and work adversaries."

Was that where this was going to end? It seemed a shame, but all signs pointed to yes. And maybe that was for the best. "It doesn't have to be that way."

"So says the guy who insists we're racing to see who can sell their apartments first."

"We're still doing that."

She closed her eyes and sucked a deep breath through her nose. "Goodbye, Michael."

"'Bye." He watched down the hall as she walked away, unable to ignore how much he loved the sway of her hips in stretchy black pants. He was definitely going to need to find a date for her brother's wedding. There was no telling who Charlotte would show up with—probably Chad from Hunks with Trucks.

No, it was time for Michael to get back on the horse and start dating again. Maybe it would help him finally get Charlotte out of his system.

Four

Charlotte's new apartment, especially her home office, was shaping up nicely. Her desk, one of her favorite pieces of furniture, was a floor model she'd picked up for a steal at a lovely designer shop in SoHo. It had weathered gray wood and legs that were heavy and scrolled, with a glass top for smoother writing. She'd never liked the idea of a rolling desk chair—too many opportunities to sit and miss—so instead, she used an upholstered side chair in linen with dark legs and nailhead trim. With a lovely bank of windows streaming in daylight, it was the sunniest possible spot to get her life back on track.

Primped by 9:00 a.m. and dressed for the day in a knee-length navy skirt, black-and-white checked blouse and black pumps, she sat at her desk and began to plan out her day. It was almost enough to make her feel like a confident and accomplished businesswoman. The only thing nagging her was the distinct sense that the clock was ticking. It would only be another ten days or so until she was starting her second trimester.

The words alone—*second trimester*—filled her with a cocktail of excitement and worry that far surpassed any bout of anxiety she'd ever had to battle. She couldn't spend too much time perched on this feather-stuffed chair in her photo-spread-ready office, casually writing herself notes. Soon a crib would need to be added, a rocking chair, a bureau for the baby's things. After that, she'd be focused on practicing breathing techniques and the best ways to navigate her environment while her belly was the size of a Smart car. Soon after that she'd be wandering the apartment in slippers and pajamas, holding her sweet little bundle, wondering what day it was and whether her breasts could ever again be used for anything fun. Or at least that was what Fran had said.

Fran had also been regularly reminding her that she only had a few more weeks before it'd be impossible to walk around in an outfit like the one she was wearing today. At some point soon, some unwitting stranger or member of the hotel staff was going to ask when she was due. Unless she wanted to blame her expanding waistline on late-night potato-chip binges, there was no getting around it. She'd have to start telling people about the baby.

Today was December 15. Ten days until Christmas, when their faction of the Locke family would be spending the holiday at Sawyer's apartment, right before he and his wife-to-be, Kendall, would be leaving for their honeymoon. If she'd sold her half of the units, she would tell them then. Visions of opening gifts before a roaring fire, sipping eggnog and enjoying family time popped into her head. What a lovely backdrop for the announcement that not only Sawyer and Kendall would be bringing a new Locke into the world, but Charlotte would be as well. She imagined good wishes, warm embraces and wide smiles. That was the response she wanted more than anything, and she knew very well that she'd have to live with the memory forever, so she'd better do her best to make it a good one. As far as she was concerned, news of a baby, no matter the circumstances, should be greeted with nothing less than pure joy.

Which was precisely the reason she had not yet told Michael. There was no telling how he would take the news, or if he would take it at all. Knowing him, he'd probably blow it off and say he had to get to a meeting with a client. She wanted to believe there was a chance he'd be open to it once he actually heard the news, but she was haunted by the things he'd said when they were together. Things like *I've never wanted to be a parent. Mine seemed to hate it.*

Charlotte's phone rang, and the caller ID said it was Sawyer. She guessed he was calling to make sure she was actually doing something productive and real-estate-related today.

"Morning, Sawyer. How are you?" she answered.

"Wow. I forget how chipper you can be in the morning."

Charlotte had always been a morning person, which was admittedly incongruous with her party-girl past. She'd never been the type to sleep until noon, even when she was a teenager and had tiptoed her way back into the house at 4:00 a.m. "I've got work to do. Phone calls to make. Luxury condominiums in the most beautiful hotel in Manhattan to show off."

Sawyer laughed. "So it's going well?"

"Great. Fantastic." Charlotte didn't hesitate with her answer, even when she knew she was only putting polish on her unproven sales skills. "I've got my home office all set up. I'm ready to sell."

"And you're okay with the Michael Kelly situation? You seemed tense around him. Is there something I should know?"

Oh, sure. You got two hours to sit down and listen to your sister spill her guts? She sucked in a deep breath and blew it out. The simplest explanation was the best for now. Sawyer would only think less of her if he knew that she and Michael had been romantically involved. She could hear it now. *Is there a single guy in Manhattan you haven't dated?* "I interviewed with his agency earlier this year. He declined to take me on as an agent."

"Oh. Wow. I had no idea. I'm so sorry. That had to have stung a bit."

There it was, that familiar sound—pity. Charlotte wanted so desperately to erase that conditioned response from her family's repertoire. "It's fine. You know. It's just business." She could give herself the it's-just-business answer one thousand times and she still wouldn't believe it. Michael's ability to turn her down for a job and still end up her boyfriend was a shining example of just how often and how easily the man got whatever he wanted. He always won. Always.

"You're right. Sometimes business decisions are nothing more than that. I just wanted to make sure there wasn't any romantic history there."

Charlotte had to think fast. Eventually, her family would know about the pregnancy. Eventually, they would learn that although they were not together, Michael was the father of her child. There was no getting around that. "There's a little romantic history, but it's old news. Done and gone."

"What does 'a little romantic history' mean?"

"It means exactly what it sounds like. A little romance, and it's history."

He blew out an exasperated breath. "I just need to know that there's nothing going on between you two. It's not good for business."

"You realize you sound like a total hypocrite right now?" Much of Sawyer's history with his fiancée, Kendall, involved blurring the lines between business and pleasure.

"I know. But I'm also thinking about the reality of the situation. My romance with Kendall messed up a lot of things for her professionally. She nearly lost her job. It's a double standard, and it isn't right, but oftentimes women are judged for these things differently than men."

He wasn't wrong. Women were judged for *a lot* of things differently than men. "Michael Kelly is in the past, I promise. Nothing to worry about."

"Okay. I just want to make sure everything is aboveboard. I want people talking about the hotel and keeping its reputation as a destination, not gossiping about the agents selling the units. I also want to keep the chance of working with Michael open. I don't want him thinking a single bad thought about a member of the Locke family."

Too late. "Got it. Loud and clear."

"I want you to know I gave the same speech to Noah. It's not just you."

"You did?"

"He has a crush on Lily, our admin. I keep telling him to back off, but he has a hard time keeping the flirtation in check. They're close friends, which makes me nervous enough. I'm amazed he hasn't managed to figure out a way to make a move on her without making me mad."

"What if she's the one for him?"

"For Noah? You know how he is. He'd get restless. She'd quit. There's just too much opportunity for things to go wrong. Kendall and I gambled and it worked out, but it almost never does."

As if Charlotte needed a reason to stay away from Michael romantically—Sawyer would be greatly displeased. Knowing this only confirmed how sensible her plan was. It was best to wait until her units were sold before telling her family about the pregnancy. No more conflict of interest, and she'd also be past the twelve-week mark. Too many pregnancy books insisted it was best to wait until then. "Look. I swear to you that this is a nonissue. Michael and I work in the same industry and we are professionals. I will sell my units and that's all you need to know. Don't you worry." *Leave that up to me.*

"You're very resourceful and there's no doubt you're determined. I know you won't let me down."

Charlotte would deserve every ounce of guilt to come if she let down Sawyer. That's why she wasn't going to let it happen. She glanced at the time on her laptop. "I actually have a showing in a few minutes. I should probably head down to the lobby to meet my client."

"Absolutely. Don't let me hold you up."

"Love you, Sawyer."

"Love you, too."

Charlotte hung up, ducked into the bathroom, brushed her teeth and checked her hair. It was time to kick some butt and charm her way into convincing the New Jersey divorcée to buy her own little piece of the Grand Legacy.

Downstairs in the lobby, Charlotte stood near the concierge desk, trying to stay out of the way as a flurry of people milled about. Folks were checking in, some were checking out and the staff catered to their every need. The holidays were always a very busy time in the city and popular with tourists. If any city knew how to do Christmas, it was New York. Between ice-skating in the shadow of the big tree at Rockefeller Center and the extravagant department-store windows and decor, there was no shortage of cheer. The city had even gotten a dusting of snow last night, although it had been meticulously cleared from the sidewalk in front of the hotel. No detail at the Grand Legacy was ever overlooked.

The lobby itself was tastefully decorated with thick swags of fresh pine garland, adorned with strands of glimmering silver and scarlet beads and studded with tiny twinkling lights. The tree, twelve feet tall and dressed with an array of glass ornaments, was tucked into an alcove next to the sweeping grand staircase, which led to the second-floor speakeasy. Christmas was most certainly coming. As was Charlotte's baby.

In through the revolving door came Charlotte's client, Marie Stapleton, bundled up in a black wool coat and a Burberry scarf. Her face lit up when she caught sight of Charlotte. They rushed toward each other and embraced.

"Marie. It's so good to see you. Let me help you with your coat." Marie had been one of Charlotte's most loyal clients when she had her party-planning business. Marie's husband, or now ex-husband, was a Wall Street bigwig, and they had thrown some seriously over-the-top bashes out at their estate.

"You look lovely, Charlotte. Are you doing something new with your makeup? Your skin looks incredible." Marie unwound the scarf from her neck and worked her way out of her coat, both of which Charlotte took from her.

Charlotte shrugged. "Nope. Same old thing. Maybe I'm getting more sleep?"

"Well, whatever it is, it's working."

Charlotte flagged one of the bellhops, who hustled over to them. "Can you check Ms. Stapleton's things in the coatroom, please?"

"Yes, Ms. Locke. Of course." He smiled and was on his way.

"Shall we go pick out your new apartment?" Charlotte asked. It was such a sales-y thing to say. It was the sort of thing Michael would say. Charlotte was proud of herself for having the nerve to presume that Marie would end up living here.

"I can't wait to see it," Marie replied as they managed to catch the elevator before the doors closed. "I'm dying to be back in the city and I wouldn't mind having you for a neighbor. Think of all the fun we could have. Two single girls, out on the town."

Charlotte smiled and nodded, even though she knew she'd have to hold off on revelry with Marie for at least a year or two unless Marie's idea of "out on the town" included newborns and strollers. They rode up to the fifteenth floor to look at the first unit Charlotte had to offer.

Marie only took a few steps into the foyer before she turned to Charlotte and said, "I'm in love already."

"You are?" Charlotte asked, quickly correcting herself. "Well, don't fall too quickly. There are other fish in the sea, most notably the top-floor units. If you're interested in looking." She flipped on the dining room lights, which included a gorgeous chandelier and four elegant wall sconces.

Marie nodded intently, looking all around the room. "It's beautiful. I can see myself throwing intimate dinner parties here. I'll invite all my single friends and we'll laugh and drink too much wine and talk until the wee hours." Marie painted an appealing picture. Charlotte committed her words to memory—she could use them on a future potential buyer if they weren't as much of a visionary as Marie. "Show me more. Then I definitely want to see one of those top-floor units."

"Yes. Of course. They're more expensive. And in fact, they're a bit outside the price range you gave me." Charlotte knew that many real-estate agents would wait until the client couldn't imagine living anywhere else before they broke the bad news that the price exceeded the budget. But she wasn't most agents. "The units are so new there isn't much room for negotiation, unfortunately."

Marie trailed into the kitchen and gasped when she saw the stunning white marble countertops. She smoothed her fingers over them. "I'm guessing they're worth every penny."

An hour later, Charlotte had given Marie the tour of three units. Now they were settling into a corner booth at the hotel restaurant, which hadn't been ready at the time of the grand reopening and had only been open for a few days. As it was midmorning, Charlotte ordered them a big pot of tea and a basket of handmade pastries. She was starving. "Well? What did you think?" she asked, scarfing down a ginger-blueberry scone in as ladylike a fashion as possible.

"I think the hardest part is going to be picking the unit. They all have different things to fall in love with. The terrace on the top floor is hard to beat, but I love the bathroom configuration in the first one we saw." She sipped her tea and tapped her fingers on the table.

Charlotte's pulse started to pick up. She'd closed appallingly few real-estate deals in her short tenure as an agent. She was still learning the art of reading people when it came to this. There had been several times when she'd worked with someone for weeks, certain they were going to buy at any moment, only to eventually discover that they weren't serious or simply weren't able to make up their mind.

"I don't think you can go wrong, if that helps at all." It was the most diplomatic thing Charlotte could think to say. "It's going to be awesome no matter what you decide. The world is your oyster, and anyone would kill to have the sort of options you do." She blanketed Marie's hand with hers. "Just envision your fabulous new life and where you'd like to be living while you embark on your new beginning."

Marie turned to Charlotte and a tiny tear rolled down her cheek. "You know, I never thought I would be here.

I really thought that Bradley and I had one of those marriages that would last."

Oh, no. Charlotte had said something wrong and now she was going to pay the price. "Of course you did. A bright and optimistic person like yourself believes in love. You'll find it again. I know you will. But you won't find it until you're ready to start your new chapter."

"You really think I will?"

"I do. There's no doubt in my mind." It wasn't a line simply to close the deal. "You're sweet and generous. You're smart and a good person. You are truly beautiful, inside and out." Charlotte's entire worldview revolved around people like Marie finding their soul mate. If Charlotte didn't believe with every fiber of her being that someone as wonderful as Marie would find love again, what was there to believe in?

"Okay, then. I'm ready to make an offer." She cut open a muffin and slipped a generous pat of butter inside.

"On the first unit?"

She smiled with a devilish gleam in her eye. "Oh, no. On the top floor."

Charlotte matched Marie's grin with one of her own. *Take that, Michael. Take that.*

Five

After only a few days living in the hotel, Michael already liked coming home to the Grand Legacy. His apartment wasn't quite settled yet, but he was happy, albeit still unsure if living in such close proximity to Charlotte was a good idea. If he was supposed to be the guy getting her out of his mind, having her so nearby wasn't going to help.

Tonight, he had the elevator to himself, which was an unexpected bonus. He leaned against the wall during his ride upstairs. He'd had such a crazy nonstop day, no moment of silence was taken for granted. When he reached his floor and the doors slid open, he got another surprise—Thor, then Charlotte, whizzing past.

He stepped out into the hall, watching Charlotte scurry after her dog while wearing heels. How he loved the sway of her hips in that skirt. "Hey, neighbor. Did Trouble make a break for it again?"

"Very funny calling him Trouble."

"It's only fitting."

Charlotte cornered Thor and scooped him up into her arms. "Bad dog," she scolded, her brows drawing together. The reprimand was followed by kisses on the nose and a ruffling of his ears. If Michael's dog, Abby, was spoiled, Thor was spoiled rotten. "I don't know what his problem is. He's still behaving like a puppy. I thought he would've outgrown this by now."

"Maybe he just doesn't like being cooped up all day. Maybe he needs a walk. I have to take Abby out if you want to go together." He wasn't sure it was a good idea, especially since he'd convinced himself the other night that moving on from Charlotte was his best course of action, but he'd already extended the invitation.

She arched both eyebrows at him. "That sounds like a social outing."

"You can wear a disguise if you're worried someone might see you with me. Sunglasses and a fake mustache, maybe?"

She swatted him on the arm. "That's not what I meant." She pursed her lips and drew in a deep breath through her nose, looking at Thor, not him. "It's just so civilized. Almost like we like each other."

"We do like each other, don't we?" He did his best not to sound hurt by her statement. He loved their biting back-and-forth and never thought of it as genuine dislike. He'd assumed she felt the same way.

"Not always we don't."

"Don't be ridiculous. Even when we argue, it still feels like we like each other. Even when you were breaking up with me, I felt like half of the anger you directed at me was out of affection."

It was true. And maybe that was why he was still so drawn to Charlotte, even when he knew that if he dared to try again, it would be no easy task. She wasn't the type of woman to let him off the hook about anything. It was both her appeal and her downside. He loved a challenge, but only when he had an excellent chance of winning. There was no winning with Charlotte when they each wanted radically different things.

She shot him another doubting look. "I'd say it was more out of affection for the idea of screaming at you."

"It's still attention, darling. I'll take what I can get from you."

"Oh, please. You get all the attention you need and more. Every time I see you, I'm surprised a gaggle of women aren't following you like stray puppies."

"Is that what a group of women are called? A gaggle? Like geese?"

"It's better than calling them a murder, as in a murder of crows."

"True. Gaggle is much more kind." He pulled back the sleeve of his wool overcoat and consulted his watch. It was nearly seven thirty. He really needed to start working less and getting home earlier. "Are we going for that walk or what?"

Charlotte bounced Thor in her arms. "What do you say, buddy? A walk with Abby?"

"Just no canine fornication, mimed or otherwise."

"I'll have to change." She looked down at herself, and her blouse flopped back, revealing the line of her collarbone. Maybe it was the way the light in the hall was hitting her skin, maybe it was the fact that he was lonely and tired or maybe it was that Charlotte had an inexplicable hold on him. That one innocent vision sent his imagination flying off on all sorts of tangents, each involving his clothes and hers mingling on the floor of his bedroom.

"Meet back here in five?" He cleared his throat if only to right his mind.

"Make it ten." With that, she sauntered toward her apartment, skirt in full sway.

He keyed into his apartment. Abby was waiting for him at the door, wagging her tail and following his every move through the foyer. "Hold on, sweets. I need a minute." He dropped his keys on the hall table and hung up his coat and laptop bag. The trip to his bedroom to change into track pants and a sweatshirt was quick. He grabbed his black fleece jacket and clipped on Abby's leash. The forecast was for snow this evening, so he grabbed a hat and gloves, too. He'd learned that Abby had no patience for wearing a dog sweater, but that was probably because she liked to walk at a clip and that kept her body temperature up.

They met Charlotte and Thor at the elevator. She'd changed into jeans and boots, wearing the blue wool coat she'd been wearing the other day when they were at Sawyer's office. It did the most amazing things for her eyes—they were always a rather piercing blue, but now they were even more vivid and breathtaking.

They rode the elevator while the dogs sniffed each other, Thor waging the most eager inspection. Despite the more negative parts of his history with Charlotte, he did appreciate that they could be quiet together without it growing awkward or painful. The elevator came to its graceful stop on the ground floor, and they walked the dogs through the lobby and out onto the street. The night air was ice-cold and clear, but calm—perfect for a brisk walk. They headed west toward the Hudson River greenway, away from the crowds they'd find if they traveled east toward Times Square.

"Smells like snow." Michael grew up in Maryland, so he'd lived through his fair share of snowstorms.

"I hope so. I love it," Charlotte replied, inhaling deeply. "Which is weird because I generally hate the cold. Maybe it's a Christmas thing."

"I can see that. A reminder of family time and presents under the tree?"

She laughed quietly. "Maybe the part about presents and trees. I avoid most reminders of family time. It doesn't always bring up the best memories."

Many of Michael's family remembrances were unhappy, too. His brother was the only bright spot in most of them. "You and Sawyer seem close. He really put himself on the line when he gave you half of my listings. I could've made it ugly if I'd wanted to."

"You made it a little bit ugly, remember?"

"What? By sticking up for myself and reminding him of what we'd already agreed to? That's not ugly. That's my whole day." Today had been particularly bad. Most of the time, he loved his job. It was the closest he'd get to the adrenaline rush of competition. But today, he'd had to remind himself that he had Abby and this walk waiting for him when he got home. It was the only thing that had kept him going.

"Okay, tough guy. I get it." Charlotte flipped up the collar of her coat as they crossed at the corner to the wide pedestrian-and-bike path along the Hudson River. "As far as Sawyer goes, we're pretty close, but not like he and Noah. Those two are really close, but they had a different childhood than I did. My father always worshipped them. Well, at least until Sawyer inherited the hotel and decided to go against my dad's wishes. Noah sided with Sawyer and that's when things went south. Unfortunately, for me, my relationship with my dad has always been bad."

Michael's father was blustery and intense, not the slightest bit pleasant. He didn't talk about him, though, not even to someone like Charlotte, who he knew quite well. He never saw the point. Discussing him felt like it gave his dad even more power over him. He wouldn't allow that anymore. He'd done his time. "I don't get that, though. You're the only girl. Don't dads love their daughters and want to protect them?"

"Maybe if they aren't the family screwup. My dad seems to view me as nothing more than a liability. Maybe if I was more successful at something he might think otherwise."

Michael remembered how eager Charlotte had been the first time he'd met her, when she'd come in to interview for a position in his agency. He'd never before encountered someone quite so desperate to work for him, although there were a lot of people who would do a lot for a spot on his team. He'd hated telling her no, but he knew from their earliest conversations that he'd struggle to reprimand her or push her to meet her sales quota. There was something about Charlotte that revealed a soft spot in him, one he'd never even known he had before he met her. The idea of delivering bad news to her was duly unpleasant. Probably why he'd merely paved the way for their breakup, rather than pulling the plug himself. He'd figured he'd let her walk away with some sense of control and her pride intact.

"You'll be successful, Charlie. You just need to hit your stride."

"So says the guy who has been hitting his stride since he was ten years old."

She wasn't wrong, but it wasn't as effortless as she made it sound. He hadn't just worked hard, he'd suffered—there was an awful lot of mental anguish wrapped up in succeeding on the highest levels. There were certainly days when he'd wondered if it had all been worth it. The high of those big achievements never lasted, and the crash that followed them was often devastating. "How are things going with your side of our friendly wager?"

"I told you I'm not racing with you. I'll never win."

"First off, you don't know that. Second, something tells me that if you did sell out first, you'd rub it in my face for all eternity."

A sheepish smile crossed her lips. "Okay. Fine. I guess we're racing, but I'm only agreeing to that because I contracted my first unit today. After only one showing, I'll have you know. It's the one time in my life I've had a perfect record at something. It won't last, of course. Somebody's going to bail on me at some point."

"I don't know. These are hot properties. In theory, they should sell themselves."

"I'd like to think I had a little something to do with it."

"I'm sure you did."

"And what about you? Had any luck yet?"

It was an unfamiliar reaction, but he really wanted to

deflect. He didn't want to be winning. "Two. But we'll see how it goes. I'd say it's anyone's game at this point."

Charlotte came to a halt. Thor kept going until his leash went taut. He rounded back to her and yipped.

"Everything okay?" Michael asked.

She looked up at the sky for a moment. Now that they were out of the forest of buildings and right by the water, you could at least see a few stars. Not many—there were too many lights for that. The cold had turned her face into an adorable patchwork of bright pink and creamy ivory. "I'm fine. I forget that I'm going up against the inimitable Michael Kelly. There's a reason my brother wanted you selling the condos."

He grasped her arm. "Don't you dare let this discourage you."

"I'm not. It's just…" She again stared off, this time out over the water, an inky mystery in the dark. She was so beautiful it was hard not to stare. But it was about more than her sweet lips or the blush of her cheeks. He'd learned in real estate, a vocation where you must become an expert in observing behavior, that most people lived in either the eye of the storm or the heart of it. Not Charlotte. She somehow managed to inhabit both at the same time. She was ironclad, and she was a marshmallow. Indestructible on the outside, but impossibly soft to the touch.

He stepped close enough that the white puffs of her breath in the cold reached his cheeks. A snowflake landed on her nose, instantly melting and leaving behind a shiny spot. He reached out and wiped it off with his glove. "It's just what?" The snow was coming more steadily now, and another flake landed on her, this time on her eyelash. It didn't melt, it just fluttered away when she blinked.

"I don't want to talk about it, okay? I have to stop thinking of every little hiccup as if it's an actual set-back. Sometimes things are just a blip on the map."

She was upset that he was one more unit ahead. He wasn't going to apologize, but at least he knew how she felt. So often in their relationship he'd had a hard time arriving at what she was saying or what she wanted. It was only since running into her at Sawyer's office that he'd started to understand that it might have helped his case if he'd done a better job paying attention.

"You're right. No big deal."

She turned to him and smiled. "Shall we head back? I love the snow, but it's really starting to come down. I'm sure you have other things you need to get to to-night."

The only thing he really wanted to get to was Charlotte. Standing there in the cold, in the dark, with a front-row view of her beautiful blend of strength and fragility, he wanted nothing more than to get lost in her. And maybe now was the time to test the waters. She wasn't mad at him right now. Or at least not that much.

He poked his hand through the loop of Abby's leash and cupped both sides of Charlotte's face. Her eyes popped wide. Her lower lip dropped. He didn't wait for anything else. His mouth fell on hers, just a delicate brush of a kiss at first, but warmth quickly bloomed between them. The softness of the kiss was a brilliant counterpoint to everything around them—the hard edges of the city, the loud noises, the too-bright lights. She leaned into him, pressed her chest against his, stoking the fire. Heat built as her lips parted and she turned her head to be closer. For an instant, it was like the breakup had never even happened. She was his again.

Until she wasn't.

Charlotte wrenched her lips from Michael and turned away. "No. We can't. We shouldn't." Funny how every word she sputtered contradicted what her body wanted, but she couldn't let him start something she wasn't prepared to finish. The old Charlotte would throw caution to the wind and worry about the consequences later, but with a baby in the mix, she couldn't afford to complicate things with Michael. Things were going to get messy enough when she finally told him.

"I'm sorry." He reached for her. His breath was jagged, coming out of him in fits and stops.

She could hardly look at him. His face made her want to do foolish things. "You shouldn't have done that. You and I are not a couple. We have no business kissing. It's just going to make things more confusing between us."

"I don't understand what exactly is so confusing. We broke up, Charlotte. Sometimes people get back together."

This was her opportunity to tell him, and the words were tumbling in her mind, but they weren't ready to come out yet. She knew Michael. He thought a romantic dinner set the bar too high. There was zero chance he'd react well to a baby, and she couldn't face the reality of that yet. Plus, with her brother's wedding on the horizon and her need to prove herself to her family a pressing matter, it was easier for everyone if she just stayed mum on the subject. "I know you and that was a let's-have-sex kiss." Good God, it really was a let'shave-sex kiss. And she had to be mad about it. "That was not a reunion. What were you thinking anyway?"

"I was thinking that you're beautiful and I wanted to kiss you."

If anyone knew how to say the right thing at the right time, it was Michael. Charlotte wasn't going to fall for it, though. The old Charlotte would've been fawning all over him. *Oh, Michael, you're so romantic.* She knew that it didn't last with him. If he got a work call right now, he'd take it and not remember what they'd been talking about before he'd picked up the phone. "Well, just stop thinking that. You know we're not right for each other. We want different things. Remember?"

He pursed his lips tightly. "I know. You're right. We do want different things. I'm sorry I kissed you."

There. Now she felt better. Sort of. "Thank you. For apologizing."

He held up his hands in mock surrender. "Yes, ma'am. Whatever you say. No more kissing. I wouldn't want to rock the boat again."

Now she knew why she was so bad at setting boundaries. She hated it. "I really think it's time to head back. I'm freezing." Of course, her lips and some of her more delicate parts were still on fire.

"Yeah. I have some more work to do before bed anyway." He blew out a breath and stuffed his hands in his pockets.

They headed back toward the Grand Legacy, walking in silence. The snow blanketed cars parked along the street and stretches of the sidewalk where no one had walked. Christmas and snow were both in the air and Charlotte had never felt more lonely. If she wasn't pregnant, it would've been easy to keep kissing Michael. She wouldn't have this monumental obstacle to get past. She also wouldn't have the one thing in her future she was truly excited about, the thing that kept her going most days—a baby.

"You know, you still never told me why you went to England." Michael looked down at her, his cheeks ruddy and wind-chapped. They were about a block from the hotel. They needed more ground to cover than that for Charlotte to explain.

"When I said I needed to regroup, it was the truth." She shook her head and concentrated on the sidewalk in front of her, kicking up snow with her boots as she went. "I won't lie, Michael. I felt a little lost after we broke up."

"Huh." He didn't say another word, he just bunched his shoulders up around his ears to ward off the cold.

"*Huh?* What does that mean?"

"I'm just thinking. Give me a minute." He shot her a look that said she needed to back off. "You know, our breakup didn't have to happen. There wasn't any reason we had to rush to get serious, Charlotte. We'd only been together three months. You were the one who was forcing the issue."

Half of a laugh left her lips. They were having two separate conversations and she had too much she still had to keep to herself. *I was forcing the issue because I loved you, you big dummy.* "I really don't want to get into the timing of our breakup." *It'll just break my heart.* "And that's not the only reason I went to England. I needed to decide what my next move was career-wise. It's not a simple thing when you're trying to make a name for yourself in an industry that is essentially a fishbowl and your ex-boyfriend is a great white shark."

Michael stopped at the hotel's revolving door. "You're perfectly capable of standing on your own."

"I know that now. I didn't know it before." Charlotte pushed the brass bar across the glass window. The rush of heat in the hotel lobby was heavenly.

"And I'm not a great white. I'm more of a hammer-head."

They made their way back to the elevator and hopped on board. Abby and Thor were back to sniffing and licking each other. Charlotte wasn't sure how it was so easy for the dogs to figure it out. After all, they'd gone from Thor only wanting sex and Abby fending him off to actually being friends. At this point, friendship was the best-case scenario with Michael, and she had to do everything to steer herself toward that.

"Thanks for the walk," she said when they arrived on the fifteenth floor. "I guess I'll see you around."

"Your brother's wedding is this weekend."

Charlotte nodded, fighting her inner sense of dread. *Please don't bring a date.* "Yes. Definitely that. I'll see you on Saturday."

Six

Charlotte walked into the Grand Legacy speakeasy at 5:15 p.m., for a prewedding cocktail with her brothers. Hers would be nonalcoholic, but she hoped no one would notice. It was Sawyer's idea to close the bar to the public and invite the wedding guests to enjoy a libation before the nuptials. Aunt Fran was in the lobby waiting for her date, an old flame she'd run into outside the hotel a few days ago.

"There's the handsome groom," Charlotte said to Sawyer, finding him standing at the bar with Noah. "How are you holding up? It's a big night."

He gave her a shaky grin, a kiss on the cheek and a warm embrace. Tugging at the collar of his crisp white shirt and straightening the sleeves of his classic black tuxedo jacket, he looked every bit the part of dashing yet nervous groom. "I'm a wreck."

"A happy wreck," Noah said, chiming in. "I told him not to worry. We have security stationed at every exit in the hotel. Just in case Kendall decides to make a run for it."

They all laughed, quite effortlessly she noticed. For a moment, it felt like old times. Noah was always making jokes. When they were kids, he regularly annoyed their father with wisecracks at the dinner table. After their mother had passed away, their dad insisted on eating every meal in the formal dining room at the Locke estate. It had seemed ridiculous and stuffy at the time, but now that Charlotte was an adult, she realized those words—*ridiculous* and *stuffy*—were an apt description of her father.

"You look gorgeous, Charlotte." Sawyer's vision narrowed as he appraised her. "Did you do something different with your hair?"

Charlotte smiled sweetly. Sawyer was as sharp and observant as a person could be, but she'd managed to dodge any pregnancy suspicion. "That's nice of you to notice. I curled it a bit. No big deal."

Sawyer nodded toward the speakeasy entrance. "Michael Kelly's here."

Charlotte was immediately hit with a flash of excitement she wanted to banish from her body. She turned and got her wish. The vision before her zapped whatever stupid part of her brain had decided there was reason her heart should flutter when she heard Michael's name. He'd followed through on his promise to bring a date.

He spotted them and waved, and the pair approached. Michael's companion, she of zero body fat, had a flawless complexion, full red lips, legs that went on forever and jet-black hair so glossy even Charlotte wanted to skim her hands down it.

"Good evening, Locke family." Michael shook hands with Sawyer and Noah, but Charlotte received only a polite nod. It was her fault for having been so adamant about no more kissing—she'd failed to be specific that an affectionate peck on the cheek in the presence of a supermodel would be perfectly acceptable. "I'd like you all to meet Louise." He presented his prize while finishing the introductions.

Charlotte had no choice but to shake the hand of the woman whose butt was in no way acquainted with gravity. "Gorgeous dress."

"Oh, thank you." A perfunctory smile crossed Louise's luscious lips. She was probably tired of fielding compliments all day.

Charlotte berated herself for being generous, especially when she caught the arrogant smirk that crossed Michael's lips. He was so handsome in a tux it made her dizzy—his shoulders were impossibly straight from swimming seven zillion miles over his lifetime, and the black jacket only accentuated the sharp line. He'd worn a traditional tie rather than a bow tie, which made his normally imposing height that much more evident. His hair was perfect, walking that sexy line between impeccably groomed and disheveled.

A waiter came by with a tray of champagne. Michael took two flutes, handing one to Louise. Why that one perfectly appropriate and polite gesture made Charlotte so mad, she had no idea. "No, thank you," Charlotte said to the waiter. She made a mental note to drink an entire bottle of champagne by herself once the baby had arrived and she was no longer breastfeeding. "I'll get something from the bar."

Noah declined as well. "Sawyer and I had better head downstairs to the grand ballroom."

The nervousness returned to Sawyer's face.

Charlotte found it adorable to see her normally unflappable brother so worked up over his wedding day. "Oh, right. You don't want to be late." She kissed him on the cheek. "It's going to be amazing. You'll do great. I love you so much."

"I love you, too," Sawyer said, returning her affection. He and Noah disappeared into the growing crowd in the bar.

Charlotte was now alone with the man who had no earthly idea she was pregnant with his child and the freakishly beautiful woman he would probably end up taking up to his apartment, down the hall from hers, in a few short hours. She should probably sleep with her earplugs tonight.

"Big day for your brother," Michael said.

"Yes," Charlotte replied. She would've said something to continue the conversation, but everything running through her head right now was appallingly impolite. *So, Louise, what's it like living on cucumber slices and ice water?*

"You have the most stunning skin," Louise said, shocking the hell out of Charlotte. "It's like you're glowing."

While putting on her makeup, Charlotte had worried that the pregnancy made her face look more like a moon. Louise's kindness was appreciated, even if it had come out of nowhere. "Thank you."

Louise tugged on Michael's sleeve. "Do you see the way she glows?"

He cast his eyes to Charlotte and their gazes connected like there was nowhere else for either of them to stare. "She's gorgeous. She's always been gorgeous."

Charlotte's heart returned to hyper fluttering. Her breath couldn't find its way out of her throat. She both loved and hated these moments with Michael, especially since they'd become neighbors. Would she ever be able to shrug them off? She couldn't even bear to answer the question. Anything having to do with the future and Michael was a crap shoot at best.

Louise smiled at Charlotte as she took Michael's hand and rested her head against his shoulder. He looked…well, it was hard to put into words. Uncomfortable, but it wasn't like he was protesting. His hand was curled in at her waist and Charlotte couldn't stop studying his long fingers. Nor could she ignore the fact that if she could have anything at that moment, it would be Michael's hand on her. Charlotte's breaths came faster and she was overcome with a deep desire to take a hunk of Louise's shiny locks in her hand and give a non-gentle pull. *Stop it. He's not right for you.* Michael wasn't hers to fight for, and this was her brother's wedding—she needed to behave herself. That meant the two minutes she'd already endured with these two was enough.

"I'm so sorry, but you'll need to excuse me. I'm going to get something from the bar." She didn't wait for a response before she scurried off. "Club soda with lime, please," she blurted to the bartender. She wondered if it would be weird to strike up a long conversation with him, just so she could tell Michael she was busy if he happened to approach her.

"Gladly, Ms. Locke." He was very efficient, almost too quick. He had her drink to her in no time flat.

"Thank you." She tucked some cash into the tip glass, then turned and nearly ran into the man behind her. "Oh, my gosh. I'm so sorry."

He cocked his head to the side. "You're Charlotte Locke, aren't you?" He was fairly good-looking, with dark hair, bright white teeth and kind blue-gray eyes.

She nodded. "Guilty as charged."

He held out his hand, but when she offered hers, he raised it to his lips. "Very nice to meet you. Gabe Underwood. I'm in real estate, too."

For a moment, Charlotte hardly knew what to say. A colleague. Someone had recognized her in the context of her profession, not just because she came from the well-known family who owned the hotel. "It's so nice to meet you, too. Are you a friend of Sawyer's?"

"I've done one project with your brothers. I'm hoping we can do more in the future. I really enjoy working with them."

"Oh, nice. I'll be sure to tell them that we met."

"I heard you snatched away half of the condo listings in the hotel from Michael Kelly. You have no idea how happy I was to hear that."

Charlotte was a little surprised she was the subject of industry gossip. It was deliciously exciting. "The family connection didn't hurt."

Gabe shrugged. "Doesn't matter. All that matters is that you left a chink in Michael Kelly's armor."

Charlotte glanced over at Michael. He made eye contact with her, then slowly shook his head and mouthed the word *no*. As to what that meant, Charlotte didn't know, but she could guess that he didn't like her talking to Gabe. She hooked her arm in his. "Were you going to get a drink?"

"Yes. Can I get you anything?"

Charlotte tossed back her head and laughed. She was mad at herself for wanting to make Michael jealous, but she couldn't help it. "No, thank you. I'm fine."

Gabe got his drink and was back at her side in a flash. He was nothing if not attentive. He cradled a glass of something suitably manly—brown liquor of some sort in an old-fashioned glass with a single ice cube. "So, I have at least one buyer who might be interested in one of the units here in the hotel."

"Oh, really?" Charlotte was starting to like Gabe more and more.

"Young couple. Married three years. He works in advertising, and she's in fashion. They have a two-year-old son and have been living in Connecticut, but they're both ready to be closer to work."

"Sounds like the Grand Legacy could be a good fit. Sawyer is dead set on resident tenants."

"Would early next week work for a showing? You'll have to let me know what your schedule is like."

"I'll work around whatever works for your clients. Evenings are fine if that suits them best."

"Perfect. I'll need your number, though. I don't think I have it." Gabe slid her a sly smile and took a sip of his drink. He wasn't as smooth as Michael, but he wasn't that far off.

Charlotte was thrilled to dig her business card out of her evening bag and hand it over, especially when she could feel Michael's eyes on her. She smiled at Gabe and remained focused on their conversation as they discussed the state of affairs in upscale Manhattan housing. Charlotte did more listening and taking mental notes than contributing, but she figured she had to start somewhere. She was quickly learning two things—real estate in New York, especially in the upper tier of high-priced residential properties, was cutthroat, much more so than she'd really understood. And the other new bit of info was that Gabe did not like Michael, and he maintained that most other agents didn't, either. That part definitely put her in a peculiar spot. However much she and Michael were working in opposition, the bottom line was that she disliked hearing other people speak ill of him.

A female bartender stepped out from behind the bar and clinked a champagne glass with a spoon several times. The chatter in the room softened. "The grand ballroom is now open if everyone would like to make their way downstairs. The ceremony will begin in thirty minutes."

The rumble of conversation resumed to its previous noise level, and guests began to file out of the bar. Charlotte wasn't ready to give up the comfort of having a companion. "I'm up front with family if you'd like to join me," she said to Gabe.

His eyes were wide with surprise. "I would love it. Thank you so much."

There. Now she wouldn't have to feel so bad about Michael and his date. They followed the flow of guests out of the speakeasy, down the grand staircase and around to the ballroom. Inside, they filed up the aisle and took their seats on Sawyer's side in the first row. The ballroom looked splendid, lights dimmed and there were plenty of candles everywhere. Sawyer had been specific about wanting a small ceremony, so there were fewer than one hundred seats. A gorgeous art deco arch had been erected, covered in white calla lilies. Tables for the reception ringed the room, with elaborate but tasteful centerpieces in an elegant color scheme of white, silver and gray.

Charlotte's parents had been married in this room. By all reports, it had been an even smaller affair, since Charlotte's mom was pregnant with Sawyer, just like Kendall would soon be having Sawyer's baby. She wondered how her mom had felt that day. Charlotte didn't really have any warm memories of her parents as a couple. They'd never been affectionate around her, or not that she could remember. She only had sweet remembrances of her mom, and those were hazy at best, worn away by time. Charlotte had been only seven years old when her mother died.

Gabe's phone beeped with a text. "I'm so sorry. I should've muted my phone."

Charlotte touched his arm. "It's okay. Answer it if you need to."

"I'll just be one second." Gabe discreetly walked to the end of their row.

Aunt Fran arrived with her date, a dashing man with a thick head of salt-and-pepper hair. "Charlotte, this is Phil. Phil, this is my favorite niece, Charlotte."

They shook hands. Phil had a killer smile and a firm grip. *Way to go, Fran.*

"Do you mind leaving a seat for my friend, Gabe?" Charlotte nodded in his direction.

Fran cocked an eyebrow and left the seat to Charlotte's left open. "Where'd you find this one?"

"He's another real-estate agent. We were chatting in the bar."

Fran nodded and looked back over her shoulder. She closed her eyes and shook her head. "Oh, no. Your father actually showed up."

"He did?" Charlotte turned to the back of the room. Sure enough, her dad was holding court with his current wife, Catherine. They were greeting several old family friends.

"I probably shouldn't stay," Fran said. "Or I should at least move back a row or two."

How Charlotte despised the drama created whenever her father showed up. "You don't think he'd make a scene, do you? It's Sawyer's wedding, for God's sake."

"I'm not your father's favorite person. You know that."

Charlotte did know that, but she'd never known the reason why. She suspected it might've been that Fran never liked Charlotte's dad and had not wanted her sister to marry him. After Charlotte's mom died, the rift had grown wider. There had reportedly been an argument at the funeral, but Charlotte was so young, she knew nothing of it. The one time she'd dared to ask Fran about it, her aunt had said that no good would come of discussing it. "I love you. That's all that matters. And Sawyer wants you here. You're not going anywhere."

Fran nodded. She was tough as nails. "You're right. If your father decides to make a stink, I'll have no choice but to put him in his place."

As if that comment had just summoned him, Charlotte's dad appeared, holding hands with Catherine, who said, "Hello, Charlotte," and took the seat next to hers.

Her dad leaned across Catherine's lap. "Nice of you to show up for your brother's wedding."

Look who's calling the kettle black. "I've been back

in town for weeks, Dad. You know I wouldn't miss this for the world."

He cleared his throat and crossed his legs. "Oh, that's right. I forget how the three of you are so tightly wound in your allegiance to each other."

Probably because we had to be that way. Otherwise we never would've made it through our childhood in one piece. Charlotte wasn't going to take the bait. If she stopped talking, hopefully her dad would back down, too.

Sawyer and Noah appeared at the archway, as did the minister. Poor Sawyer looked even more nervous, eyes laser-focused on the back of the room. The music started and everyone stood. Gabe quickly took his place next to Charlotte. "I'm so sorry."

"No problem."

Kendall's one and only bridesmaid marched up the aisle, but all eyes were drawn to the bride, who was smiling wide and waiting her turn. Kendall's father had never been a part of her life, and her mother had passed away a few years ago, so she had chosen to stride up the aisle on her own. She took each measured step carefully, as if she was savoring every minute. Charlotte couldn't blame her. She would do the same and soak up every second of the spotlight, if her big day ever came. Not that she had to worry about it anytime soon. Being pregnant and single severely diminished the dating pool.

Kendall was stunning in a gorgeous bias-cut dress of satin charmeuse. The woman wasn't afraid of showing off her curves, even the four-plus months of baby that made her belly beautifully rounded. The smile on Sawyer's face when she reached the archway filled Charlotte's heart with so much love she could hardly stand it. His shoulders relaxed the instant Kendall took his hand. A tear streamed down Charlotte's cheek. At least her brother could have this.

The ceremony was simply beautiful. Kendall and Sawyer exchanged their vows, staring deeply into each other's eyes. Charlotte kept her hands in her lap, wishing she had someone to hold on to right now, and fought back the idea that this day would be better if Michael hadn't dared to bring a date. Her brother and Kendall exchanged rings, and with the single proclamation from the minister, they put the final touch on their big day with a sweet and tender kiss.

Everyone rose to their feet and applauded. Charlotte's tears were coming faster now, and she wasn't really sure why. She wasn't the type to cry at a happy moment. Perhaps it was the sea of mixed emotions she was swimming in every day—excited by the prospect of her baby, nervous about what her family would think, thrilled that her most recent steps forward in her career had been strong, scared to the bone about what Michael would say when she finally broke the news of the pregnancy.

Charlotte turned to Gabe. "Hug?" he asked, tilting his head to the side.

She accepted his offer. She needed it. "Thank you." She then took a bigger, stronger embrace from Fran. "Happy day, isn't it?"

Fran's cheeks were just as streaked with tears as Charlotte imagined hers must be. "Very, very happy, darling." She then pointed toward the back of the room. "It appears as though your father is leaving."

Charlotte looked to see that her dad and his wife were ducking through the doors, bypassing the receiving line. "What a jerk."

"Are you surprised?" Fran asked.

"Not really," Charlotte muttered. "Although I certainly hoped for better."

They made the trip through the receiving line, congratulating Kendall and Sawyer. Meanwhile, the staff cleared away the chairs from the ceremony and guests consulted the seating chart for dinner. The music became decidedly more celebratory, waiters circulated through the room, offering champagne and hors d'oeuvres.

Charlotte caught Michael's eye again. He was definitely watching her. She didn't have much of an opinion about Gabe, but she was starting to form an opinion of Louise, who was now trying to get Michael's attention. She stood in front of him, poking his chest so forcefully that Michael visibly recoiled.

Louise abruptly turned and pointed at Charlotte, then returned her sights to Michael, waved a hand in his face and stormed off. Michael looked up at the ceiling, then went after her. Charlotte had to quiet her immense inner triumph. The truth was, she felt bad for him. She only enjoyed seeing his ego bruised when she was doing the bruising. Somewhere deep inside her was a soft spot for Michael Kelly that went on for miles.

Seven

Dinner at Sawyer's wedding had been a test, and not merely because Michael's date, Louise, had first needed convincing to return to the ballroom, only to complain extensively about the food. The sight line from Michael's seat meant that he could see Charlotte and Gabe perfectly. He'd had to endure every smile, every instant their shoulders touched, every moment of conversation the pair shared. If Charlotte was putting on a show for his benefit, it was an award-winning performance. She seemed smitten.

Now that the meal had been served, the toasts had been made and the dancing was getting underway, Michael had had enough. He couldn't watch them for another minute. And to think he'd been worried about Chad from Hunks with Trucks. This was far worse. Far. Worse.

Now they were flirting. She was giggling and throwing back her head, touching the lapel of Gabe's jacket. It made Michael want to punch a wall, but only after placing Gabe's face squarely in front of his fist. Charlotte glanced in his direction for an instant. The eye contact, the bolt of blue from twenty yards away, registered first in his chest. She knew he was watching and she didn't care. If anything, she was enjoying it.

Louise grasped his chin and jerked his face to hers. "Are you seriously going to stare at Charlotte Locke again? Because if that's what's going on, I'm leaving. I already put up with it the entire time we were upstairs in the bar, and all through dinner."

He shook his head and did everything he could to focus on Louise, but his eyes were drawn to Charlotte, and he couldn't keep them trained where they were supposed to be, no matter how hard he tried. "I'm not staring. If it seemed like I was, I wasn't." *How lame an excuse could I possibly give?*

"I'm serious, Michael. I would much rather be wearing a pair of yoga pants and drinking a glass of wine than standing in a stuffy wedding reception wearing a dress that I can hardly breathe in." She ran her fingers along the lapel of his jacket. She leaned closer, putting her mouth perilously close to his ear. "Or, maybe we could go upstairs and you can help me get out of this thing."

Normally, a proposition like that was a no-brainer. Except Michael's conscience couldn't let him do it. He couldn't leave Charlotte alone with a creep like Gabe. She might think he was a nice guy, or funny or charming—the thought made him shudder—but Michael knew for a fact that Gabe was none of those things. He had to save his dear Charlotte. Even if she might stab him in the eye with a cake fork for doing it.

"You know. I gotta be honest. I really need to work the room. There are a lot of potential clients here and I'd be a fool to pass up a chance like this."

Louise's arms hung at her sides like she was carrying pails of water. It wasn't a particularly flattering look. "You're serious. You're turning me down. Right here. Right now."

He needed to end this. "I'm sorry. I'm glad you came to the wedding with me, but I just don't think this is going to work out. I'm happy to call a car service to pick you up or pay for a cab."

She huffed and held out her hand.

Okay, then. Michael fished his wallet out of his back pocket and handed her a fifty-dollar bill, which she sharply plucked from his fingers. Thank goodness they hadn't kissed or anything more. Then he might worry about being arrested for this transaction.

"You're a jerk. Just so you know."

So I've been told. "I really am sorry. Enjoy the rest of your evening."

In a flash, the woman previously known as his date was gone. Now to get rid of Gabe. He marched over to Charlotte and placed his hand at the small of her back. "Hello, Charlotte. Would you like to dance?"

Gabe's eyes nearly crossed. He stepped in front of Charlotte, physically keeping her out of arm's reach. "Hold on a minute, Kelly. I'm with Charlotte. Back off."

Charlotte peeked around Gabe. "Michael. What are you doing? Gabe and I are having a nice time."

"Yeah," Gabe muttered.

"But is he your date?" Michael was already fairly sure of the answer. He just wanted to hear it directly.

This time, Charlotte elbowed Gabe out of the way. "What if he was my date?"

Ah, the rhetorical question. As good as a real answer. "Then I'd tell you that I was surprised and that you are on a date with a bit of a snake." He shot a look at Gabe. "No offense."

"No offense? How am I supposed to be anything but offended by that?" Gabe countered.

"I call 'em like I see 'em. You're always working an angle, Underwood. Something tells me Noah Locke won't be too happy to find out you came to his brother's wedding and proceeded to pick up his sister."

"He didn't pick me up. We were talking business." Charlotte rolled her eyes.

"See? I didn't pick her up. You can shove off, Kelly."

"Not until I get an answer from Charlotte about that dance. If you aren't picking her up, she's free to dance with any man here. Those are the rules of wedding etiquette."

"Maybe she just wants you to leave her alone."

Charlotte shot Gabe a look that Michael had been on the receiving end of a few times. Michael knew from experience that it was not fun. "Enough. Stop. I'm going to dance with Michael because he asked. Then perhaps we can resume our conversation when I'm done."

Michael knew a lot of things, but one thing he knew above all else—Gabe was not getting another shot at Charlotte while he was still breathing and still in this room. No way, no how.

"I was just trying to be chivalrous." Gabe was backing down. Michael wished he'd slither back into whatever hole he'd come out of.

"That's a nice idea, but I don't need to be saved."

What a reversal of fortune in a very short amount of time. Ten minutes ago, Michael was stewing in his own juices over being stuck with a woman he didn't really care about, but who was preserving his ego. And now Charlotte had given Gabe the heave-ho.

"I don't know that I have ever been more attracted to you," he said. He cupped her elbow and pulled her to the dance floor.

"So you were serious about dancing? I thought you were just being an arrogant ass."

He pulled her into his arms. "Of course I was serious. I wanted to dance with you."

"Was it really me? Or was it more a case of buyer's remorse over your date?"

Louise had been a mistake he was accustomed to making. He'd appraised her by the way she filled out a dress. He hadn't considered much else. "She's a nice girl. Just not right for me."

Charlotte looked up into his eyes. It was so clear she was searching for more, it felt as if she was trying to pry open his soul, one of the more frightening prospects of time with Charlotte. There were no stones left unturned with her, no matter how hard he tried. "Is there such a thing? A woman's who's right for you?" she asked. The question was even heavier than the words. It felt as though it had lifelong implications.

He sighed and pulled her closer. He couldn't handle another second of that probing look on her face. He wanted to enjoy this time with her, not endure it. "You're the closest I've come." He was surprised he could make the admission, but it was the truth. Charlotte hadn't been the one, but that was only because he was certain there was no such thing. As a couple, they hadn't been perfect together, but they'd been good, and he still wasn't sure why good hadn't been enough to make her happy.

"I suppose I should be flattered by that? I came the closest to cracking the mystery of Michael Kelly?"

"I'm not that hard to figure out, Charlotte. I'm really not."

"You're right. A dead-end road is pretty easy to decipher. At least you know where you stand."

"What do you want me to say? That I regret our breakup? Because I do." The air stood still for a moment, and the song changed, but Michael wasn't about to let go of her. If anything, he pulled her closer. He dropped his head toward hers as well, just to draw in her sweet fragrance.

"If you regretted it, why didn't you try to fix it? Why didn't you come after me?"

"You just told Gabe you don't need to be saved."

"I don't. But that doesn't mean I wouldn't have appreciated the gesture."

Michael laughed quietly. He'd never understand the logic behind jumping through hoops for show, especially when you had a reasonable expectation that it wouldn't pay off. "I thought about it, but the next thing I knew, you were in London. That seemed like a pretty obvious answer to me. I wasn't about to go after you in England."

"I always planned to come back."

"Is that why you didn't say goodbye?"

"I really didn't think you cared enough to notice."

Now the thought that had made him laugh seconds earlier only made him sigh. Should he have gone after her? Should he have fought for her? He'd never done it before and he wasn't sure he had the wherewithal to double down on a relationship. You go after a woman, you beg her to take you back, that comes with expectations of commitment. At the very least, you open yourself up to conversations about where things are going and how things are going to work. He had so little confidence in love it was impossible to imagine ever doing that.

"I cared, Charlotte. I really did. However much you think I didn't, I did." Could he say what was waiting at the back of his throat and buried deep in his head? Was he really willing to start something with Charlotte again? She'd said point-blank the other night that there would be no kissing between them, that they had no business being together. So should he try anyway? It would be no easier the second time. If anything, knowing her, she'd make things harder. "And if it makes anything better, I made a mistake when I let you go. You have to believe me when I say that."

Charlotte gazed up into Michael's eyes, his words triumphantly ringing in her ears like church bells in a tower. *I made a mistake when I let you go.* She couldn't decide which part of the statement she liked most, but there was a strong contender for first place. "A mistake?"

He nodded, not shying away from it. "I'm not an idiot. I can admit to it when I mess up. You were jumping the gun all that time we were together, but maybe I did the same thing." He focused intently on her. "Maybe we need to switch to a lower gear and see where that takes us."

Goose bumps raced up Charlotte's arms. Michael's voice had dipped to a deep, gravelly place that made her spine feel like it was made of rubber. His lips parted slightly. Hers mirrored the motion. She wished she could rewind the events of the other night and rescind the moratorium on kissing. "Have any thoughts? About where that should take us?" She knew very well what she was starting, but Michael's admission that he'd made a mistake had her second-guessing every conclusion she'd ever reached about him.

The sexiest smile rolled across his face. "I have lots of thoughts, Charlie. Not sure I should say them out loud in the middle of your brother's wedding reception. This is a fairly G-rated event."

"So we should go somewhere more private?" She licked her lips in anticipation of what he might say next.

"You kill me when you do that, you know. The lick-lipping thing."

Heat rushed to her cheeks. "I do?" No one had ever squeezed so much coquettishness into two syllables before. She was proud of herself.

"Yes. It makes me feel left out." His words made everything in her body go warm, a good ten-degree spike at least. "As for your suggestion that we go somewhere private, yes. I think that's smart."

Charlotte slyly glanced across the dance floor. Sawyer was too caught up in Kendall's eyes to notice a thing. "Yes. Now."

They walked double-time out of the ballroom and down the hall to the elevators. Charlotte's mind was running on adrenaline, which was enough to make her feel drunk, even when she was stone-cold sober. Two more people joined them for the ride upstairs, meaning there could be no touching. Charlotte was dying. That kiss the other night had not been enough. It had taken her twenty-four hours to shake it off. She just wanted more of Michael, now. The other riders got off on the twelfth floor, but that didn't give them much time. Charlotte flattened him against the wall of the elevator, popped up onto her tiptoes and pulled his lips down to hers. They hardly got started when the doors slid open.

"My place?" he asked, tugging her in that direction.

This had been an issue when they were together, but she didn't have the strength to argue now. "Sure." As they made their short trip, in the brief flashes when her brain was working, all she could think was that she should not be going to Michael's apartment. Not now, when night had fully fallen and they had just spent too much time pressed against each other on the dance floor. The heat was still present from his hand in the curve of her lower back. The tingles were still there from that moment when he'd looked into her eyes and told her that he thought he might have messed up. But she couldn't get past one burning question—had she been wrong about him?

"Drink?" Michael asked as he opened the door and they stepped inside.

Charlotte wandered over to the windows on the far side of his apartment, if only to steal a moment and make sure she really wanted this. "Just some water, thank you. I've had my fill." She'd been drinking club soda with lime all night, but she hadn't said a thing when someone suggested it might be a gin and tonic.

She simply hadn't let anyone get her a drink from the bar during the entire wedding. She'd gone so far as to sneak off for a champagne flute of ginger ale when it came time to toast.

"Good." His voice was right behind her, and before she could turn around, his hands were on her shoulders and his body heat was once again pouring into hers. "I don't want a drink, either." His thumbs caressed her shoulders, his fingers pressing into the flesh of her arms.

Tiny zaps of electricity sizzled over the surface of her skin. She sensed what was coming and she knew that she should say no, but she didn't want to. Michael was too much of a sexy, handsome package to deny herself any longer. Even when she worried that she might be nothing more than his prey, she was more than willing. She'd missed this so much. She wanted this with everything she had.

He dipped his head lower and his lips brushed her neck, his stubble scratching her. That sliver of pain put her on notice that this was happening. In the window, she could see their reflection. It was a dreamy shadow, hard edges smudged, dotted with raindrops on the glass. His hair fell forward as he kissed her neck, his mouth now open, his warm tongue making her lose her mind. It felt so good she wanted to close her eyes and languish in every heavenly sensation, but she loved watching him focus on her. For that moment, she seemed like she might be everything to him, precisely what she had once hoped to be.

He hooked his thumbs into her dress straps and pulled them down her shoulders. He gathered her hair in one hand and kissed his way across her back, sending waves of tingles along her spine. His lips weren't just warm, they were on fire. His kiss was urgent. Like he needed to get somewhere. He pressed his long body against hers, his knees met the back of her thighs, his chest met her shoulders and what she could only guess was his rock-hard erection met the small of her back. She pushed right back into him, their bodies grinding against each other as she rolled her head to the other side.

"I want you," she murmured, almost involuntarily. Michael's presence tended to do that to her. Of course, he had no way of knowing that she meant a lot more than sex. She'd be lying if she said that she didn't want him for real. She didn't want to think about how incapable he was of taking this as seriously as she did.

A rough groan left the depths of his throat. "That's a very good thing, Charlie. I'm not sure I could live through it if you didn't."

If only that was true. She pushed aside the thought as he unzipped her dress. The garment slid down her arms and slumped to the floor. She turned and reached for his arm to brace herself as she stepped out of the gown. She expected him to pull her into his arms as soon as she straightened, but he actually stepped back. His eyes were heavy with desire as they raked over the length of her body. Michael had a very big weakness for sexy lingerie. From the look on his face, the way his mouth went slack, her black bustier and panties, made of the finest French lace, had been a very smart choice for this evening.

"You're so sexy. I don't want to take my eyes off you." He yanked at his tie and threw it on the floor as if he couldn't stand the thing.

"Then don't. Don't take your eyes off me." She floated next to him and pushed his coat from his shoulders, then untucked his shirt while he unsubtly peered down into her cleavage.

"Your breasts look incredible in that."

She was about to say that he had no idea, but she'd let him figure that out for himself. Pregnancy had rounded out her endowments nicely. The truth was that she was far less concerned with what was under *her* clothes than what was under *his*. It had been months since she'd seen Michael naked and she didn't want to waste another minute. Her fingers flew through the buttons of his shirt, no small task when he wouldn't stop kissing her. How dumb she'd been that day when they'd walked the dogs and she'd told him to stop kissing her. Whatever heartache was waiting on the other side of Michael Kelly's kiss was surely worth it.

The moonlight in the living room made the sight of his bare chest that much more beguiling. Shadows of blue, black and gold hit every carved ridge of his torso and abs. She pressed her palms against his chest and smoothed her hands over his muscles, which seemed to twitch beneath her touch. She drew in a deep breath and went for his belt. The clatter of metal played nicely against the moan that came from his lips as he kissed his way down her neck. With a pop and a zip, she let his pants drop to the floor. Then she made quick work of his boxer briefs.

It was her turn to torture him, as she stepped away and admired him in the light.

"Get over here," he said.

She shook her head. "I'm enjoying the view." As heavenly as it was to touch him, looking at him was a close second. He was as solid as a man could be, a looming tower of muscle. At the moment, some parts of him were more solid than usual. She couldn't wait to have him in her hand. She couldn't wait to have him inside her.

"No more looking, Charlie. Get over here. I need you to touch me."

She took her time breaching the few feet between them. She'd spent too many nights crying over Michael. If she was going to make a mistake and sleep with him, she wanted to at least feel in charge. She pressed her chest against his, letting him get another eyeful, as she reached down and wrapped her hands around his steely length. "Like this?"

"Yes." He cleared his throat and his chin dropped. She studied his face as his eyelids fluttered shut for a moment and he seemed to grapple with the firm strokes she was taking with her hand.

He cupped the sides of her face and kissed her, fast and loose. Their tongues wound in a dizzying spiral and she didn't let go of him. She caressed softer, loosening her fingers and letting the weight of his erection rest against her palm. He buried his hands in her hair, making a huge mess of it. She couldn't have cared less.

"I have to have you." Michael dropped their kiss and reached down to shimmy her panties past her hips.

Charlotte planted her hands on his shoulders. "We need a condom." No, pregnancy was not a concern, but she had no idea who'd he been with since they'd broken up.

"Two secs. Don't move." He hustled into his room and Charlotte followed orders, staying put. He was back in seconds flat.

"All better?" she asked.

"All better. Now, where were we?" He lifted her up, his fingers sinking into the soft flesh of her bottom as he thumped her back against the wall next to the living room window.

He positioned himself at her entrance and drove inside, strong and forceful. Charlotte wrapped her legs around his waist as her body came to terms with how completely he filled her. Her hands clasped his neck, urging his mouth down to hers. Having him inside her while his lips were on hers was the full-on Michael Kelly package—hot and wet.

He had one hand at the small of her back, but the other hand went to the bustier she was still wearing. He expertly popped open the top three clips and peeled back the lace to reveal her breasts. He pulled her body closer and dropped his head, his lips taking in the taut skin of her nipple. He looped his tongue and she felt her body tighten beneath that touch. It was enough to make the pressure and heat between her legs double.

He again pulled her close and lifted her back from against the wall. He turned and sat on the sofa, Charlotte straddling his lap. Now that he no longer had to hold her, he took care of the final hooks on her garment, and the lace fell to the floor behind her. He took both breasts in his hands and cupped them, rubbing his thumbs back and forth across her nipples, building heat and pressure inside her. He was so strong and nimble, he had no problem lifting her off the couch with his hips, taking strokes that went deeper and deeper. Charlotte thought her eyes might cross from the pleasure, it was so immense.

"Are you close, darling?" His voice was rough.

She nodded, closing her eyes, concentrating on how good and primal this felt. She'd needed this. Maybe this would get Michael out of her system. Hopefully, it wouldn't make things worse. Hopefully, it wouldn't deepen her attachment to him.

He slipped his thumb against her apex and began rotating in small circles, using an ideal amount of pressure. Michael knew she needed some help, and he wasn't afraid to give it. He was definitely the kind of man who wanted her to come first, sometimes more than once. It was one of his many, many selling points. She ground her body against his hand—it felt so good, the insides of her body winding tighter, her hips feeling fitful and restless. She was so close to the edge she could feel herself unraveling, and with a jolt, she gave way. She tossed her head back and called out, placing her hands on his thighs behind her. He followed while the waves of pleasure were still rocketing through her, unleashing himself into her in strong pulses. It was as hot as she could've imagined. She collapsed forward, burrowing her head in his neck. He wrapped his arms around her waist and pulled her close, smoothing back her hair and kissing her cheek.

She'd thought making love with Michael might help get him out of her system, but after their red-hot tryst, she knew it would take at least a few more tries.

Eight

In the soft light of morning, Charlotte's eyes popped open, and she lay frozen in Michael's bed. *What did I do?* The question to herself was quickly answered by a lightning-fast barrage of images from last night—their exodus from the wedding, the kiss in the elevator, the invitation to his apartment, the moment when clothes came off and, of course, the wall.

She clutched the sheets to her chest, careful not to move or breathe too loud while she tried to sort through this in her brain. What did this mean? Did Michael want her back? She'd been very clear on their walk that there could be nothing physical between them when they were on such different pages. Had he changed his mind? Had a few minutes of Gabe Underwood–induced jealousy been enough?

If Michael did want more, it could be the answer to everything she'd spent months worrying about. Single parenthood would no longer have to be the biggest challenge to come. She could switch to regular parenthood, which would be its own feat, but at least she'd have someone to hand off the baby to in the middle of the night if things got particularly hairy. It could be amazing if Michael wanted to pick things up again, but there was only one problem. Charlotte's life did not magically work out that way.

Then there was the not-small matter of what she wanted, a priority she was still learning to put first. Did she even want to get back together with Michael? Would things be any better the second time around? Would he appreciate her? Would he ever love her? There were no guarantees. Her old inclination was to search for meaning in his words, like a woman reading tea leaves. She was such a sucker for a well-delivered line, especially when it came from a mouth as gorgeous as Michael's. Last night's, out on the dance floor, had been a doozy. *I made a mistake when I let you go.* But no. She needed to stop judging a man first by his words and second by his actions. Fran had spent a good chunk of time drilling this into her head: *It's actions first, words second, Charlotte. Not the other way around.*

Judging Michael by his actions was Job One this morning. Would he offer to bring her coffee? That would be a point in her mental "yay" column. Be sweet? Want to make love again? Yay and yay. As exciting as the prospect was of things finally moving in the right direction, she needed to temper her expectations. And get on with it already. She needed to wake him up.

Prepared to press a gentle morning kiss to Michael's cheek, she carefully and quietly rolled over.

To an empty bed.

She tore back the covers as if all six feet and many more inches of him could possibly be hiding under there somewhere. "Michael?" she called, sitting up in bed. No answer. She patted down the mattress for a hint of residual body heat, but the sheets were as cold as if no one had slept there at all. She climbed out from under the duvet and hustled over to his dresser, pulling out a soft, worn T-shirt of his and threading it over her head. It lightly skimmed her legs, the hem coming down to the middle of her thighs. "Michael? Are you up?" She used her voice a little more forcefully now, but there was still no reply.

Maybe he went out to get pastries and coffee. The passion-fruit Danish from the bakery a few blocks away. Yes, that was it. That had to be it. That was a nice and thoughtful thing to do. She walked into his bathroom, peed and washed her hands, then ventured out into the apartment, hoping to find a note. Her search for evidence of a sweet, early morning scone run turned up nothing more than a neat stack of her clothes from yesterday on the end of his couch. He'd spent enough time milling around the apartment this morning to do that? What else had he done? And where had he gone? Her heart began to thump anxiously. Her heart knew what was up, but her brain was still computing.

Abby was also gone. Aha! He'd probably taken her downstairs for a few minutes. That didn't completely warrant a note, right? Maybe a text was in order. She pulled her cell out of her handbag.

Hey. Where are you?

As hard as she stared at her phone, no answer came. With every passing tick of the clock, and every lap she took in his living room, Charlotte realized more and more that she was making excuses for Michael. If the situation had been reversed, she would've left a note. She wouldn't have slept with someone and dared to leave her apartment for more than two seconds without letting the other person know what she was doing. She would have replied to a text, no matter the circumstances. This was classic Michael and the problem with classic Michael was that he knew how to please her in bed, but everywhere and everything else was sorely lacking.

She needed to put an end to her own idiocy. She needed to stop acting like Charlotte, and start acting like Michael—cold and calculating, taking what he wanted and leaving everyone else to fend for themselves. She scooped up her clothes from the wedding and decided it wasn't even worth it to change. She and Michael were still the only residents of their floor and it was very early Sunday morning, only a few minutes after seven. She'd be fine to bolt down the hall to the safety of her apartment.

She opened the door and first made sure the coast was clear. She doubted she'd run into a member of the hotel staff, but she wanted to be sure. Holding her head high, she marched down the hall, but she began to shrink with every step. This walk of shame reminded her too much of the night she and Michael broke up. It left her with the same empty feeling, but now it was more pronounced, leaving her feeling even more hollow. That time, she hadn't been aware that she was pregnant with Michael's child.

Just as she passed the elevators, she heard it ding. Half-naked, her survival instinct kicked in and she ran to her end of the hall, but she stopped as soon as she rounded the corner and was out of sight. She poked her head out to see Michael, Abby and a woman step out into the hall.

"Do you mind waiting here for a moment?" he asked the woman. "I just need to put my dog in my apartment, then I can give you a tour of some of the available units."

"Of course. I'll wait." The woman was statuesque and raven-haired, and although there was no hint of romance between her and Michael, the fact that she was beautiful irked Charlotte.

A showing? He's doing a showing? He's impossible. Charlotte had seen enough. She keyed into her apartment and closed the door behind her, collapsing against it. She was still ruminating over what was going on when Thor yelped from the confines of his crate. She let him loose, thankful she'd thought enough to text Fran last night and ask her to take him out. He yipped and vied for her attention, so Charlotte invited him up onto the couch and endured countless licks and doggy kisses.

"Abby's dad is mean," Charlotte said to Thor. "He's a real jerk."

Thor stopped licking for an instant and cocked his head, making his ears flop.

"I don't think you should run down there anymore. Whatever it is that you think you have going on with Abby probably isn't going to happen anyway, buddy. She's too much like Michael. Too much on her own plan." The more she thought about this, the angrier she got. He'd had an appointment for a showing? That was why he hadn't left her a note. He hadn't wanted her to know what he was doing. That was Michael, though— always selling and always competing. Why she should

fault a duck for looking and acting like a duck was beyond her.

Her phone beeped with a text. She anxiously dug it
out of her evening bag while anger wedged itself in her
thoughts. She was ready to give Michael a piece of her
mind…only to see that the text was from Noah.

Meet you in the lobby in fifteen?

Oh, crap. She'd completely forgotten that the family was meeting for breakfast with Sawyer and Kendall
before they left for their honeymoon. With Christmas
almost here, they were only going away for a few days,
down to Miami. They had a longer trip planned for
January. Sawyer had been insistent that the three siblings were going to spend more time together now that
he had a child on the way. Things were not going to
be splintered just because their father seemed to want
things that way. Charlotte agreed, especially with her
surprise bun-in-the-oven.

Make it thirty? There was no way she'd be ready to
go in fifteen minutes.

Plus, she had a text of her own to send. Another one,
to Michael. Thanks for letting me know where you were
this morning. So nice to wake up to an empty bed.
Michael was fluent in sarcasm. It was one of the best
ways to get to him.

Noah replied, Moving a little slow this morning?

Charlotte couldn't help but think that a hangover
would be better than the bitter sting of reality Michael had handed her this morning. Just primping. You
know me.

Okay. I'll let everyone know you'll be late.

Where did you go? This time, the text was from Michael.

She wrestled with how to reply—she had nothing in the way of a snappy comeback, although if she could come up with one, she'd find a way to include Gabe in it. That would get under his skin. But with only a half hour to shower and get downstairs for breakfast, she decided it was better to let Michael stew in his own juices.

In world-record time, Charlotte showered, put on her makeup, dressed, zipped Thor downstairs for a pee break, begged a bellboy to return the dog to her apartment and was in the hotel restaurant, headed to the very back, where her family—Noah, Aunt Fran, Sawyer and Kendall—was nearly finished splitting one of the Grand Legacy's world-famous cinnamon rolls.

"So sorry I'm late," Charlotte said, taking hugs from her brothers, who had both gotten up from the table. Consummate gentlemen.

Sawyer waved it off. "We're used to it by now."

Charlotte took her place in between her oldest brother and Fran, then ordered a cup of herbal tea and asked the waitress if she could bring another cinnamon roll. She'd missed out on too much of that yummy action. Kendall grasped Sawyer's arm and rested her head on his shoulder. The one thing Charlotte had noticed yesterday at the wedding, which was even more noticeable now, was just how comfortable they were with each other. It was like they'd known each other their whole lives. Maybe that was the yardstick for a good relationship—when you find someone and you effortlessly fit together. It doesn't have to mean it's perfect. Every couple argues.

But some people are simply meant for each other. Sawyer and Kendall seemed to be that couple.

Charlotte couldn't help but be at least a little bit jealous. It would've been nice if she could've gotten pregnant by the one man on the planet, wherever he might be, who was right for her. But at this point, lots of things would be nice, and as Fran had said a million times, dwelling on the past was going to get her nowhere.

"Where'd you get off to last night, Charlotte?" Noah asked. "We missed you at the end of the reception."

Fran cast Charlotte a sly look and took a sip of her coffee.

Oh, yeah. That. "I was tired. I didn't want to bring down the whole party by falling asleep at the table."

"You didn't seem tired. You danced for quite a while with Michael Kelly." The tone in Sawyer's voice was unmistakable, and Charlotte couldn't help but recall the first time this subject had come up between the two of them.

"He was rambling on about real estate. He can talk about it forever. I swear the man just likes to hear his own voice. I'd tell him to shut up, but sometimes he actually shares valuable information."

"You two are cute together," Kendall added. "He's really quite handsome."

"We've been married fewer than twenty-four hours and you're already scouting out other guys?" Sawyer asked, cocking an eyebrow at Kendall.

She swatted his arm. "Shush. It's the truth. And I was talking about him in the context of your sister, not me. I'm sure Charlotte would love to meet a nice guy."

Charlotte nearly sputtered a mouthful of tea across the table. All she could do was nod and smile. Of course she wanted to meet a nice guy. She just wasn't sure where exactly a girl went about finding one.

A grin crossed Fran's face. "Speak of the devil. Look who's on his way over here right now." She gave Charlotte a little kick under the table for good measure.

Everyone at the table looked up, and sure enough, here came Michael. He was dressed in jeans and a black sweater, looking far more handsome than was fair. "I'm so sorry to interrupt your family breakfast. I was hoping to steal a moment with Charlotte."

"Can this wait until later?" she answered, looking up at him, hoping the tension in her face could convey how much she did not want to speak to him right now.

"It'll only be a minute. You haven't been answering my text messages."

Sawyer cleared his throat and that sent Charlotte into a panic. She didn't need to give her brother any more material to form an opinion of what may or may not be going on between herself and Michael. "Excuse me, everyone. I'll just be a second."

Michael blazed a trail through the restaurant and Charlotte followed. Whether she was mad at him or not had no bearing on the fact that he looked better than amazing in a pair of jeans. "What happened this morning? I was gone for twenty minutes and you disappeared. Did you not enjoy yourself last night?"

Charlotte's shoulders dropped in frustration. "I don't know how long you were gone, but I'm pretty sure it was more than twenty minutes. Regardless, I woke up, you were gone, there was no note and no explanation, but you sure took the time to fold my clothes. I even sent you a text and you didn't answer. It just started to feel an awful lot like a repeat of the old Charlotte and Michael show. I hate that show, Michael. Just so you know."

He frowned. "I didn't see the text until right before I sent one to you, which you didn't bother to answer, either. I figured I should let you sleep. I never imagined you would wake up so early."

"I always get up early, Michael. Do you really not remember that about me?"

He scratched his temple. "Yeah, I guess I remember that. I was mostly just thinking about how tired you seemed last night."

"Sex against a wall will do that to a person," she snapped. "And you had a showing this morning? Or were you trying to hide that from me?"

The look that crossed his face was pure annoyance. "I don't hide anything, ever. I took Abby for a walk, the woman I ended up showing the apartment to was in the lobby. She wanted to pet Abby, we started to talk and the next thing I knew I'd sold another unit."

Of course he'd sold another unit. How silly of her to think anything less could've happened. How these things just fell into his lap was beyond her. "I'm glad you've had such a productive morning. Look, last night was really fun, but you and I have a terrible time getting on the same page, so I think it's best if we just go back to the part with no kissing or touching."

"I thought we were spectacularly on the same page last night."

He was not kidding about that. They were. But sex wasn't enough to make her happy, just temporarily giddy. "That part is fine. It's everything else that's messed up. This morning has been the perfect illustration of that."

"I'm sorry I didn't leave a note."

"It's not an indictment, Michael. So you didn't leave a note. It's not about the note. It's about our complete incompatibility. I obviously need more than you're equipped to give, which is exactly why we broke up in the first place." She patted him on the shoulder. "Now, I need to go spend time with my family. I'll see you around, okay?"

"Around? What does that even mean?"

"The hall? The elevator? The lobby? Anywhere else and we just seem to get into trouble."

Nine

Judging by the view, being a professional woman really suited Charlotte. Michael watched as she approached him at the elevators—she was teetering on heels that made her legs far too appealing. Her skirt was full and swishy, her blouse crisp and fitted. Her blond hair was up in a twist, or was it a bun? Michael wasn't sure what it was called. He only knew that it was sexy as hell.

"Morning," she said, standing straight and looking only at the elevators.

"Morning, yourself." He was still trying to sort out what had happened at the wedding, and after it.

The elevator doors slid open and he gestured for her to go first. He had Abby with him, and he firmly believed in being a gentleman. They stood inside, shoulders a polite distance apart, neither making eye contact.

"Busy morning?" he asked.

"I have a showing at ten. Eighteen B."

"No way. I'm showing Eighteen C at ten as well. On my way down to meet the client now."

"You're taking Abby?"

"He's a huge dog-lover. I figured she could help seal the deal."

She glanced at him for a second and nodded. "Nice. This was a referral from Gabe Underwood. The Taylors. John, Jane and their little boy. I'm meeting Gabe and them downstairs in a minute."

Ugh. And I thought today was going to be a good day. "So you got some business out of Gabe at the wedding?"

She twisted her lips and shot him a look. He hadn't meant for it to come out as a suggestive comment. "I did."

A big part of him wanted to just let this go, but he couldn't. "I hate that we've gone back to our old dynamic. It was more fun when we only hated each other a little."

"I don't hate you, Michael. I'm simply trying to protect my own feelings and concentrate on my career. If anyone should be able to appreciate that, it should be you. It's exactly what I told you. Nothing has changed." The elevator slowly pulled to a stop, then dinged and the doors slid open. Out she marched without him.

Indeed, nothing had changed. Except Charlotte. She seemed different now, and it was becoming more pronounced every day. She was more confident. She stood up for herself. She put him in his place. He'd never had to live with any remorse over losing a girlfriend before, but he was definitely suffering from the effects with her. Watching her walk around the world as if she didn't need him at all was again making him wonder just how badly he'd messed up when he'd let her go. "Okay, then," he muttered to himself. He followed her into the lobby, but Charlotte took strides so long he couldn't keep up, which was saying a lot considering how much longer his legs were.

Michael greeted his client, Samuel Baker, an art dealer looking to move back to New York after a few years in Los Angeles. Michael had sold him his last New York apartment. "I hope you found the hotel with no problem."

"Yep. Yep. Is this the same dog you had the last time?"

Michael leaned down and scratched Abby behind the ears. "The same one. This is Abby."

"Hello, beautiful," Mr. Baker said, showing her affection.

"Shall we head upstairs?" Michael couldn't stand another minute in the same space with Gabe Underwood. He was across the lobby, laughing like an idiot at Charlotte's jokes. He was so flirtatious with her, it made Michael insane. Couldn't she see that he was just sucking up to her as a means of getting more business from Sawyer and Noah? Or maybe she didn't care. Maybe she only wanted to get another buyer out of him.

Michael and Mr. Baker took the elevator, but Samuel was taking the hall at a pretty slow pace once they arrived on the eighteenth floor. It wasn't long before Gabe and Charlotte caught up to them, along with Gabe's clients, the Taylors and their son, who was toddling down the hall.

"Doggie!" the little boy exclaimed.

Mrs. Taylor tugged him along. "Yes. A doggie."

Michael opened up Eighteen C and went to work. Mr. Baker loved the layout of the living room and the views, which was all fantastic news, but Michael was again having a hard time focusing when he could hear Charlotte laughing from next door.

"Are the walls really that thin?" Mr. Baker asked.

Apparently. "Oh, it won't be that bad when there's furniture in both units and artwork on the walls. Plus, I know the agent next door and she's especially giggly. Don't worry. She won't actually be living there."

Mr. Baker nodded. He seemed convinced enough by the explanation. "Is that the blonde?"

"That's the one."

"She's a cutie. I mean, I know I'm not supposed to make comments like that, but she is."

"You're not wrong, Mr. Baker. You're not wrong at all. Now let me show you the master suite."

The rest of the showing went smoothly. Michael hardly had to sell at all, and that meant he was done well before Charlotte and Gabe were showing any sign of slowing down next door. Part of him wanted to hang around and find out what was happening, and another part of him knew he needed to get a life, get over Charlotte and get back to the office. He closed the door on what would soon be Mr. Baker's apartment and locked up. He was about to press the button to call the elevator when he heard a screeching yelp. He turned and the Taylors' little boy was headed straight for him.

"No!" the child yelled. "No new house."

Michael was terrible with kids, but somewhere inside he must have some protective instinct because he crouched down and spread his arms wide to keep the boy from running right past him. "What's up, little man?"

The kid collided with Michael's arms. His cheeks were puffy and red, his brown eyes wide with shock. Then he saw Abby. "Doggie!"

Abby had a different skill set than Michael when it came to children. She loved them and had the perfect easygoing attitude to go along with it. She dutifully let the boy pet her, sitting still and putting up with some rough handling. "Gentle." Michael demonstrated the proper petting technique.

Mrs. Taylor tore out into the hall. "I'm so sorry." She took the little boy's hand and turned to Charlotte, who had come out to see what was wrong. "This is the third place we've looked at today and I think he's had enough. My husband and I really think this is the place for us, but maybe we should come back on another day when out little guy isn't so tired."

Charlotte nodded, but you could see the disappointment on her face. "Of course. Whatever you think is best."

"I'm happy to hang out here with him in the hall if you guys need to finish up." Michael wasn't sure what had come over him. He liked Charlotte, he cared about her and wanted to see her succeed, but he wasn't the guy who typically tried to save the day. He had a mountain of work to do. And yet, he couldn't walk away when he knew that one tiny favor might do Charlotte some good.

Mrs. Taylor turned back to Michael with a questioning look. "Are you sure?"

"Yeah. He loves the dog. She clearly loves him. We'll just play for a few minutes." Michael sat down on the floor and leaned back against the wall, still holding on to Abby's leash and keeping a close eye on the little boy and the dog.

"That would be amazing. Thank you so much." Mrs. Taylor turned to Charlotte and squealed. "That means we can buy a house today."

Charlotte looked right at Michael, her beautiful blue eyes pulling on him like they had their own gravitational force. "Thank you," she whispered. "I owe you one."

"I'll keep that in mind," he muttered to himself after she'd gone.

After about twenty minutes, the Taylors emerged from the apartment and retrieved their son.

"Thank you, again," the dad said.

"No problem," Michael replied, standing up and brushing his pants clean. He gave Abby a pat for her extrapatient behavior.

Gabe and Charlotte were next to appear as the Taylors took the elevator downstairs.

"She was amazing in there, Kelly," Gabe said. "I gotta tell you, she really knows her stuff, and she couldn't have been any more charming if she tried. My clients fell in love with Charlotte well before they fell in love with the unit. Which they just bought, I should mention."

Charlotte blushed and playfully knocked Gabe in the arm. "Stop. You're embarrassing me."

Michael had no doubt that when it came to charm, Charlotte could win lots of people over. Maybe that was part of the reason why he just couldn't seem to get over her—she was constantly amazing him and proving him wrong. He'd always contended that real estate was a business only for the truly brutal, but judging by the look on Charlotte's face, she was managing to do pretty well by simply being her normal lovely self.

Gabe consulted his watch. "Well, I have to scoot. The Taylors are waiting for me downstairs. You sure you don't want to join us for lunch? I'm sure the Taylors would love it."

Charlotte grinned wide. She was so full of pride she looked as though she was about to explode. Michael could remember what it was like when this was all new. Maybe he wasn't tough. Maybe he was just jaded. "I'm so sorry. It sounds wonderful, but I have two more showings this afternoon and some other work to do."

Gabe held up his hands in mock surrender. "I get it. You're busy. Not surprised. Just keep it up." He grasped her elbow and kissed her cheek. "Maybe you and I can have a meal on our own some time. Celebrate the sale, together?"

Michael was as uncomfortable as he'd ever been. He found his fingers coiling in his palm, like they were itching to unleash one well-placed punch.

"That's very sweet of you. I don't like to mix business and pleasure, but if you want to have dinner as colleagues, that would be quite nice."

The disappointment on Gabe's face was a nice reward. Michael felt like he could exhale. "Oh, sure. Of course." He didn't look at Michael at all. "I'd better head downstairs."

"Nice save," Michael said when Gabe was finally gone. "It's not easy to turn someone down for dinner."

"It wasn't a save. I have no interest in Gabe. He's a nice enough guy, but our relationship is about work and nothing else."

Michael had to temper the good feelings her statement brought about. She'd made the same argument about Michael, too. Just work. No pleasure.

"Headed down to your apartment?" he asked.

"Yeah. I need to call Noah and make a plan with him. He wants me to do a walk-through on a project he and Sawyer are thinking about taking on. They want my opinion."

"Residential?"

"Yeah. Downtown. I'm hoping this means good things for me." They made their way to the elevator. "Noah hinted that they might have another project for me to work on. At first I'd thought I only cared about the listings in the Grand Legacy, but now that we're getting down to the wire, I need to start thinking about what's next, you know?"

"Of course." He had to wonder what else or who else she saw in her future. Could he ever catch up to her and be comfortable with the idea of more than casual?

"Thank you again for helping with the Taylors' son."

"I was happy to help. It's funny, because I'm usually terrible with kids. But that little guy was pretty nice."

She shot him an indecipherable look and sighed. "Well, thank you."

"So. Another sale. How many more units does that leave for you?" he asked.

"Three. You?"

"I'm down to two."

This time, she didn't seem in any way defeated by the knowledge that he was ahead in their race. "It's close. I predict a photo finish."

They rode the elevator down to the fifteenth floor. Michael was overcome with a deep desire to kiss Charlotte. She'd always been irresistible, but right now, it went well beyond that. She seemed brighter, more beautiful, so full of life. Perhaps it was the shine of success. It looked good on her.

"Hey. I'm still hosting that cocktail party I told you about. The one on the twenty-third?"

"Ah. The family avoidance party?"

"And networking. Don't forget that. I'm having it downstairs in the cellar bar. Do you want to come? You didn't give me a definitive answer the first time."

"Is this a date? Because I'm not going as your date."

Wow. He really was in the same miserable boat as Gabe. "I'd like to be able to buy you a drink, if that's what you're asking. We could even ride the elevator together."

She thought long and hard. "Okay. Yes. I'd love it. Thank you. As long as this is about work and nothing else."

"It's nothing else. I promise."

Ten

Charlotte had to go to Michael's party. It would be stupid not to go. Downright foolish. There would be professional contacts to be made, better yet in the scope of a social gathering. Charlotte could rock a party like nobody's business. She was built for it. The trouble was the host. Michael was built for making her do stupid things.

Fresh out of the shower, hair up in a towel, she attempted to apply liquid eyeliner—no easy feat in itself—but her hand wouldn't stop trembling, leaving her with more of a fat wobbly smudge than a chic and seductive cat eye. It was all her dumb heart, nervous about tonight. It couldn't settle on the proper speed, so it was instead jumping up and down like an overcaffeinated rabbit, sending quakes and tremors through her arms and legs. She set down the tube of eyeliner on the bathroom counter and drew in a calming breath, looking at herself in the mirror. Hers was not the face of an in-control businesswoman. Frankly, all she could see was the same desperate teenage girl, her old self, clamoring for approval and love. *I have to get a grip.* She had to keep Michael at a professional distance tonight. He may have worked his way into her better graces by watching the Taylors' son, but tonight was about proving a point to herself. She had to know that she and Michael could coexist on an amicable, platonic level. The trouble was the tone of Michael's voice in the elevator when he'd reminded her of the party. Every time she'd ever heard him talk that way, they were either *in* bed or *on* their way there.

Her heart couldn't afford another trip into Michael's bed. With the baby on the way, she had to keep her lines drawn. She had no doubt that the instant she finally revealed the news to Michael, that's what he would do. *I have the distinct impression you want far more from this relationship than I am prepared to give.* Even now, the words, which were permanently etched in her memory, stung like a fresh slice through her heart. There was no mistaking just how damning those words were, especially for a woman in love. Talk about closing a door on their future—Michael had slapped a padlock on it and promptly tossed the key.

Of course, he'd had to keep tempting her with his physique and sharp wit, with his smarts and the way he looked in a pair of jeans. He had no clue what was on the line. They weren't even on the same playing field anymore. He thought they were flirting. He thought they'd had a fun night of hot sex. She had to set him straight, but not until her half of the Grand Legacy units were sold. By then, she could tell her family. By then, she could tell Michael and they would no longer have work entanglements. She didn't want him to back down from their competition because she was pregnant with his baby. She wanted to win this, fair and square, if only to prove to herself once and for all that she could make it on her own.

But first, she had to find a dress she could still fit into. Rifling through her closet, she knew on a purely practical level which one it would be—the red one. The one she'd bought a year ago at a designer sample sale. It had been a size too big, which was reason enough to buy it, as there was nothing more fun than stepping out of the dressing room in a fancy designer showroom and hearing the sales woman declare, "Oh, my! It's much too big." Charlotte had been having a skinny day that day. Probably because she'd recently recovered from a stomach virus. Regardless, the dress had been a steal, and she'd brought it home, but she'd never worn it. Now that she was a good five pounds heavier, it was the perfect choice.

She slipped her way into it and took a gander in the full-length mirror in her bedroom. The dress was professional. No ruffles, no thigh-high slit or plunging neckline. But it was off-the-shoulders, and the simple silhouette left nothing to the imagination. Of course, Michael needn't search far in his memory to recall what Charlotte looked like naked, but the dress and the idea of him seeing her in it still made her nervous. She turned sideways in the mirror and smoothed her hand over the tiny pooch. That was a baby. Her baby. For now, if anyone asked, she'd simply say she'd hit the Christmas cookies and eggnog a bit early this year.

She glanced at the clock. It was already after eight.

She believed in the notion of being fashionably late, but Michael was a stickler for punctuality. He wouldn't take kindly if she pushed things too far. She popped in a pair of sparkly earrings, stepped into the bathroom to smooth out the bad eyeliner job and then went into her closet to work her way into the only red shoes she owned—sky-high and strappy. A month from now, she probably wouldn't even be able to get her feet into these shoes and her center of gravity would be all kinds of wrong. She might as well milk tonight for all it was worth.

Charlotte arrived downstairs at the newly opened cellar bar by eight twenty. The room was absolutely buzzing with frenzied conversation, with cheerful holiday music as a softer counterpoint. Charlotte eased her way inside, scanning the crowd for Michael. This space was another of Sawyer's many triumphs in bringing the Grand Legacy to its former glory. The ceiling's soaring archways were clad in warm white mother-of-pearl tile, accented with narrow strips of black glass. The original wrought-iron chandeliers had been restored and were stunning when lit, tastefully decorated with fragrant swags of fresh pine garland and holly berries.

Off in the far corner, next to the bar, Michael was talking animatedly with another man of similar build and stature. Not many humans could claim such an impressive physical pedigree, and Charlotte was dying of curiosity to know who it was. She saw a few people she knew as she threaded a path for herself through the crowd. At least she'd have some people to talk to after she'd chatted with Michael. She didn't want to take too much of his time tonight, although part of that strategy was entirely her own self-interest. Every minute with him made her more confused.

"There he is," Charlotte said as she greeted Michael. "Our brave and fearless host."

She loved the way the utterly charming smile broke effortlessly across his face. He was enjoying himself. For a man with the world at his feet, he didn't seem to do that nearly enough. "Hello, Charlotte. It's good to see you." He put his arm around her and gave her a friendly squeeze. "Especially in that dress," he muttered into her ear. "Wow."

Charlotte was sure that people fifty feet away could feel the heat radiating from her face. Michael's compliments did that to her. "Thank you for the invitation. I appreciate it."

"Of course. I want you to meet my brother, Chris."

Charlotte felt as though a lightbulb was going off over her head. "Oh! You're Michael's brother. No wonder you're so freakishly tall and handsome."

Chris's grin and his laugh were almost exactly like Michael's. He shook Charlotte's hand, his fingers dwarfing hers. "It's nice to meet you. I've heard a lot about you."

Charlotte cast her sights up at Michael. "Whatever he said, it's a lie."

"Actually," Chris said, "he had nothing but good things to say."

Michael waved to someone in the crowd. "I think that's my cue to leave you two alone. Plus, I have a potential client on the line here. I want to get a drink or two in him and see if I stand any chance of finding him a place to live."

Chris leaned back against the bar. "He really did say

a lot of nice things about you. Which is pretty surprising. He isn't always that forthcoming with his love life."

"But you know we're not involved anymore, right?" Charlotte flagged the bartender and asked for her new usual—a club soda with lime.

Chris nodded. "He not only told me you broke up with him, I even got a phone call about it. Almost no women rank that highly with my brother. You should feel honored."

"Somehow it feels like more of a dubious distinction. Plus, it's not fair to say I broke up with him. It felt more like a set-up. He just made me do the dirty work."

"Interesting. I suppose every story has more than one side, doesn't it?"

"Yes, but my side is the right one." Charlotte smiled wide. She liked Chris. She could see that although the brothers were notoriously competitive, they were close. "So, what brings you to the big city? You live in Washington, DC, right?"

"I do. I've been coming at this time every year for a while now. I like to lend my brother the moral support, even if he insists he doesn't need it."

"Moral support for what? Christmas?"

"No. It's—" Chris stopped right in the middle of his sentence. His brows drew together in a look that Charlotte could only describe as dumbfounded. "Do you not know about this?"

The tone in Chris's voice sent shivers down Charlotte's spine. "I have absolutely no idea what you're talking about. Michael never talks about himself. I'm shocked I knew he had a brother in the first place. No offense, but he doesn't talk about your family much at all. It's mostly in the context of swimming and how much your childhood revolved around that."

Chris cast his gaze in Michael's direction. "I'm not really sure I should spill the beans. I mean, there has to be some reason he never told you. And I know it still bothers him. He and our father don't even speak anymore because of it."

Charlotte grasped Chris's forearm. "Okay. You're going to have to tell me something. I need to know that he didn't murder someone."

Chris shook his head and laughed quietly. "No. No murder. Just an engagement party that went horribly wrong and two parents who expect nothing but absolute perfection from their sons."

"I'm all ears."

As Chris told her the story and Charlotte peppered him with questions, it became abundantly clear that Michael, the guy with the bulletproof veneer, the guy who never loses or suffers, had done exactly that. When he'd retired from swimming, his parents were gravely disappointed. They wanted him to bring home more Olympic gold, but Michael wanted out. He'd been dating a senator's daughter, and his parents decided that was his salvation. They told him he had to propose. He did, even though he didn't love her. They'd thrown an extravagant engagement party, but Michael couldn't go through with it. He'd been bullied enough. Michael called it off. At the party.

In front of two hundred guests Michael hardly cared about, his father flew into a rage. He unleashed a tirade of Michael's faults, his failures and missteps. Michael couldn't take it anymore. His dad threw a punch and missed. Michael countered and his fist landed square on his dad's jaw. Everything after that spiraled down. There was no reconciliation. There was no forgiveness. Michael was an ungrateful disappointment and no longer welcome at home.

When Chris finished telling the story, he seemed so sad. There he was, stuck between his brother and his parents. And there was Michael, trying his hardest, and coming up short. Charlotte thought her childhood had been rough, but it was nothing compared to Michael's. And now that she had this giant chunk of new information, she had to wonder if she'd read Michael wrong all along.

Michael was keen to sign his potential new client, Alan Hayes, a hotshot tech whiz with very deep pockets, but he would've been lying if he'd said he wasn't distracted by Charlotte and Chris's conversation. It wasn't a bad diversion. Charlotte was jaw-dropping in that dress. He'd never thought of himself as a red-dress sort of guy. He was a bigger fan of black with a healthy dose of skin—a look Charlotte also carried off with no problem. But tonight? The red? Michael knew he was in trouble the minute she walked into the room.

He liked seeing Charlotte and Chris clearly enjoying their time together. Michael was an expert at keeping his family and friends separate. He'd raised it to an art. As close as they were, he'd even been hesitant to invite Chris to tonight's party. Normally when Chris came to town, they would go out to eat and catch a hockey or basketball game—anything that meant they could spend time together, but not get too mired in socializing. Nobody in Michael's professional life knew about his private past and he intended to keep it that way. It wasn't embarrassment. It was a topic he wanted dead and buried.

For that reason, he didn't want to leave Charlotte and Chris alone for too long. He and Chris were alike in many ways, but with one exception. Chris loved to talk, especially after he'd had a drink or two. "Hey, Alan," Michael said to his potential client. "Looks like you could use a refill on that Scotch. Why don't we go up to the bar? I'll introduce you to my brother and a good friend of mine."

Alan seemed game. "Yeah. Sure."

They made their way through the crowd. With every step closer to Charlotte and Chris, it became clear that their conversation was intense. Chris was talking a mile a minute. Charlotte's face showed everything from concern to shock. Michael hoped to hell his brother hadn't told her too much. He didn't want her thinking of him that way.

"Hey, you two. I hope those aren't long faces I'm seeing."

Charlotte looked up at him with eyes that could only be described as soft and forgiving. Considering the number of times she'd given him a look that was quite the opposite, it was more than a bit of a surprise.

"What? Us? No way," Charlotte replied, entirely too chipper. "Who's your friend?"

Michael introduced Alan, still trying to sort out what had gone on between Chris and Charlotte. Perhaps he was just being paranoid. Some old rules he made for himself might just need to be cast aside. He loved his brother and he cared deeply for Charlotte. They should be acquainted.

Alan immediately took to Charlotte. Although Michael had to wonder if the dress had something to do with it, the truth was that she was simply on a roll these days, charming and entertaining, comfortable in her own skin. She could've sold a brick to a drowning man.

"Hey, Michael," Alan began, "why should I hire you instead of Charlotte? If I want to move into a historic hotel, it seems like a no-brainer to buy from the woman whose family owns it."

Michael shrugged. "Yeah. You got me there. I have no good argument for that." He was surprised at himself. Normally he'd launch right into the long list of reasons he was a superior agent. If Gabe Underwood had been standing here, Michael would've gone for the jugular. But things were different with Charlotte. He'd figure out what to do about it, if anything, later.

Charlotte cast a quizzical look at him. "Excuse me, everyone. I think Michael must be very, very ill or quite possibly drunk." She grasped his elbow and held the back of her hand to his forehead. Their gazes connected and he endured the usual zap of electricity that came with it. He suspected that her effect on him might never go away. "Nope. No fever. I'm afraid we're going to have cut you off, mister. No more drinking until you're ready to go to the mat with me on who's the better real-estate agent."

All Michael could think was that he did want to go to the mat with Charlotte—if it meant rolling around on a horizontal surface. She was so damn sexy it boggled the mind. She wasn't second-guessing herself or trying to play off a compliment. She took everything as it came. Michael found her ability to roll with the punches irresistible.

"Personally, I think you two should work together,"

Chris said, pointing at Michael and Charlotte. "You could be the ultimate power couple. Nothing would stop you two."

"It didn't exactly work out the first time," Charlotte said.

Michael didn't know how to respond. There was a voice inside his head that kept telling him to try again with Charlotte. The voice was especially insistent tonight. The trouble was that if things didn't work out, untangling themselves as a couple would be far more complicated the second time. They lived in the same building now. She'd established herself in the same work circles. People loved to talk, especially about failed relationships.

"I think Charlotte and I might end up blowing up Manhattan if we worked together."

"Or you could end up being the biggest thing that's hit this town in a long time," his brother said.

Charlotte perched on a bar stool and crossed her lovely legs. When he looked at her for a reaction to the conversation, she was stirring her drink and stabbing ice cubes with the straw.

The party rolled on for at least another hour, but eventually the guest count began to dwindle. Alan excused himself, saying he had another party to attend. Chris was tired and headed upstairs to Michael's to crash. The bartender announced last call.

"I guess this is a wrap. Thanks for coming tonight." Michael swallowed hard, looking at Charlotte, trying to decide whether or not to listen to his inner voice. "You were the best part of the party. By far. I'm glad you had a chance to meet Chris. You two really hit it off."

Charlotte got up from her bar stool. He thought she

was about to leave, but she instead took his hand. "We had a big talk. He told me a lot. Probably a lot of stuff that you didn't want me to know. I know about your parents. I know about your dad and the engagement. He told me everything."

So he'd been right. "I see." He braced for her reaction. Would she think he was less of a man? Would she think he was a monster for hitting his own father? He sought their strongest connection and looked at her. It took more than courage to gaze into Charlotte's eyes. It took reflection. Those big, beautiful blue eyes were like a mirror, showing Michael too much—everything he'd given up, everything he'd brushed aside, everything that had ever hurt him. It was sometimes torture to wade into these waters, but he had no choice now.

"I really wish you would've shared some of that with me, Michael. When we were together. It might have made things different between us."

He watched as her eyes misted and all he could think was that he was a horrible person. Could he ever come close to matching the good in Charlotte? He had pushed her away because he'd convinced himself that one traumatic event would determine the course of his life. He just couldn't own the failure, which was a defeat in itself.

"I know. You're right. It's just difficult for me to talk about. Still."

She stepped closer and held on to both of his arms. "I seriously feel like I'm seeing you in a whole new light."

"And?" He had to know how she saw him. He didn't want to be weak, but somehow with her, he felt as though being vulnerable didn't have to be ugly. It didn't have to be a failing.

"It makes me want to take the hurt away."

Relief rushed through him. He'd worried that the truth would make her want to run away. "I'm not at all opposed to the idea."

She reached up and clasped her hands around his neck. Her fingers were soft, her touch warm. "I'm waiting for you to lean down so I can get to you. You're in a different atmosphere all the way up there."

He smiled and bowed his head, wrapping his arms around her waist. He placed the smallest kiss on her lips, but knew he would get lost in Charlotte if it lasted another second. He pulled back his head.

"That's it?" Charlotte jutted out her lower lip. He would've done anything to take a gentle nip.

"If we start something, I want to be alone with you. I don't want to stop. I don't want to have to think about anyone other than you."

Her cheeks plumped up when she smiled. "Oh. Okay. Good answer." She grabbed her evening bag from the bar. "Please tell me you don't have to settle up with the bar."

"No. They have my credit card. But I just remembered that my brother is upstairs in my apartment."

She smoothed her hand over his jacket lapel, then traced her finger down the front of his shirt. That one touch made every muscle in his body twitch. "We'll have to make do with my place."

"Will Thor even let me through the front door?"

"Thor loves you. He just doesn't know it yet."

Michael took Charlotte's hand, not caring who saw them like this. She might not have thought much of it, but it meant a lot to him. He was accustomed to being concerned with appearances at all times. His parents had trained him to think that way. He didn't care about impropriety anymore, or what people might say. He didn't care that everyone who worked in this hotel knew exactly who each of them was, or that they lived on the same floor upstairs. All he cared about right now was being with Charlotte.

They got the elevator to themselves and he didn't waste a minute. He took her into his arms and kissed her the way he'd wanted to downstairs—with intent, to send a message that he wanted her so badly he couldn't stand it. Scary or not, he wanted another chance. Her lips were impossibly soft and giving, her sweet smell the only air he cared to breathe.

They both jumped when the door dinged. He grabbed her hand again and they stole down the hall, this time to her apartment. Thor made this presence known with a bark as soon as they were inside, but Charlotte shushed the dog and Michael ignored him. Her hands were all over Michael as they kissed while practically stumbling through the foyer. They bumped into the wall, Charlotte with her back to it. She groaned her approval and dug her fingernails into his biceps, tugging him closer as he deepened the kiss, but that wasn't what he wanted.

"No wall this time. I want to make love to you."

She took his hand and they hurried to her bedroom. Charlotte kicked off her shoes and pulled Michael over to the bed, shuffling backward as she went. She climbed up onto the mattress and unbuttoned his shirt, rocking from side to side on her knees. He loved her enthusiasm. She blew her hair from her face and yanked his shirt from the waist of his dress pants. He could hardly keep up with her and he wasn't sure he wanted to. She grabbed his shoulders and pulled him into a kiss, this one more frenzied than the one in the hall. With her full body weight, she flopped back on the bed, tugging him down on top of her. She slipped her leg between his, rocking back and forth, the firm pressure of her body making the blood rush to the center of his belly and due south. Their kiss was messy and perfect, fueled, he suspected, by what was new between them—his willingness to let down his guard. They were both so inspired it was like they might never stop kissing. He wasn't sure he'd ever been so hard—not even the time they did it against the wall.

Michael rolled onto his back, taking Charlotte with him. She straddled his waist, her dress hitching up her legs until it was around her hips. He sat up, but it took every ounce of strength he had in his abs to sit like that and unzip the back of her dress. He eased back down as Charlotte smiled at him and tossed her hair to one side. She was a vision he could've soaked up forever. So sexy. So sweet. He'd never met another woman like her. Did he love her? He was starting to think he might. That would've been unthinkable six months ago, but Charlotte had worn him down, even when she'd been trying to push him away.

She crossed her arms and lifted the hem of her dress, dragging the garment up the length of her body and revealing her creamy skin to him. In matching red lace panties and a strapless bra, she could be the subject of countless fantasies, and yet here she was, with him. He'd never felt so lucky in his life. "You're so beautiful, Charlotte. Why did I ever let you go?"

"I believe we've already had that discussion, but thank you. You're pretty damn handsome, but you already know that."

The grin on his face right now had to be regrettably goofy. He didn't care. She scooted back and to the side, then went to work on his pants and boxers, determinedly pulling them down past his hips and flinging them onto the floor. Now that they were gone, she again bracketed his legs with hers, but she'd stationed herself lower, with their feet touching. Her hands traveled up his thighs while a mischievous smile played on her lips. He knew exactly where she was headed and his stomach clenched in anticipation. His breath stalled in his chest. She dug in deeper with the heels of her hands as she reached his pelvis, firm pressure on either side of his erection, making it impossible to think straight, or see straight, either. She was taking her sweet time, torturing him with every second of delay, but it made the moment when she finally gave in so much better. She shimmied closer and her graceful fingers wrapped around his length. He drew in a deep breath and sank into the sensation. She stroked hard with one hand, looking deeply into his eyes, a connection he had many times found too deep to endure. He loved the in-charge version of Charlotte. To her, and only her, was he happy to relinquish control.

A deep groan rumbled out of his throat when she took the strokes faster. If he wasn't careful, he was going to be way ahead of her. He reached around to her back and unhooked her bra, but the vision of her plump breasts and hard nipples only brought him closer to the edge. As good as her touch felt, he pulled her into his arms, flat against his torso, and wrapped her up in a kiss unlike any other. He rolled her to her back and laid on his side against her, admiring every inch of her beauty. His hand caressed her silky belly, soft and smooth, then he slid it inside the front of her panties and found her apex. She sharply sucked in a breath as he employed one finger to do his bidding, creating tiny circles and a good deal of hot friction. The tiny bundle was tight and hard, but everything around it was wet and warm. She was as ready as she'd ever been, and he was so ready to be inside her that it physically hurt to wait, but he loved watching the look on her face as she closed her eyes and gave in to the pleasure.

"We're going to need a condom," he muttered into her ear, his fingers keeping steady time.

She opened her eyes halfway. He didn't mind that his touch might be making it hard for her to think. "Bedside table drawer."

He hated to stop touching her, but this had to be done. "One sec."

"Hurry."

He did exactly that, tearing open the package and putting it on. "I'm back." He returned his hand to his previous charge, sliding his palm down her belly and starting in gentle circles.

A smile broke across her face and her eyes drifted shut. "Good."

Her breaths were coming shorter now and he could tell she was close. Considering everything Charlotte had done for him, he wanted to bring her to her peak more than once tonight. He quickened his pace and stifled a smile when her mouth softened to an O, she jerked her head back on the pillow, and several gasping moans left her lips. He didn't wait for her orgasm to wane— he pulled down her panties and urged her up on top of him. He cradled her hips as she lowered her body. He closed his eyes as ecstasy threatened to overtake every inch of his body. She was so warm, her body still pulsing, now tightening around him. They began to move together in a rhythm that felt right from the first pass. They fit together so well it was as if they'd been built for each other. He took his thrusts as slowly and carefully as he could, but the reality was the pleasure was so tightly wound in his belly, he didn't have enough time to think before white light flashed through his head and the release rocketed through his pelvis. Charlotte gasped and it seemed that she was coming again, her body grasping him tighter.

As the waves began to ebb and everything blissfully sank bank down to earth, Michael pulled Charlotte against his bare chest. He rolled to his side, carefully dotting her face and shoulder with slow, deliberate kisses. All stress was gone. As he felt his body about to give in to sleep, he snugged her closer, wanting to feel her warmth all night long. Only one thought crossed his mind—Charlotte was perfect, and he'd better not let her go again.

Eleven

With the sun shining through her bedroom window and Michael's naked body next to her under the covers, Charlotte was nothing if not optimistic. Was there anything better than waking up next to someone as smart, funny and good-looking as Michael? No. She was quite certain of that. She snuggled closer to him just to soak up his body heat. She loved the way he smelled in the morning, a faint mix of his cologne and musky man.

Michael jumped when she put her feet on his calves. "What are you made of? Ice?"

"I can't help it. I'm always cold. Especially this time of year. Just the thought of how cold it is outside makes me even more cold."

"That makes absolutely no sense." He turned onto his side, facing her, his head resting on the pillow. He had a crease across his cheek and his stubble was a little longer than it had been yesterday. She palmed the side of his face, and the feel of his unshaven jaw tickled her hand. She found herself getting lost in his eyes, so soulful and deep. Funny that she had once thought of them as cruel. That was before she knew about his past. She was sure there were more secrets to be unearthed, but it would take time to reveal everything swimming in Michael Kelly's head. Possibly years.

"What can I say? I defy all logic. You'll have to get used to it." She hadn't meant for any mention of them in the context of being a couple to slip so soon, but it had and there was no taking it back.

"I'm more than accustomed to ignoring sound judgment when it comes to you."

"Good. It's highly overrated anyway." His comment hung over her as a reminder of the words she needed to finally say to him, the potentially life-shattering news she had to share. She'd said to herself last night that she would tell him today. She had to stick to that. Sooner rather than later would be best. But she still feared his reaction. She'd just gotten him to the point where he'd sleep at her apartment, for God's sake. That was a first for the two of them. Announcing a baby on the way seemed like an impossible leap, but she could no longer exclude him from their shared reality. Not when she wanted more.

Thor barked insistently from the other room. The confession would have to wait a few more minutes. The discussion that would follow was not to be interrupted. "I'm going to run him downstairs for a potty break. I can be back in ten minutes."

Michael reined her in with his arms and kissed her forehead. "You are too beholden to that dog."

"You should talk. You wouldn't even still be here if your brother wasn't staying in your apartment."

"True. Tell you what, I'll put on coffee, you take the dog out, I'll be here when you get back."

"No note required."

"No note."

He smiled that Michael smile—effortless and sexy. So brilliant it took her breath away. All she could think looking at his face was that she loved him. But would he ever feel the same way? He seemed different this morning, much more relaxed. Everything he'd been hiding must have been weighing on him terribly. Maybe that could pave the way for happier days for them. She wanted to believe that could be the case.

She pecked him on the lips. "Perfect." She hopped out of bed, threw on some jeans and a sweater, her fluffiest hat and mittens and a big coat. She and Thor caught the elevator right away. He scurried across the lobby, bolted through the door and did his business on the very first tree. She walked him to the corner, but was too eager to get in from the cold and back to Michael, so they turned back. As they approached the hotel, she marveled at how beautiful the holiday decorations were in the daylight. Tomorrow was Christmas Day. She'd be spending time with her family and Michael had plans with his brother. They apparently always spent Christmas together since they'd been estranged from their parents. Would Michael want to change his plans when he knew what she had to tell him? She wanted to believe he would. Maybe he and Chris could come over to Sawyer's and they could start folding themselves into each other's lives.

When Thor and Charlotte got back to the fifteenth

floor, the lovely aroma of coffee hit her nose immediately. Charlotte couldn't think of a more pleasant
scenario than spending the rest of the morning with
Michael and her dog. As long as everything went well
with the pregnancy announcement. She reached for the
doorknob, knowing her moment of reckoning was upon
her. *Everything will be fine.*

She let Thor off his leash and walked into the kitchen.
Michael wasn't there, but a full pot of coffee was. He
had apparently not taken a cup for himself yet.

"Michael?"

"Yeah. In here." His voice came from the living
room. It did not sound warm or inviting. Quite the opposite, actually.

When she rounded the corner, he was sitting on the
couch, elbows resting on knees, staring at her bottle of
prenatal vitamins. They had been on the counter in her
bathroom. Right where anyone could see. He picked it
up and turned his head to face her. "Please tell me these
belong to someone else."

All the warmth drained from Charlotte's body. She
couldn't lie. It was bad enough she'd kept the secret so
long. "They're my vitamins. I'm pregnant."

Michael had sensed Charlotte might be hiding something, but there had always been an element of the unknown with her. He'd assumed it was something having
to do with her family, or the hotel, or work.

But a baby? That hadn't entered his mind once. And
to think he was going to tell Charlotte this morning that
he loved her. That had to be put on hold indefinitely.
She'd lied to him, about something so monumentally
important he couldn't comprehend it.

"How did this happen? When did this happen?" The instant the words left his mouth, he felt both idiotic and betrayed. She'd been with someone else. After him. Of course she had. He'd practically dared her to break up with him and she'd made no secret of how angry she was about it.

"I'm about twelve weeks along. I found out I was pregnant about two weeks after we broke up."

He was normally the person who moved on quickly. Charlotte was making him look like a wimp when it came to dating. "You found a new guy that quickly? Who is he? And why isn't he around?"

"Are you seriously this bad at math, Michael? Or did you just not pay attention in health class? I found out two weeks after we broke up. I was about three weeks along then…" Her voice trailed off and she closed her eyes.

Oh, God. He *was* dense. "I'm the guy?"

Her eyes shot open. It was like a blue laser beam. "Yes. You're the guy. I haven't been with anyone else."

Crushing, conflicting emotions smacked into him. Was this what it was like to be in shock? If so, it was awful. "Why didn't you call me? I should've been the first person you contacted when you found out."

"I know." She wrapped her arms around herself, and he waited for her to retreat. That had always been her reaction when things got tough or she was put on the spot—to run away. Instead, she planted her hands on her hips. "But here's why I didn't. You told me flat out that I wanted too much and you weren't going to give it to me. If being a good boyfriend wasn't on your agenda, I had zero reason to think fatherhood was going to go over well."

"Hey. I know I wasn't perfect, but you make it sound like I was the worst boyfriend ever."

"You really don't want me to go there, do you?" The blaze in her eyes was like a dragon breathing fire.

"I know. I know. We always stayed at my place and I should have paid more attention. We've been over this."

"Don't do that." She shook her head and pursed her lips. "Don't make it sound like I was being trivial or petty. Your job always came first. I was second. Or quite possibly third, after Abby."

"That's not fair. My career is important to me. And I've owned Abby for nine years. It's not like I'm going to neglect my dog."

"I understand all of that. It's still not fun to be constantly reminded of the pecking order and that you're at the bottom of it."

Michael was struggling to keep up, but rehashing the past wasn't going to help him figure out the more pressing problem—Charlotte was pregnant and she'd hidden it from him. "This is why you ran off to England, isn't it? I knew there was more to it than regrouping."

"Bravo, Mr. Detective." She rolled her eyes, making him exponentially more frustrated with her and this conversation. "You know, you make it sound like I ran away with the circus. It wasn't an impulsive thing. I needed support. Quite frankly, I needed my mom, but I don't have one, so I went to Fran and she welcomed me with open arms."

Michael had to admit he didn't like the idea of her going through this on her own, but that wasn't his fault. "You can't put that on me. If you'd just told me, I could've been your support system. I don't understand why you didn't extend me that courtesy. Isn't that just common sense?"

"Common sense is not saying anything because you already know the other half of the conversation. I was upset and confused. I wasn't about to have that talk with you. I couldn't do it. I was barely keeping myself together."

"How could you have possibly known what I would've said?" He got up from the couch and started pacing the room. Perhaps movement would help him calm down. He could feel his anger growing and he refused to let it consume him or cloud his thoughts, which were already murky enough. "I don't know what to say right now and if anyone should know what I would say, it's me."

"You need to stop being so defensive." Her voice was clear and decisive, but her eyes were doing their best to work their way into his psyche. She was being so unfair right now.

"Defensive? You hid a pregnancy from me. I don't know how else I'm supposed to act. I've had all of two minutes to wrap my head around this. And right now, I can't think past the fact that you and I have been spending time together over the last few weeks and you've had every opportunity to tell me you were pregnant and you didn't." He ran his hands through his hair. His forehead was starting to throb like he'd just hit it with a hammer. There was too much competing for attention in his head right now. *Me? A dad?*

She blew out a breath. "I know. And I'm sorry, but I had my reasons. I had to get our professional entanglements out of the way. And to be honest, I think I had to protect myself from you, Michael."

If anything stung, it was hearing those words. He hated the thought of her feeling that way. It was never his intention to hurt her when he told her he wasn't capable of giving everything she wanted. If anything, he was trying to protect her. He cared too much to let her believe that he could be her everything. Now the stakes were considerably higher. "I don't know how to respond to that. I would never hurt you."

"Whether you meant to or not, you did hurt me, and this conversation is just confirming my worst fears. I feel like you're showing me where this ends."

"So I've been saying exactly what you thought I would? Am I really that predictable? Or are you just some sort of soothsayer?"

She leaned against the wall and looked out the window. He could see the gears turning in her head. "Honestly? This is worse than I imagined."

"How could it possibly be worse?"

"Because we're arguing about why I kept the secret. You haven't said a single thing about what this is really about. I messed up. I made a huge mistake and I'm incredibly sorry. But you haven't even mentioned the baby. Not a single word."

A dark and dense silence fell on the room. He didn't want to admit that she was right. The beast inside him that refused to lose was determined to take the course where he won this argument and showed her just how much she was in the wrong. "What do you want me to say?"

"I want you to tell me how you feel. About the idea of becoming a dad."

That word was a dagger to his heart. It brought up every negative connotation he could imagine, but it wasn't as simple as hating his father. Michael's greatest successes in life and his fierce determination had come from his dad. Some of it was genetics. Everything else had come by sheer force. His dad had brutally pushed both his brother and him. Their dad accepted nothing less than perfection. His sons were going to be champions, and they would stand on that Olympic podium and raise their hands in victory after the gold medal had been placed around their necks. Their dad had pursued that at any cost—he'd thought nothing of withholding love and approval. If anything, he'd seemed to think it was precisely what they needed.

It took twenty-three years for Michael to learn that his father's expectations extended well beyond the pool. He expected it in everything, and when Michael dared to put his own feelings first and break up with his fiancée the night of their engagement party, all hell had broken loose. Michael had failed in spectacular fashion, according to his father, and for that he deserved disdain and blame. The look of disgust on his father's face was permanently etched in Michael's memory. He'd witnessed it the few times he'd seen his dad since that night. After a lifetime of doing absolutely everything his dad had wanted, Michael learned that night that it would never be enough.

He sank down onto the couch again. "I never saw myself becoming a dad. I don't know that I'm capable of it." *I'm terrified I'm going to ruin some poor kid.* "When I told you that I wasn't prepared to give you what you wanted, it wasn't to hurt you, Charlie. It was to give you an out so I wouldn't end up hurting you."

He looked up to see the color drain from her face.

"And now I'm going to have your baby. So what do we do now?"

"I need time. I need time and space to process all of this. It's a lot to heap on someone at one time."

Time? He needs time? Charlotte could hardly believe the words coming out of his mouth. And she didn't care to hear too many more of them today. "Sure. Take all the time you need." *Just don't expect me to care whenever you finally sort this out in your head.* She stalked into her room.

Michael followed. "Look, I have to go back to my place. My brother is over there all by himself. I should go be a good host."

A good host? They were never going to get on the same page. It was time to put things on her terms. She wasn't about to let Michael dictate everything. "Good. Goodbye. I'm finding it hard to look at you right now anyway." That last part was such a lie. Even when she was hopping mad at Michael, she still wanted to look at him.

"I don't really want to look at you, either, if we're being honest." He thrust his arm into his sleeve and began buttoning his shirt in a fury, his hair flopping to the side as he stared at her in anger. Charlotte paced in her room as a storm of sadness and regret churned in her head. She embraced her feelings, something for which she had quite a talent. If she was going to be miserable, might as well go all in. As much as she hated to see things end like this, at least the man was showing some damn emotion. For once, he wasn't being so closed off. He didn't even bother to put on his shoes. He simply scooped them up from the floor, grabbed his jacket from the back of the chair and stuffed his wallet back into his pants pocket. Without a word, he stormed out of the room and headed straight for the front door.

"So that's it, then?" She really didn't like hearing those words come out of her mouth. They bore too much resemblance to her final utterance the first time they broke up. At least she wasn't sobbing this time.

"For now, yes." He didn't even look at her. He opened the door, waltzed through it and let it slam behind him.

Charlotte stood there like a statue, staring at the back of her door. She loved this apartment—she loved the Grand Legacy—and she'd already had so many daydreams about what it would be like to bring the baby home here. But maybe it just wasn't meant to be. The thought of running into Michael in the lobby, the hall or, even worse, in an enclosed space like the elevator was horrible. Having to see his handsome face, breathe his beguiling smells and know that he hadn't wanted to be part of her future would be too much. How would she ever heal? She wouldn't. And that wasn't fair to her, nor was it fair to the baby.

She flung open her door and took off down the hall. Thank goodness no one had moved in to the other two units on their floor, the empty ones between them. Thor yipped behind her. The escape artist was again at work. She rounded the corner and Michael was a few steps from his door.

"Michael, wait."

"What now?" He whipped around, slicing into her with the frustration on his face.

"I can't live in the same building with you anymore. Not if this is the end between us."

He threw up his hands. "You not only think the absolute worst of me, you can't stand the sight of me, either?"

"It's too painful. I won't do it. Whoever sells their units first gets to stay. The other person has to move out." Even though it was a slightly insane idea, she was pleased that it came off sounding like something the ever-confident Michael would say.

He turned to her and shifted his armful of jacket and shoes to one side. "You don't want to do that. You love the Grand Legacy. If you make this deal, you're going to be the one who has to leave. I only have one more unit to sell and I already have a buyer on the hook. Another day or two and I win."

Of course he phrased it in that way. He thought of little else. "If that's what happens, that's what happens. I just want something resolved. For good."

"It's Christmas tomorrow. You want me to basically hand a pregnant woman an eviction notice at Christmas? I'm sure you'd love to be able to tell the world that I truly am an ass, but I won't do it."

"Stop assuming you'll win. I only have two units to sell. There's still a chance I could beat you. And no matter what happens, it was my idea. I fully own it." She felt good about dictating the rules of the game for once. She'd take any shred of control she could right now. This was progress.

He shook his head slowly and deliberately—classic dismissive Michael. "Whatever you want, Charlotte. But I still want you to at least give me some time to think. Don't go calling Chad from Hunks with Trucks."

"I'm not making any promises. I'm not going to sit around and wait forever." She patted her leg three times and Thor rushed to her side. She walked down the hall, trying her damnedest to muster an air of victory, waiting for her sense of accomplishment to kick in. As she opened the door to her apartment and Thor sidled past her inside, she realized that there was no way to win in this impossible situation. Either Michael loved her and wanted to be father to their child, or he didn't. He didn't know. He needed time. It might be cold or heartless, but something deep inside her said that wasn't good enough.

For Charlotte, love wasn't a question. It was an answer. She couldn't remember a time when she hadn't felt like that. It was her strongest need, a thirst that wouldn't go away, and she'd been working so hard to get past that, to get to a point where she didn't need so much of it. But when she thought about living her life being the sort of person who didn't need it so desperately, the future narrowed to a dark and unhappy point. She refused to accept that. She wouldn't live like that. It was okay to be who she was. It was okay that she would have love and she would give it. Every day, just as she'd always wanted. That love would be for her baby, and she would give it until her last dying gasp. Everything that had been bottled up inside her would finally come out, and she wouldn't stop until it was spent and gone.

And somewhere else in this city would be Michael, walking around with a chunk of her heart, completely oblivious to everything he had missed.

Twelve

Michael woke up at seven thirty on Christmas morning, feeling more than a little hungover. He and Chris had stayed up late, playing cards and drinking. Not smart, but Michael had been nursing his wounds. He scrounged around in the covers until he found his phone, which was tucked under the pillow on the other side of the bed. He dared to look at it—no response to his many texts to Charlotte last night.

Can we talk? The first one had gone unanswered for an hour before he sent his follow-up.

You there? I'd like to talk about this. He'd sat on that message for two hours. Then he'd gone down to her apartment and knocked on the door. She never answered. So he went home and made another plea.

You have every right to be mad, but please just answer me. She hadn't had anything to say to that one, either. Charlotte always had her phone on, and she always had it with her. The only time she ever failed to respond was when she was mad. She'd done it the other day, when he hadn't left a note. For now, he was fairly certain he had his answer. *Go away, Michael.*

He rolled out of bed and Abby followed him into the kitchen. He filled her food bowl and started the coffee. It was hard to get past the feeling that this Christmas was going to suck. Michael didn't pin much on the idea of some days being more special than others, but Christmas day was at least supposed to be happy. It had been over the last several years, when Chris and Michael spent the holiday together. Of course, it hadn't been the case when Chris and Michael were growing up.

Christmas had always been a strange day in the Kelly household. Dad was nice on Christmas, almost too nice. But as was typical for him, he had a very strong sense of the way things should be, and Christmas was tailor-made for him since it was supposed to be perfect. Dad liked perfect and hated everything else. He was affectionate with Mom on Christmas, putting his arm around her and kissing her on the temple. She soaked up every minute of it, probably because it was not their normal dynamic at all. Christmas was essentially a day for a cease-fire. His parents' marriage seemed more like a hostile business arrangement, a constant negotiation and a relentless power struggle. The only thing that kept Dad in line was that Mom held the purse strings.

Most of the family's money came from an inheritance Mom had received from her aunt when Michael was eight and Chris was six. Before that, finances had always been tight. In some ways, they'd had a happier home life before the money came along. Dad worked, which meant their exposure to his short fuse and perfectionism was lessened. Swimming was an activity driven by the boys, fueled by their love of being in the water and competing. But when the money came, Dad quit his job and he funneled every waking minute into Michael and Chris.

They were plucked from their schools and their friends, the family moved from a modest ranch in rural Maryland to a massive historic home in Bethesda. Dad had the entire backyard ripped out, two-hundred-year-old trees and all, just so they could put in a pool. A private swimming coach was hired, but only one who was willing to let Dad attend practice and micromanage everything. Their old life, which wasn't perfect but was manageable, became a distant memory. Their new life became a living hell because the bar had been raised significantly. Their parents had changed everyone's lives in order to create two Olympians. Any result short of that would be an utter failure. The pressure was on. If Michael and Chris hadn't had each other, he wasn't sure they would have made it.

Michael poured himself a cup of coffee and wandered into the living room, sinking into the couch cushions and getting lost in his view out the window. It was a gray and overcast day with more snow predicted. After a while, he wasn't sure how long he'd been sitting there, only that his coffee had gone cold. Abby was curled up with her head on his lap, sleeping fitfully, her nose and front paws twitching. "Chasing rabbits in your sleep, sweets?" he asked, smoothing his hand over her silky fur.

"You talking to the dog again?" Chris shuffled into the room, his eyes about half-open.

"I would've been talking to you, but you're the one who decided to sleep in."

Chris rubbed his face and squinted when the sun peeked out from behind a cloud, flooding the room with light. "We drank too much last night, dude."

Michael was still feeling rough, but apparently not as bad as his brother. "I had to give you a chance to beat me at cards. I didn't want you going home with your pride completely destroyed."

"Yeah, yeah." Chris waved it off. "We could've played without doing shots until midnight. That was your idea."

I was drowning my sorrows. "Coffee's on." Michael nodded toward the kitchen and Chris ambled off.

His brother returned a minute later and plopped down at the other end of the couch. "It's been a full twenty-four hours since you came back from Charlotte's apartment. We successfully avoided the subject all day yesterday, but I think your reprieve is over. You want to tell me what in the hell happened? Because you seem just as bummed out this morning as you did all day yesterday."

What in the hell *had* happened? Michael still couldn't make sense of it. Everything had snowballed so quickly. He didn't make a habit of spilling his guts to his brother, but Chris was a great listener and he really needed someone to help him sort this out. "As long as you're sure you want to hear this. I'm pretty sure I messed up and I'm not sure how to fix it."

"I will always listen, but especially if it involves you messing up." He bounced his eyebrows and took a long sip of his coffee.

"Well, things were pretty intense after you left the party the other night."

"I know I probably shouldn't have said anything, but she's the only woman you've talked about since the engagement and she cares about you a lot."

Michael wasn't sure that could be true, or at least not anymore. The disdain in her eyes had come from such a pure place yesterday, and he wasn't sure he blamed her. "I'm not so sure after yesterday." Michael craned his neck to work out a kink. The whole story was tumbling around in his head—every mistake he'd made, the way he kept stubbornly clinging to his own baggage. "But I'm glad you said something. As much as I didn't want her to know about my past, I do feel like it broke down some barriers between us."

"Good. That all sounds great."

"When we woke up yesterday morning, it felt like we were in a different place. A much better place than we'd been when we were together the first time." Just thinking about waking up next to her stirred up emotions that were most often foreign to Michael—optimism, hope, peace. Charlotte was such a positive force in his life when they were on the same trajectory. Little had he known he was throwing it away by being so damn shortsighted.

"Again. This all sounds good to me."

"It was." Michael clunked his empty coffee mug on the side table next to him. "Then she took her dog for a walk and I found prenatal vitamins on her bathroom counter. She's pregnant." Michael looked over at his brother, and watched the news sink in.

"Wow. Who's the dad?"

Michael recalled this part of the conversation with

Charlotte. He was starting to wonder why he'd ever thought *he* was the smart one. "It's me. She got pregnant when we were still together, but she didn't find out until after we broke up."

Chris ran his hands through his hair, shaking his head. "Oh, wow. That is so harsh. Finding out you're pregnant by some guy who told you he had no interest in being serious? That had to hurt."

Michael had spent much of last night tipsy and trying to imagine how Charlotte must have felt right after their breakup and during her time in England. She'd been suffering and he'd been going on with his own life, missing her, which had seemed like a big step forward in his own emotional growth. Little did he know she was running laps around him. "Yeah. I'm guessing it hurt a lot. But that didn't really occur to me yesterday. I was too mad at her for keeping it from me."

"Are you serious? Mad?" He turned on the couch, facing Michael more directly.

"Yes. I'm not proud of it. At all."

"So did she give you the heave-ho? Is that why you've been in such a terrible mood?"

"Not right away. I told her I needed time to think about it, she got mad, which is understandable, and I left." Michael sighed and shook his head. What an idiot he'd been. "But then she went after me in the hall." Michael went on to explain Charlotte's ultimatum about one of them moving out. Abby woke up and nudged Michael's hand with her nose. "Human relationships are too complicated, Abs. I like what we have. I feed you, take you for a walk, you're excited when I get home from work. Easy."

"Look, Dad did a number on both of us," Chris said.

"I know that everything with your engagement convinced you life would be easier if you didn't get serious with a woman, and I understand that, but you need to get your priorities straight. Charlotte is amazing and she's going to have your baby. Don't sit in your apartment petting your dog and talking to your brother. That's not you. You should be down the hall working this out with her."

"I tried. I keep texting her and she doesn't answer. I went down to her apartment and knocked on her door last night when you ran out for more beer, but there was no answer."

"Maybe she's doing something with her family."

"We still have big issues to deal with once she finally talks to me. What about a baby? What if I ruin everything? What if I've inherited Dad's parenting skills? I'm just as competitive. I'm just as much of a perfectionist. I don't want to do to my child what he did to us."

"Hey. You need to cut that out, now. Neither of us is Dad."

"You didn't see me yesterday. I just couldn't let go of the fact that she'd deceived me. I was so hung up on her being wrong and me being right that I couldn't see straight. It was right out of Dad's playbook."

Chris shook his head. "And what's going on right here? This conversation? This is definitely not something Dad would ever do. He never questioned his actions. You're not him, Michael. You just aren't."

Was that really true? Michael wanted to believe it. He did. "I need to figure out a way to fix this." It always stung to admit defeat, but Michael found that he felt better when he committed himself to making things better.

"Any ideas?"

He picked up his phone and again tormented himself with the unanswered texts. "I need to talk to her. That's still my first step." He might be scared out of his wits and totally unsure of himself, but he had to do right by Charlotte. He had to go back to the way he'd felt before he found out about the pregnancy. The moment when he'd been ready to tell her he loved her. "I'm going back down to her apartment again."

"Good idea. I'll hold down the fort."

Michael got up and headed straight down the hall, hoping the second time would be the charm. He wanted to try to make this work. He wanted to take on the challenge ahead, however daunting. It was funny to think that every other big challenge he'd ever tackled had at least come after unbelievable amounts of preparation. Not today. He was flying as blind as could be. Or maybe all those years of suffering at his father's hand had prepared him, but not in the way one normally does that sort of thing.

He reached Charlotte's door and knocked. He waited, tapping his foot, looking down at the floor, up at the ceiling, back at the door again. There was no answer. He leaned closer and held his ear to the door. Not a sound came from her apartment. He knocked a second time, this time a bit more forcefully. Not even a yip from Thor came in response. He had to redouble his efforts. He dug his phone out of his back pocket and sent her yet another text.

You home? I'm in the hall. Hoping we can talk.

He stared at his phone. The silence and the non-answer began to eat at him. He wasn't sure where

Charlotte was—on the other side of that door or off somewhere celebrating the holiday. But no matter what, he was quite certain she was mad as hell.

As he made his way down the hall, his brain went into work mode. If Charlotte was going to be stubborn and ignore him, he was going to have to get creative. He was going to have to get her attention. He was going to have to call Sawyer.

Charlotte didn't want to spend Christmas in utter despair, but it seemed that things were going to be that way. After the breakup to end all breakups the day before, she had zero confidence this would be a merry Christmas. *Ho ho ho and deck the halls, my butt.* Maybe next year. Next year could be merry. A baby. A career. An apartment, exact location to be determined. She could live with that. However imperfect, it would be a hell of a lot better than things had been before she met Michael.

Sawyer had invited Charlotte, Fran and Noah over for an early dinner. That left Charlotte to spend Christmas morning in bed, sleeping, even after she'd turned in very early the night before. She'd turned off her phone. She'd put earplugs in her ears. No rushing to the tree and opening gifts with loved ones while sipping hot cocoa or eggnog. It was just her and Thor curled up into a pathetic ball, a good deal of crying and a few fits of anger. She'd not only managed to lose Michael, the man she had an inexplicable weakness for, but she'd also managed to lose the father of her child. In a life littered with tragic mistakes, this one went to Number One with a bullet on the top-ten list of self-made disasters. It would undoubtedly stay there for eternity.

Going to Sawyer's place might've seemed like nothing more complicated than a friendly family gathering, but it was, in truth, a day of reckoning, when Charlotte had just lived through one. Charlotte hadn't spoken to Sawyer since the day after the wedding, when they'd all had breakfast before he and Kendall escaped to Miami for a few days. He would expect a sales update today, and although the report wasn't terrible, she hadn't reached her goal, either. She'd boasted that she would sell her apartments first, but she'd fallen behind Michael. He had one unit left, she had two. It didn't sound like much, but they weren't selling lollipops or I Love NY T-shirts. They were selling multimillion-dollar pieces of real estate. Two wealthy buyers were unlikely to suddenly appear in Charlotte's life.

Fran and Charlotte took a car together for the short ride up to Sawyer's apartment on the Upper West Side. Fran had let Charlotte bend her ear about Michael yesterday, and although she was glad Charlotte had stood up for herself, she was also very clear about two things—first, she needed to cool off for a few days, and second, she needed to finally just tell her family about the baby. No more waiting until she finished her sales. It was Christmas Day, and if anything was welcome today, it was good news. A baby certainly fell into the category of good news.

Noah was already there when they got up to Sawyer's. He took Charlotte's and Fran's coats, then everyone settled in the living room for predinner drinks.

"I love what you've done with the apartment," Charlotte said to Kendall. "It's much homier now."

"Was it not homey before?" Sawyer asked, seeming a bit insulted.

"It was always nice. Don't get me wrong. But it's nicer now with the new throw pillows on the couch and the candles on the coffee table."

Sawyer shrugged. "Sorry, but it never really occurred to me that I needed more pillows."

"See? That's why you needed Kendall." Charlotte smiled at her new sister-in-law, whom she officially adored. It was nice not to be the only girl, and Fran would be going back to England soon, so Kendall might end up being Charlotte's only real ally. With two babies between them, they'd probably have a lot to talk about.

"So, what can I get everyone to drink?" Sawyer asked, rubbing his hands together. "I'm thinking a Manhattan."

"Yes, please." Fran thrust her hand up into the air. Sawyer was speaking her language.

"Sounds good to me," Noah said.

"Water for me," Kendall said.

"Charlotte?"

She'd known her turn at her brother's question was coming, but the words were stuck in her throat. Something was apparently also stuck in Fran's throat—she cleared it in a way that could only suggest she was thinking, *Charlotte, just come out with it.*

"I will have the same as Kendall. Just water, please."

"It's not like you to pass up cocktail hour, Charlotte."

No, it wasn't. "That's because I have some news." She sat straighter in her seat and looked at each member of her family, one by one. Noah, Sawyer, Fran, Kendall. This was her support system. This was the extent of it. Every person she could absolutely count on was in this room. Michael was now strictly in the category of people she could not count on. "I'm pregnant."

What came next was a squeal from Kendall, a nervous and somewhat unwarranted laugh from Noah, enthusiastic clapping from Fran and a dumbfounded "wow" from Sawyer. She wasn't sure what to make of her family's response and she wasn't about to go around the room and ask each individual for their opinion. "I'm about to start my second trimester. Things are going well, and I'm very excited about what the future holds for me."

Kendall got up from her chair and took the empty seat on the sofa between Charlotte and Fran. She pulled Charlotte's hand into her lap and looked into her eyes sweetly. "I think it's wonderful. There will be two baby Lockes running around. They can play together and grow up together. Cousins. It will be amazing."

A picture materialized before Charlotte's eyes, one that she hadn't thought about—the baby as a toddler, a cousin, an actual person. She'd been so wrapped up in the notion of a little bundle, swaddled in a baby blanket. She'd thought only of cribs and diapers and sleepless nights. It hit her like a ton of bricks, exactly what was at stake. She would be responsible for a human for the rest of her life. It would be her job not to screw it up. Charlotte, the perpetual screwup herself. And then there was the most damning detail—this baby would be a Locke. He or she would not be a Kelly.

The tears started to flow and Charlotte couldn't have stopped them if she'd wanted to. It was surprising to say the least. She'd spent her whole morning crying. How could she possibly have any tears left? Maybe it was because she had been under so much stress with work or maybe it was as simple as what had prompted it—a glimpse of the future.

Kendall plaintively looked up at Sawyer. "I don't know what I said, but I'm so sorry."

Charlotte dropped her head onto Kendall's shoulder. "No. No. It's fine. I'm just still coming to terms with everything and trying to sort stuff out." Good God, this was exactly like the speech Charlotte had delivered every other time in her life that she'd messed up. How was it that she was still repeating this pattern? "And I should let you guys know that I've known for a while now. That's why I went to England to see Fran. I needed some time to regroup and figure out what my next step would be."

Sawyer walked across the room and dropped to his knee next to Charlotte. "Why wouldn't you tell us, Charlotte? We're your family. This is a big deal."

Noah stood directly behind Sawyer, his face full of concern. Things like this were difficult for Noah. He'd never been much for drama. Fran, Charlotte's fairy godmother, wore a reassuring smile that held an edge of "I told you so."

"I've spent my whole life as the member of the family who's constantly messing things up. I didn't want to be that person anymore. Getting pregnant seemed too much like classic Charlotte. I really wanted the chance to prove myself first by selling my units at the Grand Legacy, then I was going to tell you all."

"Prove yourself?" Sawyer asked. "Charlotte, you're my sister. I love you. You don't have to prove a thing to me."

"That's not true and you know it. I saw the hesitation on your face that morning I came in and asked for the listings. You weren't convinced I could do it. You still aren't convinced."

"If I had any hesitation at all, it was only because I could see you doubting yourself. I never want you to doubt yourself, Charlotte. You're far more resilient than me or Noah."

Charlotte let out an unflattering snort. "Yeah, right. Resilient is the last thing I am. Look at me. I'm a mess."

Sawyer shook his head. "I'm not kidding. You roll with the punches and you've had some doozies to deal with. You always had a harder time when we were growing up. You always manage to find your way through everything, and you make everyone love you while you're doing it. You might be the only member of the Locke family who doesn't have an enemy."

Charlotte laughed quietly, wiping tears from her cheeks with the back of her hands. "Yeah, I guess."

"No, he's right," Noah insisted. "As awful as Dad has been to us, he was worse with you. He ignored you like crazy. I'm sure that had to sting."

Just then Charlotte realized perhaps why it had hurt so deeply when Michael ignored her or didn't give her the attention she wanted. It wasn't just because she was a bottomless vessel for love and affection. Michael was just a continuation of a persistent theme in her life. She loved him and he didn't love her back.

"Do you want to tell us who the dad is?" Sawyer asked. "I mean, you don't have to if you don't want to. I guess I just want to know what your plans are." He turned back to Noah. "I think both of us want to know what you need from us. If someone needs to fill in."

"Yes. Of course," Noah agreed.

Charlotte examined Sawyer's face. He was such a sweet guy. She was a lucky girl to have him as her brother. Noah, too. "It's Michael Kelly, Sawyer. I got pregnant when we were still a couple. I know this makes it one hundred times more complicated, but I assure you that I have everything in hand. I'm working on it." *Even if it ends up being nothing.*

Sawyer closed his eyes for a moment. "You do not skimp on the surprise factor, do you?"

Charlotte managed a small grin. "I try not to. Makes life more exciting."

"Wait a minute. Is that why he gave you the listing on his one unsold unit?" Sawyer asked.

"What are you talking about?" Charlotte wasn't sure she'd heard her brother correctly.

"Michael. He called me around noon today and said he was giving his one remaining listing to you. He said he would work it out with you once he got a hold of you. He told me he'd been trying to reach you by text, but you weren't answering."

Crap. Charlotte dug her phone out of her bag and powered it up. She'd been running behind when Fran came to her apartment before the car arrived. She hadn't looked at her phone at all. There on the screen was a whole string of texts and missed calls from him. What did this mean? Did he want to talk because he wanted to reconcile? Giving up the listing made no sense. Unless he was simply taking pity on her.

"Excuse me. I need to freshen up." Charlotte tucked her phone back into her purse and made her way to the hall powder room. Her stomach felt all kinds of uneasy. She couldn't figure out what her response to Michael should be. Did he have something up his sleeve? Or should she stop being so paranoid? With that thought came a sharp pain. When she wiped, she found an unwanted surprise—blood on the tissue. She tried not to panic, but her heart was beating as fast as it could. She washed her hands, but they were trembling under the steady stream of water. She could hardly rub them together to work up a lather. She had to call the doctor. She might have to go in.

She rushed out of the bathroom and back to the living room. Getting in touch with Michael would have to wait. "Fran, Kendall, can I talk to you for a minute?" One thing was certain. Charlotte might have a knack for making life more exciting, but this might go down as the most disastrous Christmas yet.

Thirteen

Michael's cell phone rang and he jumped. *Charlotte?* He flipped his phone over, disappointment sinking into his belly for what felt like the hundredth time today. It wasn't Charlotte, but he didn't recognize the number, either. That wasn't entirely unusual. He received cold calls all the time, but it was late on Christmas day, not a typical time for real-estate inquiries from strangers.

"Hey, Chris. I'm going to take this." Michael and his brother were watching a movie. It was supposed to be a distraction from the Charlotte situation, even if Michael's mind kept wandering. His brain insisted on ruminating, dragging every misstep he'd made into plain view.

"You want me to pause it?" Chris asked.

"No. It's okay." He got up from the couch and walked into the kitchen. "Hello?"

"Michael. This is Charlotte's aunt, Fran. I need to speak with you." She was practically whispering. Whatever she was calling about, something was wrong. He could hear it in her voice.

"Yes. Of course. What's going on?"

"I'm at the hospital. With Charlotte."

Forget how grave and serious everything had seemed when he'd discovered Charlotte was pregnant with his child. The hospital? Had she been in an accident? "What happened?"

"She started bleeding. The doctors asked for one of us to bring her in so she could be checked. We were over at Sawyer's for dinner when it started."

Michael felt as though everything in his body had just gone cold. He couldn't believe he'd spent even a minute today moping around, feeling sorry for himself. "Is she okay?" He wasn't even sure what to ask about the baby. It was still such an abstract idea. Charlotte was hardly showing. If he hadn't seen the vitamins on the bathroom counter, he might not even know right now. Charlotte had been that good at keeping the secret from him.

"Charlotte seems very worried. She could be losing the baby. It's still early in the pregnancy. It wouldn't be uncommon."

Michael felt his body go incredibly still, his breathing slowed and his pulse felt like it was fading. How did it feel to have something go from an abstract idea to a reality in the blink of an eye? Michael was feeling exactly that right now. "Tell me where you are. I have to be there if anything happens."

"Oh, thank God. I'm so happy to hear you say that."

There was no telling what Charlotte had said about him to Fran, but he had a strong inkling now. "I care about Charlotte very much. But I am a little concerned about whether or not she wants me there. I don't want to come down if it's going to upset her. I'm no doctor, but I'm guessing it's probably best for her and the baby if she stays calm."

"You'll have to trust me when I say that it will be much worse if you don't come."

Michael wasn't sure what that even meant, but he didn't want to discuss it further. "I'm on my way out the door right now. Can you text me the address?"

He and Fran said their goodbyes, he grabbed his fleece jacket and hat, then poked his head into the living room. "I'd love to stick around and try to explain this, but I have to go. Charlotte's in the hospital. There's a chance she might lose the baby." He headed for the door.

"Michael, wait. Do you want me to come with you?"

"I'll call you if we need anything, but otherwise, I need to do this on my own. I'm sorry to bail on you."

The concern was so plain on Chris's face it nearly broke Michael's heart. "Don't be silly. Abby and I will be fine. But are you really going to go dressed like that?"

Michael looked down at himself. He'd completely forgotten that he was wearing shorts and a sweatshirt. "Yeah. It's fine. I don't want to take the time to change."

"And it's snowing, you know."

The text from Fran came through with the hospital address. It was only a few blocks away. "Yeah. It's fine. I think I'm going to run. I'll get there faster than driving."

"You're certifiable, bro."

"I love her, Chris. There's nothing else for me to do."

Michael didn't bother with the elevator, and flew down the Grand Legacy stairwell. He tore through the lobby, nearly knocking over a bellman, and bolted out onto the street. He hit the pavement at full stride, his long legs carrying him as fast as he could possibly go. The icy air stabbed at his lungs, but no speed other than lightning-fast would have seemed right. He had to get there now. He had to get there an hour ago. His brain was running just as fast. *Please be okay. Please be okay.* The thought of her being anything less than perfectly safe and healthy made his stomach lurch. In that moment, he knew not only that he loved Charlotte, but that he also wanted things to work out between them. He wanted them to be together. No, she hadn't answered a single one of his text messages. Didn't matter. He still had to try.

Fran had said that Charlotte was up on the third floor in Labor and Delivery, which sounded like a scary proposition. The baby had to be tiny. How could it have come to this already? He ran in through the main entrance. The hospital was eerily quiet, so much so that it felt like his breathing was unreasonably loud. The information desk was empty, and no one offered to direct him, which he decided was for the best. Christmas was apparently not a popular day at the hospital.

Again, he took the stairs instead of the elevator. Fran was waiting for him out in the hall.

"How's she doing?" He was huffing and puffing. His cheeks were burning.

Fran looked as though she'd aged five years since the last time Michael had seen her, which was only at Sawyer's wedding. "They have a monitor on her. They've picked up the baby's heartbeat, so that's a good sign. They want to watch her for a few more hours. They're hoping the bleeding will stop on its own."

Michael swallowed hard. He was used to dealing with all sorts of crises with work, but life and death were not a regular part of his day. "Can I see her?"

Fran nodded. "Yes. I'll walk you in."

He followed her down the hall. The hospital was certainly nicer than most he'd been to, but nobody ever chose to be here. There was no avoiding the overwhelming sense of that. Fran pushed open the door and Michael trailed her into the room. Charlotte was to his left, lying on her side, both hands tucked under her head. Her eyes were closed. She was wearing a blue-and-white hospital gown. The vision left him even more uneasy than he'd imagined it would.

"Charlotte, darling," Fran whispered. "Are you awake?"

Charlotte's eyes popped open. The instant she saw Michael, she jerked up to a sitting position. "Michael? You came?" Her eyes homed in on Fran. "Did you call him?"

Fran sat on the edge of the bed and gently pushed on Charlotte's arm until she relented and laid back down. "I called him because he's the father and he should be involved in this."

Charlotte shook her head. "You don't have to be here if you don't want to. Honestly, I don't want you here at all if you're only here out of obligation."

Michael blew out a breath. He'd earned that response. "I'm here because I want to be here. I'm glad Fran called me." He dared to step closer. Charlotte's eyes slowly went from fiercely guarded to merely skeptical. He'd take what he could get. "She's worried about you. And quite frankly, I'm worried, too."

A faint scowl crossed Charlotte's face. "I hope you didn't just come for brownie points. Or to make yourself look good."

"Never." Apparently she still thought he was capable of the worst. "I'm more of a chocolate-chip-cookie guy anyway."

She narrowed her beautiful blue eyes. "Stop trying to be clever."

"And stop arguing with me. However little I know about having a baby or being pregnant, I'm guessing that the doctor has told you to rest and relax."

Fran cast her sights up at him, then back at Charlotte. "He's right, darling. And I didn't call him to upset you. I called him because everything between you two is going to need to get worked out at some point and the sooner we start, the better for everyone. Even if it ends up being nothing more than a truce." Fran got up from the bed and smoothed the rumpled sheets. "Now I'm going in search of a decent cup of coffee. I'll leave you two to talk."

Michael watched as Fran disappeared through the door, unsure of where his fate sat in all of this. Usually, when he and Charlotte talked, things did *not* get straightened out. They typically became that much more tangled. Considering everything that had happened in the last forty-eight hours, he decided there was no way things could get any worse.

Charlotte couldn't believe Fran had interfered. Although, if the roles and been reversed, Charlotte probably would've done the exact same thing. Even that was hard to believe—it was always Charlotte in the role of being the person in a pickle. It was her job to star as the screwup in the Locke family drama, shows nightly and two matinees on the weekend.

Right now, she was about as stuck as could be. Pregnant by the hopelessly handsome guy standing next to her hospital bed who had shown little desire in being a father, which was such a shame. Michael Kelly was too hot to be a sperm donor. Maybe she needed to just be thankful that he'd given her his exceptional genetic material. If everything turned out, this baby she was already so attached to, the child she wanted more than anything, would be beautiful, strong and smart. And much of that would be thanks to Michael.

"May I?" Michael gestured to the chair next to the bed. Apparently, he was staying for a while, which actually sounded nice, even if he wasn't her favorite person right now.

"Yes. Of course."

"Thanks." He dragged it closer, his knees meeting the mattress when he sat.

"You're wearing shorts? It's December. And snowing."

He sat back and crossed his hairy legs. The man's genetic gifts were off-the-charts, but his legs might be the crowning touch—a million miles long, every muscle as strong as a horse. "This is what I was wearing when Fran called. And I figured running was the best way to get here."

"So you're all sweaty and gross under that jacket."

He nodded. "Afraid so."

"Yuck."

Michael laughed and shook his head. "I already knew

there was no winning in that scenario. Show up in basketball shorts and get crap for it, or take the time to change and get crap for that." He folded his arms across his chest and looked her in the eye, wagging his foot at the same time. "So I stayed in the dumbest clothes possible for December in New York, left my car back at the Grand Legacy and ran right over."

"You ran in the snow. To the hospital. To see me." Charlotte zeroed in on his face. It was never a simple matter to look at him. There was too much wrapped up in that incredible package. Maybe he did deserve some brownie points. "Thank you for doing that. It was very chivalrous of you."

"You had to know I would never let you down when it came to the important stuff."

She sucked in a deep breath. Did he mean *every* important thing? "That was always my hope."

"So what are the doctors saying?"

Charlotte's hand instinctively went to her belly. "They want me to stay on the monitor for a few hours, although I think what they're mostly trying to do is keep me in this bed and off my feet. Unfortunately, there's not a lot they can do at this point if my body decides to…" The word got stuck in her throat. Tiny tears stung her eyes. She didn't want to think it. She didn't want to lend the thought any credence. Too much of her life had been worrying about the worst-case scenario, only to have it come true. "You know. If the pregnancy isn't viable." Using the more clinical term was of zero comfort. If anything, it made her feel worse.

He went for quite a while without saying anything. This was probably just too much for Michael to deal with. She'd have to go with assuming that. She didn't want to imagine him having anything else on his mind. He sat forward and rested his elbows on his knees, reaching for her hand. "Then I will stay until they decide you can go home."

"You don't have to do that. Fran should be back in a little bit and I'll be fine. I know this isn't really your scene, Michael. I know this is a lot for you to deal with and you never asked for any of it."

He wrinkled his nose and pressed his lips together, staring off through the picture window on the far side of the room. It was one of the most powerful shows of emotion she'd ever seen from Michael. Normally he was so composed, so in control. Perhaps it was just an illustration of how difficult this was for him. "I want to be here with you. The thought of leaving you makes me feel like my chest is being hollowed out."

"I definitely don't want you to feel like that."

He looked at her, gazing into her eyes, but it wasn't like he was peeling back her layers. It was more like he was peeling back his own. She saw a vulnerable man behind those cool blue eyes, one with no agenda. He wasn't calculating or planning. He was the most in the moment she'd ever seen him. He raised her hand to his lips and brushed her skin with a tender kiss. "I just want to be here for you."

"And the baby?" She hated that there was so much hope pinned to her question. It felt like a plea she was throwing into the wind, knowing very well that it could fly right back into her face.

"And the baby. Of course, the baby."

There was a stiffness to his voice and a hardness in his face that she disliked so much she would've done almost anything to make it go away. Tiny victories, she decided. Michael had shown up, looking like hell, no less, which was more like a normal day for most people. Six months ago, she would've killed for this much attention from Michael.

"Do you want to tell me why you called Sawyer and told him you were giving up your final listing? Does that mean you want to move out?"

He shook his head. "No. I don't want to move out. And I don't want you to move out, either. I figured you were just trying to get my attention, and I had to figure out a way to get yours. I know you tell me I'm fixated on work too much, but you've been guilty of the same over the last few weeks."

"I know. I was just trying to cement my future and the baby's."

"I still wish you would've let me be a part of that."

That familiar and deep sense of regret rolled back over her, but she took it as it came. There was nothing to do about it now. "I know. I messed up."

He leaned closer and took her hand. "You know what? We both messed up. I kept a secret from you, too. When we were together the first time around, I should've opened up to you. I know now that you were trying to get me to do exactly that. Every day. Every nice thing you ever did for me. I just fought it."

"Because of your family? Because of everything Chris told me?"

"Honestly, I think part of me felt like I wasn't good enough for you."

"How could you ever think that?" Charlotte couldn't fathom the idea. He was so extraordinary.

"I was so afraid of being weak. I was terrified of being at a disadvantage or putting myself in a position to lose. I didn't want you to see every fault in me." He reached out and brushed the hair from the side of her face. It was then that she could see tears misting in his eyes. "It's what I always do. I put on that perfect front and I hide the mistakes because I've learned to hate them. I've been taught to hate every imperfect part of me. But I can't live like that anymore. I messed up yesterday morning. I'm not the jerky guy who blamed everything on you. I'm really not."

Charlotte choked back her own tears. In her heart of hearts, she'd hoped Michael wasn't really the guy who would push her away. "I know you're not. I never truly thought you were. I was just mad."

"I love you, Charlotte. And I'm not just saying that because you're in a hospital bed and our future feels like it's hanging in the balance. I'm saying it now because I can't spend another minute of my life knowing that I'm not sharing everything inside of me with you."

Oh, good God, how she'd longed to hear words like those. She smiled wide. "I love you, too. I was going to tell you the night we broke up. I've loved you for a long time."

"Honestly, I think I've loved you from the moment we became a couple. I couldn't admit it to myself because it meant casting aside the facade that made it easy for me to succeed."

"What changed?"

He laughed quietly, but she could see the sadness in his eyes. "You. You're what's changed me. What's changed me is walking into this room and seeing you in this bed and knowing that you are as vulnerable as a person can be and you're still you. You make me want to be a better man, Charlie. You make me want to be the real, imperfect Michael Kelly."

"Only slightly imperfect. Look at you."

He pushed his chair aside and kneeled beside the bed. He clutched her hand tightly, squeezing. "I love you, Charlotte. I mean it. I love you and I want us to be a family. I want us to build a life together. Please tell me we will try to find a way to make this work."

"I love you, too, Michael." She loved seeing the relief on his face, the way his soft eyes became impossibly warm. She could look at his glorious face forever. It would always make her feel at least a little bit invincible. "If you're willing to make it work, I am, too. We're both pretty stubborn, so I think we can take a good run at it if we're on the same side."

"I never want to be on opposite sides with you again, Charlie. That's a surefire way to lose."

Fourteen

The bleeding didn't stop, so the doctors decided it was best for Charlotte to stay overnight. Michael didn't leave her side. He told Fran to go home and get some sleep. There was no point in everyone being exhausted, he'd said. He touched base with Sawyer and let him know what was going on. The nurse brought him a blanket and he moved his chair so he could sit right alongside Charlotte, holding her hand all night long.

In the morning, she woke to a note.

Charlie,
Gone in search of coffee. Be back soon.
Love, Michael

She smiled to herself, feeling a pretty big sense of pride. She'd trained Michael Kelly to do something that fell squarely in the category of quality boyfriend behavior. Now to get herself to the bathroom.

She hadn't told Michael, since he'd been asleep and the nurse said there was no way they would discharge her in the middle of the night, but the bleeding had considerably lessened when she'd gone to the bathroom around 4:00 a.m. Fingers crossed they were on the right trajectory, that this was just a minor bump in the road. They'd had enough roadblocks. She wanted to look ahead to their future.

Sure enough, the tissue this morning had been only the tiniest bit of pink. She came out of the bathroom and a new nurse who had just come on duty was waiting for her. "That's perfectly normal. Sounds like somebody gets to go home," she said after Charlotte gave her the report.

Michael popped in a minute later. The nurse turned and was instantly awestruck, either by his handsomeness or his ridiculous height or the fact that an Olympian was standing in the room.

"Hi. Michael Kelly." He shook her hand, but she couldn't manage much of a response other than a goofy grin before she cleared out of the room so Charlotte could get dressed.

"They're letting me go home," she said. "No real bleeding since the middle of the night."

"Really?" The hopefulness in his voice was so raw and real.

"Really." She turned her back to him. "Can you untie this gown, please? I can't wait to get out of this thing."

"Gladly." He did as promised, but then he snaked his arms around her bare waist, sending a million tiny jolts of electricity through her. He pulled her back against his chest and kissed the top of her head, then her neck, making her head swim with possibilities.

"No hospital sex."

"I wouldn't think of it. Just feeling like I should take advantage of your semidressed state."

"Always a flirt." She turned and swatted him on the arm, then grabbed his shoulders and urged him down to her level for a quick kiss. "But I love it."

Charlotte dressed with a running commentary from Michael about how impressive her breasts were now and that if he'd known that was a side effect of pregnancy, he would've been on board with it from the very beginning.

After Charlotte signed her discharge papers, an orderly arrived with a wheelchair for her. Michael insisted on pushing.

"I feel really dumb in this thing," Charlotte said, taking a seat. "I'm perfectly capable of walking downstairs."

"The nurse said it's a rule. Plus, it's giving me good practice for after the baby arrives."

Contentment crept over her, but she just went along for the ride. Michael pushed her through the electric doors once they were down to the ground floor. He parked the wheelchair to the side.

"You're being so normal about this whole thing. I'm kind of amazed," she said.

"You know me. Once I'm on board with something, I want to be the best. That would be the good side of my competitive nature."

Charlotte had to smile. "Are we walking?"

"It's up to you. It's only four or five blocks, but I'm happy to hail a cab if that makes you feel better."

"Michael Kelly taking a cab? My stars, you have changed."

"I'm just trying to keep you happy."

"Good answer." She hooked her arm in his. "I vote we walk. I feel like I've been cooped up inside forever."

They started off on their walk and Charlotte was overcome with a feeling that was both unfamiliar and wonderful. She had stability. She and Michael had worked past his problems and hers. She'd made her mark in business, and she'd come to better understand the ways her brothers perceived her. She could officially stop thinking of herself as the family goof-up. From now on, she could just be Charlotte, the real-estate agent. Or the little sister. Or the new mom. Possibly Michael Kelly's wife, although she wasn't ready to put the thumbscrews on him yet about that. She'd give him a week or two to propose and then she'd reevaluate.

"You know," she began, "I know you were trying to help me, but I now have three more units to sell instead of two. You just ended up making more work for me."

"I was thinking about that." He snugged her closer and put his arm around her as they stopped at a corner and waited for the walk signal. "Not necessarily. I got a text from Alan this morning. The guy from the party? He's ready to buy. He wants that last unit on seventeen."

"Oh, wow."

"I told him to contact you about it. I hope that's okay. I gave him your number, but asked him to hold off on calling you for a few days. I want you to get your rest."

The light turned green, and they made their way across the street, hand in hand. "Are you sure? Every sale you turn down is one more chance for Gabe Underwood to unseat you as top agent in the city next year."

"I couldn't possibly care less about Gabe. If he ends up on top, that's fine. I'll just have to beat his butt the next year. And for all I know, you're going to be the one to beat me."

"That's right. You'd better watch your back, Kelly." Charlotte squeezed his hand a little harder. "That leaves the two units on our floor. We're going to have to be careful about those. I really don't want some jerky neighbor living next to us. But before that…" She stopped herself there. Michael had said he wanted to try, but that was all he'd said, and she didn't want to be the one to put any pressure on him. The man knew very well how to put himself in the hot seat. She was fine simply moving forward as a couple, taking things one day at a time.

"Before that, we have to decide if we're going to live in your apartment or mine," he said, with no prompting from Charlotte at all.

She was a little relieved Michael wasn't looking at her right now. The grin that popped onto her face would've been embarrassing. How happy she was to be on the same page. "Right. Do you have any thoughts about that?" She looked up to see him deep in thought, bobbing his head, something he did a lot when he was thinking.

"I hope this doesn't sound crazy, but I just don't think one apartment is enough. I mean, Abby needs her space. We both know Thor needs room to roam. We might even be able to convince him that he's still escaping, but we could just let him into another room."

Charlotte laughed. "I'd like to think he's too smart for that, but I'm not sure." She started to think out their options. "Are you thinking two units? And we knock down a wall in between?"

He shrugged. "I don't know. How many kids do you want?"

She stepped in front of him and held up a hand. He stopped cold in his tracks. "Hold on. How many kids? Are you sure you're feeling okay? Right now, I'm pretty stuck on the idea of one kid and we reevaluate later."

He leaned down and kissed her nose. "I feel great. But you know me. I'm a planner. I don't do anything halfway." He held up his finger, a sign he was about to make an important point. "Which brings me to the wedding."

"The wedding?"

"I know. This sucks. We're standing on a sidewalk in New York and I'm still wearing shorts from yesterday. This isn't the way I would've planned this at all. But in a day or two, when you're feeling better, I'd like to take you to pick out a ring so I can get down on one knee in some place other than a hospital room, profess my love for you and ask you to marry me."

"Wow." Charlotte nearly asked him to pinch her. If it wasn't so cold out, she would've thought she was dreaming.

"You are planning on saying yes, aren't you?" He narrowed his vision on her and one of his arrogant smirks crossed his face. "I feel like I can see the gears turning in your head."

"Yes, Michael Kelly. I'm planning on saying yes. As long as you're on your best behavior until then."

"There's always something with you, isn't there?" He took her hand. "Come on. My legs are freezing."

A block later, they arrived in front of the Grand Legacy. Something about the moment warranted a stop and a look up at the building, in all its beautiful glory. The

Christmas decorations were still up, the heavy swags of pine and the red-and-gold garland. It wouldn't be long before they'd be ringing in the New Year in the Grand Legacy. "I love the hotel, Michael. It really is perfect for us, isn't it?" This was a connection to her family that she cherished, and with the baby on the way, that felt especially important right now.

"It really is. Which is why I think we just buy the other two units on our floor and figure it out later. I'll move out of my place and we'll call an architect about connecting the units."

"Four units? Are you crazy?"

He waited for her to file first through the revolving doors. "No, I'm not crazy," he said when he'd joined her seconds later in the lobby. "It's a great investment, with no horrible neighbors to worry about, and it gives us flexibility to figure everything out." He pressed the button for the elevator. "Sound good?"

She didn't have a single complaint. Which wasn't like her when it came to Michael. So this was the new normal. "I'm sure Sawyer will be thrilled." The elevator dinged and the doors slid open. They stepped on board. "So, does this mean that our race is over? I'm not really sure how we're supposed to figure out the winner."

Michael gathered her up in his arms and lifted her off her feet, placing the softest and sexiest kiss yet on her lips. Compared to their other kisses in the Grand Legacy elevator, this was the best one yet. "It doesn't matter. I already got the prize."

* * * * *

LITTLE SECRETS: HIS PREGNANT SECRETARY

JOANNE ROCK

For my sister-in-law, Kate,
thank you for joining our family!
My brother is lucky to have you, and so are we.
Wishing you much love and happiness.

One

Sun glinted off the brilliant blue Atlantic, full of sail-boats bobbing on the calm water. For Delia Rickard, the picturesque island scene meant only one thing. It was the perfect day to ask for a raise.

Delia mentally gave herself a pep talk as she rushed around the marina in Le François, Martinique. She anticipated meeting her boss at any moment. Her father desperately needed her help and that meant forcing herself to push for that raise. Her quiet nature and organizational skills made her great at her job but sometimes posed a challenge when it came time to stand up for herself.

She hadn't seen Jager McNeill in the last six months. Would he be impressed with the changes she'd made both at his family's marina and the nearby McNeill mansion where she'd taken over as on-site property manager a year ago, on top of her responsibilities assisting Jager?

She'd worked tirelessly for months just to be worthy of Jager McNeill's trust in her. He'd given her the job as a favor since she didn't have a four-year degree—showing more faith in her than anyone else in her life. At first, it had been enough to work hard to repay Jager for giving her a chance. But now, considering the hours she put in to manage both properties and the effort she made to execute every facet to the best of her ability, she knew it was time to approach her employer about a bump up in her paycheck. Her father couldn't afford his portion of the taxes on the Rickard family lands this year and Delia needed to help to keep the small plot in the family. Her former fiancé had tried to trick her out of her share of the land once and she wouldn't give his greedy corporate backers any chance to swoop in now and take it from her or her dad. But unless she made more money, the Rickard home would be up for auction by springtime.

Delia sidestepped a family loading their cooler onto a skippered sailboat as she hurried toward the dockmaster's office for an update. Just as she got there, guests on one of the new superyachts dialed up its sound system far more than the noise regulations allowed, alerting Delia to a sunset party just getting underway.

"Cyril?" she called into the small office, raising her voice to be heard. "Any word on Mr. McNeill's arrival?"

The sun-weathered dockmaster turned to her. "His seaplane just landed. The skiff picked him up a moment ago."

"Thank you." She smiled quickly before turning to glare out toward the party boat, wishing the group would take their ten-decibel fun out to sea for a few hours. She wanted Jager's arrival to be perfect. "I'll go speak to our guest about the noise."

Cyril shouldered his way out of his office. He shaded his eyes to peer down the dock past the multimillion-dollar boat blasting house music, toward the open water. "Do you know why Jager wants to meet here?"

Delia had been puzzled about that too. Why would their boss want to step off a plane and go straight to work after being away from home for over six months?

The McNeill family had been through a harrowing year. The three brothers, Jager, Damon and Gabriel, had all relocated to Los Altos Hills, California, a year ago to establish their tech company in the heart of Silicon Valley. The software start-up had been Damon's brainchild, but both Jager and Gabriel played roles in managing the business as it grew. Shortly afterward, Damon had married. He planned to stay out West once the company took root, and Gabe and Jager would return to Martinique, where the family had a small hotel resort and the marina, in addition to the main house they sometimes rented out for upscale corporate retreats.

But then their lives had been turned upside down when Damon's new bride was kidnapped and held for ransom. All of Damon's focus had turned to getting his wife back, leaving Jager and Gabe to run the fledgling business. Eight months after the kidnapping—even after ransom had been paid—Caroline McNeill had not been returned. Damon's father-in-law insisted the ransom note had been a hoax and that Caroline had left of her own volition. Damon refused to accept that story even though police refused to investigate. Damon had left the country and hadn't been heard from since. To save his brother's company before the value dropped with rumors of instability in the leadership, Jager had quietly shopped the software start-up to potential buyers. He hoped to sell the business as soon as possible.

"I'm not sure why he wants to visit the marina first," Delia answered Cyril, her gaze trained on the water for signs of Jager's arrival. "Maybe after the year his family has had, work is the only thing getting them through the days."

Someone had threatened her family once and Delia had never forgotten the bite of betrayal. She couldn't imagine the pain the McNeills had been through.

"I just hope he doesn't decide to sell the marina too," Cyril admitted before he retreated into the dockside office, leaving Delia with a new worry to add to her list.

It was bad enough she needed to ask for a raise. What would she do if Jager unloaded his Martinique assets?

Delia felt the thrum of bass in the repetitive techno-crap blaring from the deck speakers as she rushed up the long wooden dock as fast as her wedge-heeled sandals would allow. The superyacht had only been docked at Le François for three days and Cyril had already talked to them once about the noise and the parties.

"Excuse me!" Delia called up to the bow, which was at least ten feet above her head. She waved her arms to try to catch someone's attention. A handful of swimsuit-clad couples lounged on big built-in sofas or milled around the bar. A few kids ran around the deck, squealing and chasing each other. "Hello!"

Delia backed up a step to make herself visible to the group. She could hardly hear herself shout; they were completely oblivious. She glanced behind her to make sure she had more clearance, well aware that the docks were narrow at the far end where the larger watercraft tied off.

She peered back up at the party boat just in time

to see one of the kids—a girl in a fluttery white bathing suit cover-up—lose her balance near the rail. Her scream pierced the air right before she pitched headlong into the water with a splash.

Terrified and not sure if anyone else even saw the child go in, Delia scrambled to the edge of the dock. She toed off her shoes and tugged her phone out of the pocket of her simple sundress, never taking her eyes off the ring of rippling water where the girl had landed. Jumping in feetfirst to avoid hitting her head on any hidden debris, Delia rotated her arms to pull herself deeper.

Salt water stung her eyes when she tried to open them. Her hair tangled in her face as she whipped her head from side to side. Scanning. Searching.

Fear robbed her of breath too fast. Her lungs burned as she grew light-headed. Had anyone else even seen the girl fall? What if Delia was the only one looking for her, and what would happen now that even she'd lost sight of her?

Breaking the surface, she hauled in a giant gulp of air, then forced herself to dive deeper. Legs kicking fast, she felt something tickle her outstretched hand. Forcing her body deeper, she couldn't quite catch the blur of white she spotted in the water through burning eyes.

And then another swimmer streaked past her as if powered by scuba fins. There was a rush of water as strong limbs sluiced by. Though her vision was distorted by the sting of salt, she could tell the new arrival was on target for the flash of white she'd spotted. Even as her chest threatened to explode from lack of air, she remained underwater long enough to be sure the diver retrieved the child.

Thank you, God.

The fear fueling her strokes leaked away. Relief kicked in along with a wave of weariness. By the time she got to the surface, she could barely drag in air, she was so woozy and exhausted, yet she could see through painful eyes as the victim was pulled to safety on the dock.

But now it seemed that Delia was the one in trouble. Gagging, gasping, her arms flailing, she reached blindly for the side of the boat or anything, clawing for support...

"Whoa!" A deep, masculine voice sounded in her ear at the same moment two arms wrapped around her midsection. "I've got you."

Only then did she realize she'd somehow clawed him too. The arm that held her was bleeding from three shallow scratches. Sense slowly returned as oxygen fed her brain again.

The house music had been silenced. The only sound now was the murmur of voices drifting from the marina. She glimpsed the drenched little girl on the dock, already surrounded by family. A woman—a local with a houseboat who happened to be a retired RN—was on her knees at the victim's side, lifting her gently as she coughed up water. The relief in the crowd was palpable. Delia felt the same overwhelming gratitude throughout her body. Her shoulders sagged.

Bringing her breasts into intimate contact with the arm around her. She collapsed like a wet noodle against the slick, hot body of a man built like iron. Her dress floated like seaweed around her thighs, making her suddenly aware of the way her soaked bikini panties were all that separated her from him.

"Are you okay, Delia?" The voice in her ear was familiar; she'd heard it nearly every day for the past year, even if she hadn't seen the man in person for weeks on end.

Her boss. Jager McNeill.

"Fine," she spluttered, the word ending in a cough.

Of course, it was foolish to be embarrassed since she had dived in the water to save a child. And yet, it still felt terribly awkward to be caught with her dress up around her waist today of all days when she'd wanted to make the perfect professional impression.

Also, she'd scratched him.

Coughed all over him.

If she hadn't had a crush on him once upon a time, maybe she wouldn't be tingling from head to toe right now in spite of everything. But she feared if she tried to swim away from him to escape all the feelings, she just might drown. She was surprised to notice how far she'd drifted from the dock in her search. Behind them, she noticed the transport skiff that Cyril had sent out to meet Jager's seaplane. Jager must have been arriving at the same time she'd jumped into the water.

"Hold onto my shoulders," he told her, shifting their positions in the water so he faced her. "I'll tow you to the dock."

Nose to nose with him, Delia stared up into his steel-blue eyes. She thought she'd gotten used to his good looks in the past two years that they'd known each other. His dark hair and sharp, shadowed jaw made for enticing contrasts to those incredibly blue eyes. His hair had grown longer in the past months, as if barber visits were the last thing on his mind. But the way the damp strands curled along the strong column of his neck only added to the appeal.

This close, she had the benefit of sensing the wealth of muscle in his athletic body where he held her. Feeling the flush of heat course through her, she ducked deeper into the cold water to hide her reaction to him.

"I can make it." Shaking her head, she scattered droplets from her wet hair. "I just needed to catch my breath."

She attempted to paddle away, but Jager only gripped her tighter.

Oh. My.

Feeling the warmth of his chest through their clingy clothes roused an ache she should not be feeling for her boss. Adding to the problem, the strapless bra she'd been wearing had shifted lower on her rib cage, where it did absolutely no good.

"Humor me," he ordered her, his voice as controlled as his movements. "You're exhausted and dry land is farther away than it looks." He took one of her hands and placed it on his right shoulder. Then, turning away from her, he very deliberately set her other hand on his left shoulder.

He began to swim toward the dock with measured strokes, towing her along behind him. Water lapped over them in light waves. She felt every ripple of his muscles under her palms as the light waves swished over them. She debated fishing one hand down her dress to haul up her bra before they reached land, but decided the potential scolding from Jager if she let go of him wasn't worth it. So she clung to him and gritted her teeth against the friction of her pebbled breasts rubbing against his back. By now he had to be as keenly aware of her as she was of him.

The only positive of this awkward reunion?

Any anxiety she had about talking business with him was utterly eclipsed by physical awareness. So when they reached land, she clamped onto the dock, evenly met his blue gaze and said, "I definitely deserve a raise."

* * *

Two hours later, when they were safely back at the McNeill family estate in Le François, Jager still couldn't erase Delia Rickard from his mind. After pouring himself an aged whiskey from the cut crystal decanter on his desk and taking a sip, he stared out his office window through the slats of the open plantation shutters. His gaze kept returning to the guest cottage lit by white landscape lights. He was waiting for Delia to emerge. When he'd first asked her to manage the Martinique household for him, he'd offered her the cottage on the British Colonial style property for expediency's sake.

Not only could she keep track of the staff better onsite, but at the time, she had also been trying to put some distance between herself and her past. Her former fiancé, Brandon Nelson, was a particular kind of son of a bitch Jager had run into often in business—always looking for a way to cheat the system. In this case, the guy had attempted to scam Delia out of her rightful inheritance—a plot of land belonging to her father that was in the way of a proposed landing strip for private aircrafts serving a luxury hotel development. The investors had offered Brandon a cash payment if he could convince her to sign over the rights. He'd decided to simply marry her and obtain the rights for himself.

Unethically.

Jager leaned a hip on the dark hardwood desk, remembering how Delia had discovered the truth on the morning of her wedding. She'd fled the seaside venue on a Jet Ski and run it aground on a small island where Jager had been fishing. It had been the start of a friendship that had benefitted them both.

He'd been in a relationship at the time, and Delia

had been running from an awful one, so he'd tamped down the attraction for both of their sakes. Instead, he'd offered her a job. Very quickly, she'd proven an excellent assistant, invaluable in helping him repurpose a portion of the family estate for private parties and occasional corporate retreats as a way to support local businesses—in particular, his marina. After Delia trimmed the household budget the first year and made a local farm-to-table initiative on McNeill lands a success, Jager had asked her to expand her role to review the operations at the marina as well.

Leaving things in her capable hands, he'd moved to California with his brother to take Damon's start-up to the next level. Just thinking about the hell that move had caused for all of them made his shoulders sag with grief for Damon and the loss of his vibrant and beautiful wife.

Now Damon had disappeared too. He'd left to travel two months ago and at the time, Jager had agreed it would be wise for him to get away. But days after his departure, Damon had shut off his phone and hadn't been in contact since.

To make it worse, around that time Jager had been contacted by their father, who'd barely acknowledged him as a child and whom Jager hadn't seen in fifteen years. Now, suddenly, he was offering the help of his wealthy family.

Too little. Too late.

As if Jager had any desire to spend time with the dirtbag who'd walked out on their mom. Apparently Jager's paternal grandfather—whom he'd never met—was determined to reunite all his grandsons. Bastard offspring and otherwise. Jager had told them hell no.

He finished off the whiskey and set aside his glass.

His world was a giant mess. The one moment of clarity in it all?

When Delia had been in his arms in the water just two hours ago. The dark churn of thoughts that had plagued him for nearly a year suddenly quieted, burned away by an attraction grown more intense since that first day when she'd washed up on his island. Nothing prohibited them from being together now. He was so distant from the Martinique-based businesses that he could make a move without worrying about the impact on their working relationship. Or he'd simply transfer her to another part of the company where Gabe could monitor her job performance, eliminating the conflict of interest. Gabe could make the decision about that raise she wanted.

His conscience clear, Jager watched her step from the cottage, her fair hair glowing golden under the porch light as she locked the dead bolt with a key. Now he could allow himself to think about the possibilities of being alone with her. Of forgetting the hell of the past year for a night in her arms.

Backing away from the window, Jager watched as Delia strode toward the main house. She wore a rose-colored tank dress, with a thin white sweater thrown over her shoulders. A simple gold bangle wrapped around one wrist. She worried her lip with her teeth as she stared down at the dusky gold pavers that led to the stone steps up to the house.

If he could have a taste of that soft pink mouth, he would indulge as often as possible. Was she nervous about spending the evening with him? Or was she looking forward to it as much as he? She had to have known she was getting to him today in the water. Soaking wet and hard as hell for her, he'd been unable to hide his fast reaction to feeling her breasts pressed to his chest. He'd felt her reaction too though. The attraction wasn't one-sided.

"Hello, Jager." He couldn't believe how long he'd allowed himself to ruminate over her body. She'd entered the house and his office while he was preoccupied.

Of course, she had domain over the whole place while he was gone. And he'd left the double doors to his office open. He was more than ready to let her in.

"I trust you're feeling better after the impromptu swim?" He turned to greet her but did not approach, hoping to put her at ease. She'd pinned her golden-blond hair up, leaving only a few stray pieces around her face. The rest bounced in a loose knot as she walked.

He gestured toward the seating arrangement near the fireplace. A wrought iron candelabra with fat white pillar candles had been laid in the cold hearth at some point in his absence. A homey touch. Delia perched on the edge of a wide gray twill armchair near the rattan chest that served as a coffee table, her posture stiff even though she gave him a smile.

"I'm almost warm again, thank you." She tugged the shawl sweater more tightly around her while he took a seat on the couch adjacent to her chair. "Tourists may swim in November, but I don't usually go in the water this time of year."

"Yet you didn't even hesitate." He'd been watching her from the deck of the skiff carrying him from the seaplane to the marina. "I saw how fast you jumped in after Emily fell." He'd spoken to the girl's family briefly after reaching the dock, to make sure she was going to be fine and that they would focus more on parenting and less on partying.

"You were in the water almost as quickly as me."

She shook her head and briefly closed her hazel eyes as a delicate shudder passed through her. "I don't even want to think about what might have happened if you hadn't arrived when you did. I was never so panicked as those few seconds when I couldn't find her."

"I only spotted her because you were just above her in the water." He'd swum faster than he'd known he was capable of. "Although I would have searched the whole damn marina for her if I had to. I've had enough sleepless nights thinking about how different our lives might be if someone had been there to haul Caroline out of the water."

He hadn't meant to share that, but the loss of his sister-in-law had overshadowed everything else for their family. Delia's hand on his forearm cut through some of the darkness though, providing an unexpected comfort.

"I'm sorry," she said simply, her eyes filled with genuine empathy.

Empathy that didn't even rightfully belong to him. It was Damon who'd been through hell. Suddenly Jager was reminded that he needed to focus on his family and not whatever he was feeling for his assistant right now. At least until they'd cleared up some business.

"Thank you." He acknowledged her kindness before redirecting the conversation. "Which reminds me that I won't be staying in town long, so I'd like to come up with a plan to review any new business over the next week."

"You're leaving again? Why?" Delia's touch fell away from his arm. Her lips parted in surprise.

"I need to find Damon." He'd never imagined his brother as the kind of man who might do himself harm, but Damon had been through more than any man should have to bear.

"I understand." Delia nodded, but her expression remained troubled. She spun the gold bangle around her wrist.

"I won't leave until we address any concerns you may have about the business." Or Gabe did. But there was enough time to share his plan with her. He still hoped to put her at ease first.

"Of course." She quit spinning the bracelet and glanced up at him. "I know how committed you are to this place. You're always quick to respond to any of my questions about the business."

Leaving him to wonder if she'd ever had questions of a more personal nature that he'd overlooked? He studied her features, trying to read the woman who'd become so adept at managing his affairs. A woman who had become a professional force to be reckoned with despite a lack of formal training.

She deftly changed the subject.

"Have you eaten?" she asked, straightening in her seat. "Dinner is ready. Chef texted me half an hour ago to say he'd prepared something—"

"Will you join me?" he asked, wanting her with him.

"I don't want to monopolize your time on your first day home." She scooted to the edge of her seat as if looking for the closest exit. Cautious. Professional. "I can bring you up to speed on the house and marina in the morning so you can enjoy your meal."

"My brother Gabe is in Los Altos Hills for another week," he reminded her. "There's no one else in Le François waiting to spend time with me, I'm afraid."

Still, she hesitated. No doubt about it, those chilly moments wrapped around one another in the Atlantic today had shifted the dynamic between them. She'd never been uneasy around him before.

"We can make it a working dinner, if you wish." He reached for his phone and began to type out a text. "I'm requesting that the meal be served in here."

"That's not necessary," she protested.

"I insist." He needed them to clear away an important piece of business. To remove any barrier there was to being together. "Besides, I've been meaning to discuss something you brought up in the water today."

"I…" Her eyes went wide. She swallowed visibly. If she were any other woman, he wouldn't hesitate to end the suspense and kiss her.

But he wouldn't rush this.

"You mentioned needing a raise?" he reminded her, clearing a place for their plates on the rattan chest by moving aside a fresh flower arrangement of spiky red blooms he recognized as native to the island.

Already, a uniformed server hesitated at the office door, a tray in hand. He waved the young woman in.

"Sir?" The woman's starched gray uniform was cinched tight by apron strings. She carefully set the tray down where he indicated. "Chef said to tell you there is a visitor at the gate."

"There is?" Delia tugged her phone out of a long brown leather wallet that she'd deposited on the chair beside her. The call button at the gate on the main road was hooked up to an app Delia and Jager could access. "I'm sorry I didn't hear the bell. I turned off notifications for our meeting."

Curious, Jager spun his own phone toward him and clicked on the icon for the security system while the server went to retrieve another tray from a rolling cart in the hallway.

Before Jager pulled up the video feed from the front gate, Delia gasped.

"What is it?" Jager asked.

She lost color in her face, her fingers hovering above her lips as if to hold in the rest of her reaction.

"It's not your ex, is it?" Jager shot to his feet, moving behind her chair to view her screen.

"No." Delia lifted the phone to show him. "It's your brother. Damon."

Two

Steel-blue eyes stared up into the security camera. Mc-
Neill eyes. Delia had seen the three brothers together
often enough to appreciate the family resemblance. The
striking blue eyes and dark hair. The strong jaw and
athletic build. Damon was the tallest of the three. He
looked a bit thinner than she recalled, which was no
surprise given the year he'd had.

"That's not Damon." The cold harshness of Jager's
voice stunned her as he tugged her phone from her
grip, his strong hands brushing over her fingers. "Let
me speak to him."

Confused, she let go of the device while Jager
pressed the talk button. Her skin was still humming
from his touch as he straightened.

"I've made it clear I don't want to see anyone from
your family," he barked into the speaker while he gently closed the office doors to keep their conversation

private from the staff. "If you need accommodations in town, I can send someone out to the gate with a list of recommendations."

"Jager!" Appalled, Delia leaped from her seat and reached to take her phone back. "What are you doing?"

The voice of the man at the gate rumbled through the speaker. "You're not getting rid of us, dude. Now that my grandfather knows about you, the old man is insistent that you and your brothers join the fold."

Delia froze as she absorbed the words. After hearing him speak, she questioned her own eyes. The man didn't have Damon's voice. Or his reserved, deliberate manner. The voice was bolder, more casual, even a bit brash.

Her gaze found Jager's, searching for answers. The air sparked between them, making her realize how close she was standing to her boss. She was painfully aware of how handsome he was in a pair of khakis and a long-sleeved dark tee that showed off his toned body. She caught a hint of his aftershave: pine and musk. Her heartbeat quickened before she stepped back fast.

"Not going to happen, Cam." Jager spoke softly, but there was an edge to his voice she couldn't recall hearing before. Clearly, he knew the man. "You can tell your grandfather that your father made the best possible decision when he walked out on my mother. We're better off without him."

Delia backed up another step, processing. The men looked so much alike. The man at the gate wanted Jager and his brothers to *join the fold* and said his grandfather knew about them now.

The man *was* Jager's brother. Just not the brother that Delia had assumed he was. This was a relation she'd never known about—a half brother.

"We have a lead on Damon," the visitor countered in a more guarded tone. "My brother Ian knows an excellent private investigator—"

"Damon is not your concern," Jager told him shortly, still studying Delia with that watchful gaze. "Goodbye."

He lowered the phone and pressed the button to end the connection and shut down the security app. Sudden silence echoed in Jager's office.

"You have more family than just Damon and Gabriel," she observed, feeling shaken from the encounter. From the whole day that had left her exposed in more ways than one.

It seemed as if Jager had whole facets of his life that she knew nothing about. If he didn't trust her with that information, how well did she even know him? Her former fiancé had left her more than a little wary of men who kept secrets.

"My father was a sporadic part of my childhood at best, and I haven't seen him once since my thirteenth birthday." Jager set her phone on the sofa table next to a platter of food covered with a silver dome.

She'd forgotten about the dinner, but the spices of island cooking—French Creole dishes that were Jager's favorite—scented the air.

"He had other children?" She felt she was owed an answer because of their friendship but she also needed to know about this to do her job. "This can have an impact on all your businesses. You'll want to protect yourself from outside legal claims."

"And so we will." His lips twisted in a wry expression. "But the Manhattan branch of the McNeill family is far wealthier than we can imagine thanks to their global resort empire, so they certainly don't need to alienate their own relatives by forcing their way into our businesses." He gestured to the sofa. "Please sit. We should eat before the meal is cold."

"McNeill Resorts? Oh, wow." The name was as familiar as Hilton. Ritz-Carlton. It was too much to process. She sank down onto the soft twill chair cushion.

Jager took the opportunity to lift the domes from the serving platters and pass her a plate and silverware. The scent of *accras*, the delectable fritters the McNeills' chef made so well, tempted her, rousing an appetite after all.

"Yes. Wow." His tone was biting. "I believe my half brothers expected Gabe and me to swoon when they informed us we were now welcome into the family." He dished out a sampling of the gourmet offerings onto her plate—spiced *chatrou*, the small octopus that was a local delicacy, plus some grilled chicken in an aromatic coconut sauce.

His arm brushed hers. The intimacy of this private meal reminded her she needed to be careful around him. She needed this job desperately. Her father relied on her and good opportunities were difficult to come by locally for a woman with no college degree. She couldn't afford to leave the island to find more options. Balancing her plate carefully, she shifted deeper against the seat cushion to try to insert some space between her and her tempting dining companion.

"Damon doesn't know about them?" she asked, trying to focus her scattered thoughts on his last comment.

"Only in a peripheral way. We were aware of their existence for years, but they didn't contact us until recently." Jager filled his plate as well. "Cameron McNeill and his brother Ian flew out to Los Altos Hills last month to introduce themselves and make it clear their grandfather wants to unite the whole family. Including the bastard Martinique branch."

Delia took her time responding, biting into the tender chicken and taking a sip from the water glass Jager passed her. She knew that he had no love for his father after the man disappeared from their lives—refusing to leave his wife for Jager's mother—when Gabe, the youngest son, was just ten years old. Their father had only visited the boys a few times a year before that, making it impossible to build a relationship. They'd lived in California back then. But after the father quit coming to visit, their mother sold the house and used the proceeds to buy an old plantation home in Martinique, purposely making it difficult for the boys' father to find them even if he'd wanted to. As far as Jager was concerned, however, his father had abandoned their family long before that time.

Jager had shared all that with Delia in the past, but the latest developments were news to her.

"It's the right thing for your grandfather to do," she said finally. "You, Damon and Gabe have as much claim to the McNeill empire as your father's legitimate sons."

"Not in the eyes of the law." Jager scowled down at his plate.

"The business belongs to your grandfather." She knew the rudimentary facts about the hotel giant. They owned enough properties throughout the Caribbean to warrant regular coverage in regional news publications. "Malcolm McNeill gets to choose how he wants to divide his legacy." She waited a moment, and when he didn't argue, she continued, "Have you met him?"

"Absolutely not. That's what they want—for me to get on a plane and go to New York to meet the old man." He speared a piece of white fish with his fork. "They claim Malcolm McNeill is in declining health, but if it's true, they're keeping a tight lock on the news since I haven't seen a whisper of it in the business pages."

Her jaw dropped. How could he be so stubborn?

"Jager, what if something happened to him and you never got to meet him?" She only had her father for family, so she couldn't imagine what it might be like to have more siblings and family who wanted to be a part of her life. "They're family."

"By blood, maybe. But not by any definition that matters in my book." Reaching for a bottle of chilled Viognier the server had left for them, Jager poured two glasses, passing her one before taking a sip of his own.

"And does Gabe feel the same way?" She had a hard time imagining the youngest McNeill digging his heels in so completely. Whereas Jager resolutely watched over his siblings like a de facto father, Gabe went his own way more often than not. He'd only invested in Transparent—Damon's tech company—after considerable urging from his siblings. Gabe preferred to stick close to the hotel he owned on Martinique and was renovating the place by hand.

His older brothers had scoffed at the manual labor, but Delia noticed that Gabe was having a hard time finishing the hotel work because his craftsmanship skills had developed a following, making him in demand for other restoration projects around the Caribbean, all the way to Miami.

"Gabe is outvoted by Damon and me." He took two more bites before he noticed she hadn't responded. When he turned toward her, she glared at him.

"Meaning he disagrees?" she asked.

"Meaning Damon would feel the same way I do, so if Gabe chooses to disagree, he's still outnumbered."

Delia set her plate aside on the rattan chest, then put her wineglass beside it.

"Damon might have a very different opinion about family after losing someone," she observed quietly.

Jager went still.

"You have a lot to say about something that doesn't concern you, Delia." He set aside his half-eaten meal as well, and turned to face her.

"Doesn't it?" She shifted toward him, their knees almost brushing. "I could give you an update on my plans for next year's community garden or how to increase profits at the marina, but it's hard to ignore the fact that you just turned your back on a family member who looks eerily like your missing brother."

"It's not eerie." His tone softened. "It's simple genetics. And I find you a whole lot tougher to ignore than my half brother."

She opened her mouth to deliver a retort and found herself speechless. The air in the room changed—as if the molecules had swollen up with heat and weight, pressing down on her. Making her far too aware of scents, sounds and him.

"That's good," she said finally, recovering herself—barely. She needed to tackle his comment head-on, address whatever simmered between them before they both got burned. "Because I don't want to be ignored. I would have hoped you'd listen to my opinion the way I once listened to yours when I was having some rough times."

She hoped that it was safe to remind him of the start to their relationship. She'd felt a flare of attraction for him that day too, but she'd been too shredded by her former fiancé and too mistrusting of her own judgment to act on it. For his part, Jager had seemed oblivious to her eyes wandering over his muscled chest and lean hips covered by a sea-washed pair of swim trunks. He'd quietly assessed the situation despite her tearful outburst about her thwarted marriage, and he'd given her direction, plus a face-saving way out of her dilemma at the time.

She hadn't been able to pay the taxes on the family's land that year either. Her dad had been injured in a fishing accident three years ago and couldn't earn half the living he used to selling fresh catch to local restaurants. But Jager had given her a job and the income had staved off foreclosure. Plus, Jager had given her a place to stay far away from her ex, and time to find herself.

Now, he looked at her with warmth in his blue eyes. A heat that might stem from something more than friendship.

"Maybe I liked to flatter myself that I was the one doling out all the advice in this relationship." His self-deprecating smile slid past her defenses faster than any heated touch.

"I don't think any of us exercise our best judgment when our world is flipped upside down." She'd been a wreck when they'd met. Literally. She'd almost plowed right into him on a Jet Ski she'd taken from the dock near where she'd planned to say her vows.

"Is that what's happening here?" he asked, shifting on the sofa cushions in a way that squared them up somehow. Put him fractionally closer. "The world is off-kilter today?"

The low rasp of his voice, a subtle intimacy of tone that she hadn't heard from him before, brought heat raining down over her skin. Her gaze lowered to his mouth before she thought the better of it.

"That's not what I meant." She felt breathless. Her

words were a light whisper of air, but she couldn't draw a deep breath without inhaling the scent of him.

Without wanting him.

"It's true though." He skimmed a touch just below her chin, drawing her eyes up to his. "Something happened in the water today. Something changed between us."

No, she wanted to protest. To call it out for a lie.

Yet he was right and they both knew it.

His touch lingered, the barest brush of his knuckles beneath her jaw. She wanted to dip her cheek toward his hand to increase the pressure, to really feel him.

Madness. Total madness to think it, let alone act on it.

"We can't let that happen." She needed to maintain the balance of power. Rebuild some guise of professionalism before it was too late. "This job is too important to me."

Shakily, she shot to her feet. She stalked to the window on legs that felt like liquid, forcing herself to focus. To get this conversation back on track. Why hadn't she simply spoken to him about the community garden?

"And your professional skills are valuable to me as well. But we can work around that." Behind her, his voice was controlled. Far more level than she felt. "Besides, do you really believe ignoring it will make it go away, Delia?"

She felt him approach, his step quiet but certain. He stood beside her at the window, giving her personal space, yet not conceding her point. The soft glow of a nearby sconce cast his face in partial shadow.

"If we both make an effort, yes. Of course." She nodded, hoping she sounded more sure of herself than she felt. "We're both adults with professional agendas.

We can keep those work goals front and center when we're together."

"Like we did today." His gaze fixed on some point outside the window, but his eyebrows rose in question.

"Today was an aberration." It had to be. "Emotions ran high. We were both scared for Emily." She wanted it to be as simple as that. "Just an adrenaline moment."

Her heart fluttered oddly as he turned toward her again, taking her measure. Seeing right through her.

"So what about this moment, right now?" he asked. "Adrenaline?"

She licked her suddenly-dry lips. Willed herself to come up with a logical explanation for the way the air simmered all around them. The way her skin sensed his every movement.

Any answer she might have given was a moot point, however, since Jager chose that moment to lower his lips to hers.

Jager couldn't walk away from her tonight. Not after the hellish year he'd had. He needed this. Needed her.

Her lips were softer than any woman's he'd ever tasted. She kissed with a tentative hunger—gentle and curious, questing and cautious at the same time. She swayed near him for a moment, her slender body as pliable as it had been in the water today, moving where he guided her. So he slid his hands around her waist, dipping them beneath the lightweight cotton sweater to rest on the indent just above her hips.

She felt as good as she tasted. Something buzzed loudly in his brain—a warning, maybe, telling him to take it slower. But he couldn't do a damned thing to stop it.

Instead, he gripped the fabric of her dress in his

hands, a tactic to keep from gripping her too hard. He tugged the knit material toward him, drawing her more fully against him.

Yes.

Her breasts were as delectable as he remembered from in the water today. High. Firm. Perfect. And Delia seemed to lose herself in the contact as much as he. She looped her arms around his neck, pressing her whole body to his in a way that made flames leap inside him. Heat licked over his skin, singeing him. Making him realize how cold he'd been inside for months.

Delia's kiss burned all that away. Torched everything else but this incredible connection. The warning buzz in his brain short-circuited and finally shut the hell up.

Letting go of her dress, he splayed his fingers on the curve of her ass, drawing her hips fully to his. The soft moan in her throat sounded like approval, but he was so hungry for her he didn't trust what he heard.

"Delia." He broke the kiss and angled back to see her better, trying to blink through the fog of desire. "I want you. Here. Now."

"Yes. Yes." She said it over and over, a whispered chant as if to hurry him along, her hands restlessly trolling his chest, slipping beneath his shirt. "Definitely now. If you lock the doors," she suggested right before she lowered a kiss to his shoulder, "I can get the blinds."

"I'm not letting you go for even a second." He walked her backward toward the door, kissing her most of the way until he needed to focus on the bolt. Even then, he kept one palm on her lower back, at the base of her dress's zipper.

"And the blinds?" she reminded him, her hair starting to fall from the topknot she was wearing. "The switch on your desk is closest."

"Right. Of course. Lady, you do mess with my brain." His brain—and other parts of him.

Jager moved with her in that direction, but he used his free hand to sift through her silky hair, pulling out pins and one jeweled comb, letting them fall to the dark bamboo floor. He'd been wanting to do this forever, he realized. Ever since he'd held her that first day when she wore that wet wedding gown and cried her eyes out against his bare chest.

She reached to find the switch, lowering the blinds electronically, shutting the room off from the well-lit grounds. Now just a few low lamps illuminated his office, casting appealing shadows on her creamy pale skin. With her tousled hair falling over one eye and the shadows slanting over her, she looked decidedly wanton. Altogether appealing.

He wanted her so much his teeth ached. He tugged the zipper down on her dress, peeling the cotton knit away from her body, sliding it right off her shoulders to pool at narrow hips. One quick shimmy and she kicked free of the dress; now she was clad only in ice-blue satin panties and a matching strapless bra. She was even more beautiful than he'd imagined, and he'd had some dreams where he'd thoroughly fantasized about her over the past two years.

Before he could contemplate how best to savor her, she slid a finger between her breasts and loosened the tiny clasp of her bra, baring herself. He froze for an instant to take in the sight of her—then his body unleashed into motion. His arms were already moving as he hauled off his shirt so he could feel her against him.

Kissing her, he cupped her breasts in his hands, teased one taut peak and then the other. Licking, nipping, drawing her deep into his mouth. He backed her into the desk and then lifted her, settling her there. She wrapped her legs around his waist, hooking her ankles and keeping him close.

"Do you have...protection?" she asked, her breath a warm huff of air against his shoulder.

Hell, yes. He might not have been with anyone in months, but he always kept a supply of condoms here. Pulling away, he opened the middle desk drawer. Thumbed past the last file. Emerged with a packet.

Their eyes met over the condom before she plucked it from his fingers and kissed him. No hesitation. No reservations.

He tunneled his hands through her hair, tilting her head back to taste his way along her jaw and behind one ear. She shivered sweetly against him, deliciously responsive. She smelled sweet there, like vanilla. He lingered, inhaling her, relishing the way her breath caught.

Too soon, her touch along his belt, the backs of her knuckles grazing his erection through his fly, called his attention from her delicate neck. Later, he would return to her neck, he promised himself. He wanted to linger over every part of her, but right now, the need was too fierce to ignore. While he unfastened the belt and carefully freed himself from the zipper, Delia was already tearing open the condom packet, her fingers unsteady as she rolled it into place. Her palm stroking over him there sent a fire roaring inside. He touched her through the blue satin panties she still wore, and he found the hidden dampness just inside and teased a throaty moan from her, stilling her questing hands long enough to let him catch his breath.

He wanted her ready for him. Really ready. Sinking a finger inside her, he felt the deep shudders of her release and kissed her moans quiet as she rode out the storm of sensation.

Damn, but she was beautiful. Her cheeks were flushed and eyes dazed, her hair a golden banner in the low lamplight.

When she was still again, he eased inside her slowly, gripping her thighs with his hands to guide himself home. She wound her arms around him again, nipping his lower lip before drawing it between hers. She arched against him, her breasts flattening to his chest. He knew he wouldn't last long this time. The day had stolen his restraint long before he started peeling her clothes off.

So he let himself just feel the slick heat of her body around his, her warm vanilla scent making his mouth water for a fuller taste. He cupped one breast and feasted on the taut nipple, finding a rhythm that pleased them both and riding it to...

Heaven.

His release crashed through him, trampling his body like a rogue wave until he could only hold on to Delia. He buried his face in her hair, the shudders moving up his back again and again. Her nails bit pleasantly into his shoulders and he welcomed the sweet hurt to bring him back to earth. Back to reality.

A reality that felt...off, somehow.

Straightening with Delia still in his arms, his body tensed.

"What is it?" The sultry note in her voice told him she hadn't realized what happened yet.

His satiated body was only beginning to get the message too, but his brain had already figured out what was wrong.

"It broke."

Three

Delia's brain didn't compute.

Her limbs still tingled pleasantly from the first orgasm a man had ever given her. Her whole body hummed with sensual fulfillment. And yet…panic was just starting to flood through her nervous system, rattling her from the inside out.

"What do you mean, *it broke*?" She knew what he meant, of course. But she didn't understand how it had happened. How she could have let herself be so carried away by the man and the moment. Even if the man in question was Jager McNeill.

"I don't suppose you're on the pill?" he asked, instead of answering her question, as he gently extricated himself from her arms and legs.

"No." She shook her head while reality slowly chilled the residual heat right out of her veins.

"You should stand up," he urged her, lifting her off

the desk and settling her on her feet. "Do you mind if I carry you into the shower?"

His matter-of-fact response to a potential grenade in both their lives only rattled her further, making the possible consequences feel all the more real. And frightening.

"I'll walk there," she assured him, wondering what the rest of his staff—her coworkers, for crying out loud—were going to think of her walk of shame through his house into the nearest bathroom.

She would headline local gossip for weeks. Or, quite possibly, nine months.

Oh, God. What had she done?

"We could try emergency contraception," Jager suggested carefully. "If you're amenable to taking the medication."

Would that work? She'd never had a need to investigate the option. "I can call my doctor."

Jager was putting a blanket around her. The throw from the back of the couch, she realized. Gratefully, she sank into the gray cashmere, veiling her tender body from the cool calculation she now saw in her lover's eyes. He'd pulled on his pants and shrugged into his long-sleeved black shirt. Only his dark hair, disheveled from her fingers, gave away the less guarded man who'd made passionate love to her just moments ago.

Not that it was love, she reminded herself sharply.

"I'm sure I can find a pharmacy with the over-the-counter variety." Jager was all efficiency. "I'll get you settled and make a trip to the store."

"Thank you." She would still want to talk to her doctor. Double-check the side effects given her medical history. But she wasn't sure how much to disclose about that right now with her thoughts churning.

"The guest room is closest," he told her, tucking her under one strong arm as he opened the double doors of his office and steered her into the hallway.

Of course she knew the guest room was closest. She'd been in this house every day for two years. Would she lose her job now if she was carrying his child? Or even if she wasn't? Only pride kept her from blurting out how much she needed this job.

When they arrived in the downstairs guest suite, Jager locked the door behind him and she scurried toward the bathroom.

"Delia." His voice halted her just before she shut the door behind her.

Peeking out through a crack—not that it mattered since he'd already seen her very naked—she waited to see what he wanted. And wished she saw some hint of warmth in his eyes to reassure her.

"I believe emergency contraception has a high rate of effectiveness. But based on where you are in your cycle, how strong of a chance would there be that this would have—" He hesitated, and she wondered if this was rattling him more than he let on. But he blinked, and any hint of uncertainty vanished. "Resulted in pregnancy?"

"Based solely on my cycle?" She had no idea if she was a fertile woman. But if so? "We would want to come up with a contingency plan when I get out of the shower."

Delia felt marginally calmer when she emerged from the bathroom in a pair of navy cotton shorts and a tee with McNeill Meadows printed on one pocket—promotional items given away to school groups who visited the community garden. She'd found a stack of clean items still in the packaging in the back of the guest bathroom's linen closet. Indulging herself, she'd helped herself to two tees to make up for the fact that her bra still lay on the floor of Jager's office.

She used a hand towel to dry her hair a bit more as she padded across the thick Persian carpet toward the king-size bed with its pristine white duvet. This bedroom overlooked the gardens, its deep balcony almost as large as the room itself. The sliding glass pocket doors were open now, and she followed the floral-scented breeze to where Jager sat on a padded chaise longue, looking out at the lit paths of the rock garden. The table nearby was set for two, a hurricane lamp glowing between the place settings of all white dishes. New serving platters undoubtedly held an entirely new meal. Sandwiches, maybe. Or fruit and cheese. Not even the McNeills' talented chef could turn out five-star cuisine on an hourly basis.

The travertine tiles were cold on her bare feet as she padded outside to join Jager. He turned when she'd almost reached him, then stood.

"Would you be more comfortable in your own clothes?" he asked. "I brought them from the office and put your things in the closet."

She winced to think of her wrinkled dress neatly hung in one of the gargantuan closets. "No, thank you. I've always liked these McNeill Meadows tees. I chose them last year for when school groups visit. At long last, I'll have my own."

"You wear it well." His blue gaze slid over her and she felt it as keenly as any touch. "I had some food brought up in case you're hungry. I wasn't much of a host the first time around."

Her stomach rumbled an answer at the same time she nodded. Needing to stay cool and levelheaded, she focused on slow, calming breaths. She draped the damp hand towel over one of the stone railings surrounding the balcony, then let him lead her to the table. The outdoor carpet was warm against her bare toes. He held out a chair for her and she sank into the wide seat. Once he tucked her chair in, he opened the platters, offering her each so she could help herself to a selection of fruits, cheeses and warm baguettes. Jager poured them both glasses of sparkling water over ice and lemons, then sat in the seat beside her. The hurricane lamp sent gold light flickering over the table while night birds called in the trees just off the balcony.

To a bystander, it would look like the perfect romantic setting. She guessed romance couldn't be further from either of their minds.

"Based on your comment going into the shower earlier, I thought it would be wise to discuss a plan for the future. Just in case." He slid a paper bag across the table. "Although I was able to obtain the contraception option we discussed."

She eyed the bag dubiously, but took it after a moment. "I'd like to check with my own doctor in the morning, but if he gives me the okay, I'll take it then."

"That sounds fair." He nodded.

"Thank you." She congratulated herself on her calm tone that belied the wild knot of fears in her belly. She focused on her wedge of brie, spreading the cheese on a thin slice of baguette.

Jager laid a hand on her knee, an intimacy she hadn't expected after how quickly he'd pulled away following the encounter in his office. It felt good. Too good. She couldn't allow herself to fall for him. One moment of passionate madness was one too many when she needed this job and the good will of the McNeills to help keep the Rickard home and land.

"Let me begin by assuring you that I would never abandon my child." Jager spoke with a fierceness that gave her pause. "My father taught me well the damage a parent inflicts with his absence."

The candle flame leaped and the glow was reflected in his eyes. She wasn't sure how to interpret his words, however.

"Neither would I," she told him evenly. Family loyalty meant everything to her. Her father had raised her by himself, on the most meager means, after losing his wife in childbirth.

Some of the intensity faded from Jager's expression. He lifted his hand from her knee and sipped his water before replacing the glass on the white linen tablecloth.

"Then we'll have to stick together if tonight has consequences," Jager observed. "In the meantime, I think I should fly out as soon as possible to begin the search for my brother. I want to find Damon so I can return here next month or in six weeks, whenever you think we might learn one way or another about a possible pregnancy."

Her knife clattered to her plate as she lost her grip. She fumbled to retrieve it, but couldn't hide her dismay at his quick abandonment. "I have set a new record for chasing a man out of my bed." Resentment stirred. "I can email you the test results, if it comes down to that."

"Delia." He set down his own cutlery to reach across the table, his hand circling one of her wrists. "It never occurred to me you might want to travel with me, but I can arrange for that. Our chemistry is undeniable."

Defensiveness prickled. She wasn't planning to be his mistress.

"What about my job? I need the work, Jager. My father relies on my income. That's why I asked about the raise before things got…complicated."

"I had already planned to ask Gabe to supervise your work from now on. To eliminate any conflict of interest for me. But in light of what's happened—"

"You already had a plan in place to have an *affair* and didn't tell me?" She wondered when he'd decided that. Or when he would have clued her in to the fact. It might have put her more at ease about being with him.

Then again, what did it say about the beginnings of a relationship between them when he made all the decisions?

"I wanted to be with you, Delia." His jaw flexed as he spoke and she had a memory of kissing him there. "I knew it in the water today that we weren't going to be able to continue a productive working relationship with so much tension between us."

She worried her lip, unsure how she felt about that. What if she didn't like working with Gabe? More to the point, what if Gabe didn't need her? If she was pregnant as a result of this night, how could she possibly maintain any independence when she worked for the family of her child's father?

Most important of all? She wasn't sure how she felt about an affair with Jager. Of course she was tempted. She couldn't deny their time together had been incredible. One touch from him and she'd been lost, swamped by a desire so heated she'd forgotten her common sense. But she had a few obvious reservations straight out of the gate.

"I'm not sure we can have a productive personal relationship either if we're not equal partners. I'd like to be a part of the decision-making." She nibbled a strawberry, hungry despite the anxiety.

"I agree," he surprised her by saying. But then, was he just trying to pacify her? "If there's any chance we need to parent together, we'll have to figure out how to share that responsibility in a healthy way."

Determined to at least appear calm and in control, Delia lifted her glass in a silent toast. "We're making progress then. I appreciate you hearing my opinions."

"I value your input. Would you really want to travel with me for the next few weeks? The last I knew, Damon was in Marrakesh."

She took a deep breath, steeling herself for a conversation he wouldn't want to have. But he said he'd share the decision-making power. She didn't plan on accepting his offer to extend this affair if he didn't mean it.

"Your half brother said he knows where Damon is," she reminded him. "On the off chance that it's true, shouldn't you find him as quickly as possible in case he needs you?"

Jager's shoulders tensed. "You're going to make this about my family?"

"Isn't this whole conversation about the possibility of more family? A McNeill child?" Straightening in her seat, she tried to maintain some composure, but she could see him pulling away fast. It was in his shuttered expression.

"I know Damon. That means I can locate him faster than anyone else." He'd sidestepped her question, she noticed. "The only thing left to decide now is if you want to join me in my search, or if you prefer to wait in Le François until we find out for certain if there will be another McNeill in our future?"

Four

Pacing the floor of the cottage bedroom, Delia paused to check her desk calendar for the third time, making sure her dates were right while she waited for the results of the at-home pregnancy test.

The calendar told her the same thing it had before. It was now two weeks until Christmas, and almost six weeks after that fateful night when she'd let her attraction to Jager run wild.

Nearly six weeks since she'd had unprotected sex with her boss, and no sign of her period. She'd ended up taking the morning-after contraception Jager had purchased for her after speaking to her physician, so she'd honestly thought they'd be in the clear, even though she hadn't been able to take the pill within the first twenty-four hours as would have been ideal. But it was still supposed to be highly effective within the first seventy-two hours, so she hadn't panicked when her doctor hadn't gotten back to her personally until the next day.

Still, she'd delayed this test, fearing a false negative result. Better to wait longer and be certain, even if Jager had been texting her daily from Morocco, asking her for updates, tactfully suggesting a blood test at an appointment he'd helpfully arranged. She'd been ducking his calls, which was totally unprofessional given that he still had some sway over her job, despite Gabriel McNeill now technically being the one signing her paycheck. But the longer she went missing her expected period, the more her anxiety spiked.

Because honestly, she was scared to know the truth.

In Jager's last text, he'd informed her he would fly home tonight, insisting they find out for certain one way or another. Knowing she couldn't handle discovering the result in front of him, she'd surrendered and pulled out one of the pregnancy tests she'd purchased two weeks before.

Now she just had to wait three minutes.

Thirty more seconds, she corrected herself after checking her watch. Skin still damp from her bath, Delia tightened the bathrobe tie around her waist and returned to the steamy bathroom where the garden tub was draining. The clove-and-cinnamon-scented bubble bath, which she made from her own recipe during the holidays, was a small decadence she allowed herself at times like this.

The pregnancy test lay facedown on the white tile countertop beside the sink. She'd left it there while she reread the instructions to be sure she understood. One line meant not pregnant. Two lines—however faint— meant she was going to have a child with Jager McNeill.

She'd read online that high tension and stress could

delay a period. That *had* to be why she was late. So, holding her breath, she closed her eyes. Flipped over the stick on the cool tile.

Two. Lines.

One bright pink. One paler pink.

There was no denying it. And according to the package, this was the most reliable at-home pregnancy detection kit.

"Oh, no. No." Her legs turned to jelly beneath her. She felt so dizzy she clutched the narrow countertop with both hands to steady herself. The stack of rolled yellow hand towels swayed against the wall as she stared at it.

No, wait. That was her swaying.

She stumbled back to sit on the edge of the garden tub, the last of her bubble bath gurgling down the drain with a sucking swish. Kind of like all the plans she'd had for independence once she had her father more securely settled. Plans to get a college degree one day. To travel somewhere beyond this tiny island where she'd been born.

Plans for a future where she called the shots and dictated her own life. She must not have taken the morning-after medicine soon enough, but at the time, she'd really wanted her doctor's advice about the pill considering her health history.

Wasn't it enough that she'd screwed up by nearly marrying a guy who didn't care about her? Nope. She had to compound her foolishness by succumbing to a moment of passion with a man who would never see her as more than…what? A company employee? A former friend turned sometime lover?

Her child deserved better than that.

That simple truth helped her emotions to level out.

Made the dizzy feeling subside a bit. She couldn't afford to wallow in a pity party for what she'd wanted in life. She was going to be a mother, and that was something tremendously significant.

She might have messed up plenty of times on her own behalf, but Delia Rickard was not going to be the kind of woman who made mistakes where her baby was concerned. That didn't mean she had a clue what to do next, but she sure planned to take her time and figure it out.

Deep breath in.

Deep breath out.

Before she even finished the exhale, however, a swift, hard knock sounded on the front door of the cottage.

"Delia?" The deep rumble of the familiar voice caused panic to stab through her.

Jager McNeill had come home.

Jager stood under the cottage porch light, waiting. He knew Delia was here. His housekeeper had seen her enter the carriage house an hour ago and Delia's lights were all on. Soft holiday music played inside.

She'd been avoiding any real conversations with him for weeks. He'd tried to give her some space, knowing she was even more rattled about the possibility of being pregnant than he was. Besides, the search for his brother had been intense, leading him on a circuitous path around the globe. Now he was certain, at least, that Damon was alive. But he'd seen signs that his brother was hell-bent on revenge and that scared him.

Still, Jager should have made Delia his first priority before now. Either she was delaying taking the pregnancy test for reasons he didn't understand or—worse—she'd been hiding the news from him. Whatever the truth, he needed to earn her trust. He couldn't afford to alienate her when their futures might be irrevocably bound.

He lifted his hand to knock again, only to hear the deadbolt slide free on the other side. The doorknob turned and there she was.

Delia.

Wearing a white terry-cloth robe and a pair of red-and-green-striped knee socks, she was scrubbed clean, her wet hair falling in dark gold waves onto her shoulders. Worry filled her hazel eyes. The rosy color he'd grown used to seeing was missing in her cheeks.

Hell.

He hadn't seen her look so upset since that first day they'd met. And that comparison put his own behavior into perspective. He wasn't a loser like her former fiancé. He should have come home before now. Been there for her.

"May I come in?" He hadn't even changed his clothes when he stepped off the plane. He'd flown eight hours to be here today, the six-week anniversary of the passionate encounter in his office.

Six weeks hadn't dimmed how much he wanted her. Not even when they were both stressed and worried about the future. If he had his way, she'd be in his arms already, but he didn't want to pressure her.

"That would be wise." Nodding, Delia retreated while he stepped over the threshold, closing the door behind him.

He hadn't been inside the cottage for over a year. He'd overseen the delivery of a few basic pieces of furniture when she'd first taken up residence in the renovated carriage house. But it bore no resemblance to what he remembered.

To say she painted flowers on the walls didn't come close to describing the way she'd made the interior look like an enchanted garden. Yes, there were flowers of all colors and varieties—some not found in nature—growing from a painted grass border along the floor. On one wall, a full moon glowed in white phosphorescent paint, shining down on a garden path full of rabbits and hedgehogs, all following a girl in a dark blue dress. On another wall, there was a painted mouse hole on the baseboard, with a mouse with a broom and apron beside it, as if the tiny creature had just swept her front mat. Above the couch, framing a window overlooking the garden, someone had painted an elaborate stained-glass frame, as if the window view itself was a painting. The white curtains were drawn and a holiday wreath hung from the curtain rod on a bright red ribbon. He could only imagine the effect in the daytime.

From the living room, Jager spied her small bedroom; a white queen-size bed dominated the space. A canopy made of willow branches around the headboard was covered in white fairy lights that made the whole room glow. The unexpected glimpse into Delia's private space was so distracting that for a moment he'd forgotten his purpose.

"I took the test," Delia announced, passing him a white plastic stick. "Two pink lines. I'm pregnant."

She collapsed down onto the narrow white love seat, her robe billowing out at her sides. Her head dropped into her hands, and she planted her elbows on the bare knees visible just above her knee socks.

For his part, Jager felt like he'd just taken a roundhouse kick to the solar plexus. He'd tried to mentally prepare himself for this outcome for the past six weeks, but he hadn't come close to doing an adequate job.

"You're pregnant." He stared blindly at the two pink lines for a moment before setting the test aside on a glass-topped wrought iron coffee table. He needed to focus on Delia.

Lowering himself to the love seat beside her, he placed a hand on the center of her back, hoping to reassure her. Or maybe himself. He wasn't feeling too steady either.

"I only just found out." She lifted her head from her hands. Her eyes were rimmed with red but there were no tears. "I should have taken the test weeks ago, but I was scared of a false reading. I knew I just wasn't ready for the relief of getting a negative result, only to find out three days later that it hadn't been accurate."

"It's okay." He rubbed circles on her back, trying to remember the to-do list he'd typed into his phone for just this scenario. "I was worried you've known all week and couldn't figure out how to tell me."

"No." She shook her head, damp gold strands of hair clinging to one cheek. "When you texted that you were coming home tonight, I knew I couldn't wait any longer. Bottom line, I've probably been delaying just because I was worried."

"That's why I wanted to be here for you when you found out," he reminded her, wondering how they were going to come to any agreement about the future of their child when they couldn't coordinate something so simple. "I wish you would have responded to my messages."

A determined expression appeared in her eyes. "I hope you can appreciate that we're going to have a new dynamic between us now and I can't be expected to have a sixty-minute window to respond to your texts. You ensured we wouldn't be working together when you handed over my performance reviews to your brother."

Surprised at her response, Jager realized there were many facets to this woman that he knew nothing about. Her whimsical love of gardens for one. And this steely, willful side that he'd never suspected lurked beneath her cooperative professional demeanor.

"I never said you needed to reply to my texts within the hour," he answered, his hand going still on her shoulders where he'd been touching her.

"Perhaps not, but it's a level of responsiveness I prided myself on when I was your assistant." She suddenly shot up off the cushions to pace about the small living area, her stocking feet silent on the moss-colored area rug. "Maybe you never noticed, Jager, but not once in two years was I delinquent with a reply."

He supposed that could be accurate. In truth, he'd never taken that much note. He tucked aside the information to consider later, once they'd gotten through the emotionally charged moment. For now, he focused on remembering the items on the checklist from his phone.

"Fair enough. I realize our relationship has changed radically in a short amount of time. We'll find our way forward together." He kept his tone gentle, unwilling to upset her any more than she already seemed. "I hope you'll agree our next step is a doctor's appointment to confirm the result of your test and ensure you're off to a healthy start."

She stopped her agitated pacing and stared at him blankly for a moment before she resumed.

"Of course." She nodded, but she appeared distracted. She paused beside her wireless speaker and flicked it off, quieting the classical Christmas music. "I'll call my doctor first thing in the morning."

"I'd like to go with you."

She stopped again, her gaze wary. "Why?"

Frustration ground through him at the realization that she could shut him out at any time. Sure, once the child was born he had a way to exercise legal rights. But until then, she could cut him out of a large part of the baby's life—ultrasounds, heartbeats—things he wanted to be a part of. The lack of control in this situation was alien to him.

"To be a part of the process, Delia. I've tried to give you the space you craved these last six weeks." It was tough even now staying in his seat while she paced the floor. He wanted to pull her against him, hold her and remind her how good they could be together in the most fundamental way, but he knew it wasn't the time. "This child is every bit as much my responsibility as yours. I tried to explain to you on the night we made this baby that I will take this duty very seriously." Jager would not be the kind of father Liam McNeill had been.

"Okay." Delia nodded, then bit her lip. "I should warn you though, there's a bit of medical history I'll be sharing at that time. I'm not necessarily worried, but in the interest of taking every precaution—" she hesitated, her fingers massaging her temple gently before she continued "—my own mother died in childbirth."

The revelation speared through him hard. "I should have remembered." She'd shared that with him once, long ago. He tried to recall what little he knew about her past and her family. "You said she went into labor early, while she was out sailing with your father."

He'd met Pascal Rickard once, a stern-faced fisherman who'd stared down Jager when he'd visited Delia's home village to collect some of her things. Jager hadn't wanted her to return home alone after the incident with her ex. Pascal had been in his seventies then, but even with his weathered face, gray hair and half an arm amputated, he'd been an imposing figure. His broad shoulders and burly muscles attested to the hard work he'd done all his life. The man had little to say to his only child when Delia had packed up her small room for good.

"They were having me late in life. My father was fifty at the time, and my mom was forty-two." Delia hugged her arms around her waist; there was a new level of anguish in the story now that she was going to be a mother too. "Her uterus ruptured. The doctors told my dad afterward there was nothing he could have done to save her. She would have been in critical danger even if she'd been close to a hospital at the time."

The thought of something like that happening to Delia floored Jager. No matter what happened between them romantically, she had been more than just an assistant to him these last two years. Even though they'd seen little of each other these last several months, he considered her a friend.

"Did her doctors know she was at risk?" He would spare no expense to keep Delia safe. He would call specialists. Hire extra help if she needed rest. His mental to-do list grew exponentially.

"She would have been considered high-risk anyway because of her age, but I'm not sure what caused the rupture." Delia swiped a hand through her damp hair, pulling it away from her neck. "Talking about my mother—and particularly my birth—always left my father sad, so I avoided the topic in the past. But now that the events are extremely relevant to me, I will visit him as soon as possible and find out everything I can about what happened."

"I'll drive you there." Jager would clear his schedule and look into hiring someone to follow up on the lead he had to find Damon. Until he knew more about Delia's condition, he wasn't leaving her side.

"I'll be fine." She shook her head, waving away the offer.

"I insist." He rose to his feet, needing to make it clear that he was involved with this pregnancy and staying that way. He closed the distance between them. He didn't reach for her the way he wanted to, but he stood close enough to catch a hint of cinnamon and cloves.

She smelled good enough to eat, reminding him of how long it had been since he'd tasted her. Touched her. He planned to pursue her again as soon as she had the all clear from her doctor.

"Jager, I understand you want to be a part of this, but I won't compromise my independence." Frowning, she huffed out an impatient sigh.

"Giving you a ride is hardly taking away your independence. You can drive us in the Hummer if it makes you feel more in control." He didn't use the huge SUV often, but the vehicle had just the right amount of metal to keep her safe. Delia had driven it before.

"This isn't about who's in the driver's seat." Her chin tilted up. She was stubborn. Fierce. "It's about sharing decision-making. Remember we discussed that? If we're going to be effective co-parents, we need to find a way to share responsibility."

"I remember very well." He couldn't help but feel stubborn on this subject as well, damn it. Raising a child together was too important.

Which brought him to the second item on his list, every bit as important as the doctor visit.

And even more likely to put that wary look in her eyes.

"Since we want to share responsibility, I suggest we

approach co-parenting through the time-honored legal channel that gives us equal rights in the eyes of the law."

He lifted her left hand in his and held it tight. Her gaze followed the movement, brows knitting together in confusion. As he bent over her left hand, he kissed the back of her knuckles. When he straightened, her lips had formed a silent O of surprise. But he didn't even hesitate.

"Delia Rickard, will you marry me?"

Five

Was he serious?

Delia studied Jager's handsome face, trying to understand his motive. He had to know how fiercely she would resist that kind of bloodless arrangement, especially now that she'd had a glimpse of what real passion felt like. She wasn't going to accept anything less than true love if she ever returned to the altar again.

"How can you ask me that after what I went through with my engagement?" Delia slid her fingers free of Jager's hand. Though her skin tingled pleasantly from the contact, her brain rejected his matter-of-fact proposal. She needed time to process all of this. Rushing headlong to make another mistake was not the answer, and she felt like she was hanging on by an emotional thread right now. "I already had one man try to marry me for purely business reasons."

"Our child is hardly a business reason," Jager reminded her. She noticed how he was still wearing his travel clothes: dark jeans, white tee and simply cut black jacket.

She would bet he'd driven here directly from the airport. His face was rough with a few days' whiskers too, making her wonder what his trip chasing Damon around the globe had been like.

"A legal reason then," she told him flatly. "I believe that's the very language you used when you tendered the offer. Marriage as a *legal channel* to raise our child jointly."

He drew a breath, no doubt to launch a counteroffensive, but she was simply not ready for this conversation tonight. His presence already loomed too big in her small living room, and with his child literally growing inside her, it was simply too much.

"Jager, I'm sorry." She stepped closer, hoping to appeal to him as a friend. "I'm still reeling from all of this. Since we'll be spending time together tomorrow to speak to my father and visit the doctor, maybe we could table this discussion for tonight to give us both a chance to get a handle on it?"

"I understand." He nodded but made no move to leave. His blue gaze skimmed over her. "Will you join me for dinner? We can unwind and relax. No need to talk about anything you don't wish to discuss."

She hesitated. And in the small span of silence, he picked up her hand and slid his thumb across the center of her palm in a touch that was deliberately provocative. Or maybe she was just especially sensitive to his caress.

Either way, it gave her shivers.

"Delia, we were together the last time I was here for a reason." His voice wound around her senses, drawing her in. "There is no need to deny ourselves a connection we couldn't resist then either."

She swayed in limbo, hovering between wanting to lose herself in his touch, and wanting to set new parameters for a relationship grown way too complicated. In the end, she wasn't ready to do either. Taking a deep breath, she extricated her fingers from his.

"That connection caused me to make a reckless decision that I'm unwilling to repeat."

Yet.

She knew resisting the pull of Jager McNeill was going to be a Herculean task, but for the sake of their child, she needed to sort out her feelings and make a plan before she ran headlong into another unwise decision.

"Very well." He tipped his head in the barest concession of her point. "I'll wait to hear from you in the morning. Let me know what time to pick you up."

"Thank you. I'll text you." She knew tomorrow she'd face the same temptations all over again—to simply fall back into a heated relationship with Jager and indulge herself. But maybe after a good night's sleep, she'd feel stronger. More ready to think about what kind of preparations she needed to make for her child's future.

"Until then, I hope you bear in mind that I'm sleeping close by and I'm here for you, Delia." He reached out and ran his finger along a damp strand of hair, tucking it behind her ear. Then, lowering his voice, he brushed the back of his knuckles along her cheek. "Day or night."

She felt the sexy promise low in her belly, where desire pooled, thick and hot. All at once, she was reminded of how very naked she was beneath her robe. Of how easy it would be to shrug her way out of it and take the pleasure Jager's touch offered.

For a moment, she didn't dare to breathe, her whole body weak with longing. She guessed that he knew. His blue eyes turned a molten shade for a moment, before he allowed his touch to fall away.

When he departed, bidding her good-night before he closed her door behind him, Delia slumped onto the sofa, her heart beating wildly. Resisting her former boss wasn't going to be easy. How long would he hold back because she asked him to? Another day? A week?

Because she knew with certainty that she would have lost herself in him all over again tonight if he'd pressed his advantage and used all that chemistry to woo her. That meant she needed to be smart. Strong. Resolute.

She couldn't possibly invite Jager back into her bed unless she meant more to him than a passing pleasure. With a child on the way, the stakes were too high to give him that kind of power over her since she wasn't the kind of woman who could simply indulge herself for the sake of…indulging.

Starting tomorrow, there wouldn't be any more impromptu meetings in private spaces where they could be totally alone. She needed allies. Distractions.

She needed family.

With that kind of buffer to romance, Delia would carefully insulate herself from temptation until Jager saw reason. Until he understood how much it hurt her to think about marrying for purely legal reasons. She'd already been a means to an end for one man. Now? She would never marry for anything less than love.

Jager stared at his cell phone as his call went through to the Manhattan number.

He didn't want to speak to any of his half brothers and hated relying on anyone else to find Damon.

But tonight's discovery that Delia was pregnant left him with limited options. He needed to be with her to press his suit for marriage and, even more important, to make sure she remained in good health throughout her pregnancy. The realization that her mother had died in childbirth had left him reeling far more than the news that he was going to be a father.

He wouldn't let anything happen to Delia, or to their child. And if that meant making a deal with his father's other sons in New York, Jager would do it. He couldn't search for his missing brother and win over Delia too.

"Cameron McNeill," his half brother answered. It was a name Jager might never get used to hearing.

Until two months ago, Damon, Gabe and he were the only ones in his life who shared the same last name and the same useless father.

"It's Jager," he announced, pacing around his upstairs bedroom balcony. He could see a corner of the carriage house below. Delia's lights were all out now.

"Hello, brother." The greeting wasn't exactly sarcastic. But not entirely friendly either.

Hell. Maybe it was simply awkward. Jager could totally empathize with that, at least.

"I've decided to call in the favor you offered last time you were here." He lowered himself to sit on the giant chaise longue—another new addition to the house's furnishings under Delia's supervision. Everything about the historic Martinique property was warmer and more comfortable since she'd taken over.

"The favor I offered the time you locked me out and refused to see me?"

"Correct."

While he waited for Cam to respond, Jager could hear the familiar music from a popular video game.

He'd read—during a brief, unwelcome need to acquaint himself with the other branch of the family—that Cameron had founded a video game development company.

"I'm glad you're willing to have this conversation," Cameron finally said as the triumphant music that signaled he'd completed another game level played in the background. "Gramps is going to be psyched."

Jager stared out over the cottage and the gardens beyond just as some of the landscape lights shut off for the night.

"I'm not going to New York anytime soon," he warned his half brother. His grandfather had been pushing for a visit, but he had too many things to focus on at home. "I want to see if your investigator has any more luck than I've had finding Damon."

"Fine." A series of electronic chimes sounded on the other end of the call. "But when Bentley finds your brother, you're getting on a plane and meeting Malcolm."

He'd been expecting this, of course, but didn't appreciate being dictated to.

"Or Malcolm can get on a plane and meet all of us at once." Jager made the counteroffer mostly because he didn't like caving on this point. But he knew Delia wanted him to make peace with his family.

"Not happening," Cam said flatly. "It's not his fault Liam is a tool."

That shocked a laugh out of Jager. Not enough to concede the point, however.

"We can revisit the subject after your investigator finds my brother. There's no use planning for an event that could be totally hypothetical anyhow. And I'm not going to see any of you unless I've got Damon back." It would take something major to get him to change his mind. He fisted his hand against the lounger cushion, then pounded it twice.

"Very well. I'm texting you Bentley's contact information. He has reason to believe Damon's in Baja." Even as Cameron said the words, Jager heard the message notification chime in his ear.

The words confirmed what Jager had already feared. Damon had circled back to North America without telling anyone.

"He's trying to find the men he believes kidnapped his wife." A cold pit widened in his stomach.

Though he and Damon hadn't always seen eye to eye, Damon remained his younger brother. And, to an extent, his responsibility. He'd understood that even before their mother died of breast cancer when Jager was a senior in high school. With no father in the picture, it had always been Jager's job to make sure his siblings were safe.

"Or else he believes Caroline is still alive," Cameron offered, "and he wants to find her."

The words chilled him. Mostly because he feared that wasn't possible. He'd seen for himself how in love Caroline had been with his brother. He couldn't imagine her leaving of her own free will.

"For Damon's sake, I hope the latter is true." He needed some shred of positive news. "I'm going to phone Bentley now."

"Jager?" Cam said in a rush. "One more thing?"

He waited.

"You remember the terms of Malcolm's will? That we can only claim a share of his legacy if we've been married for twelve months?"

Jager's gaze shifted back to the cottage where Delia must be sleeping by now. He felt a pang of guilt that she'd taken the pregnancy test alone, that he hadn't been with her. What would she think about his wedding proposal if she discovered that marriage fulfilled one of the stipulations Malcolm McNeill had outlined for his heirs? Would she be so enthusiastic about a McNeill family union then, if she discovered another "business reason" for marriage?

"We don't want your company." He was more interested in profiting from his own projects—work he'd invested in personally.

"Right." Cameron huffed out a long sigh. "Between me and you, I'm grateful about that, so thanks. But our grandfather is a stubborn individual and he is determined to make us all fall in line."

"You're welcome to be his puppet. But not me." He was already grappling with feeling a lack of control where Delia was concerned. He wasn't about to relinquish more power over his own life to Malcolm McNeill.

"So consider a cash settlement," Cam suggested. "Meet Malcolm, shake his hand, let him feel like you're going to be a part of the family. But if you don't want the company, let my brothers and me buy you out."

"You can't be serious." The net worth of McNeill Resorts was staggering to contemplate. Far more than they'd make on the sale of Transparent, Damon's software company.

"Dead serious. Don't rob us of the business that has his name on it. The business we've all worked our asses off to further because it means something to him."

That Cameron would even suggest such an offer brought home how much he wanted to keep his grandfather's company intact. Interesting, because all three of the New York McNeill brothers were wealthy in their own right, with diverse business interests. Quinn, the oldest, was a hedge fund manager. He was *made* of money. So good with it, he earned millions showing other people what to invest in.

"I'll talk to my brothers," Jager finally conceded, levering himself off the chaise, needing to make his next call. "No promises though."

"That's all I'm asking."

Disconnecting the call, Jager checked his texts and found the contact information for the investigator Cameron had mentioned. As much as he hated asking for help to find Damon, Jager couldn't deny that he'd benefit from assistance after spending six weeks to find out something that this investigator had apparently known about for over a month. If he'd just given in and taken Cam up on the offer for help back when he showed up at the gate that night, maybe Jager would already have Damon back home.

It seemed stubbornness ran in the family, if what Cameron said about their grandfather was true.

For the first time since learning about his half-siblings, Jager thought maybe it wouldn't be so bad to at least meet them. Especially now that he was having a child of his own. Jager's father might be a two-timing failure as a role model, but that didn't necessarily mean Malcolm would be a negative influence on his heirs.

In less than nine months, Jager would need to make the decision. But first, his main concern was protecting Delia.

A job which would be easier as soon as she was his wife.

Six

With the top down on Jager's sporty convertible roadster, the warm December sun shining on them as they headed south the next day, Delia could almost forget they were driving toward her hometown.

She slicked on lip balm from her purse to keep from fidgeting as she was hit with a small attack of nerves. She'd avoided her father's fishing village for almost two years, preferring to coax him into Le François to visit her so she didn't need to run into people from her hometown. So many of her former neighbors had been at her failed wedding, witnessing the most humiliating day of her life. Understandably, going back home made her nervous. But she took comfort from the scent of the rich leather bucket seats and the smooth purr of the new Mercedes's engine. A local dealer had been all too glad to deliver a vehicle to Jager this morning, encouraging him to take the polar-white luxury car for a "test spin" for a week or two.

The privileged life her former boss led was going to be the kind of life that belonged to her child as well. But not to her. Delia had been lured in by the comforts of excess once. She wouldn't be wooed with superficial things again.

She chucked the lip balm back into her handbag as the vehicle slowed.

"That smells amazing," Jager observed as they stopped at a four-way intersection. "What is it?"

He peered over at her from the driver's seat, his blue gaze moving to her newly-shiny lips. It took all her willpower not to lick them. She felt incredibly aware of him today and she wasn't sure if it had to do with pregnancy hormones or the fact that she hadn't spent much time with him since their single combustible encounter in his office. She knew him differently now, and she wasn't sure she'd ever be able to look at him again without heat creeping all over her skin.

She straightened in her seat, hoping none of what she was thinking showed on her face.

"It's a new addition to the McNeill Meadows gift shop." She hadn't mentioned the product line to him, hoping to see the homemade beauty and bath items start turning a solid profit first. "I've been using the flower petals from the gardens, and beeswax from our beekeeper to make locally sourced lip balms and sugar scrubs. This one is called Coming Up Roses."

His gaze lingered on her mouth. Her heart skipped a beat or twelve.

"May I see?" he asked. With no one else at the intersection, he didn't seem in any hurry to put the car back in gear.

She did lick her lips then. "Um. There's no color or anything. It's just a balm." Still, she tilted toward him slightly so he could have a better look. The consistency of the product was really nice and she was proud of it.

"I meant the packaging." A grin twitched behind those words. "Although it looks very appealing on you."

"Oh." She leaned down to dig through her purse, wishing he didn't make her feel so fluttery inside. How was she going to forge a balanced, even relationship with him when she felt like a swooning teen around this man? "Here you go."

Passing him the tin, she tried to focus, bracing herself for the questions he might ask. But he seemed distracted today. Worried, perhaps. She wasn't sure if it was about the baby news or about his brother, but she understood he was coping with a lot right now. Businesswise, he was brokering a deal for the sale of Transparent, and that alone had to be stressful when it involved so much money.

"This was a great idea," he said finally, handing her back the tin before another car arrived across from them at the intersection. Jager took his foot off the brake and they continued their trip. "I like the way you kept the farm-to-table sensibility with local ingredients."

"And," she couldn't resist adding, "I'm creating a mini exhibit in the gift area about the plantation history of the McNeill home. I think visitors will be interested that we're using our own sugarcane in the lip and body scrubs."

"We are?"

"I sent you some paperwork on it last spring," she reminded him, beginning to see familiar sights out the window as her village neared. "We made an arrangement with a small refinery in Florida, but the end product is very much locally sourced."

The private marina where her wedding would have

been held was ahead on the right. She hadn't seen it since that day she'd stolen a Jet Ski that—thankfully—Jager had returned to the owner on her behalf. It had taken her a full year to repay him for the damages to the watercraft. Her nerves knotted tighter.

"Delia?" Jager said a moment later, making her wonder if she'd missed something he'd said.

"Hmm?" She pulled her gaze off the rocky coastline and back to the too-appealing father of her child.

She had to keep reminding herself of the fact since it still didn't feel real that she was carrying a McNeill heir.

"Are you nervous about seeing your father? Returning home?"

"Is it that obvious?" Her voice was a fraction of its usual volume. She cleared her throat. "I suppose it must be. And I'm not sure what has me more keyed up—telling my father I'm expecting, or seeing that marina where I stole a Jet Ski to escape from my ex."

"Would you like me to take a detour?" Jager flicked on the directional. "We can head inland for the last mile or two."

"No." She reached for him, laying a hand on his arm to stop him. "That's definitely not necessary. It's bad enough I was too insecure to handle things differently two years ago. I won't resort to running away anymore."

Resolutely, she looked out the driver's-side window, where the first boats of the marina were coming into view, bobbing in the crystalline blue water. The scent of the sea drifted through the convertible. Her hand fell away from his strong forearm.

If she touched him too long, she might not be able to stop.

"You didn't run away," he replied, his jaw flexing as he flicked his gaze out the side window for a moment before returning his attention to the road. "You escaped a bad situation. Big difference."

"There's no good excuse for larceny." The guilt over doing something so foolish still gnawed at her on occasion, but her actions that day hadn't just been in response to her fiancé's deception. "Although I might have been able to face my wedding guests that day if I hadn't also learned that my father knew about Brandon's involvement with the investment company."

They cruised past the permanent archway installed on the pier where people traveled from all over the world to say their vows. Today, in fact, a Christmas bride carrying a bouquet of red roses stood beside her tuxedoed groom, a blanket of poinsettias draping the arch. A small crowd filled the pier to watch, just the way Delia's guests had gathered two years ago.

"Your father knew?" Jager asked, his tone incredulous. He didn't even seem to notice the wedding in progress. "Didn't he care that jackass fiancé of yours was going to try to steal away your inheritance?"

That's exactly how she'd felt at the time, but her father had been unperturbed when she approached him in tears.

"Dad said the land was always meant for me, so if I wanted to sell it to developers, that was my business." It had been the way he'd said it that had hurt the most, with a shrug as if it didn't matter to him either way.

It had confirmed for Delia what she'd feared since childhood—that her father watched over her out of a sense of duty, never a sense of love. Pascal Rickard was a hard man, and she'd told herself for years he was simply too stoic to show his softer emotions. On her disastrous wedding day, she'd been confronted with evidence that he really didn't care all that much, and it had been a hurt deeper than anything Brandon Nelson could have ever doled out.

"You never told me." Jager gripped the stick shift tightly as he slowed down the vehicle. "All this time I thought it was a broken heart that brought you to my island that day."

He'd been like a mirage in the desert that day, a too-good-to-be-true vision of masculinity and caring as he helped her out from under the broken Jet Ski. She'd thrown herself into his open arms like he was an old friend and not a total stranger. Funny how she'd worked for two years to erase the horrible first impression she'd made, only to fall right back into those strong arms at his slightest invitation.

"It was a broken heart." She breathed in the scent of spices and fish as they neared the village market near the water. "But Brandon only accounted for part of it."

When Jager didn't respond, she tried to gauge his expression. He turned down the side road that led to her father's property, a tiny white-and-blue fish shack on the corner open for business. A few tourists lined up for whatever they were frying up today, the picnic tables out front already filled.

Tourist season started in December, and even the small fishing villages like this one benefited from the extra traffic.

"No wonder you haven't wanted to return here," Jager muttered darkly. "He would have let you walk right into marriage with a guy who wanted to steal your birthright."

True. But over time, Delia had come to see her father's point of view. He'd assumed that Delia was forsaking the land for the comforts of marriage to a local businessman with more financial means than she'd had growing up. And, sometimes, she feared that he'd understood her more than she understood herself, since walking away from Brandon hadn't been nearly as difficult as it should have been. How much had she loved her former fiancé in the first place?

Clearly, her judgment in men could not be trusted.

"Do you remember which one it is?" She pointed to the bright red house on stilts. "It's over there."

Nodding, Jager pulled off the main street onto the pitted driveway that led to her father's cabin, the simple home where she'd been raised. All around them, she knew, were other families who'd wanted desperately to sell their properties to the development group that had planned to put in an airstrip for a luxury resort. Her father had been the lone holdout.

For as long as he could pay the taxes. Because even though that old deal was no longer on the table, the plans were a matter of public record. Any other developer could swoop in and re-create the plan if they were able to obtain the necessary parcels of land to make it happen.

Tension seized up her shoulders as Jager stopped the car and came around to open her door. It was easier to simply send checks home than to face her father again after all this time. But today, for her child's sake, she needed answers that only Pascal Rickard could provide.

So for just a moment, she took comfort from Jager's hand around hers as he helped her from the Mercedes. She lingered for a moment as they stood close together, her sundress blowing lightly against his legs and winding around him the way the rest of her wanted to. She breathed in the scent of his aftershave—woodsy and familiar—before forcing herself to step away.

She'd allowed too many men access to her heart, and the price for her lack of judgment had been high—broken relationships and too much hurt. She wouldn't make the same mistake with Jager. As the father of her child, he was someone she needed to remain friends with. Only friends.

Forever.

Jager could practically see the mental suit of armor Delia put on as they entered her father's house. Hell, he'd done the same thing long ago himself, back when his family had still been living in the United States and he'd been young enough to care what his father thought of him.

Delia's careful mask of indifference reminded him of things from his own past he didn't want to recall.

So while she made awkward small talk with the serious, graying fisherman, Jager focused on his own agenda for the day. He needed to find out as many details as possible about the cause of her mother's death. Once he had ferreted out all the information, he would consult physicians independently.

Because while Delia had made a doctor's appointment for that afternoon, he didn't trust the local obstetrician to be on the forefront of prenatal and preventative healthcare. The one benefit he could see of a trip to New York—and to the home of the McNeill patriarch—was to ensure Delia had the best possible doctors for this baby.

Their baby.

The idea still threatened to level him every time he thought about it.

Now he followed Delia and her father outside to the deck overlooking the water. The red cabin on stilts was one of many brightly painted houses the village website touted as "charming," but Jager knew Delia's upbringing had been rough. She'd worked hard to help her father make a living, checking nets and making repairs almost daily, manning the fish market when he needed to go back out to sea and cleaning fish for demanding customers.

Still, there was beauty here in the simplicity of a lifestyle rooted in a sense of community. Jager envied that, especially after the McNeill wealth had attracted the kidnappers who'd taken Damon's wife.

Jager would never forget the naked pain in his brother's eyes the day she'd gone missing. The day she'd been presumed dead by the police.

Taking a seat beside Delia, Jager ached to touch her. Hold her hand and tell her father in no uncertain terms that he would be taking take care of Delia from now on. But until she agreed to marriage, what right did he have to stake that claim?

Clamping his jaw shut tight, he studied the older man. Even in his seventies, Pascal Rickard possessed a much younger man's vitality. His half arm didn't seem to hinder him much, and he used the partial limb efficiently enough, easily swinging an extra chair into place at the rickety patio table so that they could all have a seat. When her father didn't offer them anything, Delia returned inside, emerging a minute later with a pitcher of ice water and clear blue glasses. Jager stood to help her pour, passing around the drinks, and then they both sat again.

Had she always taken care of her father that way? Jager wondered. The older man sipped his water without comment while Delia spoke.

"Daddy, I'm here today because I need to ask you a

few questions about my mother. About how she died."
Leaning forward in her rusted metal seat, Delia clutched
her water glass in both hands, the tension in her arms
belying the calm tone of her voice. "I know you don't
like to talk about her. But it's important to me now because I'm pregnant."

Jager hadn't expected her to launch right into the
heart of the matter. He guessed it must have been nerves
that propelled the words from her, because she wasn't
the kind of woman to shock an old man on purpose.

Pascal's face paled for a moment while he sipped
his drink. Then he lowered the glass to the lopsided
wooden tabletop.

"That's why you're here?" Pascal asked Jager, his
hazel eyes the same shade as his daughter's but without any of the tenderness.

"I have asked Delia to marry me," Jager pointed out,
reaching for her hand on instinct. "I hope that I will convince her to accept before our child is born."

Long before then, actually. Tomorrow wasn't soon
enough as far as he was concerned.

Pascal grunted. Some of the color returned to his
face, but his expression remained stony. Delia, at least,
allowed Jager to hold her hand.

"I'm seeing an obstetrician later today," Delia continued as if Jager hadn't spoken. "And I need more details
about mom's medical history in case there could be genetic factors at work we should know about."

The idea punched through Jager again as he turned
to watch her. He'd lost his own mother too early, and
Delia had never known hers. He guessed the vision of
a child growing up without a mother was equally real
for both of them. The thought had him twining his fingers through Delia's slender ones, gripping her tighter.

Pascal thrust his lower lip forward in an expression of disapproval before he turned to address Jager again. "Delia doesn't want to get married. Didn't she tell you? She could have been settled by now, but she didn't want to share her inheritance with developers."

Defensiveness rose in him, all the more when he heard Delia's soft gasp of surprise.

"Her fiancé had no plans of 'sharing' it," Jager reminded him. "Something he failed to mention to your daughter. She had to discover on her own." He pressed on, remembering how hurt Delia had been the day she'd wrecked that Jet Ski on the beach. "Didn't it occur to you she'd want to know Brandon's reason for marrying her?"

The old man shrugged, settling his empty water glass on the peeling, planked floor. "She seemed happy enough to put this life behind her when she was dating her big spender."

"That's not fair." Delia shot out of her chair, stalking to the half wall surrounding the deck. "I thought Brandon cared about me."

"And I thought you cared about making a better life for yourself," her father retorted, tipping back in the wooden dining chair he'd dragged outside from the kitchen. "Brandon offered you more than a life as his mistress."

Anger flared hot. Jager deliberately remained seated, facing her father head-on before he replied, "I am prepared to give Delia my home, my name and my life. I thought I made that clear. Right now, I would appreciate your help in protecting her health, so I'd like to know if this pregnancy poses a serious risk for her."

"And if it does?" Pascal set the feet of his chair back on the floor with a thud. "What then? Are you still prepared to give my daughter your life and your name if she can't carry your child to term? Or are you only willing to marry her for a McNeill heir?"

"Daddy, please." Delia stepped closer, not quite between them, but definitely in an effort to placate her father. She touched his knee and dropped down to sit on an overturned milk crate beside him. "I will decide my future, but I need to know what I'm facing. If you don't know about my mother's medical history, maybe you could tell me the name of her doctor—"

Pascal cut her off with a quick shake of his head. "Celine didn't have anything genetic." The words sounded raw in his throat, far different from the taunting tone he'd taken with Jager a minute ago. "She never even told me until that night on the boat when you were born, but Celine had a cesarean as a young woman when she gave birth to a stillborn child. She'd been frightened of something going wrong again. Worried she'd disappoint me." He swallowed hard and looked out to sea, unable to continue for a moment. "By the time I knew about it, it was too late. We'd only been married for two years."

The anger Jager had been feeling toward him seeped away then, his own fears for Delia making it too easy to identify with him.

"Afterward," her father continued, "when I got back to shore with you, the doctors said a cesarean can cause a uterine rupture later in life. It's rare, but it happens. Your mother had no idea of the risk, I'm certain of that, because she wanted you. Desperately."

Jager waited for Delia to ask him more, but she'd gone quiet. She studied her father, who remained silent.

Leaving Jager no choice but to step in again.

"Why was Celine's first child stillborn?" he asked,

wanting to give Delia's doctor a complete picture of any relevant medical history.

Delia spun away from them on the milk crate, grabbing her bag and riffling through the purse before coming up with a tissue.

Had he said something wrong?

Pascal shook his head. "I couldn't tell you. Celine never told me anything about that time in her life until the night she died."

Damn it. Jager kept digging. "Was she from this village? Maybe we can speak to her doctor."

Pascal folded his good arm over the injured limb, his mouth set in a thin line. Delia seemed to read this as a rejection of the question or refusal to reply, because she stepped closer again, slipping her hand around Jager's elbow.

"I can find out about those things," she assured him quietly. Her eyes were bright but there were no tears. "We should go."

Jager wanted to argue, to find out what else they could glean from her father. But seeing the hurt in Delia's eyes—a hurt he didn't fully understand—he followed her outside after a terse goodbye to Pascal. He didn't want to gainsay her in front of her father, a stunt that definitely wouldn't help his efforts to win her hand. He would simply call in every resource to learn more about Celine's medical condition. For now, they had enough information for Delia's obstetrician appointment.

It was good news that the uterine condition wasn't genetic. Yet there was still the worry of why her mother had a stillborn child when she'd been a younger woman. Jager's gut knotted as he opened the passenger door of the convertible for Delia.

No doubt she was upset about that news too, because she retreated to her side of the vehicle and didn't have a single word to say on the ride to her doctor's appointment.

Seven

Stepping out of the exam room an hour later, Delia smoothed a hand through her hair, still windswept from the car ride with the top down. While she was in the cold, antiseptic-scented room with the nurse and her new doctor, Delia had been very aware of Jager's presence in the waiting area outside. The nurse had said she would bring him back to the doctor's private office so they could both speak with the obstetrician at the same time.

After their meeting with her father, Delia had had a fair idea of how that encounter would go. Jager would ask the questions and push for answers.

With the doctor, she wouldn't mind so much. But with her father...

She paused a few steps from the doctor's office, closed her eyes and pulled in a deep breath. Remembering how close she'd been to hearing her father confess something—love for her? That she'd been loved by her mother?—pinched her emotions hard. Today had been the closest her father had ever come to showing some paternal warmth for her when he'd said that her mother had wanted her *desperately*.

How long had she yearned for scraps of his affection, even if that fondness was only a pale reflection of the love her mother might have given her? But the moment when he might have said more had evaporated forever when Jager interrupted, pushing the conversation in a more pragmatic direction.

He didn't know, of course, how much those few words from her father had meant. How much she craved even a few. So she couldn't blame him for stamping out any possibility that the stoic Pascal would share some tender memory from his past.

And yet, she did.

She'd wanted to see her father alone, but Jager had insisted on being a part of her pregnancy. She needed to start building boundaries with him fast before she lost her sense of self to the strong will of this McNeill male. The past two years had been full of hard work to prove to herself she was smart, independent and capable. Being pregnant couldn't take that away from her.

"Ms. Rickard?" The voice of the doctor, a young woman fresh from her residency in Miami, startled Delia.

She opened her eyes and faced Dr. Ruiz. Tall and willowy, the physician wore a light-up reindeer pin on the lapel of her white lab coat over a red tartan dress.

"Yes." Straightening, Delia told herself to get it together. "Sorry. I'm just…excited. About the baby news." She babbled awkwardly, embarrassed to be caught doing relaxation breathing in the middle of the hallway. "It's a lot to process."

"Come on in the office," the doctor urged, opening the door to the consultation room. "I'll do what I can to help you both."

Dr. Ruiz introduced herself to Jager and they settled into chairs around the obstetrician's desk as she talked through the preliminaries. Yes, they'd confirmed her pregnancy. Delia was given a piece of paper with her summer due date written on it in black marker.

Her hand crept to her flat belly while she tried to take it all in. Once more, Jager took the lead with questions, sharing his concerns about her mother's health history and the stillbirth. But when he launched into more questions about the uterine rupture too, Delia interrupted.

"My father made it clear that wasn't a genetic condition," she reminded him before turning to Dr. Ruiz. A filing cabinet behind the obstetrician had a magnet that said Keep Calm and Get Your Pap On caught Delia's eye.

Jager reached over and rested a hand on the back of her chair, so that he was barely touching her. "But your father's not a physician. Perhaps Dr. Ruiz will view the information differently."

Delia felt the sting of defensiveness despite the inevitable rush of heat from Jager's touch. Did he think she was incapable of relating her own medical history? "My mother had a cesarean. I've never had one. I've never even been pregnant."

Dr. Ruiz gave a brisk nod and glanced down at her notes. "I think we'd all rest easier with some more information about your mother's medical history." Her red-polished fingernail trailed down over the chart. "She's from Martinique?"

"Yes. She moved to Le Vauclin after she married my father, but she was raised in Sainte-Anne." Delia knew so little about her mother or her mother's family. According to Pascal, Celine's parents had died in a car crash when she was in high school.

The doctor scribbled a note on a Post-it while her reindeer pin blinked on and off. "I may be able to requisition some more information."

Jager squeezed Delia's hand. "Thank you."

She should be relieved. They did need more information about her mother's health history. Perhaps fear for her baby was making Delia unreasonably prickly when it came to Jager taking command of the conversation with both the physician and her father. He had every bit as much reason to be concerned about this baby's health as she did. Still, something about the way the events had unfolded today made her feel like an afterthought.

He would never cherish her the way he cherished his child, of course. It rattled her to think that; in some small corner of her heart, she nursed a hope that she could be more than just a surrogate for a McNeill baby in Jager's eyes.

He took her hand in his. A show of tenderness for the doctor's sake? Or did the paternal feeling he fostered for his child come through in the way he touched her?

His blue gaze found hers for a moment before flicking back to the physician. "We will be looking for the most advanced care for a possible high-risk pregnancy. Can you recommend the best doctors or hospitals for this?"

Frowning, Delia slid her hand out from under his. "High risk?" Her heart rate sped up. Since when did she need the most advanced care? "We don't have any reason to believe I'm high risk."

"Not yet," Jager conceded with a nod. "But until we

know the rest of your mother's history, it would be wise to have a plan in place."

The doctor paused in her note taking. "We've handled many high-risk pregnancies here. However, the most respected maternal fetal medicine facilities will be in the States. If you'd like a list—"

"We don't need a list," Delia informed Jager.

At the same moment, he nodded. "Thank you."

After a few more tense minutes in the consultation room, they departed. Delia stalked out ahead of him, clutching her file of papers about pregnancy with the due date and a prescription for prenatal vitamins.

She'd left Jager to take the paper containing names of maternal fetal specialists he'd requested.

"Delia." His voice was close behind her as she hurried through the parking lot with its lampposts connected by green garland swags dotted with red berries. "Please wait."

Her toes pinched in her high-heeled sandals. She wanted to be home with her feet up, surrounded by the fairy-tale paintings on her living room walls, a cup of tea in her hand. How had her life spun so far out of control so fast? She slowed her pace.

When he reached her side, he turned her to face him, his gaze sweeping over her in a way that shouldn't have incited a physical reaction and damned well did anyhow. It was like that one fateful encounter with him had stripped away all her defenses where he was concerned. Now she felt naked every time they were together.

"You're angry with me," he observed while a French Christmas carol hummed through a speaker system connected to the lampposts.

The chorus of "Un Flambeau, Jeannette, Isabelle" celebrated the beauty of a newborn child while he lay

sleeping in a cradle. Something about the image reso-
nated deeply. The lyrics were so familiar Delia could
visualize the villagers admiring the new baby. Soon she
would have a child of her own. More than anything she
wanted to be a good mother. To stand beside the cradle
of her newborn and protect that fragile life with a fierceness no one had ever showed to defend her.

"I'm frustrated that you commandeered our important conversation today." She wondered what Christmas
would be like this year.

"Commandeered?" His brows swooped down. "I par-
ticipated. The same way you did."

"I realize you are used to taking the lead," she continued, feeling more sure of herself as she spoke. If
she was going to be an equal partner in parenting, she
needed to lay the groundwork for it now. "But we'll need
to find a way to rework our relationship so that you're
not still trying to be my boss."

"I'm trying to protect you," he clarified. "And our
child. That's different."

"And you were so focused on your own agenda that
mine fell by the wayside." She straightened the strap
on her sundress and felt his gaze track the movement.

She didn't like this confusing intersection point between attraction and frustration.

"I thought we shared the same agenda." Jager covered her bare shoulder with one hand, his fingers stroking a gentle touch along the back of her arm. "To find
out answers that could help us protect your health, and
the health of our child."

Unwelcome heat stirred from just that simple touch.
The classic Christmas carol gave way to a holiday
love song.

"I've waited my whole life to have a meaningful con-

versation with my father about the night I was born."
In the past, she'd always backed away from the talk
that he didn't want to have. "There were more answers
I wanted from him."

He'd been close to saying more about that night. She
was sure of it.

"I'm sorry." Jager's simple reply stole away her
anger. She might not be able to read him all the time,
but she recognized the remorse in his voice now, the
obvious sincerity in his eyes. "I didn't know."

Behind them, a young family emerged from the doctor's office. The husband held the door for his wife as
she pushed a toddler in a stroller. The woman's pregnant belly filled the front of a floral maternity dress.

Delia touched her own stomach, still flat. But she
could see that ultrasound image so strongly in her mind.
Would her child ever have a sibling? If she didn't accept Jager's offer of marriage—and she would not accept a business proposal—how soon would he move on
with someone else?

"Come on." Jager wrapped an arm around her waist
and guided her toward the convertible. "Let me apologize by taking you out for dinner."

"That's not necessary," she assured him, ready to
retreat from the world. And the temptation he posed.
"Thank you. But I'm tired."

Discouraged.

She strode ahead toward his car, hearing his steady
steps behind her even as he seemed to take the hint and
respect her need for silence. She needed to be stronger
and smarter tomorrow. To be a worthy advocate for her
unborn baby and weigh her options moving forward.
If she was indeed a high-risk pregnancy, what did that
mean for her? For her father? Would she have to quit

working? Would she and her father lose the family lands after all she'd done to try to protect it?

The plot of Rickard acreage felt like one small offering she had to bring to her baby that was all hers, separate from the McNeill wealth. Perhaps because she had nothing of her mother's, Delia felt the need to be able to give her child something tangible. Something beyond the love she would bear this baby.

Opening the passenger-side door of the bright white vehicle, Jager helped her inside, passing her the seat belt buckle while she tucked her dress around her legs for the breezy ride with the top down. After he closed her door and came around and settled into the driver's seat beside her, he paused before switching on the ignition.

"Can I ask you something, or are we still not talking?" Jager rattled the car key lightly against the gearshift.

"Not funny. But say what you need to." Delia pressed deeper into the leather seat, tipping her neck back into the molded headrest.

"What else were you hoping to learn from Pascal?" He lowered his voice even though there was no one else parked nearby. The family they'd seen earlier was packing into a minivan on the other side of the lot.

She figured she might as well tell Jager the truth since they would be sharing parenting one day and this was very relevant. "It might sound juvenile, but my father has never once said he loved me." She forced a shrug so the words didn't come across as pathetic as they sounded. "I thought today might be the day."

In the moment of silence that followed, she appreciated Jager's restraint. If his response had hinted at any form of pity, she wasn't sure how she could have handled it on such an emotional afternoon.

"Our fathers are very different from one another," he observed finally. "Yours is stoic and undemonstrative even though he was with you throughout your childhood. Mine was fun and fully engaged when he was around, but for the vast majority of time, he was absent." His hand slid over her forearm where it rested on the leather console between them. "I guarantee you I'm not going to be like that with our child. I will be a presence. And I'll do whatever it takes to be a welcome one."

For a moment, she allowed herself to be comforted by the words. This man had been a good friend, after all, before she'd given in to her attraction to him. She could still admire his desire to be a better person.

"We have nine months to figure out a way to be good parents." She had no role model for motherhood, but if she could figure out how to manage and grow McNeill Meadows, which included the historic McNeill mansion and a successful farm-to-table community garden, she would learn about parenting too.

"Less than eight, according to your due date." Jager's hand slid away from her forearm as he moved to start the car. "Since we have a limited amount of time and a lot to accomplish, I'm going to suggest we schedule a trip to New York as soon as possible."

"New York?" The warmth she'd been feeling for him chilled. "Didn't we go over this in the doctor's office? I'm not going to see a specialist or be stressed about a possible high-risk pregnancy until we have some concrete reason to be concerned."

"I completely understand." He backed the car out of the spot. "But you've been adamant that I meet the rest of the McNeills and establish ties with my half brothers." He shot her a sideways glance as he shifted into first, his hand grazing her knee through the thin cotton of her dress. "My relations are going to be our child's relatives too. It makes sense that you visit New York with me and get acquainted with the extended McNeill family."

His words stunned her silent.

Six weeks ago, she had lobbied hard for him to meet his grandfather, Malcolm McNeill. That didn't mean she wanted to be introduced to one of the wealthiest men in the world as Jager's baby mama.

Holding up a trembling hand, she searched for an excuse, any excuse. "I have a lot of arrangements to make here. Things to do to get ready for the baby. And I can't afford to quit my job—"

"Delia." He shook his head. "As the mother of a McNeill, you can afford to do as you please. We'll close up the house in Martinique and spend some time in Manhattan getting to know the rest of the McNeills. If you thought it was a good idea for me to foster those relationships, you must think it's a good idea for our child."

How neatly he'd turned that argument around to maneuver her now. She couldn't think of an appropriate retort as Jager turned the vehicle back onto the westbound road toward Le François. As much as she wanted to retreat into her fairy-tale-painted cottage with her books and dreams, she knew her life would never be the same again. She needed to think like a mother.

Jager slipped his hand over hers, threading their fingers together now that he'd reached a cruising speed and didn't need to shift for a while.

He continued to speak, undeterred by her surprised silence. "If it turns out you need the added care of a specialized facility, we'll already be in New York. If not, you can dictate where you want to be when it comes time to give birth." He gave her hand a gentle squeeze.

"You don't want to be traveling anywhere near the due date."

His words sent a chill through her. Her mother had been out on a boat the night she'd delivered prematurely and had paid the ultimate price. Delia felt sure that she wasn't going to be a high-risk pregnancy. But if she was thinking like a mother—putting her child first—she conceded that Jager had a point.

Accepting his help was in the best interest of their child.

She took a deep breath and let the wind whip through her hair as she tipped her head up to the blue sky. "When do we leave?"

Eight

Stepping off his grandfather's private jet onto the snowy tarmac of Teterboro Airport outside New York City eight days later, Jager wondered if he'd made a deal with the devil to coax Delia out of Martinique.

Jager hadn't wanted any of the McNeill red carpet treatment, and would have damned well preferred making his own travel arrangements, but wily old Malcolm had pulled strings to ensure the trip was exceptionally easy. With his connections, Malcolm had found a way to fast-track Delia as a trusted traveler, a designation Jager already had for himself. That streamlined their arrival process so efficiently that they didn't even need to clear customs in the airport. The minute they got off the plane and went into the terminal, the limo driver was already visible with his white sign bearing the family name.

Jager hadn't been able to refuse his grandfather's

help when it made things easier for Delia. No matter what her doctor said about her pregnancy being normal, he would continue to worry about her health and the health of their baby until they found out more about her mother's medical history. So far, Dr. Ruiz hadn't had any more luck unearthing facts about Celine's first pregnancy than Jager had, but the Martinique physician anticipated speaking to one of Celine's former doctors this week.

"What about our luggage?" Delia asked, shivering slightly as she peered back over her shoulder to stare up at the sleek Cessna, where the two crew members lingered.

Jager tugged her red plaid scarf up higher. He'd bought her warm clothes for the trip, including the long blue wool coat she wore belted tight. At seven weeks pregnant, she looked thinner to him, even in the coat. She insisted she hadn't experienced any morning sickness, but he'd checked it out online to make sure that was normal.

"The driver will make sure they're loaded in the car," Jager assured her, grateful for the cold so he had an excuse to wrap an arm around her and pull her to his side.

The past few days had been busy with preparations to spend Christmas in New York, and he'd tried to give her room to breathe. But he missed her now even more than he had after they'd spent those six weeks apart when he'd been searching Europe for Damon. Seeing her every day, knowing she was carrying his child, only made him want her more. He hoped spending the holidays together would bring them closer.

"Do you always travel like this?" She ducked her head toward his chest, her silky blond hair brushing the lapel of his gray overcoat that hadn't been out of his closet in two years.

"Definitely not." He'd traveled around the world on his own dime—an experience he'd been fortunate to afford—but never with an army of personal staff members. "The added luxury is courtesy of my grandfather."

Did Malcolm think he could bribe him to come into the family fold? Pay him off to accept his father back into his life?

Not happening.

"I know you're only having this meeting with him for our child's sake." She matched her pace to his while the driver hurried over to greet them and send two sky-caps out to take their bags.

"And for yours." Jager couldn't help but point that out since he was doing everything in his power to convince Delia he would make a good partner. A good husband. "I wouldn't be in New York right now if it wasn't for you." It was something Delia had really encouraged since she wanted their child to have a bigger family than she'd known growing up.

They walked quickly through the terminal. Christmas trees decorated the crowded lobby, filling the soaring space with the scent of pine. With just a few days left until Christmas, Jager needed to move up his timetable to convince Delia to marry him. Ideally, he'd have a Christmas Eve proposal—one that she'd accept—and a New Year's wedding. Once that was settled, he'd be able to turn his attention back to the sale of Transparent and finding Damon, both of which needed to happen before he could have any kind of meaningful conversation with Malcolm McNeill about their position within the family. Jager couldn't make those decisions without Damon's input. But for now, he could at least meet his grandfather.

"I hope one day you'll be glad you made this concession to come here." Her cheeks were flushed from the cold as they stepped back outside again toward the waiting Mercedes sedan.

The driver, Paolo, directed the loading of their bags while Jager helped Delia into the passenger area in back. Her high-heeled black boots were visible beneath the hem of her coat, the soft suede molded to slim calves. For nearly two weeks, he'd been attuned to small details like that, from the way she tipped her head back when she laughed, to the delicate habit she had of brushing her fingers over her flat belly when she thought no one noticed. As if reassuring herself there was life inside her.

He looked forward to the day she was cleared for intimacy by her doctor, and to the day she trusted him enough to welcome him back into her bed, so he too could lay his palm on the soft expanse of skin between her hips.

Once she was safely inside the vehicle, Jager took Paolo aside.

"We're staying at The Plaza," he informed him. "That's our first stop."

The tall, athletically built driver looked like he could serve double duty as private security on the side with his dark coat and sunglasses. "But Mr. McNeill said to bring you directly to the house."

"Miss Rickard has had a long journey." Jager moved closer to the vehicle. "I'll call my grandfather to explain personally."

The driver's bronzed forehead furrowed, but he nodded. "As you wish."

They had been invited to stay at the McNeill home, a private fourteen-thousand-square-foot townhouse on the Upper East Side. It was a historic piece of local architecture that Jager would normally look forward to seeing, but he had no intention of taking up residence under the family roof. He had tried explaining that to Cameron without much luck. Jager had yet to converse with Malcolm directly.

Inside the limousine, he realized Delia was listening intently to her cell phone.

"Dr. Ruiz?" she said into the mouthpiece as her eyes lifted to meet Jager's gaze. "I'm going to put you on speakerphone. Could you repeat that last part for Jager's sake?"

The obstetrician must have news. About Delia's health? Or about the mystery of Celine's medical history?

"Yes. Hello." The lightly accented voice of the doctor came through the phone. The sound quality was tinny and diminished, but Jager was so glad to hear from her. "Mr. McNeill, I was just explaining to Delia that her mother suffered from lupus. She didn't see a doctor regularly for the condition, and was unaware of the disease with her first pregnancy."

Jager sat knee to knee with Delia in the wide leather seat. At some point, he'd taken her hand, and he squeezed it now. A smile kicked up one side of her mouth, reminding him that it had been too long since he'd seen her happy. They'd both been so worried about this.

"What about Delia? Could she have the condition and be unaware?" His heart lodged in his throat.

"No." Dr. Ruiz sounded certain. "We did a complete blood workup when she was here and I had enough to run additional tests once we received the news about her mother. The test for lupus is one of the most sensitive diagnostic indicators for the disease, clearing Delia with 98% certainty. And since she has virtually no other symptoms—"

Relief coursed through him with a *whoosh* in his ears that drowned out whatever else the obstetrician had to say. He'd been concerned for Delia's health, and for their child's, but he hadn't fully understood how truly scared he was until that moment. His chest constricted. He wrapped his arms around Delia and held her tight. To hell with giving her space.

Inhaling the warm vanilla fragrance of her hair, he smoothed his cheek along the silky strands. Even through the layers of their coats, he could feel the gentle swell of her curves. He traced circles on her back with one hand, soothing himself even as he offered her comfort. Connection.

"Mr. McNeill?" Dr. Ruiz's tinny voice echoed in the limo. "If you have any other questions for me—"

"Just one," he answered, turning his head to be better heard since he wasn't ready to release Delia yet. "I want to be sure I understand. You're saying that Delia is healthy enough for all normal activity?"

Delia turned her face up and peered into his eyes. Her gaze was quizzical for only a moment. And then she must have read his mind, because her cheeks colored with a heat he remembered well. It occurred to him how much he enjoyed her pale complexion that betrayed her so easily.

"Absolutely." Dr. Ruiz's smile was evident in the tone of her voice. "Congratulations to you both. You have all the signs of a healthy pregnancy."

Delia's forehead tipped onto his shoulder, but she

didn't move away from him as Jager thanked the doctor for the good news and disconnected the call.

As the Mercedes sped south on I-95, Jager stroked Delia's hair, the strands clinging from static. When she lifted her face to look at him, her hazel eyes were greener than usual—bright with a mix of emotions he couldn't read.

"Looks like Manhattan is good luck for us." He couldn't help the heated edge in his voice as he unfastened the belt on her bright blue coat and slid a hand over her waist.

Her long gray sweater dress skimmed her subtle curves. If they weren't riding in a car, he would have slid a hand under her knees and tugged her onto his lap.

"Because I'm healthy enough to carry a baby to term, or because I just had the green light for intimacy?" She arched an eyebrow at him, but the rapid tattoo of her pulse at her neck gave away how much the idea intrigued her too.

"My concern is for you and our baby. You know that." He had battled bad dreams for the last week and a half. Every time Delia was in a boat out to sea where he couldn't reach her. Each time, he'd awoken sweating and tangled in his sheets. "But I won't deny that I've thought about being with you again."

She tensed beneath his touch as the limo jockeyed for position on the way into the Lincoln Tunnel. The last rays of afternoon sun disappeared when they descended. Shadows played over her face between flashes of the tunnel's fluorescent lighting.

"I've thought about being with you too." She didn't sound happy about it, and he noticed how she was nervously twisting a button on his coat cuff with her fingers. "But I can't afford to lose perspective where you're concerned. Not when our relationship is already so convoluted and I can't trust my judgment with men."

He hated that her ex had made her doubt herself so much. Jager willed himself to find the right words that would make her see his point of view.

"Delia." He took both of her hands in both of his. "You've known me for two years. I gave you a job because I admired the way you didn't let the pressure of society sway you into marrying Brandon. I thought escaping your wedding on a Jet Ski was kick-ass."

She shook her head. "I was scared."

"But you didn't let fear stop you. You set a course and got the hell out of Dodge."

A tiny ghost of a smile appeared on her face. "You're being generous."

"I'm being honest. I liked you right away, and I believe that feeling was mutual from the very first day." He tipped her chin up when she looked away, needing to see her eyes to track her reaction to his words. "You know my brothers. You know my business dealings. Have I ever given you reason to think I've tried to hide something from you the way Brandon did?"

"Never." She said the word softly but with a fierceness that made his heart turn over.

"Then trust me when I say that you are the most important part of my life right now." He brought one of her hands to his lips and kissed it, then the other. "The last thing I want to do is hurt you, and I can promise if anything makes you unhappy, I'm going to do everything in my power to fix it."

His heart beat harder, as if he could somehow hammer home the words with the force of his will. He could see the struggle in her eyes. The worry that another man had put there. Hell, even her father had made her doubt herself, so he couldn't blame Brandon for that.

Slowly, however, her smile reappeared as the limo hit Midtown. A sexy glimmer lit her hazel eyes as if she'd just started thinking something…naughty.

"I'm going to hold you to that promise, Jager McNeill."

"I hope you do." Desire for her thrummed in his veins, a slow, simmering heat that had him hauling open the door of the vehicle as soon as it pulled up to the curb in front of The Plaza Hotel.

Helping her from the car onto the red carpet underneath the flags that waved over the iconic entrance to the hotel across from Central Park, he was more than ready to bring her to their room. To kiss every inch of her.

And remind her how good they could be together.

But he'd forgotten she'd never been to New York. Let alone Central Park. Or The Plaza Hotel.

At Christmastime.

Her eyes glowed as she stepped out of the limo, and the pleasure he saw there didn't have anything to do with him.

"It's so beautiful!" she exclaimed, doing a slow twirl to take it all in, just like every starry-eyed tourist to ever clog up a city street at rush hour.

Despite his thwarted libido, he couldn't resist the chance to make Delia Rickard happy.

"Would you like a tour?" he asked her, waving off Paolo and the hotel doormen, who were ready to assist with their every need.

"Yes!" She was already gazing at a horse-drawn carriage across the street, her body swaying slightly to the strains of a Christmas tune emanating from a trio of musicians near the park entrance.

Jager forced his gaze away from her and told himself to get a grip. This was the chance he'd been waiting for, and he wasn't about to waste it.

"Don't let go." Delia wrapped a hand around Jager's waist and her other around his neck. "Please. Whatever you do? Don't let go."

Teetering on thin blades, she let Jager tug her around the slippery ice skating rink while other holiday revelers whizzed past them. Even knee-high children skated quickly past, their blades making a *skritch*, *skritch* sound in the cold ice, cutting tiny swaths and sometimes lifting a fine, snow-like spray in their wake.

Her first time on ice skates was a little scarier than she'd anticipated. After a tour of the Christmas lights around Central Park and down Fifth Avenue, she and Jager had stopped at a food cart for gyros. She'd been entranced by the sight of the huge Christmas tree in Rockefeller Plaza. Even better? The ice-skaters skimming the expanse of bright white below the noble fir. She hadn't hesitated when Jager asked if she wanted to test her skills on skates.

Clearly, she'd been too caught up in the holiday spirit to think about what she was getting into. Now Dean Martin crooned about letting it snow on the speaker system, but even with all the laughter, happy shouts and twinkling lights around her, Delia couldn't recapture that lighthearted joy. She was too terrified she'd fall.

"I'm not letting go." Jager whispered the soft assurance in her ear, nuzzling the black cashmere stocking cap he'd bought her in one of the glittering department stores lining Fifth Avenue. "I've been looking for an excuse to touch you for weeks."

Her attention darted from her wobbling skates to his handsome face. He'd been so good to her, helping her to tie up her work responsibilities at the McNeill estate in Martinique by hiring a temporary replacement. His younger brother Gabe—now technically her boss—had given her a surprise holiday bonus that was based on revenue growth for the property. It had given her enough of a financial cushion that she could send the money home to her father to pay the taxes on their small piece of land and keep it safe for another year.

Which was a huge worry off her mind.

Each day for almost two weeks, Jager had asked how she felt, asked what he could do to help make her life easier so she could focus on her health. She'd been touched, especially in light of the pregnancy worries she'd had—at least up until today's call from Dr. Ruiz. And more than anything, she appreciated that he'd given her time to come to terms with being pregnant, without pressuring her about marriage.

That window of time had ended, however. He'd made that clear in the car ride from the airport when he said he wanted to be with her again. That exchange was never far from her mind even as they were sightseeing and enjoying all the Christmas hubbub of New York City just days before the big holiday.

"Are you trying to distract me so I don't fall?" she asked, her heartbeat skipping to its own crazy rhythm.

The scent of roasted chestnuts spiced the air. As the music shifted to an orchestra arrangement of Handel's *Messiah*, Jager swayed on his skates, effortlessly gliding backward so she could remain facing forward.

"I'm one-hundred-percent sincere about wanting to

touch you." The look in his blue eyes sent a wave of heat through her, warming her from the inside out. "But if it helps to keep you distracted, I can share some more explicit thoughts I've been having about you."

She swallowed around a suddenly-dry throat. The sounds, the scents, the night fell away until her world narrowed to only him. Her heart thumped harder.

"I don't want to get so distracted I fall on my face." She was only half kidding. Too much flirting with Jager could be dangerous. "But maybe if you told me just one thing."

Because she had a major weakness where he was concerned.

"Wait until we turn this corner," he cautioned, slowly drawing her body against his while he guided them around the end of the rink in a wide curve.

Pressed against Jager's formidable body, Delia didn't move. She didn't even dare to breathe since breathing would mold her breasts even tighter to his chest. Their wool coats and winter clothes didn't come close to hiding the feel of the bodies beneath. His thigh grazed hers as he skated backward, hard muscle flexing.

She felt a little swoony and knew it wasn't just the skates keeping her off balance.

"There." He checked the skating lane as he moved onto the straightaway for another slow circle around the rink. "You're doing well."

He loosened his hold without letting go and her skates seemed to follow him without any help from her.

"I'm not sure that not falling is synonymous with doing well." Her voice was breathless, a barely there scrape of sound after the close encounter with the sexy father of her future child.

"So we'll get right back to distraction tactics." He

slowed his pace again, letting her close the small gap between them before he lowered his voice. "Do you want me to tell you how sexy you are in the dreams where you pull a pin out of your hair and it all comes spilling down while you straddle me—"

"No." She shook her head, unprepared for the details he seemed only too happy to share. "That is, not here."

He lifted a hand to her cheek and rubbed a thumb along her jaw. "Seeing you blush might be the sexiest thing ever."

"I'm just not used to hearing things like that from the same man who used to demand the Monday morning business briefs by five o'clock the Friday before."

He threw his head back and laughed. "I knew you were secretly opposed to those."

She liked making him smile, something that happened more rarely this year after tragedy had struck his family. Out of the corner of her eye, she saw Santa and a pretty elf walking through the brightly lit café that flanked one end of the skating rink. A family with small children posed for a photo with them.

"Employees want to be out the door at five o'clock on Fridays, not planning for Mondays." She'd been committed to the job though, and to improving herself. She'd never complained.

"I didn't keep you late *every* week." Jager loosened his hold a bit more, but it was okay since she felt steadier on her feet now.

"Only most Fridays," she teased. Despite their light banter, she kept seeing the dream image he'd planted in her mind.

Her. Straddling him.

She might not stop blushing for days at this rate.

"Then I have a lot to make up for." He drew her near

once more so they could navigate another turn. "I hope this trip will be something special that you'll never forget."

"It already is." She lifted her hand from his neck long enough to gesture at the impressive ninety-foot Christmas tree covered in lights above them. "I've always wanted to travel, and New York is...magic."

Certainly, she'd never had a Christmas like this. The holiday had never been easy with her father the fisherman making little effort to spend the day at home most years, let alone play Santa or give special gifts the way other fishing families did.

"I've flown in and out of this city so many times for business, but I will admit I've never had as much fun as seeing it with you."

Her first thought was to argue with him—to call him out on a line meant to romance her. But hadn't he pointed out that he'd never given her a reason to doubt his honesty and sincerity with her?

It was her insecurity that made her not want to believe him. The doubts she felt weren't his fault. If she was going to make this relationship work, with a balanced approach to shared parenting of a child, she needed to start laying the groundwork for trust. More than that, she needed to start trusting herself.

"This has been one of the most fun days of my whole life," she told him honestly.

The fairy-tale images painted on her walls weren't all that different from this—the twinkling lights combined with the myth and magic of New York. In fact, the statue of Prometheus in Rockefeller Center was staring down at her right now, his gilded facade reflecting all the glow.

"Look at you," Jager observed quietly, making her realize she'd been quiet a long time.

"What?" Blinking through the cloudy fog of worries for the future, she peered up into his eyes.

"You're skating."

She glanced down at her feet to confirm the surprising news. Jager still held her, true. But she was gliding forward under her own power, the motion subtle but definite.

Happiness stole through her. She wasn't going to count on Jager being there for her forever. Not yet, anyway. This Christmastime trip would help her decide if he wanted her for herself, not just for the sake of their child.

But no matter what happened for them romantically, she realized that this man had given her a precious gift no one else ever had. He'd believed in her from the moment they met, giving her the courage to have more faith in herself too.

Whatever the future held, she was strong enough to handle it. To move forward. Even if it was on her own.

Nine

Later that night, Delia turned off the gold-plated faucet in the bathroom of their suite at The Plaza.

Gold-plated faucets. Twenty-four-karat gold, in fact, according to the detailed description she'd read in a travel review on her phone while she soaked in the tub.

After toweling off, she shrugged into a white spa robe embroidered with the hotel crest. Everything about the legendary property was beautiful, from the lavish holiday decorations throughout to the tiled mosaic floor in the bathroom. Delia took mental notes, knowing she could upgrade some of their offerings at McNeill Meadows when they hosted private parties and corporate retreats in the public portion of the historic house.

After padding from the bathroom into her bedroom, she scanned the contents of the spacious wood-paneled closet with built-in drawers. The butler service had unpacked for them while they were out sightseeing; her nightgown was neatly folded with the lavender sachet she'd packed on top of it. Even her scarves and mittens were folded.

Dispensing with the spa robe, she dressed in her own nightdress, a wildly romantic gown that had been a rare splurge purchase after her first raise. It was probably the kind of thing a bride wore—diaphanous lemon yellow layers with a satin ribbon through the bodice that tied like a corset. Although it was as romantic as any of her fairy-tale paintings, knowing that she'd acquired it through her own hard work always made her feel like a queen when she wore it. She'd come a long way from the girl who'd nearly bartered her future for a slick businessman who said pretty words but didn't really love her.

Switching off the light, she stepped quietly back out into the living room to admire the view of Central Park. She'd already said good-night to Jager, refusing his offer of room service for a bedtime snack.

She had the distinct impression he was trying to fatten her up, feeding her at every opportunity.

"Did you change your mind about a meal?"

The voice from a dark corner of the room nearly made her jump out of her skin.

"Oh!" Startled, she took a step back, heart racing even though she recognized Jager's voice right away. "You scared me."

"Sorry." He unfolded himself from the chair near the window, a tall shadow that became more visible as he stood in front of the ambient light from the street and the park below. "I thought you saw me."

"No." She became very aware of her nakedness under the nightgown. She hadn't even bothered with underwear, an oversight that made her skin tingle with warmth. "I didn't realize you were still awake."

"I ordered room service while you were in the bath. Just in case." He moved toward the wet bar, where she could see a tray of bread, cheeses and fruits. A champagne bucket held two large bottles of sparkling water chilling on ice.

She was tempted.

Seeing him tempted her even more. She remembered how he'd felt against her in the water that day he'd saved the drowning girl. The way they'd moved together later that same night when desire had spun out of control. She cleared her throat and tried to block out the memories of how his hands felt on her naked skin.

"That was thoughtful of you. Thank you." She reached for a water to quench her sudden thirst; her throat had gone very dry.

"Here, let me." He moved behind the bar, retrieving two crystal glasses. "Do you want me to switch the lights back on?"

"No," she blurted, immediately thinking about the lightweight nature of her nightgown. "We can see the view better this way. That's why I came out here."

While he poured their drinks, Delia walked to the window near the sofa and stared out into the night. The sounds of the city drifted through the closed windows. Horns, brakes, a distant siren provided a kind of nighttime white noise, the unique city sounds all muffled though, since their room was on the eighteenth floor.

Behind her, she heard rustling. Something heavy scraping across the floor. When she turned, she saw Jager had pivoted the couch to face the window, keeping the low coffee table in front of it.

"Come. Have a seat." He was placing the cheese

board on the table, no doubt to tempt her. "We can see for ourselves if this is the city that never sleeps."

The invitation sent pleasurable shivers along her skin as if he'd touched her. The sensation was so vivid she debated scurrying back into her room with her glass of water and half a baguette to prevent a rash decision fueled by this insane chemistry. But running away from him every time this man enticed her was not going to lead to productive parenting for their child.

She bit the inside of her cheek to steel herself, then joined him on the sofa.

He'd never had to work so hard to win a woman's trust before. The way Delia's chin was tilted up and her shoulders were thrown back gave her the look of someone stepping into battle rather than just sharing a couch with him.

As she settled onto the tufted blue cushion, she tucked her bare feet beneath her, her sheer yellow nightgown draping over the edge. His brain still blazed from the way she'd looked while standing in front of the window a moment ago. There'd been just enough light coming through to outline her curves.

Her absolute nakedness underneath.

That vision would be filed away in his memory for a lifetime.

"I love how the lights run in a perfect straight line up either side of the park." Her attention was on the view and not him, her face tipped into the dull golden light spilling through the window. "It's so pretty here."

"You didn't mind the cold today?" He focused on slicing the fresh baguette to keep from thinking about touching her.

"Not one bit. I felt energized. More alive." She

reached for a piece of kiwi and dropped it on a small plate. "I can't believe how much we did today after we landed."

"I think the cold makes you want to move faster to keep warm." She'd looked adorable in that hat he bought her.

She'd told him it was one of the most fun days she could remember, and it had been for him too. He'd never been the kind of guy to cut loose; he was always aware of his responsibility as the oldest brother in a family with no father. And later, no mother.

With Delia, it was different.

"Maybe that's the secret to New York ambition." She added a few more pieces of fruit to the pile, then extended the china toward him for a slice of bread.

"Frigid temperatures?" He layered on multiple pieces of bread and cheese before she pulled the plate back.

"Could be." Her smile faded as she peered out the window into the darkened park. "I never got to ask you much about what it was like to live out on the West Coast. Did you like it there?"

The question chilled him far more than the northeast winds had during their sightseeing. Perhaps some of his reluctance to talk about it showed on his face, because Delia spoke up again.

"We don't have to talk about that time, if you don't want." She chased a slice of cheese around the dish with her bread. "I was just curious how California compared to New York, since it's my first time out of Martinique."

He was never going to put her more at ease if he didn't share some part of himself that wasn't business-related. She knew plenty about his work life. But he'd kept many of the details of what he and his brothers had been through private.

"At first, I was excited to return to California since I'd lived near LA until I was thirteen." He'd been happy enough there, until he understood how unhappy his mother was. Until it occurred to him how his father never visited them anymore, abandoning his illegitimate family for his legal wife and kids.

"That's when your mom decided to ditch Liam and start over somewhere he couldn't find her."

"Right." Jager ground his teeth, the impulse to keep the past on lockdown stronger than he'd realized. He set down his plate and refilled their water glasses to give himself something to occupy his hands. "She'd had enough with his sporadic visits and she knew by then that he'd never leave his wife and other sons."

"Did you know about them back then?" She set aside her plate to lift the heavy crystal goblet. "Your father's other family?"

He studied the way her lips molded around the glass to distract himself from the old anger he always felt thinking about Liam McNeill.

It had been one thing to abandon his kids. Abandoning the mother of his children? Jager found it unforgivable, especially since their mother had fought cancer and died without a partner by her side. Just three devastated sons.

"Not really. As a kid, I had the idea that Liam had another girlfriend and that's why he didn't stay with us more." Remembering the confusion of those years, he had to give his mother a lot of credit for what she'd done when she left the country. "Before she died, Mom told us everything—about Liam's connection to McNeill Resorts, about his other family. But by then, we hated him for not being there when she was battling cancer.

We all agreed after she was gone that we didn't want anything to do with him."

"I can't imagine how hard that must have been for all of you." Delia bit her lip for a moment before continuing, "Liam never knew though, did he? About your mom's illness?"

"No. But keep in mind he lied to two women for over a decade, pretending to his wife that he was faithful and pretending to my mother—at first—that he was a single man, and later that he would leave his marriage for her." Much later, he'd heard that Liam's wife left him shortly after Jager's mother, Audrey, decided to end their affair. So he'd been free. He could have come for his other family, married his mistress if he'd wanted. But he'd never even bothered to search for them.

"After my own experience being deceived, I know that must have hurt both of them deeply." Delia placed the water goblet on the glass coffee table. The soft glow of light from the window played over her delicate features.

"I'll never forgive him," he told her truthfully, unwilling to give her false expectations for their visit. "I'm in New York to meet my grandfather, because I respect that it's important to you that we know my family."

On an intellectual level, he understood that it wasn't Malcolm's fault that Liam had wronged his mother. But Jager couldn't help feeling a sense of disloyalty to his mother for setting foot in Liam's world.

"It is important to me." Her eyes widened as she reached out to lay her hand on his forearm. "But maybe once you reconnect with Liam, you'll feel differently."

"Impossible." Jager knew his own heart, and it was cold where his father was concerned. Still, he regretted his quick response when her hand slid away. Swiftly, he changed the subject before she pursued the topic any further. "But you asked about life in Los Altos Hills. I was looking forward to it when I first got there last year, but after the hell Damon went through soon afterward, I don't think I could ever live on the West Coast again."

His sister-in-law had vanished without a trace after her honeymoon. Damon had punched holes in most of the walls of that big, beautiful home he'd built. Then he'd left town and shut off all means of communication.

Delia smoothed the embroidered satin cuff of her nightgown with one hand, fingering the embellishments stitched in pale blue thread. A placket on the bodice covered her breasts, while two layers of something gauzy and thin created a barely there barrier between his eyes and the rest of her. The urge to touch her had been strong all day, but now—remembering the way Damon's life was falling apart without his wife—the need for Delia was even more fierce.

"I've always wanted to see the Pacific." She had a faraway look for a moment before turning back to him. "Maybe it has to do with being a fisherman's daughter, but I'm more curious about the water than the land."

"I couldn't see the Pacific from the house Damon built in the hills, but the view of San Francisco Bay was impressive."

"There's a lot about the McNeill lifestyle that's impressive," she noted drily, straightening.

It was a welcome change of subject.

"We've been fortunate financially," he admitted, wondering how he could tempt her into eating some more. To keep her strength up. "But I hope you know I'd trade it all to see Damon happy again. Hell. I'd trade it all to *see* him." Jager worried about him. Damon wasn't himself when he'd left.

Jager grabbed the white china plate Delia had set aside and refilled it. It might not be a high-risk pregnancy, but she still needed to take care of herself. He'd read online that exhaustion would kick in over the next few weeks and she could lose her appetite even more.

"I wonder where he went?" She frowned down at the plate as he handed it to her, but she took a raspberry and popped it in her mouth. "Do you think he had a plan?"

"I think he was going to look for Caroline himself. Visit places her credit card was used in the last year. I spoke briefly to the investigator Cameron told us about—the one who said he could find Damon. But ultimately, I know my brother wants to find the men responsible for his wife's disappearance."

"That sounds dangerous. Can you stop him?" Delia set her plate aside again, worry etched in her features. Damn it. He hadn't meant to upset her. "Before he does something rash?"

He hesitated. The truth would only make her more uneasy. But Delia had been lied to before. He had no option besides being completely forthright.

"I'm not sure I'd want to, even if I could." The police had honored a request from Caroline's father that they "respect his daughter's wish for privacy." But Jager didn't believe for a moment that she'd left by her own free will, and neither did Damon.

Unfolding herself from the couch cushion, Delia rose to her feet. Clearly agitated, she paced around the sofa before returning to the window.

"But he could get in serious trouble." She laid a hand on the back of Jager's. "I didn't have time to get to know Damon very well before you all left Martinique, but I spoke with him often enough to realize he's a good person. If you could talk to him, you could convince him to speak to the police again."

Jager came to his feet, wishing he had more comfort to offer her. But his words were unlikely to ease her mind.

"Men came into his house. Took the woman he loved. And, as far as we can tell, those same men let her die alone at sea rather than return her to him after he did everything they asked." Talking about it made him agitated. Putting himself in Damon's shoes lit a fiery rage inside him. "If someone hurt you, I'd turn over heaven and earth to find them too. How can I blame my brother for doing the same?"

His heart slugged hard as he wrapped his arms around her, drawing her close.

"What if he finds the men he's searching for? He could get hurt. Or killed. Or end up in prison for the rest of his life if he—" Delia objected.

He gently quieted the torrent of worries with a finger on her lips.

"He's already suffering more than we can imagine. I'm not sure there's any punishment worse than what he's going through right now."

When she sighed, her shoulders sagging, he shifted his finger away from her soft mouth, feeling his way along her smooth cheek. His hand traveled down her warm neck to the curve of her collarbone, mostly bare above the square neck of her nightgown.

"Damon's in hell." The truth had been apparent to Jager when they parted. "He may never have the chance to touch his wife this way again."

He meant to comfort Delia somehow, but as he glanced up into her hazel eyes, he wondered if he was the one who needed the warmth of this connection. The solace of her touch.

The vanilla scent of her skin beckoned him. Her hair, still damp from a bath, was beginning to dry in soft waves. And damn it all, no matter who needed who, he couldn't deny himself the feel of her any longer.

Gently, he tipped her head back, giving her time to walk away if she chose. But her eyelids slowly lowered, her lashes a dark sweep of fringe fluttering down. He kissed her there. One press of his lips to the right eye. One press of his lips to the left.

Her raspberry-scented breath teased his cheek in a soft puff of air. Her fingers trailed lightly up his arm through the worn cotton of the well-washed Henley shirt that he'd pulled on along with a pair of sweats after his shower. The light, tentative feel of her hands on him seared away the conversation they'd been having. All he cared about was touching her.

Tasting her.

Cradling her face in his hands, he waited for her eyes to open again. He wanted to see acceptance there. When her entranced gaze found his, there was more than just acceptance. He saw hunger. A need as stark as his own.

Ten

Delia's world tilted sideways, her breath catching as she stared up into the laser focus of Jager's blue eyes. She felt herself falling and she was powerless to stop it.

If this night had been just about passion, maybe she could have walked away. But she'd glimpsed Jager's heart tonight, and the stark emotions she'd seen there had ripped her raw too. As the self-appointed head of his family, he took his responsibility to Damon seriously.

How could she argue with him when he would one day give their child that same undivided loyalty that he showed his brother? The power of that devotion was foreign to her, and it took her breath away.

"Kiss me." She whispered the command softly, knowing he awaited her wishes.

The two simple words unleashed a torrent.

He drew her into him, sealing her body to his, chest to thigh. Sensations blazed through her. Her breasts molded to the hard plane of his chest, her heartbeat hammering against him in a rapid, urgent rhythm. He bent to wrap an arm around her thighs, lifting her higher so his sex nudged her hip. Her belly.

She melted inside, the hunger becoming frenzied. Imperative.

When his lips met hers, she speared her fingers into his dark hair, holding him where she wanted him. Every silken stroke of his tongue awakened new fires in her body. A nip to the right made her breasts ache. A kiss to the left caused her thighs to tremble.

The fevered urgency spiked higher. Hotter.

"Delia." He reared away from the kiss abruptly, his eyes blazing. "A kiss won't be enough." His eyelids lowered, shuttering the raw hunger she'd spied. "That is, if you don't want things to proceed—"

"I do want. This. You." Tracing the line of his bristly jaw with her fingers, she inhaled the musky pine scent of his aftershave, then licked a spot in the hollow of his throat to breathe in more. "Very much."

Returning his mouth to hers, he palmed a thigh in each of his hands, wrapping her legs around him. Never breaking the kiss, he charged toward the bedroom. His bedroom. The feel of his muscles shifting against her as he walked provided a sultry prelude to the pleasures she knew came next. Her silk nightgown was a scant barrier to the feel of him, and he felt every bit as amazing as she'd remembered from their first time together.

"I thought I dreamed how good this felt," she murmured, keeping her arms looped around his neck while he toed open the bedroom door and strode into the darkened interior.

His blinds were drawn, the blankets turned down the

same way hers had been. He paused near the dimmer switch on one wall to turn a sconce to the lowest setting.

"It was no dream." Carrying her over to the king-size bed, he lowered her slowly to the center. "Although I've been reliving that night often enough when I close my eyes."

"Me too." The harder she'd tried to forget about it, the more often every touch and kiss replayed in her brain.

He stood up and dragged his shirt up and over his head. Tossing it aside, he untied the drawstring on his sweats, the waistband dropping enough to reveal his lower abs. And…more.

He wasn't wearing boxers.

Lured by the sight of him, she pushed herself up to her knees. Her palms landed on his chest before he could join her on the bed, and she held him there, wanting a chance to explore, needing to imprint the feel of him in her memory.

Hands splayed, she covered as much of him as possible, skimming her palms down his chest, then turning at an angle to line up her fingers with the ridges of his abs. His breath hissed between his teeth, but she couldn't stop until she tested the feel of his erection, trailing her fingers down the rigid length then back up again.

She bent to place a kiss there, her lips following the line of the raised vein.

The harsh sound Jager made was her only warning before he hauled her up by the shoulders. "You play with fire."

"I'm already burning." She reached for the tie on her nightdress, a single yellow ribbon that wound through the satin bodice. "I need to be naked."

His gaze dipped to her body, his hands tunneling under the diaphanous layers of pale yellow to draw the fabric up and over her head, bringing with it the lavender scent of the bath oils she'd used.

Jager set the gown aside and stroked her arms. Shoulders. Breasts. There was a slow reverence in his touch that made her heart turn over, stirring feelings she couldn't afford to have yet. Not with so much uncertainty between them.

So she wrapped her arms around him and dragged him down to the bed with her, losing herself in a mind-drugging kiss. He covered her gently, keeping an elbow on the bed to ensure he didn't put his full weight on her. But she wanted, needed, to feel the full impact of being with him. She kissed him harder and skimmed her leg up one side of his, snaking it around his thigh until she could roll him to the side and lie on top of him.

"You said you had a fantasy about having me here," she reminded him, rubbing her cheek on his chest, soaking up the feel of him. "Straddling you."

"The real thing surpasses it." He captured her hands and held them on either side of his head.

To make sure he remembered it, she rolled her hips against him for emphasis.

He reversed their positions in an instant, flipping her to her back. His move surprised a giggle out of her. When his erection nudged between her thighs, she gripped his shoulders, fire rushing through her veins.

"Please." She needed this. Him. "Come inside me."

"Do you want to use protection? I have it, but—"

"We're both clean." They'd shared medical records for the sake of their child. She shrugged. "And I'm already pregnant. Let's enjoy the benefits."

The last words were muffled by his kiss before he licked his way down to her breast, drawing on the taut crest. She arched against him, wanting more. Everything.

He came inside her then, edging deeper. Deeper.

He lifted his head to watch her, his blue gaze fixed on her eyes. She bit her lip against a rush of pleasure so sweet it threatened to drag her under. She tingled everywhere, her pulse an erratic throb at her throat. Clamping her thighs around his waist, she let the sensations roll through her. Poised on the edge of an orgasm, she simply held on and let herself feel it all.

Jager. Pleasure. Passion.

When he reached between their bodies to tease a finger over the slick center of her, she went completely still. He felt so good. So. Impossibly. Good.

Her release rolled over her like a rogue wave, tossing her helplessly against the bed, having its way with her. She was so lost in her own pleasure that his almost took her by surprise. But his hoarse shout of completion let her know she wasn't alone in the powerful throes of passion.

She clutched him to her hard, her head tipped to his strong chest as she slowly became aware of his heartbeat. It raced faster than if he'd run sprints. She placed a kiss there, smoothing her hand over his skin gone lightly damp.

Closing her eyes, she waited for her breathing to return to normal, her own heart to slow. With the flood of happy endorphins running through her, she couldn't imagine a time when she would regret what they'd just shared. It was nothing short of beautiful. But that didn't mean she could simply allow an affair to continue indefinitely.

She needed to think about her child's future. About maintaining a relationship with Jager that would never put them at odds. Not for all the world would she subject her child to the kind of confusing upbringing Jager had, never seeing his father after his thirteenth birthday.

"Can I get you anything?" His voice broke in on the crowd of worries creeping up on her, his hand tender as he stroked her tousled hair. "Something to eat or drink before bed?"

"I feel like Hansel and Gretel in the witch's cabin," she murmured, exhaustion from their long day starting to take hold.

"Okay. Did I miss something?" He sounded so baffled that she laughed.

"You're trying to fatten me up, Jager McNeill. Don't deny it."

"I've been reading." He tried to fluff the pillow under her head without moving her, then he straightened the blankets as they untangled themselves. "You might experience extreme fatigue in the upcoming weeks. I want you to be ready for it."

Imagining this all-business corporate magnate on his computer doing Google searches of pregnancy symptoms made her smile. He would be a good father. Would she ever measure up as a mother with so little to guide her?

A nervous flutter tripped through her belly at the same time his hand landed there. Right where their baby was growing. Her eyes stung at his tenderness.

"I'll be fine," she reassured him. "And I think the fatigue is starting. I'm so tired all of the sudden."

It was true. Yet she also wasn't ready to think about the implications of what had just happened. About how important it was that she get her relationship with Jager right. Because no matter how tenderly he'd touched her, she had to ask herself if it was really *her* who mattered to him.

Or was he simply honor bound to care for the mother of his child?

Once Delia had fallen asleep, Jager could no longer ignore the notifications on his phone. Or, at least, that was what he told himself; he wanted to let Delia get her rest and he was still reeling from their encounter.

He'd wanted her, that much was damn certain. Still did, even after sex that satisfied him to his toes.

But he hadn't expected being with her to rattle him this way. There had been something deeper at work between them than sex. Knowing the whole time that she carried his child had been powerful.

So maybe he scrambled out of the bed a little too fast once she'd dozed off. But there were a hell of a lot of messages and missed calls on his cell. He'd noticed them earlier, beginning shortly after Paolo dropped them off at The Plaza. Messages from Cameron, Quinn and Ian.

His half brothers were all looking for him. Apparently they'd been summoned to the McNeill mansion to greet him tonight, and he'd never shown. In his defense, he'd tried to warn Cam he needed to have space of his own in New York. And he needed to meet with the family on his own terms. On his timetable. Now, stalking around the dark living room, he debated whom to text first. Before he could decide, the phone vibrated again.

Gabe.

Jager clicked the button to connect them. "I hope you're calling with good news."

"What good news could I possibly have for you?" his brother drawled. Gabe was as unhurried in life as

Jager was Type A. "I know better than to think you'll get excited about the new crown molding I installed in the McNeill Meadows gift shop."

Dropping onto the sofa where he'd sat with Delia earlier, Jager stared out over the lights dotting Central Park and the few low buildings that broke up the dark expanse of trees.

"This is the woodwork you were making?" He'd visited Gabe when he returned from Europe, wanting to update him on the search for Damon.

As usual, Gabe had been in his workshop in the converted boathouse on the small hotel property he ran. The Birdsong had come into his hands as a teen when the older woman Gabe worked for had died. Her family had fought the inheritance for months, but the will had been airtight. Gabe had renovated every square inch, bringing guests from around the world to the Birdsong. He'd either restored or handcrafted all the woodwork himself and quickly got a reputation as a master. Now he had more work than he could handle from businesses that appreciated an artisan's touch.

"That's the stuff." In fact, Gabe had started the project based on a long-ago memo from Delia, when she'd been trying to make over the McNeill Meadows gift shop into a more period-appropriate space. "But I wasn't calling about that. I wanted to see what happened today. Did Cameron have an update on Damon?"

Leaning back into the couch cushions that still held a hint of Delia's scent, Jager ground his teeth at Gabe's impatience. But then, he could hardly blame Gabe for wanting to think about something besides his personal life. Gabe's songstress wife had told him their marriage was over while pregnant with their firstborn. She'd abandoned Gabe—and their son—two weeks after giving birth so that she could pursue her career.

The only thing keeping the guy's bitterness in check was his eight-month-old son.

"I didn't go over there today." He pounded a fist on the arm of the couch. "I'm not going to start reporting to Malcolm McNeill's every summons, and the quicker the old man understands that, the better."

"You went all the way to New York because they said they knew where Damon was, and now you choose to get in a pissing contest to prove some kind of asinine point about how we don't need them?" Gabe's voice lowered, a sure sign he was angry. "We all want the same thing. Bring Damon home."

Frustrated, Jager closed his eyes and counted backward until he could rein himself in.

"They don't want the same thing as us, because they don't even know him. The only reason they're helping us is to flex their muscle and bring us into the fold."

"Dude. This isn't a mob family or something where they're asking us to be part of a gang or start offing their enemies." Gabe's voice broke up on the last few words, probably as a result of poor reception on the island. "They are blood relatives and they'd like to get to know us. It's not their fault Dad is an ass."

Jager had tried telling himself that before, but there was some latent protectiveness of his mom that he couldn't quite shake.

"Still feels disloyal." He didn't have to explain why. Gabe understood him.

"Mom was tough as they come, bro, and she would never hold it against them." Gabe sounded so certain. And he'd had a different relationship with their mother. He hadn't necessarily been the favorite. But the two of them had been alike in a lot of ways. They were more generous and kindhearted than other people.

But you didn't cross them.

"I'll go over there tomorrow." Jager needed to speak to Delia about it, and see what she wanted to do. "I promise."

She'd stressed the importance of meeting his family, and keeping that connection open for their child's sake. But did that mean she wanted to meet all the McNeills too? If so, did he introduce her as his girlfriend? The future mother of his child?

He wished she was already wearing his ring. He had no idea how to tell her that one of the stipulations in Malcolm McNeill's will was that his grandsons had to be wed for at least twelve months to inherit their shares of the family business. Would she view that as him pressuring her? She had to know he didn't want any part of an inheritance from Malcolm, but then again, it seemed too important a detail to omit given that he was going to keep asking her to marry him until she said yes.

"I'll call you tomorrow for an update. If Damon is stirring up trouble somewhere, we either need to talk some sense into him or—"

"Or help him. I know." Jager disconnected the call, and quickly texted with Cameron to make arrangements for visiting the McNeill mansion the next day.

Still, he shut off the phone feeling even more unsettled than when he left Delia's bed.

He had a lot to do to make a more secure world for the child coming in less than eight months' time. Tomorrow, he'd see the McNeills and demand answers about his brother. But first, he needed to have a conversation with Delia about the future. Now that they'd renewed their physical intimacy, she must have recognized how strong their chemistry together could be.

They needed to stay together because he wouldn't be the kind of failure at fatherhood that Liam was. More than that, Jager would never give Delia cause to feel betrayed the way his mother had been. He would be there for her. They could have a Christmas wedding in New York. At The Plaza, if she wanted, surrounded by all the Christmas decorations she loved.

It was a damn good plan. But as he slid quietly into bed beside the beautiful, vibrant woman who'd set him on fire an hour ago, he feared he didn't have enough to offer her.

He had homes. Money. More security than she could ever want.

Yet after hearing about her upbringing with her stoic father, Jager wasn't sure how to convince her he could provide the one thing she wanted most. She longed for love after not receiving it. Jager knew how it felt and understood the way it devastated you when you lost it.

Planting a kiss on Delia's bare shoulder before he covered it with the sheet, he closed his eyes and tipped his head against her back. She sighed sleepily, curling into him. Fitting there perfectly.

Somehow, he would make her see there was more real security in shared goals. In a strong relationship based on trust. And in chemistry that would keep them both satisfied for a lifetime.

Eleven

Sinking deeper in her soaking tub the following afternoon, Delia tipped her head back against the soft bath pillow she'd discovered in a gift package from the hotel spa.

From Jager, of course.

After sleeping soundly for ten hours, she'd awoken to a room service cart near the bed with a veritable breakfast buffet just for her, including two plates of hot food on their own warming stands. She'd also discovered an assortment of gifts lined up on the bedroom's bureau. Jager had gone out to do some Christmas shopping, but left her a note telling her to enjoy herself until he returned. How on earth had she slept through his departure?

She lifted one arm from the water to examine her fingers for their level of pruning and decided she'd probably soaked long enough. She emerged from the bath and stepped into the shower stall to rinse off the spa oils from her skin and deep conditioner from her hair, deciding the only possible explanation for her heavy sleep was the pregnancy. She hadn't experienced any nausea and her breasts seemed to be the same size as normal, so she hadn't felt many effects of carrying a baby. But she wasn't one to sleep so soundly or for so long, and even when she awoke she'd been heavy-limbed and a bit foggy.

The bath and shower were welcome indulgences after the big breakfast. Jager would have been pleased to see how hungry she'd been.

Of course, the voracious appetite might have resulted from the late-night extracurricular activity. She stretched languidly in the shower, remembering the feel of Jager's hands all over her. She was still hyper-sensitive everywhere, her body pleasantly warm and satiated.

Shutting off the spray, she wrapped herself in fluffy white towels and breathed in the heady fragrances from the bath oils and hair products. The spa package had inspired her to try some new herbal combinations when she got back to work at McNeill Meadows. She would also have to give a lot of thought to how she would balance the responsibilities of her job with the care of her child.

Returning to the spacious closet in her bedroom to choose an outfit, she heard rustling in the living area.

"Jager?" Barefoot, she hurried toward the door adjoining the rooms. Then, recognizing how eager she was to see him, she forced herself to slow down.

"Delia." His voice was teasing. Good-humored. Had he been as stirred by their night together as she?

Cracking open the door, she peered out to see him scoop up a small package gift wrapped in gold foil printed with red holly berries and tied with a red velvet bow.

"I got you a pre-Christmas present," he announced, approaching with the gift held out in front of him.

He wore dark pants and a white dress shirt she happened to know was custom-made for him since she'd been in his office one long-ago day when his tailor had arrived with a garment bag containing that season's wardrobe update. No surprise, it fit him perfectly, molding to his shoulders and tapering to accommodate his athletic frame.

She heated all over remembering how well he'd used that sexy body of his last night.

"That was nice of you," she offered after a pause. "I should dress first."

"Please don't think that's necessary on my account." He stopped just inches from the door but didn't open it the rest of the way.

Letting her set the pace.

"I'm not sure we should make a habit of this." She didn't sound remotely convincing, especially since his nearness made her all hot and breathless.

"Of gift giving?" He arched an eyebrow, a wicked grin curling his lips.

Sweet. Heaven. She wanted his mouth on her.

She released her hold on the door, letting it fall open a bit more.

"Forget what I said." She tipped her head sideways against the door frame. "How about if I thank you for the present first, and then I'll unwrap it?"

His eyes narrowed. His nostrils flared. And he set the package aside on a narrow console table as he understood her meaning.

"That hardly seems fair, but I live to please you."

He reached for her, circling her waist and pulling her close.

His woodsy aftershave acted like an aphrodisiac, calling to mind all the ways she'd kissed him the night before.

Having his hands on her only deepened her hunger.

"I do believe pregnancy is finally increasing my appetite." Delia grazed his mouth with hers once. Twice. Then she tugged his lower lip gently between her teeth. "At least one kind of appetite."

With a growl of approval, he bent to lift her off her feet and cradled her in his arms. He headed for the bed.

"It could be *me* that's driving the new hunger." His fingers flexed lightly against her, squeezing her closer. "Either way, I'm going to be the one to satisfy it."

Her eyes fell shut with the need to concentrate on all her other senses, especially the feel of him. The feel of his powerful body levering over hers when he lay with her on the bed. Of his hips sinking into hers, even through the damp towel around her waist.

He kissed her with a care and attentiveness they'd been too impatient for the previous night. He caressed her face, pressing his lips to her eyelids. Then he slid aside her towel to trail more kisses down her neck. Between her bare breasts.

Lower still.

Pleasure spiraled out from a fixed point inside her, sending ribbons of sensation to every hidden spot on her body. A trembling began in her legs before he laid a kiss on the most sensitive of places, taking his time, clearly in no hurry. Ah, but she was. Eager to ride the tension to completion. She saw stars and never opened her eyes, the pinpricks of light flashing a warning of the pleasure to come. He tasted her and she was lost, her hips arching helplessly against the sensual waves of sweet release.

He didn't let go until the spasms slowed and she sagged into the downy duvet, opening her eyes. Only then did he peel off his clothes and join her on the bed again, seating himself deep inside her. His presence there set off more aftershocks, and she wrapped her arms and legs around him tight.

He held himself still for a long moment, letting her adjust to him. He stroked her hair, kissed her neck. And then he began to move.

She wouldn't have thought it possible to build the hunger again, but when he dropped a kiss on one tender breast, she felt pleasure swell for a second time. Seeing his perpetually shadowed jaw in contrast to the creamy pale skin there made her breath catch. Her nipples tightened more. Had she thought her breasts weren't sensitive from pregnancy? She almost shuddered with release from his tongue's careful attention to each peak.

But then he reversed their positions, letting her sit astride him the way she'd started to do the night before. Now, she didn't take the moment for granted, enjoying the way he let her take control.

She delighted in seeing what pleased him, savored the sensation of his hands on her hips, guiding her when he was ready for more.

And then he stole the rhythm back for them both, taking her where they both wanted to go until her orgasm broke over her. Her thighs hugged his hips, drawing a shout of completion from him. The muscles along his chest contracted against her palms and the knowledge that she pleased him as much as he pleased her sent a fresh ripple of bliss over her tingling nerves until, finally, she slumped against his chest, spent.

Cracking open an eyelid to peer up at him, she was taken aback by a sudden swell of tender emotions. She wanted to wrap her arms around him tight and keep him in her bed for days. She wanted to feed him. Make him smile.

On instinct, she shut her eyes again, knowing she couldn't let herself start caring for him that way. She hoped it was just pregnancy emotions making her so tenderhearted. When she thought she had a handle on her feelings again, she opened her eyes.

Unbelievably, the sun was starting to set again by the time her heart settled into an even pace once more.

"How can it be dark already?" she whispered against his bare shoulder, grateful for a neutral topic to speak about when her heart was beginning to hunger for a different kind of fulfillment. "I only woke up shortly before noon."

"I'm wearing you out." Jager frowned his concern, his blue eyes bright in the slanted rays of the setting sun.

"No. I'm just surprised how much shorter the daylight hours are here versus back home." She hadn't given much thought to it, but it made sense because they were so much farther north. "It's only a little after four o'clock."

He glanced away, and she could see his jaw flex.

"We're invited to the McNeill mansion for dinner tonight, but I will call them and reschedule."

She felt very awake then. A bolt of panic did that to a woman.

"Dinner? As in a meal with your brothers and grandfather?"

"I think they'll all be there, yes. Everyone but my father. They know my feelings where he's concerned." He gripped her shoulder when she would have leapt from the bed. "Delia, we can go another time. You're tired—"

"No. I want to go." She also wanted to look her best. To not embarrass Jager. "I was afraid you wouldn't invite me to go with you when you met them."

He stilled. "You're certainly under no obligation to attend."

Would he have preferred to meet them alone? She was torn between wanting to let him find his own way with his half brothers and wanting to understand the world her son or daughter would one day move in. Maternal concern won out.

"I want to be there. I just need a little time to get ready." She would assess for herself what kind of family her child would have.

She had so little to offer a baby in that regard.

"I'll leave your gift on the bed," he called after her while she hurried to her closet to find something to wear. "You might want to wear it tonight."

She heard the bedroom door open while she took stock of her half-dried hair. She couldn't deny a stab of envy for this baby she carried. A McNeill heir would be surrounded by more than just wealth and luxury, both of which she'd lived happily without.

Her child would have a large, caring family to love him or her, something Delia would never know. Even her father, never a demonstrative parent, seemed to have forsaken her. She'd been hurt by his reaction to her baby news.

She was having a child and, at the same time, her family seemed to be dwindling. Unless, by some chance, Jager McNeill started to feel the same new emotions that she'd experienced.

Christmas was a time of miracles after all, and tomorrow was Christmas Eve. Delia couldn't help a quick, fanciful thought.

What if Jager fell in love with her?

The question halted her, stilling her hand as she reached for a brush. What on earth was she thinking?

She had no business thinking those kinds of thoughts. The fact that the question had floated to the surface of her brain reminded her why it was so dangerous to indulge in a physical relationship. She was already falling in love with him.

Closing her eyes, she acknowledged the simple truth that complicated her life so very much. She'd hoped to use this trip to make a smart, reasonable decision. She was going to be a mother, a duty she took seriously. She couldn't afford to fall victim to foolish, romanticized notions. Again.

She wasn't here because she was Jager's girlfriend, or significant other, so she couldn't allow her new feelings to show. In Jager's eyes, she was simply the mother of his child. She would be wise to remember it.

"The jewelry is stunning, Jager." Delia fingered the diamond drop earrings shaped like snowflakes as she stood beside him in the foyer of Malcolm McNeill's expansive mansion in one of the most jaw-droppingly pricey parts of New York.

The maid who answered the door had taken their coats and then disappeared to announce them. Or so Jager guessed.

He thought he had been prepared for the family's wealth. But he wasn't anywhere near ready for a Cézanne in the foyer or the sheer size of the place in a city where tiny patches of real estate went for millions.

If the house caught him off guard, he could only

imagine what Delia was feeling in her first trip outside Martinique. She was definitely in an unusual mood, something he'd noticed as soon as they'd settled side by side in the back of the chauffeured Range Rover his grandfather sent for them. Jager had watched her open the gift on the ride over, and while he was sure she'd been genuinely pleased, there was something reserved about her this evening. Restrained.

He hoped it was just nerves at meeting the more famous branch of the McNeill family.

"I hope the earrings make you think about how much fun we had watching snowflakes fall on the ice at Rockefeller Center." He kissed her temple just as the maid returned to the foyer, pulling his attention back to the impending encounter with his grandfather and half brothers.

"The family is waiting for you in the library." The older woman gestured to her right as she stepped out of their way. "The elevator is down this hall, and it might be easier than the stairs with your beautiful dress, ma'am."

"The skylight is so lovely over the stairs though, I wouldn't have minded a closer look." Delia peered up the formal staircase to the stained-glass window six stories above. She turned to smile at the woman. "I'll bet you see amazing displays of light depending on the weather."

"Some days are truly breathtaking." The woman nodded before disappearing down a corridor toward the back of the house.

"Speaking of breathtaking." Jager slid an arm around Delia's slender waist, careful not to wrinkle the silk taffeta skirt she wore while he guided her down the hall toward the elevator. "Have I mentioned how incredible you look tonight?"

She was vibrant in the ankle-length crimson skirt, a designer confection he'd bought for her with the help of a shopping service. They'd sent an assortment of outfits particularly fitting for the holidays and the long skirt with beadwork and appliqué was a festive choice. She wore a simple creamy-colored angora sweater with it, letting the skirt shine. The earrings went well with her outfit, dangling against her pale neck since she'd swept her fair hair into a smooth twist.

"You clean up well yourself." Her hazel eyes darted over his crisp white dress shirt and tie, as if scanning for anything amiss. She smoothed her fingers down the lapel of his black jacket and he wondered if she did so to soothe herself or him.

Either way, the caring gesture touched him as they stepped into the elevator cabin and he hit the button for the third floor. When the door closed silently, Jager picked up her hands and kissed the back of one and then the other.

It wasn't until that moment—halfway to the third floor—that he remembered he hadn't informed her about his grandfather's will. Swearing softly, he hit the elevator emergency button, halting their upward progress and making the cabin lurch awkwardly as it stopped.

Delia stumbled a bit, but he caught her against him easily.

"What are you doing?" Frowning, she righted herself by gripping the lapels of his jacket.

An alarm blared inside the car, a red light flashing inside the emergency knob.

"I forgot to tell you something important and I don't want you to be surprised, or think I was trying to hide it." He hated sharing it with her this way. "I meant to talk to you when I got back from shopping, but then we got so distracted—"

"Tell me what?" There was a flatness to her voice. An edge.

He didn't blame her for being upset. The flocked red paper on the walls around them seemed to close in as the alarm kept up its insistent wail.

"My grandfather is determined to bring all his grandsons into the business. To carry on his legacy."

She nodded, her hold on his suit jacket loosening. "I remember your half brother talking about that when he came to the gate the first time you and I were together."

"Right. What Cam didn't mention was Malcolm's insistence on his heirs being married for at least a year to inherit."

"Married." She pursed her lips.

He couldn't read her expression, but it seemed like the damn elevator alarm was getting louder.

"Yes." He tensed, willing her to understand it meant nothing to him. "I didn't want you to think that my proposal to you had anything to do with that. I don't care about the hotel business—"

"Don't you think I know that?" Delia shook her head, resting her hands on his upper arms as she faced him. Her words were reassuring but her expression remained tense. "I know you don't want anything from this family, Jager, but I'm glad you're at least in their home, hearing what they have to say."

He stared into her hazel eyes, trying to find out if he was missing something. "You're not upset with me?"

He would swear there was a stiffness about her shoulders. Then again, maybe he was seeing trouble where there wasn't any. This damn meeting had him uptight.

"I'm a little embarrassed about what your family

might say about our elevator mishap, but other than that, of course I'm not upset with you." She offered a tight smile.

He hurried to explain himself, knowing time was running out and not just because of the elevator. "You know I asked you to marry me because—"

"Because of the baby," she finished for him, straightening as her hands fell away from his arms. "Yes. I'm very clear about that, I assure you."

She pressed the elevator alarm button to set things back into motion again and Jager breathed a mental sigh of relief. She understood him.

And she said she wasn't upset with him.

So he wondered why she seemed to bristle when he touched her as the doors swooshed open on the third floor. He hoped it was simple embarrassment for the awkward situation, as she'd mentioned. He would do whatever it took to ensure this visit went smoothly for her. Because in spite of his grandfather's maneuvering, Jager had his own reasons for wanting to make certain he was married before the New Year.

Twelve

If Delia hadn't been upset about his insistence that he only proposed for the sake of their child, she might have been more appreciative of his anxious attempt to tell her about his grandfather's will. That had been kind and considerate, proving to her that he was a far different man than Brandon and—more important—showing her that he understood how hurt she'd been by her former fiancé's deception.

But instead of putting her more at ease for this first meeting with his grandfather, the conversation only brought home for her that Jager was thinking solely about social convention and his legal claim to their child. That hurt all the more tonight since she'd just come face-to-face with the realization that she loved him. And since she'd made it clear she wouldn't marry for anything less than love, his reminder that they should wed for the baby's sake only deepened the raw ache inside her.

Jager had asked her to marry him because she carried his child. It had nothing to do with any feelings for her.

The blunt truth hurt, but it certainly helped her to be less nervous about meeting the rest of the McNeills. She didn't need to worry about impressing people who would never be *her* family. She could focus on taking their measure because they would be her child's relatives.

"Seriously?" Cameron McNeill, the tall half brother who bore a striking resemblance to Damon, was waiting for them on the third floor when the mansion's elevator doors swished open. "Don't they have home elevators where you come from?"

"Funny." Jager extended his hand and the two men shook. "I figured the old man got wind there was an imposter McNeill in the house and hit the reject button."

"There are no imposters here." Cameron clapped him on the shoulder. "Although I'm more interested in your lovely guest." Expectant and charming, he turned to Delia.

"Delia, this is Cameron. Cam, meet Delia Rickard." Jager wrapped a possessive arm around her waist. "And she is special to me."

She swallowed back the automatic thrill that danced through her at his words, his touch. She tried to focus on his half brother instead. Now that Delia could see Cameron more clearly, she realized she'd never again mistake him for Damon. Though both men were unusually tall, Cameron was probably on the high end of six foot four. And whereas Damon had been a serious man even before his wife's disappearance, Cameron seemed a lighter spirit.

"A pleasure to welcome you, Delia." He grinned as he squeezed her hand briefly. "And no need to worry.

Now that I'm happily wed, I won't be issuing any more impulsive marriage proposals to the beautiful women I meet."

"I'm sure your new wife is glad to know it," Delia replied, remembering well the tabloid frenzy about Cameron's public proposal to the New York City Ballet dancer who later married Quinn—the eldest McNeill. Months afterward, Cameron had wed a concierge who worked for one of the McNeills' Caribbean hotels. The rush to wed made all the more sense in light of what Jager had confided. "And thank you for having me."

"If you're special to Jager, you're special to us. Are you ready to meet the rest of the clan?" Cameron held an arm out, gesturing toward the double doors flanked by carved wood panels at the end of the corridor.

The panels were the kind she'd seen in historic plantation homes, the sort of things that Gabe enjoyed restoring or even reproducing from scratch.

Grateful to have that first encounter behind them—and to have easily brushed aside the matter of the stuck elevator—Delia accompanied the men toward the library. She needed to tamp down the hurt and unease from her conversation with Jager mere seconds earlier.

When Cameron opened the double doors, she only had a moment to take in the richness of the room, with its walls fitted with historic Chinese lacquer panels between the windows overlooking the street. Quickly, she shifted her attention to the six other people she hadn't yet met.

Delia was glad she'd taken time to read up on the family—again—before the trip to New York, since the tidbits she recalled about the various members helped her to keep them straight. Ian was the first to step forward and introduce himself to her. Jager had already met Ian, the brother who was most involved in the hotel business, developing his own specialty properties in addition to his work with McNeill Resorts. Ian's wife, Lydia, a dark-haired beauty with deep furrows in her pale forehead, eyed Delia with an assessing gaze. She was dressed elegantly in a green tartan skirt and black silk blouse, and a velvet choker with an emerald pendant at her throat.

Cameron's wife, Maresa, perched on the arm of a wingback chair, composed and elegant in an ice-blue sweater dress that drew attention to honey-colored eyes, a shade paler than her deeply tanned skin. She was the only one in the group to hug Delia, a gesture that put her a bit more at ease for meeting the rest. Maresa no longer worked as a concierge for one of the McNeill Resorts hotels, but her warm manner made it obvious why she'd been so good at the job in her native Saint Thomas.

The last of the brothers was Quinn, the hedge fund manager who had married the exotic ballerina.

"Good to have you in New York," Quinn greeted them, his navy suit and light blue shirt conservative without being stodgy.

It was interesting to view Jager side by side with this man since each was the oldest of his respective group of McNeill brothers, and she recognized a similar way they had of sizing each other up. While Cam had been open and friendly, Ian was tough to read but warm, and Quinn, the oldest, clearly reserved judgment. That was Jager too. She'd seen it in business meetings.

She saw it in how he related to her.

He held back. He sure didn't rush to embrace people. He'd been as scarred by people in his life—the loss of his mother, especially—as Delia had been. Seeing him that way helped her to understand him better, even if it wouldn't change him.

"Good to be here," Jager replied, offering the barest nod of acknowledgment. "I hope to work more closely with your investigator while I'm here. Bentley."

From the back of the room, the gray-haired gentleman seated in a leather club chair—the patriarch himself, no doubt—finally spoke up. "Bentley will be here before dinner is served."

The crowd of relatives shuffled to give Jager and Delia a better view of Malcolm McNeill. His bearing commanded the room.

With all the attention turned toward Malcolm, the petite blonde beside Delia whispered to her. "I'm Sofia, by the way."

Delia glanced down at the speaker. So this was the ballerina Quinn had married. She was even more beautiful than her photos online, and she didn't even seem to have any makeup on. She certainly had a natural look, and her outfit was a simple black dress, long sleeved with a floor-length skirt that might have been severe on someone else.

Jager strode forward to shake his grandfather's hand, and Sofia continued to speak quietly. "Meeting Quinn's family was more terrifying than any audition I've ever had," she confided, forcing Delia to hide a smile by biting her cheek. "But they're not so bad."

Nearby, Lydia must have overheard because she softly chimed in, "When they're not brawling."

"She's teasing," Sofia rushed to explain, fixing her loose topknot that was slipping from its clasp. "Mostly."

At the other end of the room, Jager conversed quietly with his grandfather. Delia couldn't help but be curious about the exchange; the older man was smiling as Jager held out a hand to help him from his chair. Malcolm shook off the gesture, however, pointing to a silver-topped walking stick nearby.

When he stood, even with his slightly stooped back and bent knees, he was every bit as tall as Cameron. It was clear the brothers had inherited their grandfather's genes. He wore a smoking jacket, of all things, made of dark silk and belted over a pair of black trousers and wing tips. With his thinning hair still damp but combed perfectly into place, he had a debonair quality about him.

"My dear, I'm eager to meet you." His voice boomed the length of the room, and his blue eyes—that matched all the other men's eyes in the room—turned to Delia.

She swallowed hard, grateful for the reassuring pat on the elbow from Sofia.

Stepping forward, she braced herself to meet her child's great-grandfather.

"Hello, sir." Pasting a smile into place, she reminded herself she was good at this. In the same way that Cameron's wife had a warm manner from being a concierge, Delia had honed her skills making people feel comfortable at McNeill Meadows. She could do this. "Thank you so much for inviting me tonight."

Malcom paused a few feet from her, steadying himself on the cane. She wondered if his strength was waning after the heart attack Cameron had mentioned.

Jager might not have believed the story, but Delia did. She guessed the older man's failing health had prompted him to act fast to unify his family.

"I am delighted to know you, Delia." Malcolm McNeill enveloped her hand in his larger one and kept hold of it. "You might have heard that I'm very committed to meeting all my grandsons and ensuring the McNeill legacy lives on through a strong family tree."

Family tree? Delia shifted her gaze to the floor, afraid her face would betray her secret.

"Gramps." Cameron exchanged a look with his wife and then edged forward to stand by Malcolm. "Maybe we should go in for dinner first."

"We haven't even offered our newest members a drink yet, have we?" Malcolm glanced around the room. "Lydia, love, would you bring me mine so we can have a toast?" He let go of Delia's hand to point at the half-empty glass by his abandoned club chair. "And for pity's sake, let's get Jager and Delia something." He nodded toward Ian.

Lydia hurried over to do her part, making no noise in her stilettos. How did some women manage that trick? She had a graceful walk that Delia envied. Delia felt more out of her element with each passing moment, and she most certainly would not have a cocktail to toast anything. Why hadn't she thought of that before she asked to attend this gathering?

"No need to wait on us." Jager beat Ian in his move toward the bar, a freestanding antique that held a few bottles of high-end liquor and three cut crystal decanters. "I'll get it."

Delia touched one of her snowflake earrings to calm herself. She had thought she wasn't nervous when she walked into the room, but Malcolm McNeill's reference to the "strong family tree" stirred anxiety. She felt certain Jager wouldn't have shared their secret with his grandfather.

But was there a chance he'd told one of his brothers? The way Cameron quickly cut off Malcolm's line of conversation made her wonder. Everyone would know soon enough, of course. But she wanted to discuss how to broach the news with Jager before they revealed it to his family.

"What would you like, my dear?" Malcolm asked her suddenly, fixing her with his clear blue gaze. "If Chivas isn't to your taste, there's a bottle of Tattingers we can open."

From the bar, Jager spoke up. "I know her preference. We're all set."

She could see that he'd poured tonic water into a highball glass with an ice cube and a lime wedge. Perfect.

Turning her attention back to Jager's grandfather, she saw the older man's gaze was fixed on Jager's actions as well. And was it her nervous imagination, or had everyone else noticed his discreet pour?

"You're not drinking this evening." Malcolm's observation confirmed her suspicion. He'd seen, all right. "Good for you, my dear." He patted her forearm and then accepted his glass from Lydia as she rejoined the group. "Very good, indeed."

Could he be any more obvious in his implications? Delia felt her cheeks heat and remembered Jager saying how easy it was to read her because of those blushes.

"What did I miss?" Lydia asked, frowning as she peered around at the family.

The men tried to look elsewhere. Sofia gave her sister-in-law a quick headshake as if to discourage a follow-up question.

Jager returned to Delia's side with two drinks, passing her the water before answering Lydia. "Only that Malcolm seemed pleased Delia isn't much of a drinker." He gave Delia's cheek a kiss. "I think we're as ready for that toast as we'll ever be."

Her skin warmed from the brush of his lips. She knew that Jager would have rather skipped the whole formality of a toast that put them at the center of attention. No doubt he'd only redirected the conversation to forestall speculation that she could be pregnant. It was kind of him, and yet the damage had already been done. Malcolm had all but shouted it from the rooftops in his own subtle way.

Unless, of course, Jager really had told his family that she was expecting without letting her know? That was hard to believe given the importance he'd placed on informing her about his grandfather's marriage ultimatum. And yet, she already knew he viewed this baby very differently than he viewed marriage. The former meant the world to him.

The latter? A formality. Different rules might apply in his mind.

She found herself touching the snowflake earring again and forced her hand down to her side. Why should she allow his family to make her feel so uneasy? She might never see them again after tonight. Once the holidays were over, she'd be back on a plane to Martinique.

Around her, the assembled guests retrieved their beverages. Malcolm shuffled backward a step so he could lean against the sofa and set aside his cane. He lifted his tumbler, the crystal glass acting as a prism and reflecting light from the overhead chandelier. Jager's blue gaze landed on her with an unfathomable look. Did he regret bringing her here?

Jager tamped down the urge to tuck Delia under his arm and haul ass out of the mansion and the whole McNeill realm. Although Malcolm McNeill had seemed genuine enough in his words of welcome earlier, Jager didn't appreciate the way the older man put Delia on the spot. What the hell had he been thinking?

Clearly, she was upset. Jager had seen the splotches of color on her cheeks, noticed the way she fidgeted with her earring. He kicked himself for not insisting he meet the family privately first, but she'd surprised him with her emphatic decision to attend the dinner. Besides, his number one goal this week was to make her happy, to change her mind about marriage so they could start building a future together as a family.

Damn. This was not helping.

His grandfather's hand—a surprisingly heavy weight—landed on his shoulder. "I'd like to propose a toast to every person in this room." The older man's voice rumbled with gravelly authority. "My grandsons and the women who stand beside them. I am proud to call you family." His gaze scanned each face around the library. "Tonight, we celebrate a joyous occasion, welcoming even more McNeills into the fold." He nodded at both Delia and Jager. "Cheers to you."

Jager watched Delia, hoping she wouldn't be too upset the toast made it sound like they were already married. Perhaps the family patriarch was referring to Jager's brothers when he mentioned welcoming *more McNeills*. But Jager could see her uneasiness grow even as she raised her glass along with everyone else during shouts of "Cheers!" and "Here, here."

Maybe he was the only one to notice the signs of her agitation. Her time dealing with the public at the McNeill Meadows property had given her easy social skills that hadn't been so apparent when he'd first hired her as an assistant. But he'd known her before she'd developed the ability to put on a public face. He spied the way she waited until she glanced down to bite her lip, hiding the sign of nerves.

The women in the group congregated around Delia; he hoped whatever they had to say distracted her from this debacle in a good way. Quinn moved to speak to Malcolm, shaking his hand and complimenting the toast.

"I should have told you to bring an engagement ring with you to this thing," Cameron muttered in Jager's ear, his tone dry. "We've all been on the marriage fast track here."

"You warned me," Jager admitted, feeling more trapped by the minute. And they hadn't even sat down to dinner yet. "But I underestimated his commitment to his approach."

Cam sipped his drink, his gold wedding band glinting in the light, while he studied his grandfather. "I think when you reach his age, you say what you want and don't give a rip."

"If he sends Delia running, I'm done with him." Jager meant it. Seeing a tentative smile on Delia's face while one of the women spoke to her made him grateful to the females in the group. "I'm only here because of her."

She was all that mattered to him.

And, of course, their child.

It occurred to him that he thought about them—Delia and their baby—in the reverse order of how he'd been used to weighing their importance in his life. Ever since their first impulsive night, when he knew there was a chance she could be pregnant, he'd put all his focus on making plans for an heir.

But there was more to Delia than just her role in this pregnancy, and he wasn't sure how to contend with his growing feelings for her. They were a distraction from the goal. An inconvenience that made him second-guess himself, and he couldn't afford that when he was so ready to close the deal.

Forever.

He had that engagement ring Cam mentioned after all. He'd been working on a Christmas Eve proposal she'd never forget.

Quinn moved away from Malcolm to speak to his wife, and Jager noticed Malcolm retrieve his cane. Jager strode over to intercept him, making sure his grandfather didn't corner Delia to press his family agenda.

"Thank you for the welcome." Jager leaned against the back of the couch beside Malcolm, thinking to keep the two of them separate until the meal. Or to change the subject of conversation.

But Delia was already moving toward them, her diplomatic smile firmly in place.

"It was nice of you to include me," Delia added as she came to face them both. "Even though I'm not family."

There was an edge to her words. No doubt, she'd been pushed to her limit tonight. Jager itched to take her hand. To kiss away her frustrations and make sure no stress touched her. No matter what the doctor said about her pregnancy not being high risk, it couldn't be good for a woman to be upset like this while she was expecting.

It should be a happy time for her.

"Well, I hope my grandson will change that soon." Malcom grinned broadly, unaware of the nervous energy practically thrumming through Delia. "I predict it won't be long until we have another McNeill wedding."

Delia's sharp intake of breath was audible. Jager put a placating hand at the base of her spine and felt for himself how tense she was. The room went silent.

Jager drew a breath, prepared to make their excuses and depart.

Delia beat him in responding.

"We won't be marrying." She smiled sweetly, but her hazel eyes were filled with a steely determination he recognized.

He'd seen it the day she jumped in the sea to save a drowning child.

"My dear." The furrow in Malcolm's brow indicated that—finally—he understood he was out of line. Or that, at the very least, he'd upset his guest. "I only thought, since you are glowing at my grandson's side and you didn't imbibe tonight—"

"You were mistaken," she fired back, standing tall and proud and ready to do battle. "I may be expecting. But we have no plans to wed just for the sake of our child."

If Jager's future didn't hang in the balance of those words, he might have taken some pleasure from seeing this woman, once prone to being insecure, take on the intimidating Malcolm McNeill.

Instead, he felt a kick to the teeth. It reverberated squarely in his chest and every part of him. In spite of his every effort, he'd now be living out his father's legacy of bringing a child into the world without benefit of marrying the mother. That worried him.

But unexpectedly, the pain ran deeper, beyond losing out on a chance at a real family, one with Delia and their child. He was completely leveled by the fact that he'd lost his chance to win over Delia.

The only woman he'd ever loved.

Thirteen

Delia wondered if she would blame this moment on pregnancy hormones later.

It was unlike her to gainsay anyone, especially her host on an important night for Jager. But what made Malcolm McNeill think he could maneuver his family like chess pieces, especially after all these years? Is that what family was about?

In the heavy silence that followed her declaration, she became aware of Jager beside her. His face was a frozen mask she did not recognize. No doubt she had embarrassed him, and she regretted that. Deeply. But he could not have been surprised, as she'd already confided her deep need to marry for love. He, of all people, must understand that. He'd been there for her when she'd been falling apart from Brandon's betrayal. Jager had met her father and seen how that need for authentic emotions went back to her childhood.

Delia became aware of the deep, resonant ticking of the vintage grandfather clock while everyone around her seemed to grapple with what to say next. She understood the feeling, since Malcolm McNeill had put her in that precise awkward position from the moment he'd acknowledged her presence.

"I see that I've upset you, my dear." Malcolm found his cane with one fumbling hand and set down his drink with the other. "And I'm so sorry for that. You should understand I am accustomed to being far too abrupt with my grandsons about my hopes for the future, a flaw they have overlooked because of my age and my health. But that should not excuse poor manners."

When he reached Delia's side, he squeezed her forearm. There was sorrow in his eyes, and she felt contrite. For all she knew, he could still be manipulating her emotions, but she wished she hadn't spoken out.

"Perhaps we should leave," Jager interjected with a terseness that alerted her to how much this had upset him too.

Exhaustion hit her in a wave, making her acutely aware of the stress, the lateness of the hour and a sudden hunger. Her pregnancy hormones may have been late making themselves known, but these last two days had rocked her on a physical level. She felt a bit faint, her vision narrowing to two pinpricks of light.

"I may need to sit," Delia told him, done with caring about how well-liked she was among the McNeills. She'd been foolish to try to be a part of Jager's world. As much as she longed for family, she was not cut out for this.

As one, the McNeills moved to clear a path to the sofa. Jager offered her his arm and steadied her, guiding her toward the couch near the bar.

Ian's wife was suddenly beside her, holding her hand. "Have you eaten? Would that help?"

Delia nodded and someone, Maresa maybe, said, "I'll get it," and left the room. Delia let the soft hubbub of voices wash over her as her vision slowly returned to normal.

"It has to be stressful meeting us all." That voice belonged to Sofia. "Especially everyone at once."

"It's okay, Gramps." That might have been Cameron. "When I'm upset, it always helps me to clear the air. Say what's on my mind and then move past it. She won't hold it against you."

"Delia, would you like me to call for a car?" Jager asked in her ear, his voice kind and yet…distant. "You'd be more comfortable at the hotel."

"I'm fine," she assured him, her vision beginning to clear. "We can't leave now after I put everyone in an uproar."

"Your color is returning." She realized Lydia still held her hand on her other side. Or, rather, Delia was gripping Lydia's hand for dear life.

"Sorry." Delia let go and sat up straighter. "I am feeling better."

"Maresa went to get you something to eat." Lydia lowered her voice for Delia's hearing only. "And we're excited for you, no matter what your plans might be. Babies are the best news."

Sliding a sideways glance to gauge her expression, Delia found a wealth of sincerity in those pretty green eyes. And, maybe, a touch of envy. Did Lydia hope to get pregnant herself? she wondered.

"Thank you. And I am very happy," Delia assured her, realizing how much more attached she grew to this child every single day. What started out as a shock had come to mean more to her than anything else in her life. Although, she had to admit, winning Jager's love would have come very close. Thinking about raising their child separately, losing the close relationship they had, made her heart hurt. But the notion of subjecting herself to a loveless marriage hurt worse. She'd been rejected enough by the people in her life.

Sitting beside him and feeling so apart from him was far worse than any dizziness and exhaustion she may have experienced because of the baby.

Maresa returned with a plate for Delia at the same time two servers entered with hors d'oeuvres for the group at large. The family all seemed as thrilled to see the food as her, probably grateful for a diversion after the tense start to the cocktail hour. Ian asked Jager about McNeill Meadows and the changes he'd made to the property to highlight its plantation history.

She breathed a sigh of relief as Jager allowed himself to be pulled into conversation. Hopefully they could get through the rest of the evening on a more positive note. She crunched into a cracker topped with warm brie and a slice of glazed pear, wondering how many she could devour without raising eyebrows.

As if reading her mind, Lydia winked. "Want me to find a few more of those?"

"Thank you." She nodded. "That would be great."

With Lydia's spot vacated, Delia had a clear view of her host in the club chair, which was situated at an angle to the couch. With both hands folded on top of the cane that rested to one side of his knee, he stared out a window, the lines in his face deeper with his frown.

Unable to leave things festering between them, she set her plate on the coffee table and slid down so that she sat closer to him.

She felt Jager's eyes follow her movement, but she knew what she was doing.

"Mr. McNeill, I began to feel faint while we were speaking and didn't get a chance to say that there is nothing to forgive." She patted his hands awkwardly. "You apologized to me, but I realize that I was unusually prickly, especially at what should be a wonderful reunion for your family. This is about you and your grandsons."

"It's about family. All of us." He shook his head. "I should not have been so forceful."

"But at least I could tell that you were enthused about this baby, and I'm glad for that." She had come here tonight, telling herself the visit was about her child when, really, she had wanted to be a part of Jager's world. To feel the embrace of a long-lost family. Did he know how fortunate he was to have people who wanted to claim him for a brother? For a grandson? "My own father has never expressed much joy in his family, so I may not be adept at navigating the nuances of..." She peered around the room, taking in the faces of so many McNeills, so many people who truly did care about welcoming yet another generation. "All this," she finished lamely.

"And I am so eager for family, I unwittingly push them away. It wouldn't be the first time." When the older man turned his blue eyes toward her, they were bright and shiny. "The mother of any McNeill is family to me," he said quietly.

Malcolm had spoken softly, but Delia could feel Jager's attention focused on them from the other end of the couch. He was listening. She hoped what his grandfather said meant something to him—at least in regard to his own mother, if not to Delia.

"For that, I thank you." The words certainly warmed her heart, even as they underscored all that she would miss by not marrying Jager.

"I had hoped to see all my grandsons married, so I put it in my will." He shook his head, bent in defeat. "Maybe it was not so wise."

She realized it wasn't just Jager who now strained to listen. Conversation around them had stopped once more. This time, Delia didn't feel the need to cross swords with him though, even though she guessed each McNeill in the room wanted to shout that his dictate was horribly unfair.

Yet it seemed to have netted three happy marriages so far.

"You might be better off letting your heirs decide what's best for their future," Delia suggested, reaching for her water glass before remembering she'd left it near her former seat. "Don't forget Damon already lost a wife he loved dearly. A dictate to marry again would only drive him away."

"You make a very good point."

All heads turned toward the open double doors to find the source of the comment.

Damon McNeill had entered the room.

Jager sat with his brother later that night in a second hotel room he'd booked for Damon at The Plaza. Between Delia nearly fainting and Damon showing up unannounced with Bentley, the McNeills' investigator who'd made good on the promise to deliver him, everyone agreed they would share a meal together some other night. Even Malcolm had been too stunned to argue, perhaps feeling abashed between his pushy tactics with Delia and then having Damon, quite possibly a widower at this point, overhear their discussion of the old man's matchmaking tactics.

Jager had had more than enough of the Other Mc-Neills for one night. Cameron had let it slip at some point that that was how they referred to their half brothers. The shoe fit the other damned foot just fine.

Now, as he shared a beer and watched an NBA game with the brother he'd always been closest to, Jager realized his happiness at having Damon back was only dampened by Delia's insistence they wouldn't marry.

And yeah, it dampened his happiness a whole hell of a lot. Still, he was glad to have Damon's big, ugly boots planted in his line of sight on the coffee table while they watched a game being played on the West Coast. He needed this time to decompress after Delia's rejection. Decompress and regroup. He wasn't giving up, but he wasn't sure how to move forward to win her over. She was a confounding, complex and amazing woman.

"If we were still in Los Altos Hills, we'd be at this game right now," Damon observed, looking thinner and scruffier than he had in the fall before he left on his trip. He looked like he hadn't shaved since then; his dark beard hid half his face. "We left behind some good season tickets, didn't we?"

They'd left behind much more than that, but he wasn't sure how to broach the subject with his brother. Jager sucked at expressing himself lately, it seemed. He'd fallen short with Delia when he'd tried his best to be honest and forthright with her—which was exactly what she'd said she'd wanted.

On the TV, a player went for a slam dunk and got rejected at the hoop. It was a perfect freaking metaphor for this day and the ring that burned a hole in his jacket pocket even now. He leaned forward enough to tug his arms from the sleeves and tossed the jacket aside.

When they'd arrived back at The Plaza, he mentioned wanting to spend some time with his brother, and Delia seemed only too glad to find her bed for the night. She was exhausted and happy to have a tray in her room, something he'd ordered for her before he left her two doors down.

"I waited around for you to come home," Jager said now, not sure how much his brother knew about events that had transpired in the past few months. "When I couldn't get in touch with you, I figured I'd better put the business on the market before it lost all value. You know how rumors of the founder's disappearance can make investors nervous."

"I'll take over with the business now. There's no need to sell." Damon clinked his longneck against Jager's bottle. "I just got held up."

Thinking about all the nights he'd been convinced his brother was dead, Jager set the beer down and sat up, barely restraining his anger and—hell, yes—hurt.

"That's all you have to say? After months of not answering your phone and letting us all think the worst?"

Damon traced the outline of the name of the craft beer molded into the glass.

"I needed to find out what happened to my wife." His words were flat. Emotionless. "Unfortunately for me, I've come to agree with the police. She must have wanted out and didn't know how to tell me."

Jager was too stunned to reply for a long moment. Damon had been so certain she'd been kidnapped. "What about the ransom note?"

"Must have been a scheme for cash by someone who

knew she disappeared. I still need to get to the bottom of that."

"You could have called. Or taken me with you. Or—" Jager shook his head. "You shouldn't have left us wondering what happened to you."

"Next time I lose my mind, brother, I'll try to communicate more." Damon tipped back his drink.

Jager stewed for another minute, hoping his brother would offer up the full story. Or at least a few more details. But he didn't want to push him.

Yet.

He'd find out what had happened soon enough. For now, he was so damn glad to have him back and wouldn't risk pushing him away again. There'd been enough screw-ups on that account tonight.

"So what's next for you?" Jager asked, wishing he had a wedding to invite him to. He would have asked him to be his best man.

Then again... No. He couldn't have done that. Not when Damon had been preparing for his own wedding just a year ago.

"I need to launch my software." Damon lifted his bottle to peer through the dark glass. He closed one eye and then the other, watching the TV through the curved surface. "Get Transparent off the ground."

"Sounds good." Jager liked the idea of Damon getting back to work. Before Caroline, he'd been able to lose himself in the business for months at a time.

Jager wished he could be on the West Coast for him. But he had already spent too much time away from McNeill Meadows. Would Delia keep the cottage if she didn't marry him? he wondered. But not marrying was unacceptable. Thinking about her pronouncement during the cocktail hour was driving him out of his mind.

He needed to get back to their room and talk to her if she wasn't asleep.

And if she was, he needed to figure out a way to change her mind about marrying him and convince her first thing when she woke up.

"So." Damon set aside the empty bottle and glanced over at him. "You and Delia Rickard?"

"Yes." Jager ground his teeth. He had been irritated that his brother hadn't said much about where he'd been the last few months, and yet he realized he didn't feel like talking about how he'd spent his time recently either.

They'd never been an overly chatty family. And since their mother had died, they'd been quieter still.

"She's changed since the last time I saw her," his brother observed. "I almost didn't recognize her voice when I heard her from out in the hallway. She's feistier."

Jager had wondered what his brother thought about how she'd confronted Malcolm.

"She contradicted the McNeill patriarch all night long and still won the old man over somehow." Jager had only heard snippets of their conversation as they'd said their goodbyes, but he had overheard his grandfather wresting a promise from her to stay in touch.

The dynamic there was lost on him.

"Did they win you over?" Damon asked, pointing at the television and making the call for a flagrant foul a moment before the game ref did. "Are you going to be joining the petition to merge the families?"

There'd been a time when Jager would have simply barked a *hell no* in his brother's face. But maybe his time with Delia, thinking about a future and family of his own, made him view things differently.

"I think Malcolm is the only one who is psyched

about it. Quinn was polite, but I got the impression he'd rather swallow glass than compromise the empire."

Damon chuckled, a sound rusty from lack of use. "I was there for twenty minutes, and knew in about ten seconds he's a carbon copy of you, dude. That's exactly how you look to the rest of the world."

Jager laughed it off to end the night on an easy note. Finishing his beer, he left Damon to watch the rest of the game on his own. He needed to check on Delia. Make a plan for tomorrow.

But as he strode through The Plaza's empty hallway shortly before midnight, he couldn't help thinking about what Damon had said. Did Delia see him that way? Uncompromising? Unyielding?

If he could figure out how to change her mind, maybe he still had a chance to win her back. Clearly, introducing her to his family had been an epic fail, but he had one last strategy that still might work. A plan he'd put in place before he even left Martinique.

Because to help Jager make his case to Delia, Pascal Rickard was on a flight bound for New York tonight.

Fourteen

Delia slept late on Christmas Eve. She'd been so tired and heartbroken the night before after the failed dinner at the McNeills; she'd forgotten that time was ticking down to the holiday.

And now, it was Christmas Eve and she was alone in her bedroom at The Plaza Hotel.

Through parted curtains, she could see snow falling outside. Fat, fluffy flakes danced down from the sky, taking their time on the way. Her first thought was to share the beautiful view with Jager. Until she remembered their awkward parting the night before.

She'd told his whole family they weren't getting married. She'd hurt him on what had to be one of the toughest days of his life.

He'd been cold and distant, barely speaking to her directly afterward. Of course, he'd had a shock seeing his brother walk into the library. She hadn't blamed Jager for wanting to spend time with Damon when they returned to the hotel. She'd felt deeply tired anyhow. But a part of her had also recognized that Jager was pulling away from her.

From them.

He'd said all along their chemistry was off the charts. He'd made no promises about having feelings for her.

Rolling to her side, she noticed the time—almost 10:00 a.m. *Wow.* She scrubbed her hand across her eyes. She'd slept half the morning away, the pregnancy sleep deep and heavy, as if her body needed plenty of quiet time to nurture the life inside her. Moving a hand to her flat stomach and touching it through the silk nightgown she wore, she marveled to think that her child grew there. One day, she'd be able to share the wonders of snowfalls and Christmases with this baby.

Or Christmases, at least.

Of the many things she would miss when Jager was no longer in her life romantically, snow seemed like a small, frivolous addition to the list. How many times a day would she think about ways she would regret not having him in her life?

As she sat up, her forearm crumpled a piece of paper on the pillow beside her.

Puzzled, she reached for it and discovered Jager's handwriting on hotel stationery.

There is a breakfast tray outside your bedroom. Please take your time getting dressed. I left an outfit for you as I invited a special guest I think you will want to see this afternoon. —Jager

Special guest?

She wondered if he meant Damon. Or someone else in his family. Key word being *his*. Not hers.

Although for a surprisingly touching moment last night, she had wanted to hug Malcolm McNeill tight for his kindness to her. She'd started off the evening so irritated that the older man had put her on the spot, implying she was pregnant when she hadn't been ready to announce anything. Yet by the end of their eventful time together, she'd felt a keen understanding and affection for Jager's grandfather.

Was it the overdose of hormones that made her so emotional? Or was she so hypnotized by the idea of a paternal figure that even Jager's bossy grandparent could win her over that fast?

Planting her feet on the floor, she waited for any sign of morning sickness, but she felt good. Solid. Padding to the door, she opened it and peered out to see if Jager was around, but she spotted only the silver room service tray, as he'd promised.

She also saw a huge, decorated Christmas tree in the living area that hadn't been there the night before. Red ribbons festooned the branches along with multicolored lights and ornaments that looked like...skyscrapers?

Unable to resist, she hurried closer, hugging her arms around herself to ward off the chill from seeing snow outside.

The ornaments were all New York themed. The Empire State Building and the Chrysler Building shone bright in the glow of tree lights. The Statue of Liberty hung from another branch, along with taxicabs, hansom carriages and even The Plaza Hotel with the flags flying on the front. Some of the decorations she'd seen at Rockefeller Center were represented, including the white angels blowing their trumpets and the gilded bronze Prometheus statue that presided over the ice skating rink.

The tree, the scent of pine that filled the room, it all mesmerized her, putting her in the holiday spirit. And outside in Central Park, that dizzying white snowfall coated the trees.

Had Jager done all this? Well, all this except the snowfall? Even a McNeill couldn't make demands of Mother Nature.

Delia wondered if this was his way of... No. She squelched the hopeful thought as she ignored the breakfast tray and jumped in the shower. She was unwilling to build up her expectations all over again. She would speak to Jager. Ask him about realistic goals for co-parenting in the future and plan accordingly. He might break her heart, but she couldn't afford to indulge that hurt. She had to be mature and responsible for her child.

No more running away from her problems on a Jet Ski.

An hour later, she finished drying her hair and dressed in the outfit she'd found on the lower shelf of the room service tray: a simple red velvet dress with a black ribbon sash. As if that wasn't decadent enough, there were red velvet heels with skinny ankle straps. Both boxes were stamped with designer logos from exclusive New York boutiques. And everything fit her perfectly.

She checked her reflection and wondered if it was wrong of her to wear the gifts after what she'd done the night before. Then again, maybe wearing the clothes was a conciliatory gesture. She didn't want to appear ungrateful after all Jager had done for her.

They'd been friends first. She wished there was a way they could maintain that friendship somehow. But there would be no going back now. Not after everything they'd shared.

Blinking fast before her emotions swallowed her whole, she braced herself for whatever awaited her in the next room. She thought she'd heard Jager return when she first emerged from the shower, but she'd done as he asked and taken her time getting ready for whatever special guest he'd brought. Fully expecting to see Damon when she opened the bedroom door, her brain couldn't process what—who—she saw.

Her father?

She blinked, but sure enough the vision stayed the same.

Pascal Rickard sat on the couch in front of the Christmas tree, a glass of eggnog in his hand.

"Dad?" she asked so softly she wasn't sure how he heard.

But he shifted on his cushion, turning toward her before getting to his feet slowly. Behind him, Jager rose as well. It was a sign of how stunned she was that she'd missed him sitting there.

"Hello, Delia." Her father placed his drink on the coffee table to greet her, but didn't move closer.

She looked over at Jager, seeking an explanation, something to account for this visit.

He cleared his throat. "I'm going to leave the two of you to talk." Jager grabbed his long wool coat from a chair by the door. His face was freshly shaven, but there were shadows under his eyes, making her wonder how late he'd stayed up with his brother the night before. "I told Damon I'd meet with him today about the sale of his company. Bring him up to speed."

She nodded, too dazed by her father's presence to think beyond that. When the door closed behind Jager, she moved toward her father, arching up on her toes to kiss his weathered cheek in a rare display of affection between them. But if he left his boat to fly halfway around the world to see her, she thought the moment warranted it.

To her surprise, he wrapped her in a hug with his good arm. She laid her head against his chest, noticing his clean new sweater and the heavy sigh he heaved.

She levered away to look up at him. "I can't believe you're here. Is everything all right back home?"

"Things are good. Better than good, actually." He pointed to the couch. "Let's sit."

"I didn't know you were coming." She dropped onto the cushion beside him, facing the Christmas tree that cast a warm golden glow on both of them.

Outside, the snowfall made the day feel cozy, the lack of sunlight making the tree lights more prominent in the room.

"I spoke to Jager last week." He picked up his eggnog and had another sip. Beside his glass there was a plate of sugar cookies shaped like snowmen that must have been delivered by room service. "He came back to town to ask if I would visit you here for Christmas."

"Jager." Of course that accounted for her father being here. He could have never afforded the plane ticket otherwise. "Why? I mean, I'm glad to see you. I'm just surprised he didn't mention it."

"He said he wanted it to be a surprise." Her dad's face had aged in the last few years—more than she'd noticed when they visited to announce her pregnancy. The weathered lines from his years in the sun were deeper, his pallor grayer. "I know I was surprised myself when he showed up. He apologized for being abrupt in the other visit when you both came to see me that day. Asked how he could help out. He said he wanted to provide for you and—for me too."

"That was thoughtful of him," she said carefully, not sure how her proud parent would view that kind of offer.

"It was a damn sight more than thoughtful," he grumbled, swiping a snowman cookie and crunching into it. After a contemplative moment, he said, "He offered to have my boat fixed and my roof patched. And made a deal with me and a few of my friends to provide the seafood for the Birdsong Hotel."

Gabe's resort property.

"He did?" She knew what that meant. Her father could take it easy. There would be no more stress about selling what he caught. Thinking about Jager doing those things for her father—for her—made her eyes sting with sharp gratitude. He'd never even mentioned it to her.

"I told him no—about the boat and roof, not about the seafood deal because I'm still a businessman and I've got bills too, bills I can now afford to pay." He pointed at her with the cookie, the half-eaten snowman taking some of the fire out of his emphatic words.

"But he insisted on the rest too, didn't he?" She already knew the answer. Two years of working for Jager McNeill had shown her that he drove a hard bargain. Weeks of being his lover, even when she'd been ducking his texts and afraid to face him, had shown her he was persistent and caring where she was concerned.

She was so touched. She couldn't stop loving him if she tried.

"Wouldn't take no for an answer. What's more, he gave me this passbook for a bank account with both our names on it—yours and mine." He dug in the pocket of his jacket he'd draped over the couch arm and then slapped a bankbook down on the coffee table. "It's got a balance in it already. Enough to pay the Rickard property taxes for years to come, so we don't have to worry each year about how we'll hang onto the land."

He sounded indignant. But also…amazed.

Her father, the stoic fisherman, had been bowled over by Jager's kindness. She was too. Yet she wasn't at all surprised.

"He's a good man." Her eyes stung more, as she wished there was a way for her to reach Jager's heart.

And wondered now if it was too late.

Had she been foolish to reject him when he had so much to offer beyond the words she longed to hear?

"I wasn't convinced." Her father passed her the tray of cookies. "Have you eaten? These are good."

She took one even though she craved the rest of this story more than the sweet. "What do you mean you weren't convinced?"

"I told him my daughter couldn't be bought." He set the tray down awkwardly, with cookies sliding every which way but somehow managing to stay on the plate. "You know what he said? He said you'd earned far more than what the land was worth doing a CEO's job over at that mansion of his. Any truth to that?"

A flutter of pride swelled her chest to hear Jager's praise. To know that he'd shared it with her father. "I'm not sure, Daddy. But I did run the property for almost a year while he was away."

No doubt about it, she still craved her father's approval.

"Sounds like a CEO to me." There was an assessing light in his eyes. "I told him my daughter and I are cut from the same hardworking cloth. You're like me in that we don't need a lot of recognition or praise. We just quietly get our jobs done."

Is that what he thought? That she didn't need to be told how important she was? Or special? New understanding slid into place.

"I think everyone likes to be recognized sometimes." She set her cookie aside, unable to eat until she told her father how she felt. If she could blurt out her feelings to a total stranger like Malcolm McNeill, surely she could tell her dad. "When I was growing up, I wondered some days if you even noticed what I did to help around the house or prepare the boat for your trips."

"Ah, kiddo," he said brusquely, shaking his head. "I bragged to everyone in town that I had the hardestworking daughter for miles." He stared down for a minute and she didn't say anything.

Waiting.

Needing more from him.

"Delia, I know I wasn't the best father. I was already so damn old when you came along, and I missed your mother so much. Still do. It sounds crazy when I only knew her for a few years before you were born. I've been without her so much longer than I was with her. But I loved her so hard she left a hole."

The anguish in his eyes was the deepest, truest emotion he'd ever let her witness. And while she was grateful for the insight into her father's heart after a lifetime of wishing for his love, a flash of deep self-realization hit her.

She also understood in that moment why she couldn't walk away from Jager.

What if something happened to him and she was the one left with a hole in her heart? How much would she regret the time she wasted that she could have been loving him?

For that matter, maybe instead of worrying about

how her father felt about her, she could simply share how she felt for him. She covered his hand with hers and squeezed.

"Thank you for sharing that. I love you, Daddy," she told him. "I'm going to be so proud to introduce you to your grandchild."

He closed his eyes for a long moment. When he opened them, she saw a new tenderness there. "Love you too, missy. And I never did deserve such a good girl, but I sure am proud of you."

He wrapped his arm around her and kissed the top of her head. Delia let herself rest in the moment, in the gift of finally having a connection to her dad.

"Can I ask you a question?" She angled back to look at him.

"Sure thing." His gaze darted around, as if he was embarrassed by the emotion. When his focus landed on the cookies, he seized another frosted snowman.

"What did Jager say to convince you to come to New York?"

"He said he wanted to give you the best Christmas ever and he thought—for some crazy reason—that meant you might like to see your old man."

"He was right, you know. This is the best Christmas gift he could have given me." Well, one of the best. Having Jager's heart for a lifetime...that was something she couldn't deny she deeply craved and wasn't sure he could give.

But for the first time, she knew she had to risk it.

Her father shook his head. "I know I behaved badly when you told me about the baby, Delia. But you did shock the stuffing out of me when you showed up with that news."

She remembered the way he'd paled at her announcement, no doubt remembering his beloved wife who'd died in childbirth. "I was still reeling myself or I wouldn't have sprung it on you that way. I'm so glad you're here though."

"I got a new sweater out of the deal too." He rubbed a gnarled hand over the cream-colored wool. "It's a fisherman's sweater, you know. And I'll be damned but I never had one before." He flipped his wrist over suddenly to look at his watch. "That reminds me though. I made a deal with Jager to let him know when we finished our talk."

Straightening from the sofa, he reached for his jacket. So soon? She felt off-kilter from this day and it had only just started. But she'd already gotten two wonderful gifts.

An acceptance from her father she'd craved her whole lifetime. And a new determination to share her heart with Jager, no matter the cost.

"I hope we'll have more time to visit than that." She stood too, wondering what kind of arrangement Jager had made with her father. Apparently they'd been conversing often in the last weeks. "You just got here and I've been a neglectful daughter these last two years."

"Nonsense." He brushed aside her worry with a wave. "You had a plantation house to run, for Pete's sake. Besides, I've got some sightseeing to do today while you...do other things." He pointed toward the door. "I've got a room down the hall, you know. And tomorrow is Christmas."

She followed him to the door, the red velvet skirt of her long dress swishing pleasantly around her legs. She'd worn the snowflake earrings too because it was Christmas Eve, after all, and the dress called for festive jewelry even if it was only noontime.

"See you soon then?" she asked, fitting in one more hug before he left.

"For sure. We'll see each other tomorrow. Merry Christmas, Delia."

She smiled, inside and out, to have a holiday to look forward to with her father. How many other Christmases had he spent at sea while she'd been at home by herself?

Peering down the corridor after him, she watched his slightly bent form and his wide-legged seamen's walk as he departed. He barely paused his stride to knock twice on a door down the hall. Damon's room, she guessed, where Jager was visiting with his brother.

Her mind swirling with thoughts, her nerves alight with apprehension, she ducked back into their suite, shutting the door behind her and pressing her spine to it for a moment while she caught her breath. Was Jager on his way back now?

And what should she say about last night and her public refusal to marry him? He'd arranged for her father's trip and the tree before the blow she'd dealt him in front of his family. Had she damaged beyond repair what little chance they may have had together? She wished she could take those words back.

All she could do now was not waste whatever time they had left. To make his Christmas as special as he'd tried to make hers.

Jager knocked before he opened the hotel door with his pass card, wanting to warn Delia he was here. Things had ended so awkwardly between them last night, so he wanted to be as considerate as possible.

Bringing Pascal to New York had been a shot in the

dark, and he had no idea if the surly fisherman had mended his relationship with his daughter. But after hearing her dad's quick knock at Damon's door, Jager knew the time had come for him to face Delia himself. To salvage whatever he could of their relationship.

And while he wanted that to be marriage and forever, he was going to try to be patient. Hear her out. Understand her misgivings before he tackled them, one by one, to show her how good they could be together.

"Delia?" He didn't see her in the living area by the noble fir he'd ordered before dawn. The hotel staff had been excited to help him decorate while Delia slept.

"Coming," she called from her bedroom. "I'm just finishing up something."

"How are you feeling?" He laid his overcoat on a chair, noticing the flurries still swirling outside. It was picture-perfect, snow globe weather.

"Good." Her response was quick, coming a moment before she breezed into the room, looking so beautiful she took his breath away.

"You look...so very lovely." He couldn't imagine not having her in his life—as his wife. Not being there with her to share moments in their child's life.

"It's a gorgeous dress." She swayed slightly, a sweet, feminine movement that sent the skirt swirling around her legs. "I love how it feels."

"It's not the dress." He wanted to reach out to her. To hold her. "It's all you."

Her hazel eyes tracked his, as if she was trying to gauge his mood. He remembered what Damon said about how he was hard to read—like his half brother Quinn. So, digging deeper, he stepped closer. Picked up her hand.

She held a paper, still warm from the in-room printer.

She set it hastily aside, making him curious, but mostly grateful that she let him touch her this way. He bent to kiss the back of her fingers.

"I'm so sorry for the fiasco at my grandfather's last night."

"I'm not." She bit her lip. "That is, I'm sorry that I got upset and blurted out words I didn't mean in front of your family. But I'm not at all sorry I moved past that and got to talk with them and get to know them. I actually think Malcolm is kind of great."

Jager hung on to the first part of what she said— about being sorry for blurting words she didn't mean—so he almost missed the rest. Did she regret her announcement that they wouldn't marry? Or something else?

He backed up a step so they could sit near the tree, bringing her with him and drawing her down to the couch.

"You don't mind that Malcolm rudely called out your pregnancy in front of a room full of strangers?" He started there, dealing with the less thorny question first.

The one less inclined to shred him.

"They weren't strangers though. But yes, I did mind. That's why I gave such a knee-jerk response, and I'm sorry for that. Very sorry." She squeezed his hand in both of hers. "Whatever happens with our relationship, I do think it's between us and none of their business, no matter how many wills and contracts he draws up to try to maneuver his grandsons."

"Whatever happens," he repeated carefully, sounding out the words like a kid reading his first book. Damn, but he was far gone for this woman. "Meaning, you haven't closed the door on a marriage down the road."

"No," she said breathlessly, before looking down for

a moment, and when she met his gaze again, her hazel eyes were a brighter green, lit with some new emotion behind them. "All this time, I've been so determined to avoid a loveless marriage. But what I realized today, while I was talking to my father, is that a union between us could never be a loveless marriage. Not even close. Because I love you, Jager."

His chest swelled with love for her, even as he regretted he hadn't been the one to say those words first when he knew how much they meant to her.

Her declaration leveled every plan he'd made to win her back. Detonated the elaborate presents and gestures he'd orchestrated for the best Christmas. Because she'd just given him the most perfect gift of all.

"Delia. My love." He shook his head, scrambling to get this right without all the plans. To go off script for the most important moment of his life. "I have been planning for days to prove my love to you. To *show* you how I feel so that you would believe it, deep in your heart." Damn, but she humbled him. "Yet in a single moment, you showed me how powerful those three simple words are all on their own."

Her smile was happy. Secure. Certain.

"I was almost afraid to hope when I saw the tree. And my father." She bit her lip, but it wasn't nervousness. It was like she was trying to hold back her excitement before it burst right out of her. "Your gifts inspired me to take a risk on that hope and to give you something too."

She started to reach for the paper she'd set aside and he stayed her hand.

"Wait. It's my turn to give you something first." He withdrew the ring he'd had made for her. "Delia. Love of my life. I would be more honored than I can say if you would be my wife."

Eyes wide, she gasped when she saw the ring. "It's a heart."

"You've had mine in the palm of your hand ever since the day you nearly mowed me down on a Jet Ski." He held the ring over her left hand, waiting for her permission to slide it in place. "It's only fitting you wear it here, where you can see it every single day, and remember how much I love you."

"Yes." She nodded, and then kissed his left cheek and stroked his right with tender fingers. "Yes, I will marry you, Jager, and be your wife."

As he slid the ring home, he realized he'd been holding his breath. She did that to him.

"I'm going to remember, every day, how powerful those words are," he vowed, so grateful to have her in his life and in his heart.

Forever.

"Do you want to see my present?" she asked, curling into him, her silken hair clinging to his cheek.

"You've already given me more than any man deserves. But I'd be glad for any gift from you."

She reached for the paper that she'd been printing when he walked into their suite. In the warm glow of the Christmas tree lights, he could see that she'd printed the application for a marriage license.

"I wanted to show you that I didn't mean what I said at your grandfather's house." She peered up at him.

Jager kissed her nose. "You're going to be the most beautiful Christmas bride."

"Can we invite your family?" She straightened on the couch, so full of hope and happiness that he felt too.

"We'll invite *our* family," he assured her. "Every last one of them."

She wrapped her slender arms around him, and he wondered if she'd ever know how much he loved her. Thankfully, he had a whole lifetime to show her. Starting right now.

Epilogue

One week later

"You may now kiss the bride." The young, ruddy-faced justice of the peace closed his officiant's book and grinned broadly at Delia and Jager.

They stood side by side for their New Year's Eve wedding at The Plaza Hotel in the famed Palm Court, which Malcolm McNeill had bought out for a few hours to enjoy a private, late-afternoon ceremony. Delia wore a specially designed gown from an up-and-coming designer friend of Lydia's, who had fully delivered on Delia's request for a fairy-tale dress. Off-the-shoulder chiffon, fitted through the bodice and waist, the dress had a full skirt and short train worthy of any princess. Delia carried red roses and poinsettias, her heart-shaped ring firmly in place on her finger for a lifetime.

"My wife." Jager's quiet words, spoken as his lips

hovered just above hers, gave the happy moment a power and meaning that she understood deeply. "My love."

The kiss that sealed their promise made her light-headed with joy. Or maybe it was the sentiment he expressed, since it was echoed in her own heart.

"Congratulations, Mr. and Mrs. McNeill." The justice of the peace's words called her back to the reality of the wedding day, and reminded her that they weren't just celebrating their marriage.

Turning toward their small group of assembled guests, Delia knew that promise she'd just made was also a celebration of family. A wonderful new chapter for all of the McNeills, who had taken the first slow steps toward making peace. Toward giving Malcolm McNeill the united kin he dearly craved.

She glanced his way now, and saw the happy tears in his eyes. He didn't even bother to hide them. He was the exact opposite of her father, who of course chose that moment to put his fingers between his teeth and let out a wolf whistle. Cameron McNeill seemed to like this salute to the new couple, and he did the same thing, filling the air with their whistled approval.

"I think that means they want us to kiss again," Jager suggested in her ear. He hadn't let go of her hand since they'd exchanged rings.

Or maybe it was she who couldn't let go of him.

"I think you're right." She kissed her husband again, for longer this time.

She kissed him until the room broke into applause and cheers. But soon decorum prevailed and her cheeks heated just a little.

Jager must have noticed, because he gave one warm cheek a kiss before he drew her over to the dance floor, where they had agreed to share a first dance as man and wife before a meal with the family.

"Shouldn't we thank everyone for coming first? Mingle?" Biting her lip, she peered back at the group seated under an archway of palms outlined with white lights for the holidays.

They hadn't spent a lot of time planning their wedding since they'd only invited family, but Delia was new to having so many siblings-in-law and she wanted to entertain them well. Do things right. Make sure they had fun.

"We'll visit with them soon enough." Jager's blue gaze was for her alone.

And from the heated flame in their depths, she knew he wasn't thinking about family.

"Then I guess I'll follow your lead, husband." She set her bouquet aside as the chamber orchestra began the opening strains of their wedding song.

"I wouldn't steer you wrong," he assured her, nibbling at her neck as they turned together on the small parquet floor. "I taught you to ice skate after all."

It was such a happy memory. And they had so many more left to make together.

"I trust you." She followed his steps, letting him guide her as they twirled past a waiter bringing in the wedding cake, which consisted of layers and layers of red velvet iced in white. She didn't need to see the cake to know the bride-and-groom topper danced inside a snow globe. She'd adored the magical romance of the pretty decoration, so fitting for how she'd fallen in love.

"Should we make New York a yearly trip at Christmastime?" Jager asked, and she guessed his thoughts were following the same line as hers. "We'll have to introduce our child to his or her great grandfather next year."

She couldn't wait for her second ultrasound appointment two days from now, before they flew back to Martinique. It was too soon to determine gender, of course, but she wanted to see their baby.

"I'll be surprised if Malcolm waits that long for a meeting." She'd had fun visiting with the older man in their two trips to the McNeill mansion since that dubious first meeting. He had been overjoyed at the news of the marriage, all the more so since he'd been afraid he'd driven a wedge between Delia and Jager.

"He is a family man, through and through," Jager admitted. He and Damon had agreed that they would try salvaging a relationship with this branch of the family.

Gabe, with his own child to consider, had been game all along. He was already in discussions with his half brothers about taking over some of the Caribbean properties.

"How do you think your brothers will fare with the marriage maneuvers?" She was worried about Damon.

He had stayed in New York to attend the wedding, but there was a deep sadness in his eyes even at happy times.

"They'll set the old man straight," Jager said with certainty as the closing bars of their song filled the room. "Malcolm McNeill might be growing on me as a person, and as a grandfather. But that doesn't mean he controls us."

Delia glided to a stop, peering over at the patriarch surrounded by grandsons who obviously adored him. Even Damon sat close by, listening intently to something Malcolm had to say.

It warmed her heart. But then, everything about this day did.

"I love you so much, Jager." Happy tears welled up, as they had all week, and she knew it didn't have anything to do with pregnancy hormones.

Jager kissed her, giving her a moment to compose herself. A moment to savor how perfect and special this day was.

"I love you, Delia." His words wrapped around her as surely as his arms. "More than I can ever say."

* * * * *

COMING SOON!

We really hope you enjoyed reading this book. If you're looking for more romance, be sure to head to the shops when new books are available on

Thursday 27th June

LET'S TALK

Romance

For exclusive extracts, competitions
and special offers, find us online:

f facebook.com/millsandboon

🐦 @MillsandBoon

📷 @MillsandBoonUK

Get in touch on 01413 063232